DEDICATION

For the fighters, the survivors, and the ones who clawed their
own way out-
To the quiet rage that built you,
and the strength that remade you.
This one is for us.

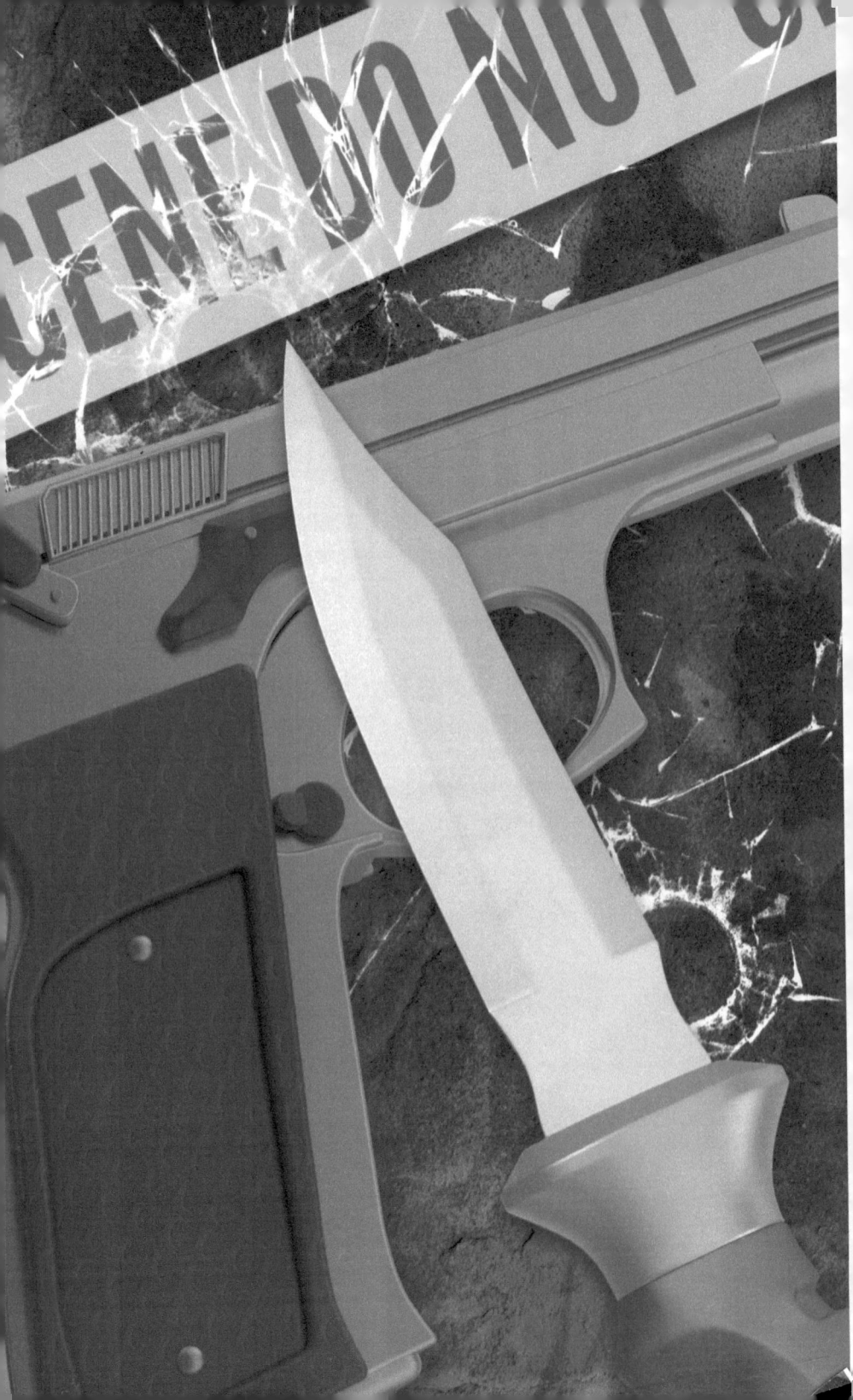

SINNERS OF SUNBRIDGE

IDLE HANDS

ANDI BLACK

Edited by Mallory Day Editing
Cover and interior design by The Bloodied Soul Creative

Contact: Authorandiblack@gmail.com
Socials: TikTok, Tome, Instagram and BlueSky

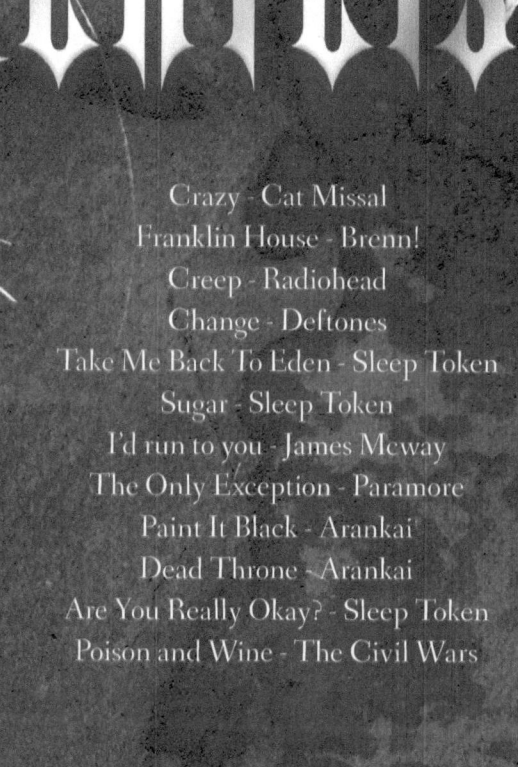

PLAYLIST

Crazy - Cat Missal
Franklin House - Brenn!
Creep - Radiohead
Change - Deftones
Take Me Back To Eden - Sleep Token
Sugar - Sleep Token
I'd run to you - James Mcway
The Only Exception - Paramore
Paint It Black - Arankai
Dead Throne - Arankai
Are You Really Okay? - Sleep Token
Poison and Wine - The Civil Wars

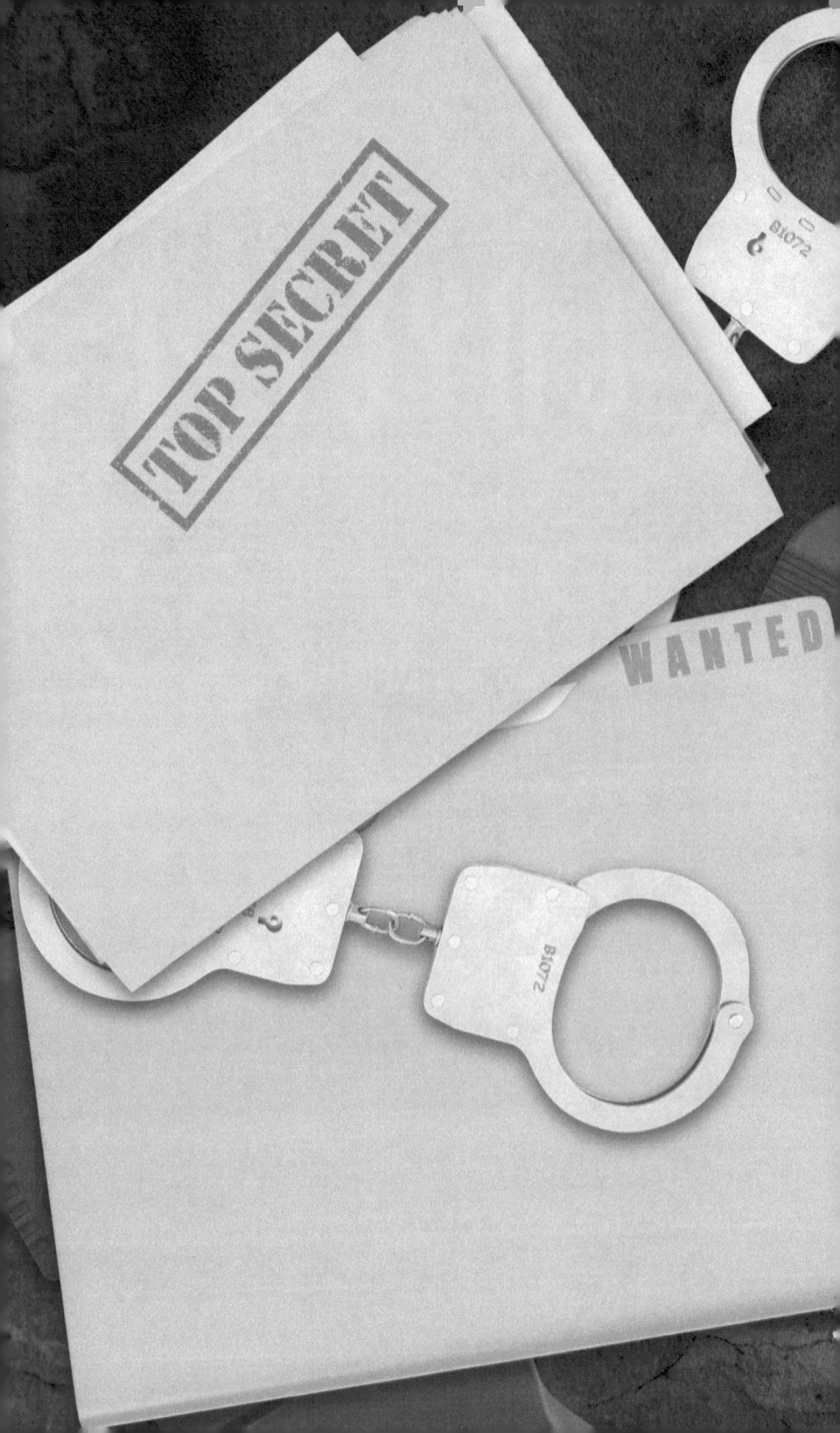

TRIGGER WARNINGS

While SA will never be written out in detail in one of my books, there are mentions of it. Please take a moment to check the list of possible triggers below and decide if this book is for you.

Mentions of SA (vague)
Murder
Torture
Panic attacks and PTSD
Blood
Gore
Adult Content
Profanity
Knee cap removal
Kidnapping
Sex Trafficking
Death
Bone snapping
Stabbing
Drug use
Betrayal
Stalking

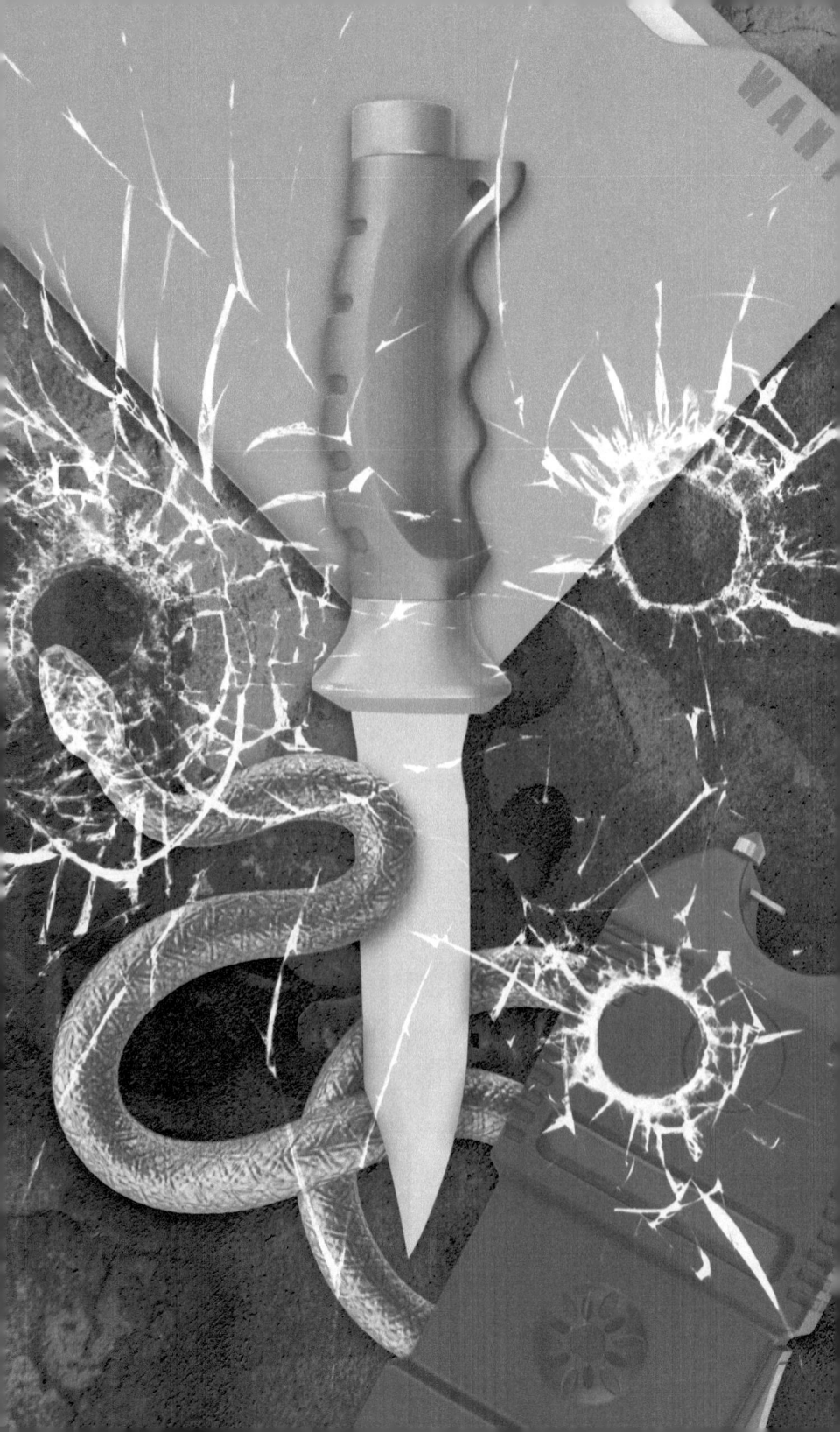

CHAPTER ONE

SHILOH

"First floor clear, moving up."

"Copy. Shy, move in," Aaron's deep voice rumbled through the static of my earpiece.

I grit my teeth against the response forming on my tongue and hit the timer on my watch.

"Moving in."

I had exactly fifteen minutes to get up the balcony to the second floor and maneuver through the window leading into the target's bedroom. I stood on top of the perch I'd been crouching on for the last couple of minutes while everyone else got into place, a thick retaining wall that was just close enough to the balcony that I could make the jump if I was careful. I rolled my neck, bringing my arms over my head and leaped. My heart stuttered as the soles of my boots scraped against the wall. My hands found purchase on the railing, and I heaved myself over it, ignoring the pounding of my heartbeat and adjusting the thin mask over my face.

This house was massive, but old. Our intel team figured out their security system within minutes of receiving the mission briefing. The fact that it hadn't been updated in over a decade meant bypassing it wasn't going to be a problem. Intel had planted a small cam facing the master suite window, which had shown the owners as they stumbled in two hours ago and promptly passed out in their California king. Given the circumstances, it should be an easy mission.

Keeping my steps light, I moved toward the large window in front of me, noting the small light in the corner of the room, but other than that, the dark stretched quiet and unbroken, like the rest of the world was sound asleep.

"In place." I checked my watch, ten minutes left. I slipped the jammer from my belt and stuck it to the top right-hand corner of the glass pane, directly underneath the security sensor, making it completely useless as I wedged the window open and slid it up enough to get my body through it. I held my breath, waiting for an alarm that didn't sound. I trusted our tech, but one small slip up is all it would take in a neighborhood like this one. Nosy neighbors with too much time and money on their hands would flock to the front lawn if we tripped an alarm in here.

My boots hit the plush carpet without a sound and the light in the corner caught my attention again, making my stomach drop as my eyes adjusted to the darkness.

"Are you in?"

"Yeah."

My voice caused the body in the bed to stir, the comforter rustling as they rolled over.

"Be quick, Shy. It's easier that way." That was bullshit, and we both knew it.

Nothing about it was easy.

I moved to the corner of the room, reaching down and plucking the unicorn nightlight out of the wall and placing it carefully on the dresser before walking to the bed and pulling back the covers.

She was tiny. Maybe seven? Eight years old? Too young to ever experience this, all of them were.

I pulled off the thin black mask I'd been wearing, pulling my hair free from the knot I'd tied it in, and letting the long red strands flow over my shoulders. Anything to make this less intimidating for her. I sat on the bed next to her, clicking my earpiece off and keeping my voice as soft as possible.

"Hey, I need you to get up, honey."

Bright, round blue eyes stared up at me, illuminated by the moonlight streaming in through the open window. They were nearly the same color as mine, a shade darker, her hair lighter, but I saw the reflection of myself in her eyes.

The same way I always did on a mission.

It always felt like the air was being stolen right out of my chest.

"Who are you?"

"I'm a friend, but we have to go, okay? Can you be a big girl for me and keep really quiet?"

She hadn't been awake for more than ten seconds, and here was a stranger trying to lure her out of her bed. The only thing working in my favor was that rich kids typically bounced between so many nannies and handlers that strangers weren't all that scary to them by this age.

"Okay." She slipped out of bed, stuffing her feet into a pair of sparkly pink boots and snatching the night light off the dresser.

"Ready?"

She nodded. So terrifyingly trusting.

Guilt stabbed at my chest, the disgust I felt at pulling her from the safety of her bed cloaking my skin like mud. There was no way to justify this, we were monsters. Simple as that.

"Okay." I smiled, reaching down and scooping her small frame into my arms.

I clicked the earpiece back on. "Coming out."

"Copy, on the balcony."

I helped the girl through the window and climbed out after her, positioning her behind me as we approached Aaron.

"Scared?" he mumbled, glancing behind me.

I shook my head. "Not even a little." It wasn't comforting. It made the job easier, sure. But after tonight, she would never trust another stranger again.

Disgust covered his face, but he quickly wiped it away, turning away from the small child behind me and speaking into his comm.

"Target secure, coming out."

I quickly stepped over the railing, jumping back down to the retaining wall and holding my arms out for the girl.

"Close your eyes, sweetheart. She'll catch you," Aaron told her.

The girl did as she was told, scrunching her eyes tight and not letting out so much as a yelp as he dropped her into my arms. Once he was beside me, we made quick work of getting through the backyard and out to the service entrance where the van was waiting.

Someone slung the back door open, and we filed in as the van lurched forward and took off down the road.

I snatched the comm from my ear, tossing it into the open duffle bag full of equipment by our feet and leaned my head against the cool metal of the wall behind me.

"Where are we going?" Her words made my skin crawl, the lack of terror in her voice leaving a hopeless pit in my stomach.

"We'll see when we get there, sweetheart."

"No pet names," the driver, Jason, bit out. We weren't supposed to be friendly with them, we weren't even obligated to be kind. This was a job, they were a mission, and there was no room in either of those for basic human empathy.

I met Aaron's narrowed brown eyes across the van, and he

gave me a careful nod before sliding his phone from his belt and sending off a text. I let my eyes roam over his face, the tight line of his lips, the furrow in his brow. His posture stayed relaxed, but the tension was there. He had pulled his mask up, resting it on top of his head, dirty blonde strands of hair peeked out from the corners to contrast the dark stubble dusted across his jaw. Aaron was three years older than me, and the only thing keeping me going.

And he was the only one who I trusted to execute this mission the way it needed to be done. Aaron tucked his phone away, gesturing toward his thigh and displaying three fingers there, out of sight of the rearview mirror. Three minutes. He tossed me a small red bag, and I pulled the two child-sized foam earplugs from it, turning back to the girl.

"We're going to play a game, okay? But you have to be super quiet." I pressed my forefinger to my lips, forcing a smile to form around it.

"Okay," she whispered back, her eyes bright with excitement.

"I'm going to put these in your ears, and when I do this," I held up a peace sign, "I want you to close your eyes as tight as you can and keep them that way until I tap your hand three times. Can you do that?"

"Uh-huh!" She pushed her hair back, allowing me to wiggle the plugs into her ears with only a scrunched face to show her displeasure. A text alert sounded from Aaron's phone, and I rested my hand over the girl's seatbelt buckle as his eyes met mine.

Steady and determined.

"Hey," I leaned down and whispered to the girl, careful not to let my words travel past our little bubble.

"Let's get you strapped in real quick, okay?" I waited for her to bob her head before reaching across her and securing the lap belt and then bracing my arm behind her to protect her head.

"What do I get if I win?" the girl asked.

"Everything," Aaron grunted as he slipped his mask back over his face.

The impact to the van came with the sound of crunching metal, and the screams of a little girl who finally felt the fear that had been creeping toward her all night.

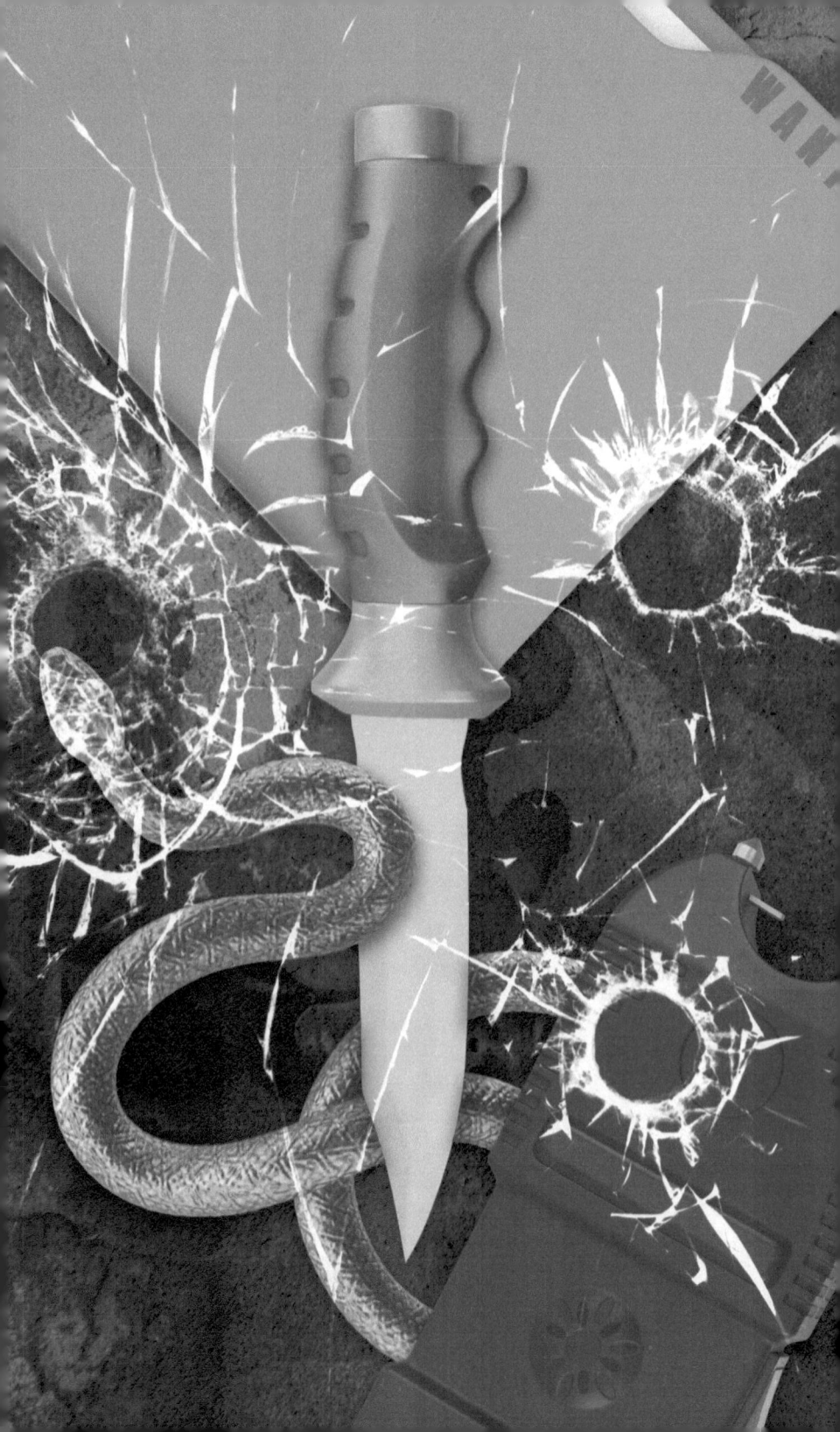

CHAPTER TWO

SHILOH

Aaron jumped to his feet, moving to the front of the van and pulling his gun from his belt as I laid my hand over the little girl's leg to get her attention. Her eyes were wide with fear as she looked at me, and then the peace sign I held up in front of her face. A tear tracked down her face, her small hand reaching up to clutch mine as she squeezed her eyes shut.

The doors to the back of the van flung open seconds later, three men in tactical gear similar to ours rushed in, bypassing both me and the girl to get to the driver. Aaron moved out of their way, watching with cold eyes as one of the men shot our driver in the back of the head.

"Let's move." One of the men spoke, but the voice was muffled through his mask which covered everything except his eyes.

"She'll take the girl back in, we'll meet you in five."

I gathered her into my arms, jumping from the back of the van and jogging back to the house with Aaron on my heels.

I pulled the plugs from her ears, placing my hands on either side of her face.

"You can open your eyes now, honey."

She cracked one eye before opening them and looked around.

"Why did you bring me back?"

"This is where you belong. When we leave, there is going to be a really loud noise. We'll make sure your mommy or daddy comes and checks on you, okay?"

"Okay."

"Lay back down, it's okay."

I watched her climb onto the bed, snuggling under her thick pink comforter. I hoped she wouldn't remember much of this night. Maybe she was too young, maybe it wouldn't be something that stuck with her throughout her life.

Maybe I was delusional.

I slung one leg out of the window, waving to her before reaching up and pulling the jammer free. The alarm sounded almost immediately, blaring throughout the house.

I slipped through the rest of the way, dismounting from the balcony and running through the yard behind Aaron. When we made it back to where we had left the van, it was already gone. No trace of it left, including the body of our former driver. I followed Aaron around the block to find the three men waiting for us in front of a massive Jeep.

"Cleanup was successful. We'll make sure they get the message."

Aaron nodded.

"We need to get back. It's gonna be hell when we get there."

"She's safe though. That's all that matters. Thank you," I added, nodding my head to the men in front of us.

The one across from me nodded, his sharp blue eyes scanning my face as he cocked his head to the side. "Don't mention it. Aaron owes us a favor now, anyway. We'll cash in."

Aaron cleared his throat, glaring at the man as he turned and pulled me along with him.

We walked a few blocks over before he pulled out his phone and texted for a retrieval team.

"You know I'm going to ask what he meant."

"You know I'm not going to tell you."

True. Aaron was the person I was closest to in all of this, but he was still a closed book ninety percent of the time. We all learned early on to keep our mouths closed about our backgrounds. The younger recruits would break down over every little thing and the leaders would use any information they could against you. The less the people here knew about you, the better. Information was leverage, and Aaron and I had made sure these bastards didn't have any on us.

"Stick to the story," Aaron said as a sleek, black SUV approached us.

"I know."

His eyes found mine, his lips pulled into a tight line. The weight of what we had done tonight was heavy on both of our shoulders. We had a story, we knew what we would say, but they weren't going to just let this go. 'Losing' a target was probably the worst thing we could do. There's no telling how much Ruben would have gotten from her, and knowing him, he was already planning on how to spend that money.

No, we were going to be punished for this one. Aaron and I had been sabotaging missions for the last six months, since I was moved up to the same rank as him.

The family was home and alert when we got there? Must have been bad intel.

The van got a flat on the way to the target's house? Coincidence.

The target was taken from us after we had secured her? There wasn't a story we could come up with that would satisfy them on that one. We would just have to take whatever they gave us and be more careful the next time around.

A few blocks from here, a little girl was sleeping safely in her bed. That was what I would focus on when Ruben came to take his pound of flesh from me.

The SUV came to a stop, and Aaron opened the back door, ushering me inside before climbing in behind me. I didn't recognize the driver, but that was typical. Our drivers usually weren't as... immersed in the organization. They were typically paid for a day or so at a time and rotated out often enough that I hardly ever saw the same one more than a few times.

The drive back was silent, the tension in the car growing with every mile we inched closer to the manor.

When we finally came to a stop and filed out, I made a beeline for my room. Reaching into my top drawer and snatching the orange bottle out, I dumped three little white pills into my hand and swallowed them dry. They wouldn't erase what was about to happen, but at least the memories would be blurred.

I walked back to the front of the house and found Ruben already there waiting for me with his hands clasped behind his back.

"Shiloh. Follow me please." He turned without waiting for a response and moved down the hallway to his office.

I followed the clacking sound of his expensive shoes, each step making my heartbeat ratchet up higher.

He opened the door and motioned for me to go in ahead of him. I took a few steps into the room, closing my eyes and forcing myself not to jump as the lock clicked into place.

"Shiloh, do you know why I have kept you this long? Why you were moved into Ranks, when I could have easily cashed in on you?" He prowled around me in a circle, his hands still locked behind his back as he studied me.

"Because I'm your favorite." The words had been beaten into me for so long, they came out on instinct.

"Because you are my favorite," he agreed, stopping in front of me and brushing a rogue strand of my red hair behind my ear. The gesture made my stomach roll, everything I ate for dinner earlier threatened to make a quick exit through my mouth due to his proximity. The expensive cologne he always wore stung my nostrils. The sharp, pungent smell of it imbedded in all of my worst memories.

I braced as best as I could, knowing what came next.

"Sometimes, even our favorite toys need to be taught a lesson. Broken in. I thought we had accomplished that years ago, but if you need a reminder, Shiloh, I will give you one."

I closed my eyes a fraction of a second before the back of his hand connected with my cheek, the thick golden ring on his middle finger no doubt leaving a gnarly imprint on my skin.

"Undress."

The human instincts that used to urge me to run when I was in his presence had disappeared sometime over the years. There were no warning bells—no alarm going off in my head.

Compliance was the best option.

The pills were quickly working their way into my system, creating a warm buzz in my head that dulled my stinging face.

Another twenty minutes, and I wouldn't even be in this room with him. Not mentally, at least.

Big blue eyes flashed through my mind, the picture of a tiny girl resting in her home where she belonged, and my shoulders relaxed.

It was worth it. I repeated that over and over as I stripped the clothes from my body.

I reached for the button on my pants, ignoring the sound of Ruben's belt clinking as he unfastened it, popping the button free just as the window behind him began slowly sliding open.

I froze, my eyes locked on the masked figure that moved silently through the window and into the room, coming to stand behind Ruben without making a single sound. His hand moved to his waist where he pulled out a small gun.

Ruben finally caught on that we weren't alone when the barrel was pressed against the back of his bald head.

"Go ahead and put your clothes back on, Red," the man said, nodding to my shirt on the floor at my feet.

Man wasn't quite right. He didn't seem much older than me by the sound of his voice. He was tall, lean, but every bit of his skin was covered in black fabric. I was positive he was one of the guys that had stopped the van earlier, the piercing blue eyes that looked back at me gave him away.

I hesitated a moment before bending to gather my clothes to my chest, turning my back to whatever the fuck was happening over there and hastily pulling my shirt over my head, followed by the tactical gear I had on from earlier.

"Whoever you are, you are making the biggest mistake of your life right now."

"Not even close."

The gunshot was nearly silent, like the sound of a thick book hitting the ground, followed by Rubens body *actually* hitting the ground.

I turned to look over my shoulder, noting Ruben's body in a heap at the man's feet, blood pooling around his head.

He tucked the gun into the back of his pants and sighed, looking at me from across the room. "You alright?"

Was I? Maybe I was just high and imagining all of this. I pinched the skin of my forearm hard enough to bruise. He was still there, as was Ruben's lifeless body.

"Sure." I shrugged.

"Sure? You're an odd little bird, aren't you?" he mused, a smile evident in his voice.

"I'm on drugs," I blurted the words out, unsure if I regretted them or not.

He nodded. "Fair." He turned around, making long strides back toward the window.

"You were there, right? Earlier, with the van?"

He hummed, straddling the windowsill with his head cocked to the side. "Your hero is on his way in. See you soon, Red."

He slipped out of the window and into the darkness beyond it, leaving me alone to watch the blood pooling on the expensive carpet beneath my feet.

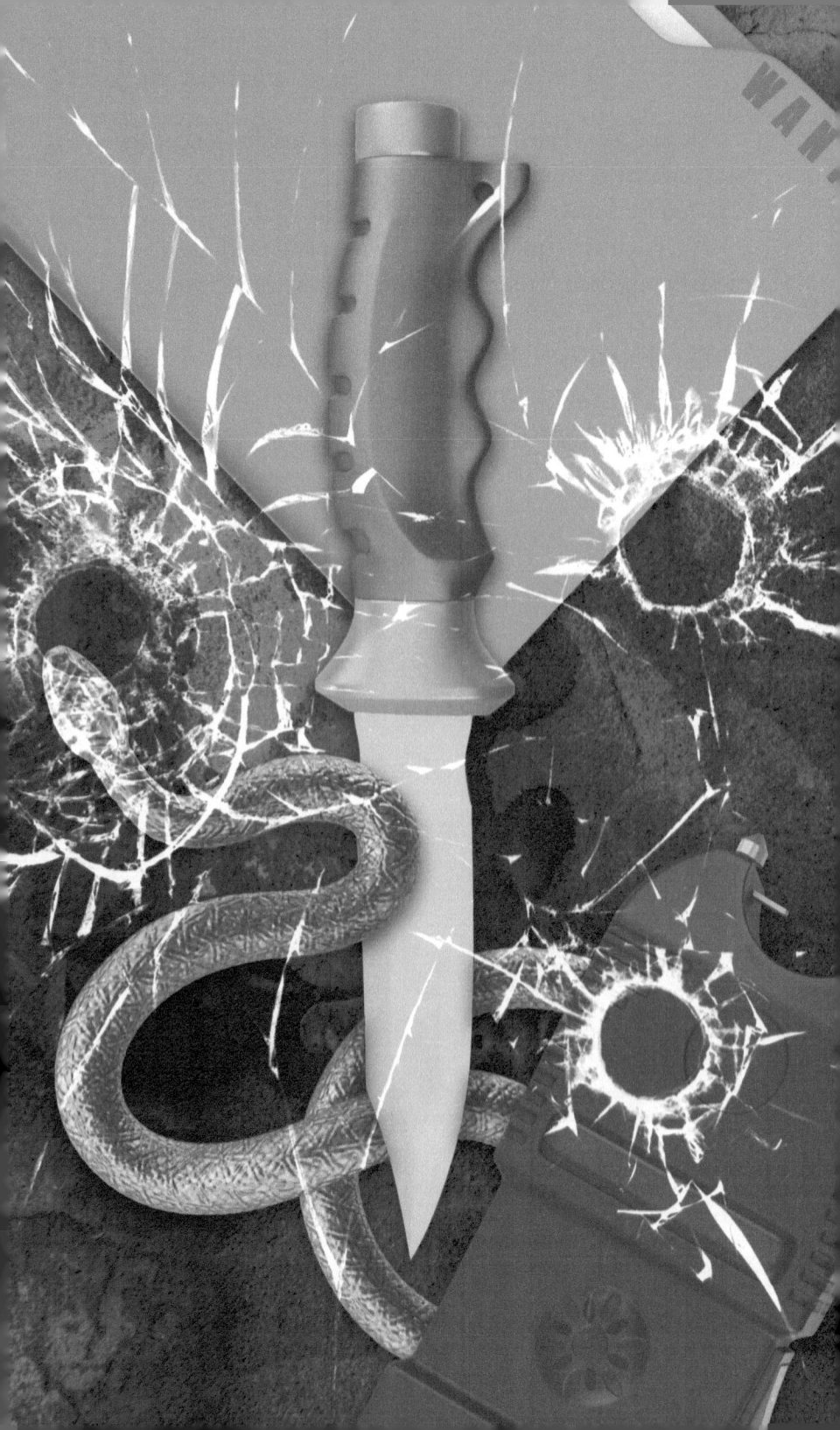

CHAPTER THREE

SHILOH

I blew a breath out of the corner of my mouth, flinging a strand of hair back as I looked around the room. What now? No doubt I was going to go down for this, no one was going to believe that a masked assailant came in through the window, popped the most important man in this building with a single bullet, and then exited without a trace.

I was dead.

I scrubbed my hands over my face, grateful for the drugs in my system that made all of this seem more like an inconvenience than the death sentence it actually was. Footsteps sounded throughout the hallway on the other side of the heavy oak doors behind me, followed by the sounds of shouting from a dozen different voices. I walked over to the plush armchair that sat in the far-left corner, curling up in it and closing my eyes against whatever evil thing was coming for me next.

I had been in this hellhole for five years now. Five years of being Ruben's favorite toy had taken every ounce of energy I had and sapped it straight from my body. There was no leaving this place, not in one piece. Every kid that came through those doors was equipped with a tracking implant, given a merchandising number, and shuffled through the sales floor like cattle. The 'lucky' ones joined what we referred to as Ranks. We helped facilitate newcomers, helped prep for clients, and eventually moved up to missions. I had managed to wiggle my way to the top just two months ago.

And I had purposely fucked up every mission since.

Ruben would have killed me himself if he had known the work me and Aaron had been doing behind his back—the number of kids we had saved from ever knowing this place existed. As it was, I just got the shit kicked out of me after each failed retrieval and went about my day.

While I didn't have a single shred of hope left for my own well-being, I refused to pull more innocents into this place. This wasn't the kind of thing you survived and went on to lead a normal life after.

From the moment you crossed the threshold here, everything essential to who you are as a person would be systematically stripped away. Your dignity, your pride, your hope.

Until you were just a shell, full of pain pills, nodding off in front of a dead body.

Bleak as fuck.

My eyelids drooped shut, the warmth running through my veins lulling me into a semi-peaceful sleep as I sunk further into the chair. At least I could get a good nap in before they came to burn me at the stake.

A loud pounding echoed off the marble of the hallway, growing louder and louder with each passing second. The shouting hadn't stopped either, I realized, forcing myself to sit up straighter and listen.

The large doors to the office suddenly flung inward, and a rush of uniformed officers barreled in with their guns drawn.

"GET ON YOUR KNEES!" The light of at least a dozen flashlights blinded me as I fumbled to the floor, raising my hands in surrender.

How the fuck did they find out that fast?

No, wrong question.

How the fuck did the police get in here?

Aside from the fact that Ruben had the entire local police department in his pocket, the security around The Manor was tighter than Area 51. There was no way they could get in here without setting off a hundred different alarms.

"Face down, put your arms behind your back."

"Not her, she's with me." Aaron? I shielded my eyes from the flashlights and caught a glimpse of his face as he moved toward me, the badge on his hip glimmering in the bright lights.

"Am I higher than I thought, or is that," I pointed to the badge, "a fucking police badge?"

The apology written all over his face was all the confirmation I needed.

He was a cop.

The last hour really was going to be what snapped my sanity in half.

"I will explain everything."

"Cool. Officer Aaron, could you please tell your friends to turn off the goddamn flashbangs before I go blind?"

He winced at the choice of title, but motioned behind him, the lights dimming immediately as I attempted to blink the spots from my vision.

"Shy, I need you to come with me, okay?"

"I don't see that I have much choice. Lead the way."

He shook his head with a sigh, and reached for my hand, pulling me into his side as we weaved through the crowd of armed officers that filled the office and hallway outside of it.

There were more of them in the foyer, guarding a row of men who rested on their knees with their hands cuffed behind their backs. I recognized most of them. Ruben's assistant was at the front, followed by a handful of butlers and one of the men that ran the sales floor on the basement level of the house.

Aaron pulled me along with him out the front doors and all but shoved me into the front seat of a car, before getting in the driver's side and hauling ass down the long driveway.

"They will need to question you, Shy. But considering the situation, that will take place at your house."

"My house?" Those two words didn't go together. My mind couldn't conjure up an image of what they meant.

"Your parents' house. They've been alerted. We're on our way there now."

My parents. My house.

I had spent the last couple of years forcing any recollection of my old life out of my mind. There was no use dwelling on things I'd never see again. Now the idea of my old bedroom sounded foreign, my parents' names rolling around my head like shards of glass.

They weren't going to get back the daughter they had lost.

She was gone, and me, *this*, was in her place.

I had thought about running when I first moved up to Ranks, but Ruben had people monitoring the tracking implants nearly 24/7, and the second I had gotten within 100 yards of my parents' house, all hell would have broken loose. Combine that with the efforts Aaron and I were making to keep other kids out of this place, and running just wasn't worth the risk.

I tucked the events from the day into neat little boxes and shoved them as far back in my mind as I could manage. I would wake up in the morning livid that Aaron had been lying to me for as long as I'd known him, but right now I couldn't muster the energy to tell him what I thought about it.

The thought of going 'home' made my stomach turn, and memories of Ruben's blood splattering across the room still floated around my mind.

The rest of the drive was silent. Turns out, I had been less than three hours from where I was taken this entire time. It occurred to me as the landscape started becoming familiar that I never asked where The Manor was. The first week in that place was hell, and then after that I think you're so firmly locked into a state of survival, that details just don't seem to matter. We pulled into a gated community, and the massive houses lining the streets looked like the ones most of our targets came from. Long driveways, perfectly manicured lawns, towering multiple story mini-mansions.

It wasn't hard to figure out which one was mine, given the news vans we had to weave around and the mob of reporters that had converged on the front lawn. Aaron swore under his breath, calling someone and demanding that they open the gates.

The wait wasn't long, but reporters and men holding massive cameras still swarmed the car, knocking on the windows with their microphones in hand while lights flashed all around me. I sunk down in my seat and squeezed my eyes shut, only opening them when Aaron let me know we were in the garage and they could no longer see us.

My relief was short-lived as the door leading into the house opened, and my parents stepped out.

They looked roughly the same as I remembered, just... older. Streaks of gray had taken over my father's previously jet-black hair, peppering throughout the short beard and mustache on his face. My mom was skinnier. Not in a 'went to the gym' kind of way, but in a way that made her appear frail. Delicate in a way she hadn't been when I left.

Her hair, just a few shades lighter than my own, hung low down her back, nearly reaching her hips. Wrinkles had formed on both of their faces, making the amount of time I had been gone both apparent and painful. I knew I had to look different to them too, enough that I was terrified to leave this car.

My hair was still flaming red, but shorter than it had been.

The freckles along the bridge of my nose had faded into my pale skin thanks to the lack of sun exposure I'd received over the years. I was a pre-teen the last time they saw me. I was in training bras and sketchers and now I was here with a busted face and a tactical belt around my waist.

I forced myself out of the car, watching every miniscule twitch of their features as they took in the scars and bruises that lingered on my arms. My father broke first, covering his sob with his hand.

I wanted to say something to comfort them, but what was there to say?

'I'm okay?' I wasn't. Far from it.

'I missed you?' That wasn't entirely true either. The first few years I missed them so much it made me sick. After that, I forced those thoughts away. They were doing more harm than good in the corner of my mind they resided in; I had to get them out.

"Let's go inside?" my mother asked, her voice soft and unsure. I nodded, following her as she placed a hand on my father's shoulder and guided him back inside.

Whatever they had expected this reunion to be, they hadn't gotten it.

And the disappointments were going to keep coming for them after tonight.

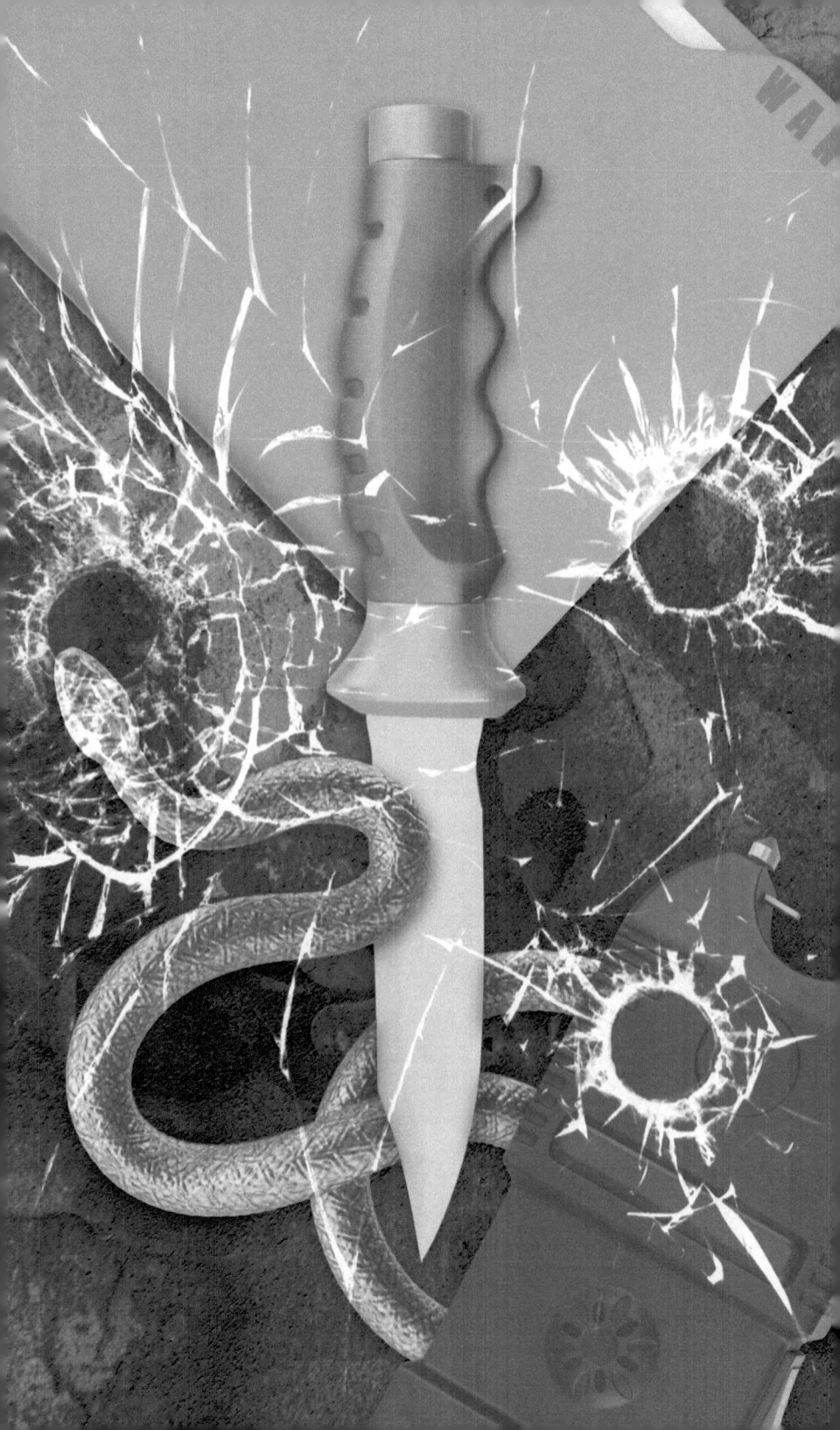

CHAPTER FOUR

SHILOH

The next couple of hours went by in a blur. My parents were visibly torn between giving me space and asking the questions that had accumulated over the years I had been gone. They sat within reach on either side of me on their plush white sofa that hadn't been there before, gently probing with carefully constructed questions.

"When was the last time you ate?"

"I don't know. I'm not hungry."

"We can call the doctor to the house; would that be more comfortable for you?"

"Sure, whatever is easier."

"Are you feeling okay?"

"I'm fine."

My responses were robotic, each answer that left my lips seemed to deepen the creases around my father's eyes. I was sorting through what I would actually tell them in the coming weeks.

There were parts of the last five years that needed to be kept from them, for everyone's sanity. I couldn't imagine the turmoil they had been in, even now, with me sitting between them.

I wasn't the little girl they had lost. Regardless of what

those years had been like for me, they had missed out on key years of my adolescence. I got my first period in a cramped room I shared with six other kids. Giada, one of the women assigned to keeping track of the kids, tossed me a bag of various supplies and told me "congrats" before turning around and leaving me to figure it out.

Puberty had hit me like a ton of bricks, changing my frail thirteen-year-old frame into something more closely resembling a woman. My chest and hips had filled out, my cheeks hollowed from stress and the lack of appetite that comes with being held captive during your formative years. I was heart-breakingly... different.

I blew a strand of hair out of my face, glancing to the large windows and noting the lights that still flickered around the property.

The flat screen tv across from us had been left on the local news station and flashes of The Manor flitted across the screen, along with images of some of Ruben's buddies that had been taken in after the raid. I watched as they showed each of their pictures, recalling every interaction I'd had with each of them. None were good.

The feed switched to what looked like a press conference; reporters were crowded around a podium as a handful of officers filed in.

One of them moved to the podium, and I reached for the remote, turning the volume up over whatever conversation my parents were attempting.

"After years of investigative work, and with the help of local agencies and independent organizations, we were able to bring down the sex trafficking ring known as The Manor. During the initial raid, the head of the ring was killed in a standoff with our officers. All of those working under him have been taken into custody."

Reporters yelled over one another, raising their hands and shoving microphones toward the podium.

"Officer Giles, how many children were rescued in tonight's efforts?"

"We retrieved seventeen minors from the residence, along with ten young adults who were there against their will. We are currently working to get as many of them back to their families as possible."

"Can you give us some names?"

"We will not be releasing any of the victims' names at this time."

"Is it true that police chief Hale's daughter was among the children rescued?"

"That's all for tonight. We will keep the community updated on any breaks we have moving forward." He nodded to the reporters and walked quickly off the stage.

"Police chief?" I asked. Last time I had seen him, my father had worked for an insurance company.

"Yes. After... well after we lost you, I knew I couldn't find you from behind a desk. So, I joined the police force and worked my way up over the years. I've been the chief for a little over a year now."

Something in his words worked hard to puncture the cement case I'd constructed around my heart. The idea of my father working through the ranks, his sole mission to find his daughter.

It would have hurt, if I'd let it.

"What about you?" I asked my mom.

"Still a nurse, specifically in the E.R. Same as when you left. Some things stayed the same, honey," she whispered the last part, like she was trying to convince herself more than me.

"I'm going to go to bed now." I stood, shrugging the blanket from my shoulders.

"Do you... remember the way to your room?" My mom's voice cracked along each syllable.

I nodded, even though I wasn't sure I really did, and moved toward the stairs. The soft carpet under my feet felt nice. I focused on the feel of it as I made my way down the long hallway, letting my feet lead me instinctively while refusing to let myself think about it.

I stopped in front of the last door on the right, turning the knob and rushing in.

This was definitely the room of a pre-teen girl. A small pile of laundry sat in the corner, right next to an empty laundry basket. Stuffed animals lined the bed and the top of a white wicker dresser along the wall to my left. Pink paint. Glow in the dark stars along the ceiling. Tiny bottles of nail polish and body glitter cluttered a vanity.

They hadn't touched a thing in this room; it was as though it had been turned into a shrine in my absence. I flipped the light switch off, plunging the room into a comfortable darkness and flopped over onto the bed. I wiggled my phone out of my back pocket, and kicked off my pants, flipping to my back as the screen illuminated my face.

Six missed calls from Aaron, two of which he left voicemails on. I wasn't ready to talk to him. I didn't want to know how long he had been undercover in The Manor. How many times I had left his side to go to Ruben's office, watching the grimace on his face as he turned and walked the other way. I tossed my phone on the bed, folding my hands over my stomach and staring up at the stars that covered the ceiling above me. This was good. I was away from that place; I was safer than I had been in years.

I was home.

It's a shame Ruben had broken anything worth having inside me before I got here.

CHAPTER FIVE

SHILOH

One Year Later

"Shiloh! You're going to be late, honey!" Mom's voice echoed off the hallway outside my door as I stepped into my tennis shoes.

"Coming!" I was running late, as usual. In my defense, the sleeping pills I started last week had actually been working, a little too well considering the number of alarms I had slept through, but I was finally getting more than a couple hours of rest at night so being late for work seemed like a fair trade off.

I had nightmares almost every night for the first few months when I got home. Dreams of Ruben sneaking in my window and dragging me back to The Manor, dreams that felt more like memories of the trips to his office. More often than not, I woke my parents up screaming in the middle of the night. The pills helped, even if it meant I overslept the next morning. Aaron owned the gym anyway, so the chances that I would be written up were less than zero.

I grabbed my bag off the dresser and hustled down the stairs, stopping in the kitchen to grab a bottle of water and snag a piece of French toast off the plate on the bar.

"Shiloh, you need to start waking up earlier. You never eat

a full meal in the mornings." Mom tsked her tongue at me, a frown settling in the corners of her mouth at my choice of breakfast.

"I know, I'll get up earlier tomorrow."

She gave me a small smile, gently patting the back of my hand before returning to whatever she was cooking on the stove. The news was playing on the small countertop TV Mom had insisted she needed last month. She stood at the stove, one hand on her hip, a spatula forgotten in her hand as she shook her head at the headline that scrolled across the bottom of the screen.

SERIAL KILLER STILL AT LARGE IN SUNBRIDGE.

The Red King. Mom had been following the case for weeks, every new update she would watch, her lips tight as she shook her head back and forth. "There's just too much evil in this world, Shy," she would say.

I rubbed at the scar on the back of my neck. My dad had called in a doctor to remove the tracker the morning after I got home. It wasn't a pleasant experience and although no one was around anymore to use it, I still wanted it out of my skin. The thick purple scar served as a constant reminder that my mother was right. There was a lot of evil in the world.

I yelled out a goodbye as I entered the garage and climbed into my car. It had been the first big thing they bought me when I returned, a black Camaro with interior that very nearly matched my hair color. I got my driver's license the same week, and since then I've looked for any excuse to drive.

After years of my every move being tracked, the freedom I felt behind the wheel of my own vehicle felt like lightning in my veins. I could go anywhere, do anything.

I hit the button for the garage door and started down the

long driveway as I clicked on Lottie's name on my phone and set it in the cupholder. It rang four times before she picked up.

"Why are you calling me at the ass crack of dawn?" She croaked into the phone. Lottie was a lot of things, but a morning person wasn't one of them.

"It's 9:45 in the morning, babe." I laughed.

"My point exactly. You on your way to work?" I could hear her rolling out of bed on the other end of the phone, probably hungover from whatever party she had been at last night.

"Yeah, I was just calling to check in, make sure you weren't passed out in a field somewhere."

"Nah, just my bed. The party was a bust, so I stole a bottle of tequila from the frat boy hosting it and came home to get hammered solo."

"Charming."

"I'm a delight. It's crazy that I'm single, honestly."

"No man could handle you, Lottie Lou. I'll call you when I get off."

"Ooooh, dirty."

I rolled my eyes and hung up as I pulled into my usual spot in the back parking lot and quickly made my way to the locker room, stuffing my bag into a locker and tying my hair into a ponytail. The gym was fairly dead this morning, only a handful of cars in the parking lot. Perfect. I slid my headphones on and got to work on the laundry that had piled up in the back, working for hours without having to interact with any other humans. By the time I checked my phone, four hours had flown by.

"Shy!" Aaron's voice boomed from the other side of the gym. I glanced up to see him dangling his keys, his eyes motioning to his truck outside. "Lunch?"

I was over the counter and halfway to the door before I heard his chuckle behind me.

"Where do you want to go?"

I buckled my seat belt, resting my feet on the dash and tapping my fingers against my knees as we drove.

"The mall."

"The mall?" He scoffed.

"Yes, I want a pretzel. Actually, I want a bunch of pretzels. The little ones with the cheese sauce."

He shook his head. "You have the diet of a six-year-old."

"I don't see anything wrong with that. It's better than the protein pancake red meat nonsense you're always eating."

He flexed his arm with a raised brow. "That's how I keep this physique, Shy."

I forced a gag, swatting at his arm. "Put that thing away, Superman. You're going to scare the children."

Coming home had been a rocky adjustment. The relief of being away from Ruben was heavily dulled by how out of place I felt in my own room. The relationships with my parents were tentative at best for the first couple months, all of us tiptoeing around each other, afraid to say something that would send the other spiraling. I had to relearn the layout of the house I had taken my first steps in, continuously remind myself that I didn't have to ask permission to eat and see the devastation on my parents' faces when I did it anyway.

Things had been smoother lately. I spent less time in my room and more time with my mom in the kitchen or shopping when she asked. I sat on the sofa in my dad's office and read while he worked most weekends. On the surface, we looked whole, healed.

If you were to peel back the layers though, you would see the truth.

I haven't felt more than a fleeting connection to anyone since I returned. Not for lack of trying, either. It's like there's a wall between me and where my ability to form connections lies, and I can't break through it, no matter how hard I try.

Aaron and Lottie had been my only sources of hope lately. The only people I can *feel*.

With Aaron, it had everything to do with the circumstances our friendship was forged under, but being around him is the only thing I have that makes me believe I'm not a complete loss. At The Manor, he was always by my side when he could be, pulling strings to keep me out of missions. The only time he left was when he was made to, but it was his comfort I sought out as soon as I was excused from whatever Ruben had decided to put me through.

As for Lottie, we had grown up in the same neighborhood and attended the same school since pre-k. Everyone needed a Lottie, and mine was still waiting for me when I got home, no questions, just ready to pick back up where we left off. So, we did.

The mall was packed, as usual, Aaron's truck rumbling as we made it to the third level of the parking garage and finally found an empty spot. Conveniently, the food court was on the same level, so it wasn't a long walk to get to my beloved pretzels. Aaron ordered and paid for our food while I went in search of Icee's for both of us.

I ended up at the pizza place across the food court, ordering two large blue raspberry Icee's for us, one of the few 'treats' Aaron never turned down. I stood to the side of the counter, scrolling through my phone while I waited, when I noticed the amount of security lingering around. On either side of the doors Aaron and I entered, two security guards stood with their hands behind their backs, their eyes tracking over the court like hawks. Three officers were walking around the entire area, casually strolling between tables, speaking into their radios in low voices.

We had been to this mall at least a hundred times over the last year, and I couldn't remember ever seeing more than maybe one single mall cop throughout the entire building.

My heart rate picked up, the slow trickle of fear coiling at the base of my spine.

When you live in fight or flight for years on end, your body learns to warn you the instant something feels off. Small things most people would probably overlook become warning signs, allowing a steady trickle of adrenaline into your body.

"Ma'am." I spun around so fast I nearly launched my phone, looking into the confused eyes of the man holding my drinks.

"Thanks," I muttered, stuffing my phone into my pocket and taking the cups, making a beeline for the table Aaron was sitting at.

"Aaron, did you notice all the cops?"

His brow furrowed as he looked around us, I watched as the line of his lips pulled tighter with each uniform he counted.

"It's a little odd. Could be anything though, Shy. Maybe they've had a spike in shoplifters lately." His tone was light and joking, but the tension in his shoulders told me I wasn't the only one concerned.

I chewed at the inside of my cheek instead of responding. I wasn't a paranoid or nervous person, but I was cautious out of necessity.

We decided to walk down to the sporting store and stock up on the protein powders Aaron used for the gym. His phone rang as we entered, and I nodded at the finger he held up and continued toward the back of the store where the tubs of powder were. I grabbed the flavors I knew he liked, adding in a couple new ones just for fun, then took my time weaving up and down the aisles to kill time.

"We had to move Grace's birthday to the house. It just doesn't feel safe to have them out in public anymore."

"Who could blame you? Abigail was taken from cheer practice, can you imagine? Broad daylight, and no one saw a thing."

"It's awful. I can't stomach the thought."

I leaned closer to the shelf on my left, eavesdropping on the conversation two women were having on the other side.

"Six girls, just in the last two months. They have got to catch whoever is doing this soon, or we're going to have to lock our girls up in the house."

Six girls.

Six missing girls.

My pulse pounded in my ears.

Flashbacks of the day I was taken ripped through my mind like broken glass.

It's not the same.

Not the same. Not the same. Not the same.

Aaron entered my line of vision, his expression flat. He didn't have a quip about me standing with my head pressed against a shelf of yoga mats. He just took the basket from me and set it on the floor before guiding me out of the mall and into the parking garage.

Aaron opened my door and ushered me into the truck, pulling my seatbelt across my chest and buckling it before shutting the door softly.

My head was swimming.

The last thing I saw before I passed out was the man standing on the other side of the parking garage, the black mask covering everything but his eyes.

Which were looking right at me.

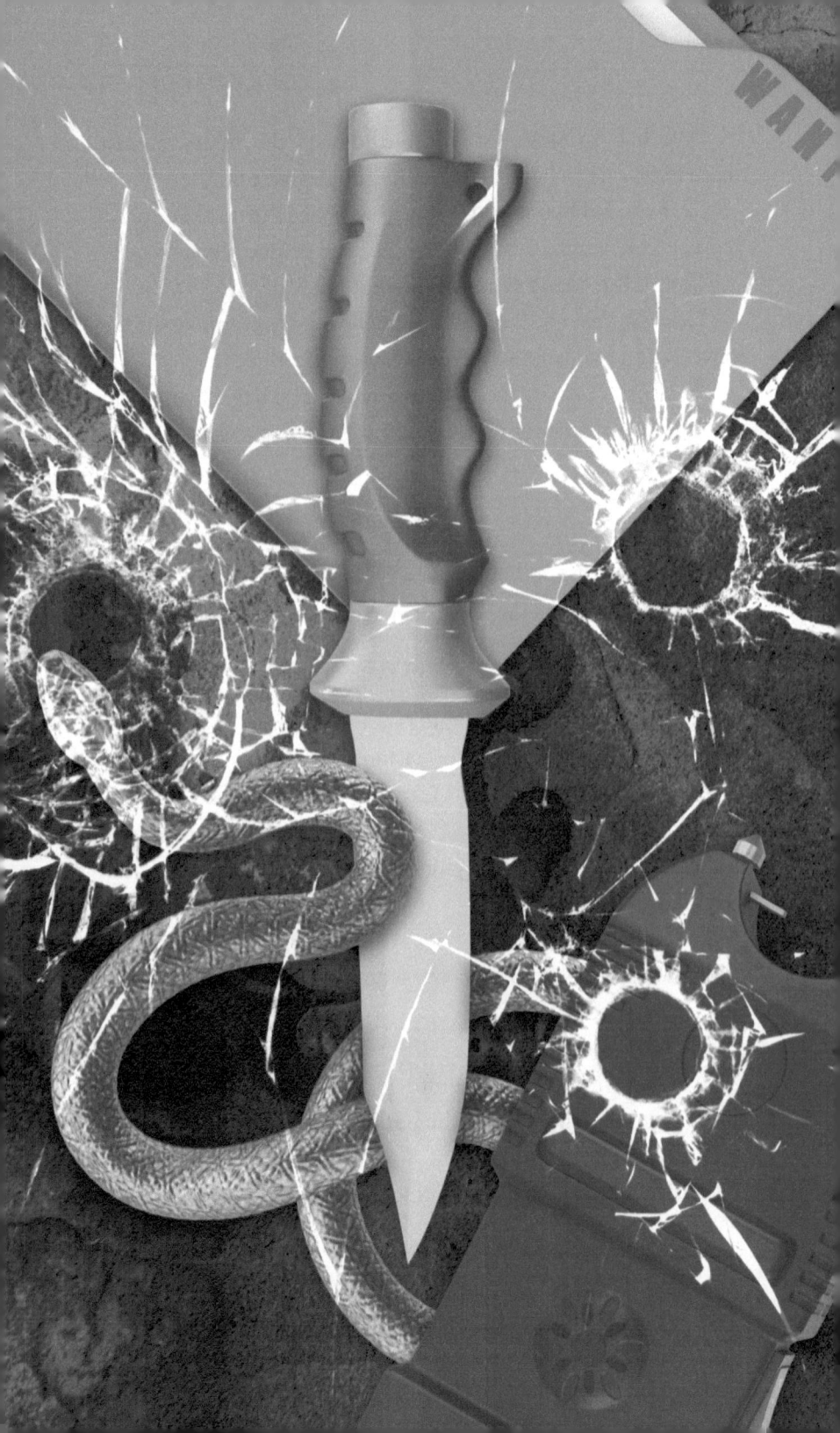

CHAPTER SIX

SHILOH

The sound of a door slamming downstairs jolted me awake; the clock on my nightstand told me I had been out for over an hour. I could hear muffled voices downstairs; it sounded like they were arguing. I rolled my neck as I climbed out of bed, sliding my feet into my slippers and tiptoeing toward my bedroom door. As I cracked it open, the voices became clearer. I heard Aaron and my dad, a few other distinctly male voices that I couldn't quite place interrupted here and there as they all argued about something in hushed tones. Keeping my steps light, I left my room, creeping slowly down the staircase until the living room came into view.

There were at least ten people; some of them sat on the edge of the couch, files spread out on the coffee table in front of them. The rest of them stood, or paced, around the far side of the room. My dad and Aaron were in the latter group.

I noticed my mom, sitting in a chair next to one of the large floor to ceiling windows, her fingers rubbing at her lips as she stared outside. Her leg bounced violently, but I don't think she heard a single thing that was being said around her. For such a present woman, she was a million miles away right now.

"We can't just wait around, David. We need to get her out

of here. I can find a safe house. I'll take her myself and stay with her until all of this blows over."

"These things don't just 'blow over,' Cross. You know that."

My eyes flicked to the TV; a picture of a young girl in a cheer uniform displayed behind a reporter's head.

The headline at the bottom of the screen read 'Another abduction in Sunbridge. What police are doing to stop the spree of kidnappings.'

Spree of kidnappings. The words strung together on my tongue as I whispered them, but they didn't make any sense. My brain refused to wrap around them.

"They left a picture of her on the doorstep, David. Someone is trying to come back for her."

My heart stuttered in my chest, a vile, icy kind of dread leaking into my bloodstream. Ruben was dead; the rest of them were in prison. Who was left? Who would come looking for me?

"She is safest here, Cross. You are not the voice of authority here," my uncle Miles barked.

"And you are? Where the fuck were you when she was taken the first time, huh? Weren't you the one who had taken her to the park?" Aaron scoffed.

"That's enough."

I watched as Aaron stared down my uncle, which wasn't hard considering Aaron was a tall, mean looking motherfucker and my uncle looked like he spent his days hunched over a desk.

I barely remembered him from when I was younger. I don't think he was around all that much. Once I turned back up though, so did he. He visited a few times a month now, even though he lived a few towns over. I never got any closer to him than I did anyone else, but I also didn't care much about forging that relationship. He was disappointed when I didn't run into his arms the first time I saw him and went out of his way to force a bond there. For my birthday a couple months ago, he gave me a pearl necklace that probably cost close to what my car did. I didn't wear pearls, nor did I want jewelry from some man I barely knew, so I had tossed them in my jewelry box where they had sat collecting dust ever since.

"She will stay here. We'll hire a private company to keep watch at the house."

"I'll take care of it," Aaron said, leaving the room with his phone pressed to his ear.

My dad turned, his eyes catching mine, and a frown formed on his mouth. "Shiloh. We didn't mean to wake you."

I stood straighter, bracing myself for the answer to the question I needed to ask. "Is it them? The same people from The Manor?"

"We don't know that for sure."

"But you think it is." That one wasn't a question, but a statement. I could see the fear I felt inside mirrored on all their faces.

"We're just being cautious."

"What picture was left on the doorstep?"

My dad swore under his breath; the rest of the men in the room looked to the floor rather than at me.

"Shiloh, let's go talk in my office, sweetheart."

I walked down the stairs, ignoring the motionless people in the room who averted their gaze when I passed, and followed my dad into his large home office, closing the door behind me.

He sighed heavily as he sat down in the chair behind his desk, his head falling into his hands before he raised it to look at me.

The way his hands clasped in front of him and pressed against his mouth told me what I needed to know. Anger, fear, and anxiety were so palpable in the space between us I could have plucked each feeling from the air and held it in my hands.

"It was me, wasn't it. A picture of me?"

"Yes."

"Do you know who sent it?"

"No. The feeds to the security system were down when it was delivered; we aren't sure why."

I nodded. There was the slightest tremble in his words, a shake to his voice so delicate I would have missed it if I hadn't been searching for it. He was terrified. Which meant I should be too.

The initial wave of panic had struck hard and fast, seizing me with a strength so violent I thought it would swallow me whole. And then... it passed. The numbness I had grown accustomed to returned, and the fear ebbed away.

"The girls that are missing, is it connected?"

"We believe so. I won't lie to you, Shiloh. I will never lie to you. But there are things that it might be better if you are kept in the dark about, for your own mental health."

My mental state hadn't been healthy since I was prepubescent, but he didn't need to hear about that. I gave him a small smile and nodded my head like a good daughter would.

"I'll stay with Aaron if I'm out, and I will only go places I need to for now. Okay?"

He smiled, though it didn't reach his eyes, and came around the desk to pull me into his arms. His short beard scratched along the top of my head as he placed a soft kiss to my crown. "I love you, my girl."

"I love you too, Daddy."

He pulled back to look me over, as if checking I was still present and whole. "I need to go clear everyone out. How about a movie night when I get done?"

"Sounds good."

He squeezed my arms before releasing me and leaving the room. I listened to the sharp click of his expensive loafers as he walked down the hallway, waiting until the sound had faded before I went to his desk. The stack of files was small, but I had counted when we first came in.

Six files. Six missing girls.

I started from the top, opening the file and checking the name, age, and date of abduction before moving to the next. The second to last file made my hands freeze in place. A picture was pinned to the inside of the file of a little girl with bright blue eyes and blonde hair. She smiled in her cheer uniform with her pom-pom's raised.

Name: Abigail McCarthy

Age: 8

She was taken over two months ago. Her face was burned into my memory—the trust in her eyes as she climbed through her bedroom window with me, clutching her little nightlight. They had gone back for her. A rage so hot I thought it would burn me alive erupted inside me. Anger like I had never felt before consumed every free inch of my mind. I spent weeks coordinating that mission and how to throw it so it wouldn't be obvious.

I made sure she was safe, and they went back for her? I snatched the file, tucking it under my shirt before rushing back to my room and locking the door. I pored over every word in her file, her parents' names and occupations, her hobbies and what she was last seen wearing.

A name was written in sloppy cursive on the last page, with the word 'suspect?' underneath it.

Joseph Waynes.

DNA evidence had connected him, but it was only on the outside of the house, the same balcony I had used to take her. He claimed he had done maintenance around the property and the parents, being the typical rich assholes they were, couldn't remember the faces of all the people they had hired over the years.

He was still being investigated, but it wasn't looking good. I had promised that girl I would keep her safe, that everything would be okay. Who knew what she had seen since they had taken her? It was a split-second decision, an understanding more than it was a choice. Maybe my psyche had finally broken. Whatever it was, I had decided.

I was going to find Joseph Waynes, I was going to get whatever information he had out of him, and then I was going to kill him.

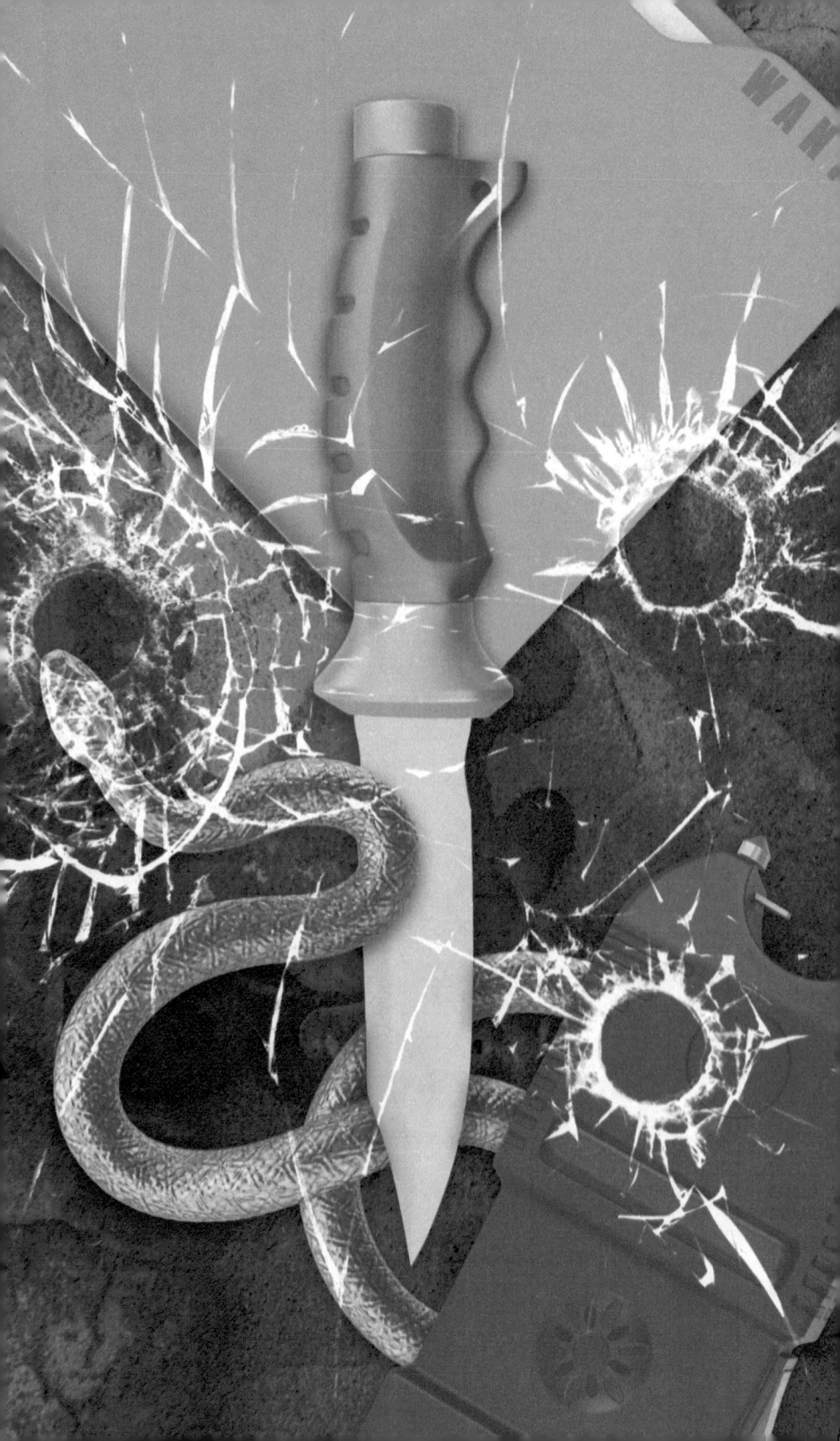

CHAPTER SEVEN

SILOH

Finding someone was incredibly easy when you knew everything about them that the local police force did. The last piece of paper in Abigail's file had the last known address for Joseph, along with his phone number and a handful of other personal information.

I was tucked away in the shadows across the street from his apartment complex, my eyes glued to the window I was sure was his, waiting for my opening. I convinced my parents I was staying with Lottie, and although they were reluctant to let me leave, my age and the life experience I carried around with me at nineteen made it hard for them to outright tell me no. I made a quick trip to a little army surplus store right outside of town, and turned the location off on my phone, and my car was parked three blocks away in front of a sushi spot Lottie loved, just in case they decided to check up on me.

A delivery driver parked in front of the building, juggling brown paper bags of food as he got out and walked toward the door. There was my opening. I walked quickly across the street, slowing my steps as he punched in the code and started attempting to get the door open.

"Here, let me get that for you," I said, reaching out and pulling the door open for him to step inside.

"Thanks, got my hands a little full here."

"Not a problem, have a good night."

He walked toward the elevator, which meant I would be taking the stairs. I didn't need any small talk to occupy my focus tonight. Three floors up, apartment 307. I slipped my mask over my face, the thin black fabric covering my bright red hair and concealing everything but my eyes. I began pulling my gloves on as I reached the third floor, and by the time I got to his door, I already had my knife in my hand.

I stood close enough that I covered the peephole, knocking softly. Footsteps sounded inside, growing closer as my heartbeat notched up. The door swung open, and I took just long enough to make sure the face in front of me matched the one in the file, before I slammed the hilt of the knife against his throat and barreled forward, shoving him backwards and kicking the door shut behind me.

"Who the fuck are you?!" The words came out broken, in between hacking coughs.

I pointed toward one of the dining room chairs with my knife.

"Sit."

He looked from the chair, back to me. I could see it in his eyes, he was measuring me, trying to decide if he could take me down, even though I was the only one armed. I looked from the chair to his face, trying to decide the best way to actually make this man do what I wanted him to.

I sighed, pulling the taser my dad had gifted me last month from my back pocket and letting it crackle between us.

"Easy way or hard way, Joseph. I do not have a preference."

He ground his teeth together, but moved to the chair and sat down, his eyes tracking me as I moved around the space in front of him.

"Let's just get right to it. I need information, and you are going to supply that information."

"And if I don't?"

"Then we will see how long it takes for you to bleed out once your dick is detached from your body."

He scoffed, but I noticed the way his thighs pressed together tightly.

"What information?"

"There was a little girl, one of six actually, who was abducted two months ago from her cheer practice at Jones Elementary. Ring any bells?"

His face blanched, but he shook his head.

"Joseph, I don't have time for you to lie to me. For starters, you aren't good at it, and I'm on a bit of a time crunch here."

I pulled out my phone, pulling up the picture of Abigail and turning it around so he could see it.

"This is Abigail. This is the girl I am looking for. You're gonna need to tell me everything you know about her, quickly."

He stuttered over his excuses, nothing coherent enough to form a full sentence.

"Alright then, hard way it is."

I lunged forward, pressing the taser against his crotch before he could process the movement and hit the button. The crackle of electricity was muffled against his groaning, the veins in his neck thick and prominent as his body was forced into a stiff position. I pulled back, quickly grabbing the two sets of handcuffs from my bag and snapping each wrist into a cuff, and the other cuff to each arm of the chair.

"You're fucking crazy!" he spat, his face an ugly shade of red.

"You know what? You might actually be right. Unfortunately for you, I'm here instead of seeing a shrink. Who took her?"

"I'm not telling you anything. You can kill me, but I won't talk."

"Don't tempt me."

"Go ahead, they'll come for me if I rat them out anyway."

I let out a heavy sigh. Why were men so difficult?

"Joseph?"

"What?"

"I'm going to need you to put this in your mouth." I pulled two bandanas out of my bag, rolling one into a ball and folding the other.

"Fuck you."

"You can open your mouth on your own, or I will tase you until it opens for me. Choose."

He muttered a string of curses, but his mouth slowly fell open.

"Good boy." I stuffed the bandana in, tying the other one tight around his head to hold it in place.

His eyes were little more than slits as he glared at me, though the intimidation was lacking due to his current predicament.

"So, here's what we're going to do," I said, twirling the knife in my hand. "I'm going to start poking around on you, and when you get ready to talk, you just tap your foot and let me know. Got that?"

He mumbled uselessly around the fabric in his mouth, rolling his eyes when he heard his own words coming out muffled.

"Nod your head to tell me you understand."

He didn't move, just sat there glaring like his eyes could cut through me if he stared hard enough.

I shrugged. "Good enough for me."

I flipped the knife in my hand, gripping the hilt and driving the blade into the flesh of his thigh. What I'm sure would have been a very loud scream attempted to leave his mouth, the sound barely loud enough to be heard in the next room.

Oh. Ew?

I wasn't expecting the wave of nausea that hit me when the knife sunk into him. In my defense, I'd never stabbed anyone before, but holy shit, that was gross. I shook my head and ripped the blade free, trailing it up his stomach and over his chest, leaving a streak of crimson along the dingy white shirt he wore. I settled on his shoulder, tapping the cool steel against his skin before plunging the knife in once again.

Nope. Not any less disgusting the second time.

Tears formed in the corners of his eyes as I slowly slid it free. Blood ran in a steady stream from his shoulder, rivaling the wound on his leg that had formed a small puddle of blood beneath his feet.

"More? Alright."

I traced his jaw with the knife, reveling in the way his entire body shuddered and his eyes squeezed shut.

"How many fingers do you think you can lose before you pass out, realistically?"

I tapped the blade against the knuckles on his left hand, watching as he curled his fingers into fists, trying to escape the thought of them being amputated in his own kitchen.

"No? Not into that?" I pouted at him.

I moved the blade back to his face, pressing it firmly just above his cheek and dragging it down, following the curve of his jaw and leaving a long slice across his flesh. The blood was everywhere, dripping from his face in sticky streams.

Slicing isn't as bad. I need to write that down somewhere.

"What about an eye? Surely you could live with just one. I'm not exactly a surgeon though, and this knife is getting slick, so let's hope this doesn't slip and turn into a lobotomy." A manic cackle left my mouth, I think it surprised me as much as it did him.

He shook his head back and forth, tapping his foot frantically against the floor.

I tucked the knife into the back of my pants by the hilt, grasping each side of the knotted fabric around his head and forced his eyes to meet mine.

"If I take this off and you don't talk, I will take out one of your eyes and I will stomp on it like a grape."

He nodded weakly, gagging as I pulled the fabric from his mouth.

"I don't know where she is."

I reached behind me, pulling the knife free and swinging it toward him.

"WAIT! I'm telling the truth! Okay? I took her. But I don't know where she went after that. I was paid to grab her and deliver her to an address. Everything was done anonymously. I don't know who these guys are, I just needed the money."

"Where did you drop her off at?"

"Feller's Mill off the old access road that runs behind the lake. I didn't see anyone there. I put her in the building and grabbed the bag of cash, and I left. That's it."

"How did they find you to do the job?"

"I don't know."

I swung the knife out, slicing a small line against his arm.

"Fuck! I don't! I was at Sinner's, and someone slipped me a piece of paper, it had a phone number and that's it. I called it and they set everything else up."

"Do you still have the paper?"

"It's in my wallet."

I tossed the knife aside, kicking his chair with full force so that it landed on its side with a thud. I slipped my hands behind him and fished out his wallet, shoving the whole thing into my bag before righting his chair.

"Alright, Joseph. One more question."

He swallowed hard but nodded.

"Did you hurt her?"

Was he pale from losing blood, or was he afraid to answer that question?

"It's a yes or no question," I prompted him, waiting for him to find the balls to answer.

"I mean, not on purpose? I had to knock her out, she wouldn't come with me, you kno—"

I ran the knife across his neck in a steady line, pressing hard enough to hit anything vital. The shock on his face was quickly replaced by fear as he felt the blood flood down and coat his chest. The wide, terrified look in his eyes told me he knew he was dying. I watched the blood drain from his neck with my head tilted to the side. It was slower than I thought it would be. He thrashed around in his chair, trying to scream, though nothing came out. His movements grew sluggish, his color draining to an ashy gray as I watched.

I pulled the mask from my face, stuffing it along with the taser back in my bag before retrieving the handcuff keys and bending to unlock both sets. I opted for wiping the knife clean on his pants. He was already covered in blood anyway, so it didn't seem like it mattered. Once I had everything packed away, I slipped out his door, down the stairs, and out into the fresh air.

I held my hand out in front of me, expecting to see it shaking from adrenaline or fear, or... anything. It was steady, my heartbeat even and calm.

There was a moment where I thought those things should concern me, considering what I had just done, but I pushed that thought aside. I was definitely fucking insane. But who wouldn't be at this point? Maybe I'd go see a psychiatrist when I was done with all this, but for right now, I was going to find that little girl, and then all the others.

And I was going to cut down anyone who stood between us.

CHAPTER EIGHT

CREED

"My god, she's lost it," Kane's voice rumbled in my earpiece.

"She's incredible." How could he see anything else? Was she a little messy? A little sloppy with the clean up? Sure. But for her first kill, she did damn good. There was no hesitation; she didn't question herself once. We had installed a small camera in Joseph's apartment last week to keep an eye on him, but nothing we did came close to the show she gave us. She gave herself over to her instincts, letting them guide her hands as she carved her rage into his flesh.

"Let's get this cleaned up so we can get out of here, please." Kane got out of the van and slammed the door, hefting his bag over his shoulder. Nate and I exchanged a look before following behind him.

Kane had always been a grumpy fucker, but lately he seemed to have an abnormally large thorn in his ass. We made it into the apartment, getting to work on wiping down any prints she may have left behind. Nate ran a small handheld vacuum over the area in case there were any strands of hair we had missed, while Kane wormed his way into the building's security system and erased both her entrance and ours from the tapes.

The job only took roughly twenty minutes. I was the last one to leave the apartment, pulling the fresh pack of playing cards from my pockets and shuffling through them until I found the one I was looking for. Shiloh had no idea she had caught our attention, to my knowledge, she was only recently aware she had caught the attention of anyone at all.

Cross had called me when the third girl had been taken, and again when Shiloh's photo was delivered to her house. It wasn't hard to call in that favor he owed us and get us on board with Shiloh's father as private security for their house.

Kane had been doing under the table surveillance since he was in high school, eventually turning it into a legitimate business. He hired Nate and I after we turned eighteen, and we had been working for him ever since. Aaron and Kane were raised in the same foster home from the time they were in diapers, eventually getting adopted together and they've been a package deal ever since. While Aaron decided to join the police force, Kane opted for a more direct route. On the surface, Kane, Nate, and I operate a private security company. Our side gig is hunting down the morally corrupt predators that reside within our state and eliminating them.

Aaron feeds us information when it comes across his desk, or we find it ourselves. We had already been investigating The Manor when Aaron was assigned to go undercover, which made our work a little easier. Until I saw her.

I'd heard Aaron talk about her plenty of times. The redhead that had moved up the ranks, Ruben's favorite girl, the daughter of the police chief. Nothing he said had ever stood out to me, but then again, not much did.

I wasn't what most people would classify as 'all there.'

There was no traumatic backstory for me, no abusive parents, no real reason why I was the way I was.

Maybe seeing what my friends had gone through snapped something into place for me; maybe I watched too many super-hero movies. Whatever it was, nothing brought me more joy than seeing the fear on a grown man's face, knowing he had instilled just as much into a child before he got to me.

I tucked the edges of the card into the slit in his cheek so that it stuck out of his face, my calling card. Kingston Creed, or The Red King, according to the news stations. We had taken out thirteen men in the last two years, each one of them guilty of the vilest of crimes.

The justice system was a goddamn joke, and none of us were willing to let them handle these cases.

After each target, I left a card, the news reported on it, and then the 'secure' group chats would go wild, and Kane would record every single message. It was like shooting fish in a barrel.

Was this my kill? No. Part of me hoped she would see the news tomorrow morning, recognize his face, and *not* recognize the card they would say was found. We were scheduled to start patrol at her house at five tomorrow morning. If I was lucky, I would be in the same room when the realization dawned on her —she hadn't been alone in that apartment. If I had it my way, she would never be alone again.

No, I would be around. Even if she didn't see me. I climbed back into the van and shut the door as Kane took off, heading for our shared apartment across the city.

"You need to keep it professional with her, Creed. Aaron will kill you if you try anything."

"I will not 'try' anything. I will 'do' as she lets me."

Nate snorted from the front seat.

"Don't waste your breath, Kane. He watched her commit murder; he's probably already planning their wedding."

"I'm thinking carrot cake, what do you think, Nathaniel?"

"Creed, I'm serious."

"I know. I'm not planning on listening to you, but I am aware of your grave warning."

He scoffed at me, dismissing me with a wave.

Aaron would absolutely try to kill me. Fortunately, I have a much higher body count than him. Something about her had crawled beneath my skin the first time I saw her—her face twisted in disgust as she cradled the small girl in her arms, so much self-hatred written across her face for anyone to read.

She hated what she was doing, what she was, but there was no life left in her to fight it. I saw the smallest spark in her tonight, a miniscule twinkle in her eyes that gave her away. She was in there, somewhere. That place had beaten everything about her into a box and locked it up tight, but I was going to help her break it open. She was realizing the freedom she possessed, the ability to eliminate the threats around her, and I wanted to be the one to help her see who she could be when she was untethered.

Aaron Cross be damned.

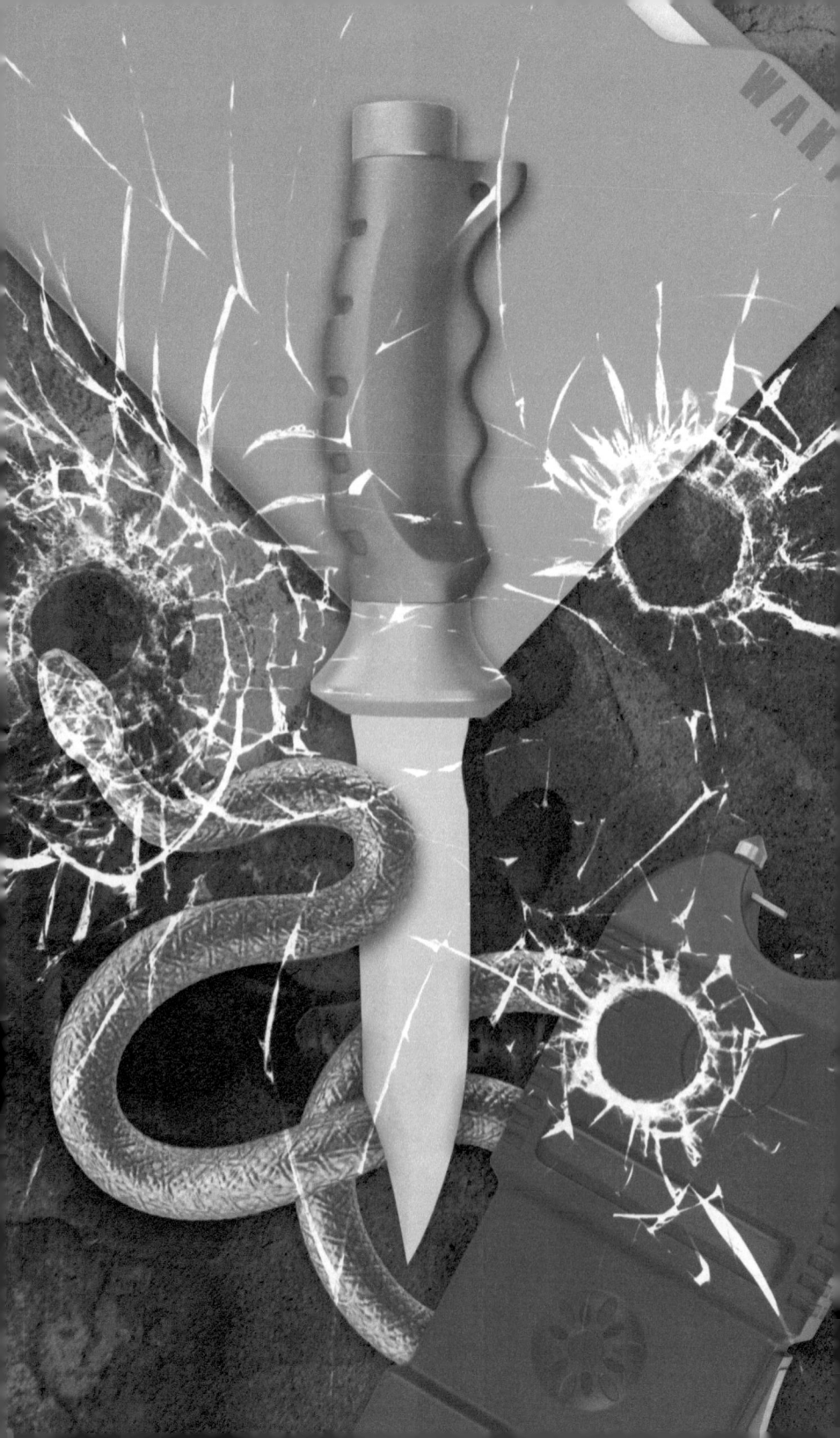

CHAPTER NINE

SHILOH

I pulled into the garage and shut off the engine, relaxing into the leather seats of my car and enjoying the moment of silence before I went inside to lie to whichever parent would inevitably be waiting up for me. I was going to have to figure out a way to get out of the house again this weekend. The place Joseph had mentioned, Sinner's, was a dive bar downtown and the second place I was going to look for answers.

I think my father would spontaneously combust if I told him I was going there, so lying was the only option. I also needed to get a fake I.D., but Lottie could help with that. She lived in a house twice the size of mine and had driven a Bentley since she was fifteen, but she hated every minute of it. All her free time was spent downtown in the only club in Sunbridge, or at some house party in the middle of nowhere. She would know someone who could get me what I needed. I rehearsed my lines in my head as I entered the house. My mom was sitting on the couch in the living room when I passed through, a book in her hands as she looked up at me.

"Hi, honey. Have fun?"

"Yeah, just watched a movie and talked. I'm gonna head on up."

"Alright, see you in the morning."

"Night, Mom."

I walked straight to my room and entered the ensuite bathroom, stripping off my clothes and dumping them into the bathtub, filling it with cold water and an entire bottle of peroxide.
The water turned a pinkish color almost immediately. Must
have gotten more blood on me than I thought.

I scrubbed the clothes together, wringing and rinsing over
and over until the water ran clear, and then sticking them in the
laundry basket in the corner. I would take them down in the
morning before I left for work and get them in the washer
before Mom did. I didn't want to answer any questions about
why my entire outfit was soaking wet.

Once the bathtub was clean, I slipped into the shower. I
stood under the stream of hot water for a while, enjoying the
cool tiles pressed against my forehead. There was considerably
less blood on my actual body than there had been on my
clothes, which made washing up easy. I dried quickly, ignoring
the myriad of scars decorating my midsection and pulled on
one of the huge t-shirts I'd stolen from Aaron at some point, the
worn fabric nearly grazing my knees, and crawled into bed to
stare at the stars on the ceiling.

I wonder how long it will take them to find him. He's still
under investigation so surely, they won't leave him alone for
long. He had a nice long criminal history too, so the suspect list
should be nice and long. I was one step closer to figuring out
who was taking the girls, one step closer to saving the only
person I had ever made a promise to and meant it.

Wherever she was, I hoped she was safe and that she knew
I was coming.

I had always thought of Ruben as the most powerful man
on earth, he snapped his fingers and people jumped to do whatever heinous thing he told them to. I had just figured The

Manor had ended when he did; everyone else involved was still sitting in prison awaiting trial.

The missing girls were concerning on their own, but I don't know that I would have made the connection as quickly as I did if it hadn't been for the picture of me. I couldn't get any details out of my dad about it, not even when it was taken. Was it a picture from before? A school picture or a Christmas card photo? Was it one of the hundreds that Ruben had taken of me over the years? The thought made my stomach churn. I guess it didn't really matter, the only important thing was that we got it. It was a message; someone wanted me to know they were watching.

I mentally worked through every person I could remember from The Manor, from the hired hands to the maids to the drivers. None of them had an ounce of the influence that Ruben did, nowhere near enough to conduct an operation like that. Maybe it was a copycat? Someone who saw what he had created and destroyed and thought they could do it better? It made more sense than someone carrying on the organization for him. Ruben would never pass the torch willingly; there were parts of that operation that only he was allowed to deal with.

When I was ready to talk to Aaron again after I got back, he took me to get a milkshake and explained everything. How he had joined the police force and why, everything leading up to the day he was given orders to infiltrate The Manor undercover, the day he met me. I saw the shame and guilt on his face as he explained why he couldn't just grab me and run. The investigation had been over a year in the making, and while they could have busted it at any time, they needed as much proof and evidence as possible to make the charges stick. I understood, but it didn't make it any easier to stomach.

Now the thought of someone rebuilding Ruben's empire

from scratch gnawed at my mind, sending waves of unease through my body. Dad had hired a private security company to start tomorrow, which should have made me feel safer, but it didn't. The idea of strange men in the house made my skin crawl, but Aaron had approved them which meant he either knew them or had done an in-depth background check and decided they were safe enough to be here.

As long as they stayed out of the way so that I could continue my own surveillance, I guess it didn't really matter.

My next step was to call the number on the paper I had taken from Joseph's wallet. The chances that it wasn't a burner phone were slim, but it was the best lead I had right now. Aaron would likely be breathing down my neck until they figured out who left the picture, but Lottie was always a good cover. All I had to tell her was that I met a guy somewhere and needed her to cover for me, and she was all over it. I just needed to get to these guys before the cops did.

Easy.

CHAPTER TEN

CREED

We pulled up to the massive house fifteen minutes before we were expected to be there. Aaron was already waiting for us on the front steps. He jogged down to meet us, shaking Nate's hand and hugging Kane before turning to me and extending his hand. I shook it, gripping it as firmly as he gripped mine.

"Morning, gentlemen. Mr. Hale is waiting for you in his office, I'll show you the way."

We entered into a large foyer and followed Aaron through the living room to a room at the end of the hallway. Chief Hale sat behind his desk with his phone pressed to his ear, holding a finger up in our direction as he mumbled into the phone and then hung up.

"Sorry about that," he said as he stood, "I'm David, nice to meet you all."

Kane was the first to speak, as usual. "I'm Kane, this is Nate, and Creed."

"You will meet my wife and daughter in a little while. Shiloh usually sleeps in a bit, but Jennifer should be down any minute. Can I get you gentlemen anything to drink?"

"We're good. Can you show me where your security moni-tors are? I'd like to take a look at your system."

"Of course, follow me."

We followed him across the hall, into a room that looked like a gamer's wet dream. The far wall was made up entirely of large monitors, all showing different corners of the house from the outside. A desk to the left had three that displayed the kitchen, living room, and entry way.

"Does anyone monitor these?"

"Not all the time. We didn't find it necessary until recently. I'd like one of you to be in this room at all times. If you want to rotate or assign positions, it doesn't matter to me."

"We can do that. Are there any other cameras in the house?"

"No, Aaron and I have been discussing adding some, but we would need to inform the girls."

"Understandable. I would recommend having a camera at every entry point. You can't be too cautious."

"You boys add whatever you need. Aaron will be around if I'm not, so just let one of us know."

"David?" Mrs. Hale entered the room behind David, her features so similar to Shiloh it looked like she had herself cloned and aged down.

"Jen, these are the men from the security team—Creed, Kane, and Nate. This is my wife, Jen."

"Nice to meet you, though I wish it were under different circumstances," she said, a sad smile on her face as she shook each of our hands. "I've had the guest rooms cleaned up, two upstairs and one right across the hall here." She pointed to a closed door behind her. "Please make yourselves at home. I can't tell you how much we appreciate you coming on such short notice."

"We're going to have this place locked down tight, Mrs. Hale. Don't worry about that."

"Aaron trusts you, so that's good enough for me. Have you met Shiloh yet?"

Yes.

"Not yet. We need to do a perimeter sweep and check for blind spots in your cameras, first thing. How many entrances are there?"

"Front door, two on the left side, the garage, and the utility room."

"Nate, go with Mr. Hale and check the side doors, I'll handle the garage, Creed can take the utility room. Figure out the best camera placement and mark it."

"Utility room is down the hallway, all the way at the end, last door on the right."

"Yes, sir."

"Let's get it done." Kane clapped his hands together.

"Aye aye captain." Nate gave him a salute, following behind David as Kane turned and headed for the garage. I made my way down the long hall, admiring the borderline obnoxious level of pictures hanging along the walls. It was a shrine to their family, before Shiloh had been taken. Dozens of family photos dotted with picture frames showing her as a baby, a toddler, messy red hair and a freckled face smeared with the remnants of an ice cream cone as she smiled at the person taking her picture.

The frames trailed all the way down the hallway, the last one was a snapshot from what I'm assuming was her eleventh birthday, judging by the candle on the cake in front of her.

The hum of the washer was barely audible as I cracked the door open and peered inside. The room was small, a washer and dryer to the left side. And her.

She had her back to me, her hands braced against the edge

of a deep sink to the right of the washing machine. Wet clothes —last night's clothes if I wasn't mistaken—were piled inside. A slow drip of water slid down her wrist before she shook it off, blowing a breath out of the corner of her mouth that tossed a piece of hair off her face. She hadn't noticed me yet.

I pushed the door open further and leaned against the doorframe, crossing my arms as I watched her scrub at the shirt in her hands. *Adorable.*

"You know," I drawled, breaking the silence in the room, "most people let the machines do the washing."

She jumped, twisting around, her breath catching in her throat. Wide, sharp blue eyes landed on me, flashing with something that looked dangerously like intrigue. Her eyes trailed up and down my frame, sizing me up.

I liked that.

"Jesus," she muttered, wiping her forehead with the back of her wet hand, "ever heard of knocking?"

"Ever heard of locking doors?" I countered, smirking.

Her lips parted slightly at the nickname, realization dawning on her face.

Yes, Doll. I'm the one who snuck in the window and shot Ruben in front of you.

She turned back to the sink, wringing out the soaked fabric. "I don't need an audience."

"Too bad," I said. "You've got one."

She huffed out an annoyed breath. "Are you just going to stand there?"

I pushed off the doorframe and stepped inside, taking slow, deliberate steps into her space. Just enough to watch as her hands gripped the edge of the sink a little tighter.

"Depends," I said. "You gonna tell me why you're in here playing maid instead of tossing those in the washer like a normal person?"

She hesitated, tipping her head side to side like she was trying to determine if she wanted to tell me the truth or not. The lack of hesitation didn't have anything to do with me; I honestly think she just didn't care all that much.

"They needed extra attention."

I glanced at the water, the faint pink swirl draining from the fabric. Blood. *My girl.*

I smiled, slow and knowing. "Rough night?

Her jaw tensed. "None of your business."

I chuckled, the sound coming out low and dark in the quiet room. "You sure? I've got quite a vested interest in your nights now. I'm your new *personal* security guard."

Her hands stilled in the water as she turned her head just enough to look at me. "I don't need a babysitter."

I stepped closer. Close enough to feel the warmth radiating off her, close enough that she would have to make a choice— hold her ground or back away.

She stayed planted where she was.

"Then who will keep you off the drugs?" I widened my eyes, concern in my words, though my tone was drenched in humor.

She slit her eyes at me, flipping me the bird with a wet finger before tossing the bundle of soaking clothes into the washer, hitting the start button, and slipping out of the room.

I barked a laugh as she slammed the door.

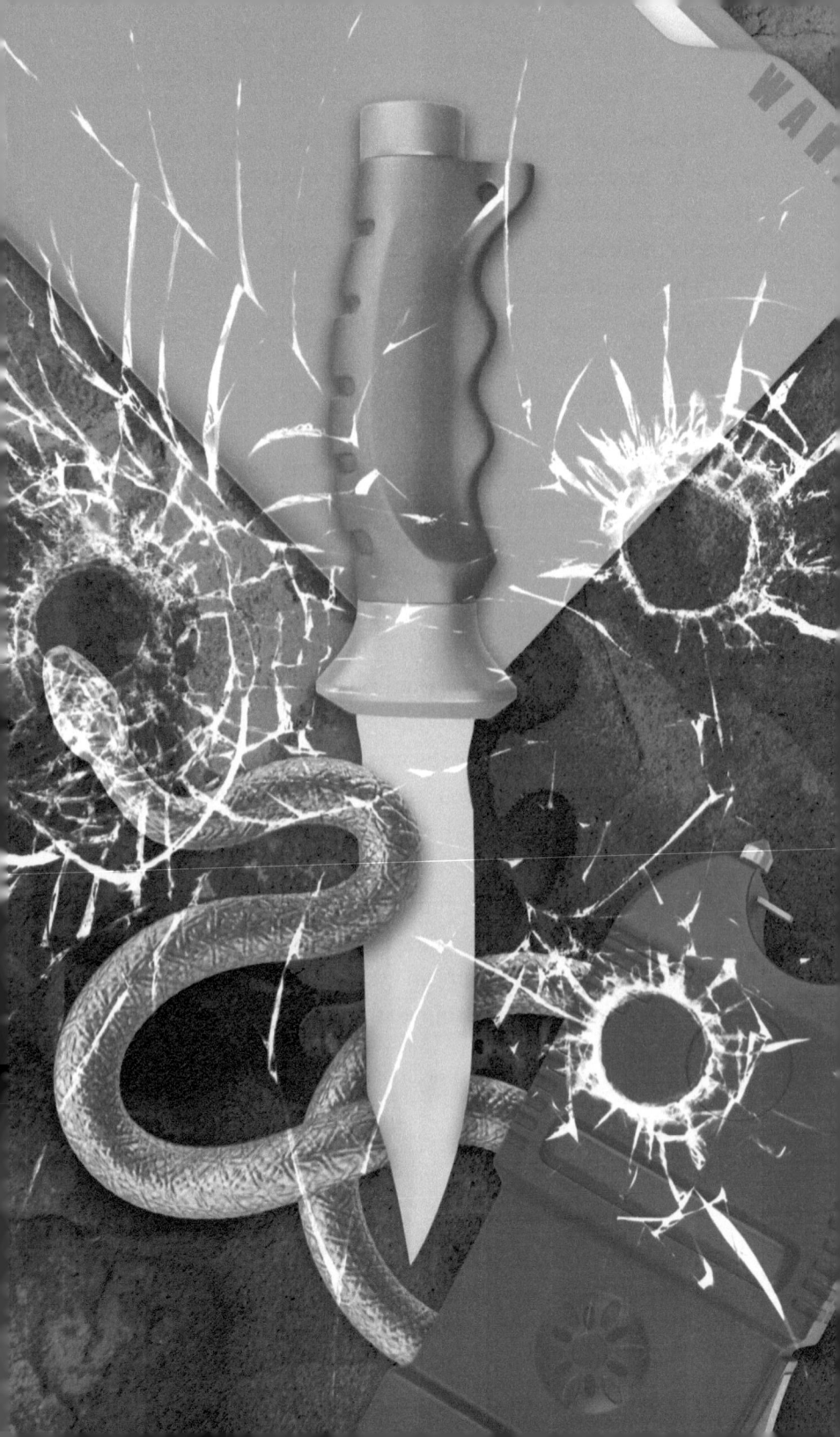

CHAPTER ELEVEN

SHILOH

I hustled down the hallway, my heartbeat surprisingly erratic after that interaction. I don't know how he managed to get hired on here, but Aaron had to have something to do with it. Were they actually a security company? When I found Aaron, we were going to have a long talk about why the man who shot Ruben stood in my laundry room right now. I slowed my steps as I approached the living room; the scent of the chamomile tea Mom always made when she was home hung in the air, so she had to be nearby. She didn't know the gritty details of my time away, or about the rescue. Aaron and I agreed to tell my parents what they needed to know and leave out the rest.

Mom sat in her usual chair by the window wearing wrinkled scrubs, dark circles under her eyes and a book resting open in her lap as her fingers absently traced the worn spine. Sunlight slanted through the glass, making the silver in her hair glint like diamonds, but her focus wasn't on the book anymore. It was on the TV. I followed her gaze.

The morning news flickered across the screen. A reporter stood outside a very familiar looking apartment complex, the entrance behind her marked off with bright yellow crime scene tape.

"—body of Joseph Waynes was discovered this morning by

his neighbor. Authorities have yet to release a statement, but sources claim Waynes was well known in Sunbridge for his criminal activity."

I exhaled slowly through my nose. They had found him quicker than I had expected.

"In a strange twist, an anonymous source present at the scene reported a calling card left on the body—"

Pardon?

"Though unconfirmed, rumors are already swirling that a playing card was left at the scene, giving way to speculation that this may be one in a string of murders committed by a serial killer known as The Red King. More than a dozen bodies have been found within one hundred miles of Sunbridge with a single king of hearts playing card left somewhere on or near the body. We will have more on this story as it develops."

I pressed my lips together. Was this some kind of message? Who else could have been there? And why claim my crime as their own? Honestly, it was a little offensive. A serial killer taking credit for my one kill really was so shitty it was border-line hilarious.

A strange mixture of irritation and intrigue consumed me. I had gone there alone, finished the job alone. So why did it feel like I wasn't the only one involved in this?

"Awful, isn't it?" Mom's voice pulled me from my thoughts, her lips pressed into a tight line. "There's always something going on in this city. It's scary."

If she knew he had lured and kidnapped a seven-year-old girl last year, I wondered if she would still feel sympathy for his death. I met her gaze, forcing my expression into something mirroring empathy.

"Yeah, it's terrifying."

The screen flickered again, switching from the reporter to the weather. Someone else was there last night. I just needed to find out who. I was still turning the king card over in my head when I heard voices in the kitchen. Low, familiar. One of them was my dad, the other was Aaron.

I followed the sound into the kitchen, where my dad stood with Aaron and three other men.

Aaron noticed me first. "Morning, Shiloh."

I ignored him, my attention sweeping over the others. Kane, I recognized from pictures Aaron had shown me, was standing just behind his brother, arms crossed, looking like he'd rather be anywhere else. They looked nothing alike. Kane was taller, more muscular, and where Aaron's hair was dirty blonde, Kane's was so dark it was nearly black, buzzed short to show off his brown eyes. A thin layer of stubble coated his jaw. Next to him stood another guy, bleached blonde hair, bright green eyes, a tall, lean build, and watching me like I was the most interesting thing in the room. God given intuition told me that one had some screws loose, so I quickly averted my gaze. And then there was *him*.

Leaning against the wall, a smirk playing at his lips. His dark hair hung just above his blue eyes, tattoos covering most of his exposed skin, and enough muscle that it was obvious he worked out when he wasn't laying underneath a tattoo gun. They all looked like they walked off an assassin modeling shoot, and it made my skin itch.

Dad gestured between us. "Shiloh, this is Kane, Nate, and Creed. They'll be helping with the security while we deal with the current... situation."

Security. Right.

I gave them each a short nod, though my gaze lingered on Creed for a second longer than I meant it to. He noticed and his smirk deepened while the squirrelly one grinned like a lunatic.

I looked back at Aaron. "Can I talk to you, please?"

His brow lifted slightly. "I don't know, can you?"

I turned on my heel and started toward the stairs. "That was awful. Do better."

He chuckled and followed me up.

I didn't say anything until we were in my room, door shut behind us. Aaron barely had time to lean against my dresser before I turned to him with my arms crossed.

"You hired him?!"

He didn't bother pretending he didn't know who I meant. "I did."

"The guy who killed Ruben."

"The guy who saved your ass before me and half the police force showed up."

"Semantics." I narrowed my eyes. "Is this really security, or is that just the word you're using to keep my dad comfortable?"

Aaron sighed, running a hand through his hair. "It's security, Shy."

"Uh-huh." I arched my brow. "And how exactly does killing people factor into *security*?"

"On an as-needed basis?" He shrugged.

"Right." I exhaled sharply. "So, we're not just talking cameras and locked doors, you hired men who—"

"Who are going to keep you safe," Aaron interrupted, his voice calm but firm. "Shiloh, you have a target on your back, and we both know it. I don't care if they kill a hundred people as long as you're safe. So, yeah. I hired men who won't hesitate to do what needs to be done, because I care about you."

I stared at him for a second. "You really trust them?"

"With your life," he said confidently.

I dropped my arms with a sigh. "You're lucky I like you."

Aaron smirked, wrapping his arm around my shoulder and squeezing me into a tight hug. "I am pretty great."

I punched at his side and smiled at the "ooof" he let out. "That's a stretch."

But I didn't argue it any further. Because as much as I hated to admit it, he wasn't wrong.

And now I had even more questions about Creed.

The rest of the day went by in a blur of noise and movement. Cameras were installed in nearly every corner of the house, and the sound of drills and conversation floated constantly in the background. I didn't have the energy to participate in either activity, so I mostly stayed out of the way.

Every so often, Creed would catch my eye, always with that crooked little smirk on his face. On my last trip to the bathroom, he was just leaning against the wall in the hallway like he had all the time in the world. He didn't say a word, just gave me a wink that had a pulse of unwanted heat flaring in my chest, immediately followed by a wave of annoyance. I flipped him off and kept walking.

The chaos of the house was unsettling, and the feeling that everyone was here to watch me, to guard me, made my skin crawl. I found Nate standing by the kitchen counter. He was holding a banana and staring right at me. His gaze never wavered as he took a bite, straight through the peel. I felt my face twist up in horror, but I couldn't look away.

His eyes were wide and unblinking, locked onto mine as he chewed, like he dared me to say something. No thank you. I just blinked and looked away. Then, in the most serious tone, he spoke.

"Can I take off your jacket?"

I blinked again, looking behind me to make sure I was alone, before realizing he wasn't talking to me. He held the banana in front of his face, staring at it like he was actually waiting for it to respond.

He peeled the skin slowly, with the utmost care, and

repeated, "Can I take your jacket, sir?" He paused, as though listening to the banana's response. "No? You're not in the mood?"

I spun on my heel and power walked away, trying desperately not to lose it at how absolutely absurd the entire situation was. What a group Aaron had assembled here.

I went back to my room, shutting the door behind me and leaning against it.

The sound of the house—the noise, the chaos, the lunatic in the kitchen, all faded away. For the first time today, I felt alone again. I wasn't sure how long I stayed there like that, just soaking in the silence, but it was long enough that when I checked the clock on my nightstand, it was already late afternoon. I moved to the bathroom and ran hot water in the tub, adding in a healthy pour of bubble bath and sinking into the warm water. Across the hall, I could hear them in the guest rooms, laughing between each other while they invaded my space.

The only thing I could do now was wait to see what the hell happened next, and plan how the fuck I was going to get out of Fort Knox to continue my investigation without alerting the damn Avengers downstairs. God knows I couldn't call Lottie to come break me out, she would have Aaron's entire crew stripped down to their underwear and playing poker before I could blink.

No, I was going to have to figure this one out on my own.

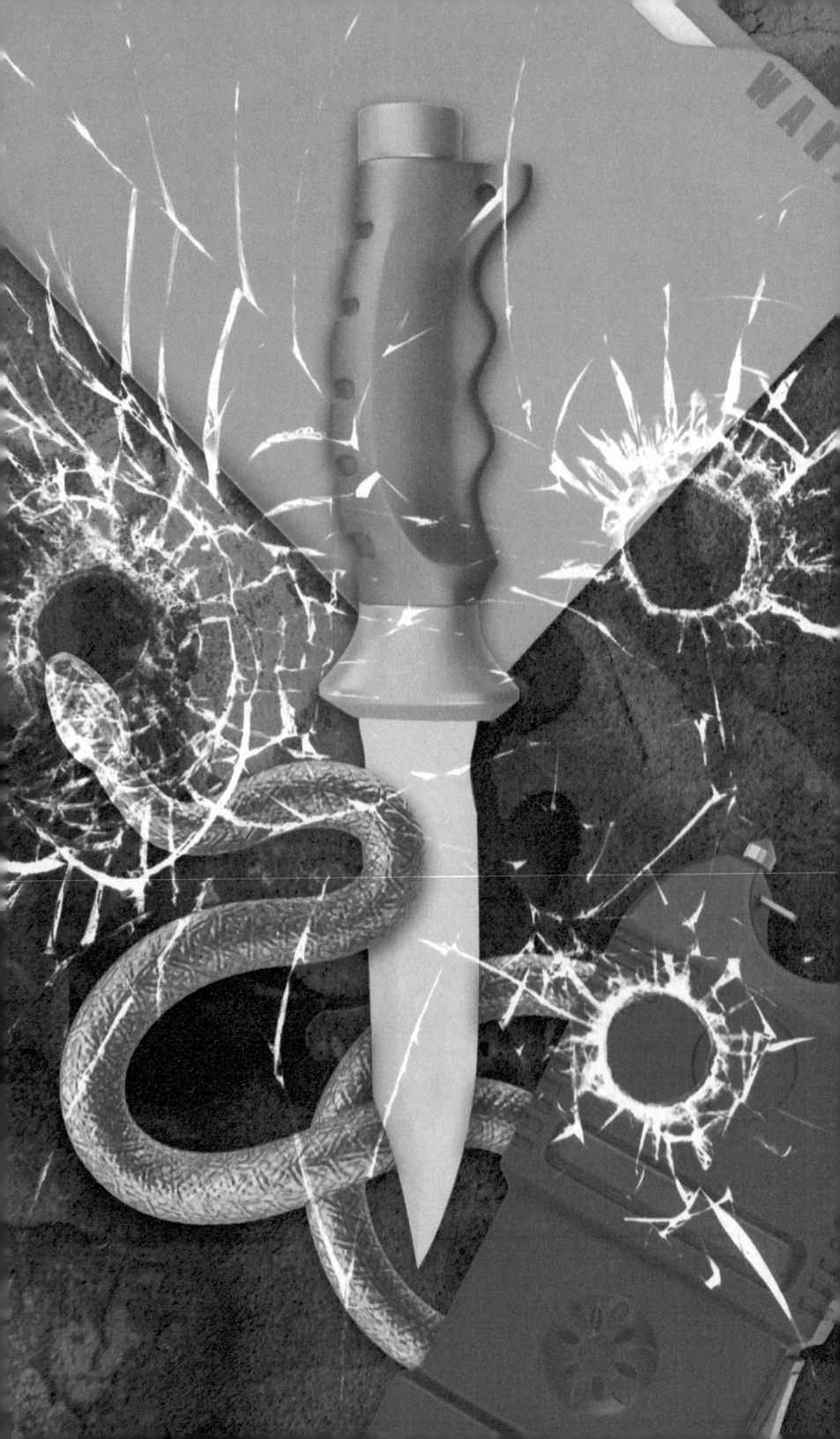

CHAPTER TWELVE

SHILOH

I flipped the worn piece of paper around in my hand, the edges already beginning to fade from how often I had folded and unfolded it. I sat cross legged on my bed with my phone in one hand and the slip of paper in the other, debating if I really wanted to do this alone.

Someone was already looking for me, and I had enough common sense to know that hunting these people down wasn't exactly helping me stay off their radar, but I couldn't stop it. The need to wipe the entire ring off the face of the earth was its own living, breathing thing that had taken up residence inside me. It didn't feel like a choice, it just felt right.

Before I could talk myself out of it, I dialed the number and lifted my phone to my ear, my lip tucked tight between my teeth as I waited for it to connect. It didn't. My first assumption had been correct: it was a burner phone and whoever Joseph had called was no longer using this number. I balled the paper up and tossed it across my room in frustration. Okay. Think, Shiloh. We still have another lead, so it's not the end of the world.

Getting in and out of Sinner's would be its own beast, but Lottie could help with that. I sent her a quick text letting her know I was on my way, then rushed to get ready, carefully creeping around the hallways of my house. I waited just around the corner by the back door for Nate to go outside for his patrol, slipping through the door a minute after him and veering right where he went left. Timing was everything, and since Kane and Creed were in the basement gym with Aaron, and Nate was on the other side of the property, I had just enough time to get in my car, and be sitting in Lottie's driveway in under twenty minutes without any of them noticing my absence. The irony of Lottie rebelling against her parents' wealth, while also living in one of the biggest houses in our neighborhood never ceased to amuse me. The front of the three-story structure was decorated with white marble columns, a massive fountain in the middle of the circular drive, and a balcony to either side of the house that overlooked immaculate gardens. None of it matched the foul-mouthed girl I knew; she was more likely to sneak a thermos full of bottom shelf vodka into a church service than to attend her parents' garden parties.

Lottie answered the door barefoot, a hoodie swallowing her small frame. "You got here fast."

"I need a favor"

That got her attention. Her brow lifted, and she stepped to the side, motioning for me to come in.

We went straight to the kitchen, Lottie pulling out two glasses and pouring them full of orange juice while I took a seat at the kitchen island.

"So, murder or mischief?" she asked, all teeth and curiosity.

"Fake ID."

Her smile didn't fade but sharpened. "Well shit. And here I thought you were going to start small."

"I'm serious."

"I know." She sipped her juice. "That's why I'm not laughing."

My fingers drummed against my glass. Lottie wasn't a nosy

person; it was just in her nature to go with the flow. Still, I didn't know how to explain why I was asking her for this if she asked.

"So do you know a place?"

"Babe." She scoffed. "Of course I do. What kind of reformed rich kid would I be if I couldn't procure you counterfeit identification?"

She leaned forward, elbows on the counter, watching me like she was trying to see past my face.

"But you're gonna have to give me something here, Shy. You don't ask for this kind of stuff, ever."

I didn't meet her eyes. I don't want to lie to her, but I can't tell her everything either.

"There's a bar, Sinner's," I said. "I need in."

She whistled. "Classy joint. Smells like piss and tequila in there and a new fight breaks out every three minutes."

"Perfect."

She paused, giving me a quick glance. "Ominous. Are you looking for trouble?"

"I'm looking for answers."

The words came out harsher than I meant for them too, but she didn't even flinch. Lottie knew about the same amount that my parents did about what happened, but she never once pushed for more information.

She nodded her head, pulling her phone out. "Alright. What name do you want?"

"What?"

"For the ID, genius. You don't want to go in there as Shiloh the-Police-Chief's-Daughter, right?"

I blinked. No, I don't. "I didn't think about that."

She rolled her eyes, smiling to herself as she typed. "Veronica. Would you like to choose your last name?"

"Knock yourself out."

"That would make a terrible last name, silly. Let's do Smith."

"Original," I laughed.

"Look, I would be surprised if Sinner's even checks your ID, so don't worry about it. Do you want me to come with?"

Yes. But there was no way to drag her along without bringing her in on everything, and I wasn't ready for that.

"No, I'm okay. I'll call you if I need you."

"Promise?"

"Promise."

Lottie tapped her nails against the counter. "You don't have to do anything alone, Shy."

I stared at my drink. I could tell her. I could tell her about the note, and the picture, and the blood. I could tell her I killed someone and plan to do it again. But if I did, I'm pulling her down here into this world of putrid people, and I refused to do that to her.

So instead, I just smiled. "Thanks for helping me."

She wiped the concern off her face, giving me an easy smile instead. Her immediate acceptance of my boundaries was just another reason why she's one of only two people I let in.

"You'd do the same," she said.

And I would.

"I'll go pick it up for you in a few hours; the guy that makes them is a little squirrely around new people."

"Can you just stick it in the mailbox? I'll grab it on my way out tonight, it'll be late."

"Sure thing, babe. I'll let you know when it's done."

Lottie wrapped her arms around me in a tight hug that conveyed the things she wouldn't say out loud. She was worried about me. Honestly, so was I.

CHAPTER THIRTEEN

CREED

I fucking hated suburbia.

Each house looked like it was picked out of a catalog specifically catered to billionaire assholes. Everything... clean. The angles on the houses were too sharp, the white interiors too clinical. The hedges were all trimmed just right, the flower beds pristine, hundreds of thousands of dollars' worth of security systems just to leave their doors unlocked.

The wealthy were an enigma.

We were stationed in the surveillance room in Shiloh's house. Despite the cozy touches, this house felt like all the others on this street. Upper-middle class layout, rooms that echoed when we walked through them, and not a single sign she once crawled through hell to make it back to this place. She fit here on the surface, but it was an illusion. Just like the way she smiled at her parents; just like the way she pretended she slept.

She didn't.

I knew, because I heard her moving around in the room above this one all hours of the night. She frequently had what sounded like violent nightmares. Her father let us know she had stopped taking her sleeping pills, and to just let her work through it. It made my skin itch, listening to her scream into her pillow. Eventually, she would give up and I'd hear her pacing above me.

Her feet moved from one side of the room to the other, just pacing like she was trying to outrun the thoughts that kept her up.

"I'm putting motion detectors around the back," Kane said, crouching by the window with a tool kit and no patience for small talk.

"Already set two on the east side," Nate added, flopped across the small sofa in the corner.

Aaron sat in the kitchen with David, going over the list of suspects. None of us said it but we knew this wasn't just a clean-up job anymore. The second Shiloh killed that man, we stopped being watchers. We became part of the plan.

"Lucien Scott," Aaron said, walking in and dropping a photo onto the table. "He was in with some of the guys on Ruben's outer circle but never had his hands in The Manor directly. He's our next suspect, and he's been seen around town in the last two days."

"You connect him to the abductions?"

Aaron shook his head. "Not fully, still working on it. I'd bet money on it though."

I leaned over the table, examining the man in the photo. Sharp, calculating eyes, no soul to be found in them.

"He has motive. His ties to The Manor are gone, but the network isn't. Someone is trying to assemble it."

"We'll look into it, just help keep tabs on her," Kane told him

Aaron sighed. "She shouldn't be dealing with this shit."

"But she is."

"She's too young for it."

"She's nearly twenty," I reminded him.

Aaron shook his head in defeat. "Still."

"We all have a vested interest in taking these guys out." Kane said calmly.

Aaron scoffed at that. "You also have a 'vested interest' in Shiloh."

Nate made a choking noise and sat up straighter. "*Interest?* That's what we're calling it?"

Kane snorted, actually snorted, from across the room, which is how I knew he agreed.

"I'll thank you to leave my personal interests out of this discussion. You're making it weird."

"She is pretty," Nate said with a shrug.

I didn't even look at him. "You say that again and I'm going to amputate your thumbs."

Kane let out a low whistle. "There it is."

Aaron's eyes ping ponged between the three of us, his wheels probably spinning while he tried to decide if me having personal feelings for Shiloh was a good or bad thing.

On one hand, she'd always be safe. On the other, I was fucking insane.

They didn't understand it either way. I didn't want her the way they thought I did. It wasn't about sex; it wasn't even about the affection. It was the proximity, getting to see a side of her most people never would when she was in her own home with her guard down.

She put her weight on her toes when she walked, forcing her steps to be as silent as possible, even at the cost of her comfort. She breathed like the air hurt her lungs, her shoulders moved up on each exhale, and there was the slightest tremble when she let it out. I watched her watch others more times than I can count, absorbing her mannerisms and the way she tracked the people moving around her like a hawk. No, they didn't understand because they didn't see what I saw. I saw everything.

"Look," Aaron said, holding his hands up. "Whatever the fuck is going on with your personal feelings, don't let them get in the way of the job. Got it—"

He was cut off by the sound of chips crunching in the corner. Nate sat cross-legged on the back of the sofa, spooning chips into his mouth by the handful.

"Can you not eat in the middle of tactical briefings?" Kane grumbled.

"Can you not brood like someone banged your prom date?"

Aaron rubbed his temples. He was used to our antics, but the added stress must make our group dynamic incredibly stressful. I pulled my knife from my pocket, flipping it between my fingers—something to focus on as they bickered.

We still had no lead on who left the picture of Shiloh. Our suspect list was maddeningly short, and I could feel the clock ticking. The girls that were being taken were abducted at a sporadic, but frequent rate. There was no foolproof way to time it, the abduction sites varied from schools to recitals to parties thrown by their parents. Whoever was doing this wasn't an amateur; they knew how to get in and out without drawing attention to themselves. We had informants spread throughout the city, watching and listening for anything that might give us a lead, but so far, we hadn't heard anything substantial.

"Creed," Aaron said, pulling me out of my thoughts. "Be smart tonight. No bodies unless necessary."

"Define necessary."

"Not your default setting."

I smiled. Just a little. "No promises."

Aaron sighed. "We're not assassins."

I sheathed my blade. "I mean, we kind of are, though."

Nate raised a chip in the air like a toast. "Amen."

We finished going over the last details—shift rotations, camera feeds, backup signals. Shiloh had snuck out earlier, the tracker I put on her car showing her friend Lottie's house on the other end of the neighborhood. I may or may not have tapped her phone, giving me access to their conversation and her plans for the evening. A fake ID? She was really going all out for a bar that didn't care if you smoked crack in the corner as long as you paid your tab.

I had arranged with the guys to be out of the house tonight; they knew where I was going before I told them, and after some light ribbing, Kane agreed to cover my shift. I needed to see what she was up to. Sinner's was in a rough area, so either way, I wouldn't have let her go without me.

Whether she knew I was there or not.

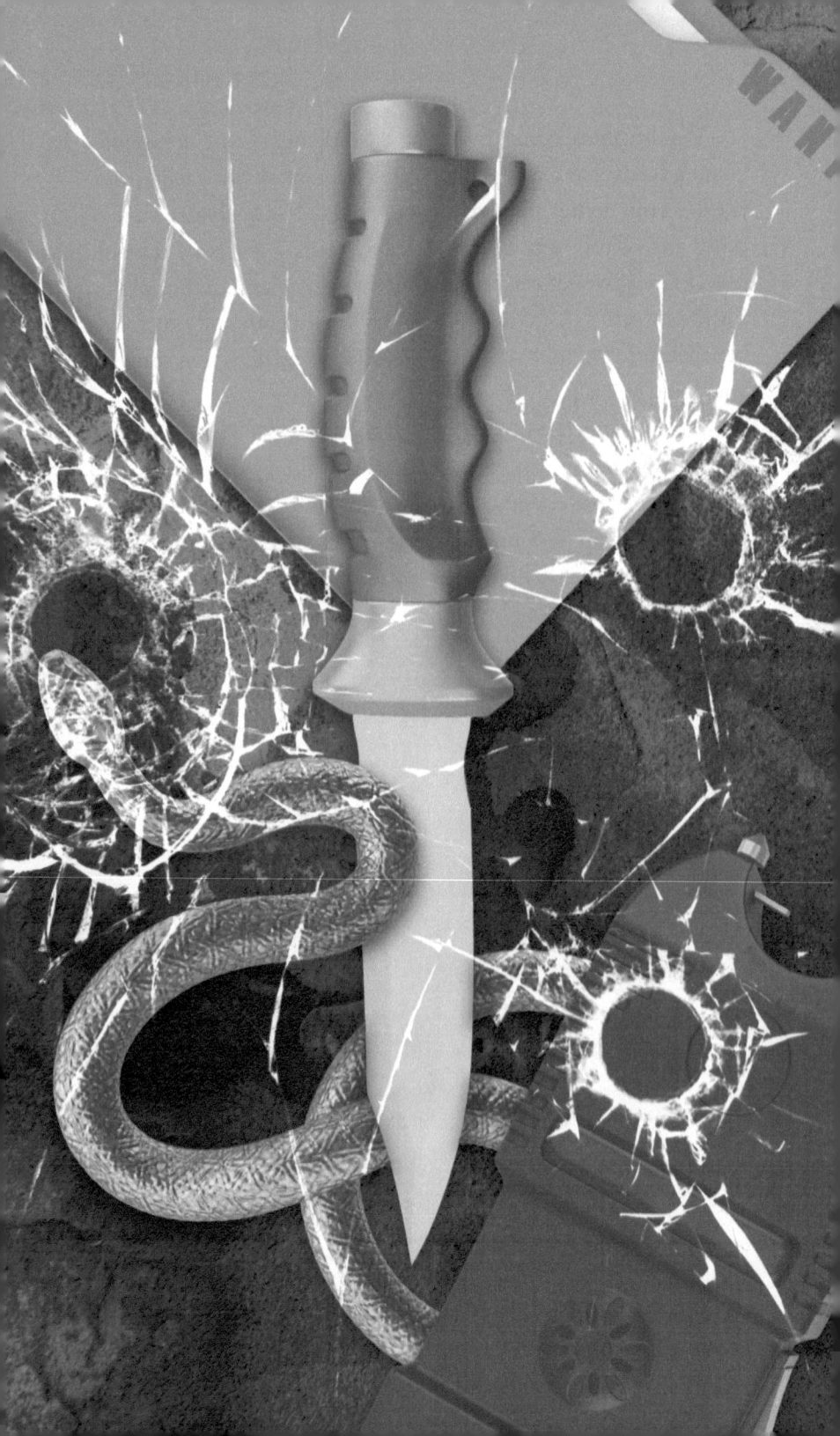

CHAPTER FOURTEEN

SHILOH

The ID was taped to the inside of the mailbox and, honestly, it looked incredibly real. Whoever Lottie was in cahoots with had found their calling.

She had also offered to be my cover for tonight, vowing to tell my parents I was with her unless I didn't check in at the designated time, in which case she would send my 'mom, dad, and the wrath of god herself' after me. I believed her. She was a petite thing, but my god was she intimidating.

I made the drive to the block downtown where Sinner's was tucked away, parking down the street and power walking toward the bar. I slipped my hand into my pocket, clutching the ID as I approached the giant of a man sitting on a stool outside the door.

That had to be a bouncer, right?

I stepped up in front of him, grinding my teeth against the feeling of his eyes roaming over my exposed skin. I needed to blend in here. So, taking Lottie's advice, I had gone for a cheap black slip dress that hit above my thigh, the slit on the left side dangerously close to revealing the color thong I had on. I didn't own much in the way of high heels, so I had gone with a pair of black heeled boots and a long coat. A little dark eye shadow, lipstick the color of my hair, and I was out the door.

As Lottie had predicted, the man never bothered to check my age. He was content to just leer as he motioned for me to go inside. Walking through the door was like getting smacked in the face by a porta potty. The smell of stale beer and cigarette smoke clung to the air, and I forced down a gag as I moved to the bar and claimed the first open stool I saw.

A tall, lanky bartender came over as soon as I was seated.

"What'll it be, sweetheart?"

Fuck, I didn't drink.

Think. What do people drink?

"I'll have a whiskey, neat please."

His smile grew as he nodded approvingly.

"My kind of girl." He winked and poured the amber liquid into a short glass, sliding it across the bar with a napkin.

"Holler if you need anything else, name's Tim by the way."

"Thanks, Tim."

I let out a breath as he moved further down the bar to attend to the other people crowding the small space. Forcing my shoulders to relax, I surveyed the room with a bored gaze.

I didn't have a solid game plan when I came in here; I just knew I needed to be here. It was packed tonight. I grabbed my glass and walked to the back wall and the line of booths there. It wasn't as well-lit back here, so it would be easier to blend in and people-watch. With any luck, I would see or hear something that would stick out.

I slid into the booth, scooting all the way to the inside, just out of the overhead light and relaxed into the shadows there. I reached for the glass in front of me, breathing through the burn as I swallowed. I traced the rim of the glass with my fingers, decidedly done trying to drink its contents, but happy to have something to do with my hands.

"Didn't peg you for a whiskey girl."

My hand froze.

He was here? I turned my head to the left, letting my eyes adjust in the dim light.

There was Creed, sitting so close I should have felt him, one arm draped along the back of the booth like he belonged there. Like he hadn't just materialized out of nowhere.

I turned my head back to the glass in my hands. "How long have you been there?"

"Long enough to see you come in. I could visibly see the moment the smell hit you, you know."

"How did you know I would choose this booth?"

"It's the only one in the dark, Red."

I didn't have a response for that. I hated that he could read me so easily. That he could guess at what I would do in a situation this far out of my comfort zone and be right.

"Why are you here, Creed?" I asked, the exasperation I felt leaking into my voice.

"Same reason you are. I'm looking for something."

"Like what?"

"Show me yours and I'll show you mine." His grin was bright in the dim light of the booth, his teeth on display like a predator cornering its prey.

"Pass." I rolled my eyes, glancing around the room before my gaze landed back on him.

He leaned forward, allowing the light to fall across his face. God, he really was handsome. Not in the traditional, model kind of way. He was gorgeous in the same way a poisonous snake was. On the surface, you couldn't help but admire it. His midnight black hair shone like scales in this light, his eyes tracking mine as they traced over him. But there was a danger there that was so potent, so salient, that it radiated off him in waves. His head cocked to the side slowly as I studied him.

"Red."

My eyes snapped to his.

"What?"

"If you could take a short break from eye-fucking me, you would notice what's going on at the bar over there."

That fucking smirk was going to be the death of me. He leaned in slightly, the smell of him invading my senses.

"The guy at the bar, far end. Brown jacket. He just dropped a phone into the coat pocket of that woman in the red dress."

I glanced over, as subtly as I could manage. He was right. The woman didn't even notice. She picked up her glass and took a long swig as the man turned and disappeared into the crowd.

"Did you recognize him?" he asked.

"No."

He hummed. "Interesting. I did."

I turned on him with narrowed eyes. "Who is it?"

"Wouldn't you like to know?" he said, leaning his elbow on the table and resting his head on his hand, amusement dancing in his eyes.

"Creed," I warned.

"*Red*." He wasn't even trying to bite back his smile.

"Why did you follow me here?"

"I follow you everywhere." His voice was a sinister murmur.

"Sounds like something a stalker would say."

"Only if you say it in the wrong tone," he said, grinning.

I sighed, running a hand through my hair. Did he actually know who that man was, or was it a ploy? I didn't have any other leads, so I determined it was worth the risk.

"Okay, what do I have to do for you to share what you know?"

"Let me drive you home."

"What?"

"Let me drive you home. Aaron dropped me off; we'll take your car." He was already sliding out of the other side of the booth, coming to stand in front of me and offering his hand.

"Why?"

"Keeping you safe is part of my job, Shiloh. I take it very seriously."

I hesitated a moment before sliding my hand into his, ignoring the first spark of something other than mild friendly affection that I had ever felt in my life.

We walked to my car in silence. He hopped in the driver's seat and pulled onto the nearly empty street, heading toward my neighborhood.

"How did you know I would be here tonight, Creed?"

"I always know where you are. Don't worry about that."

I didn't respond. Because part of me hated that he was always around. And part of me *didn't*.

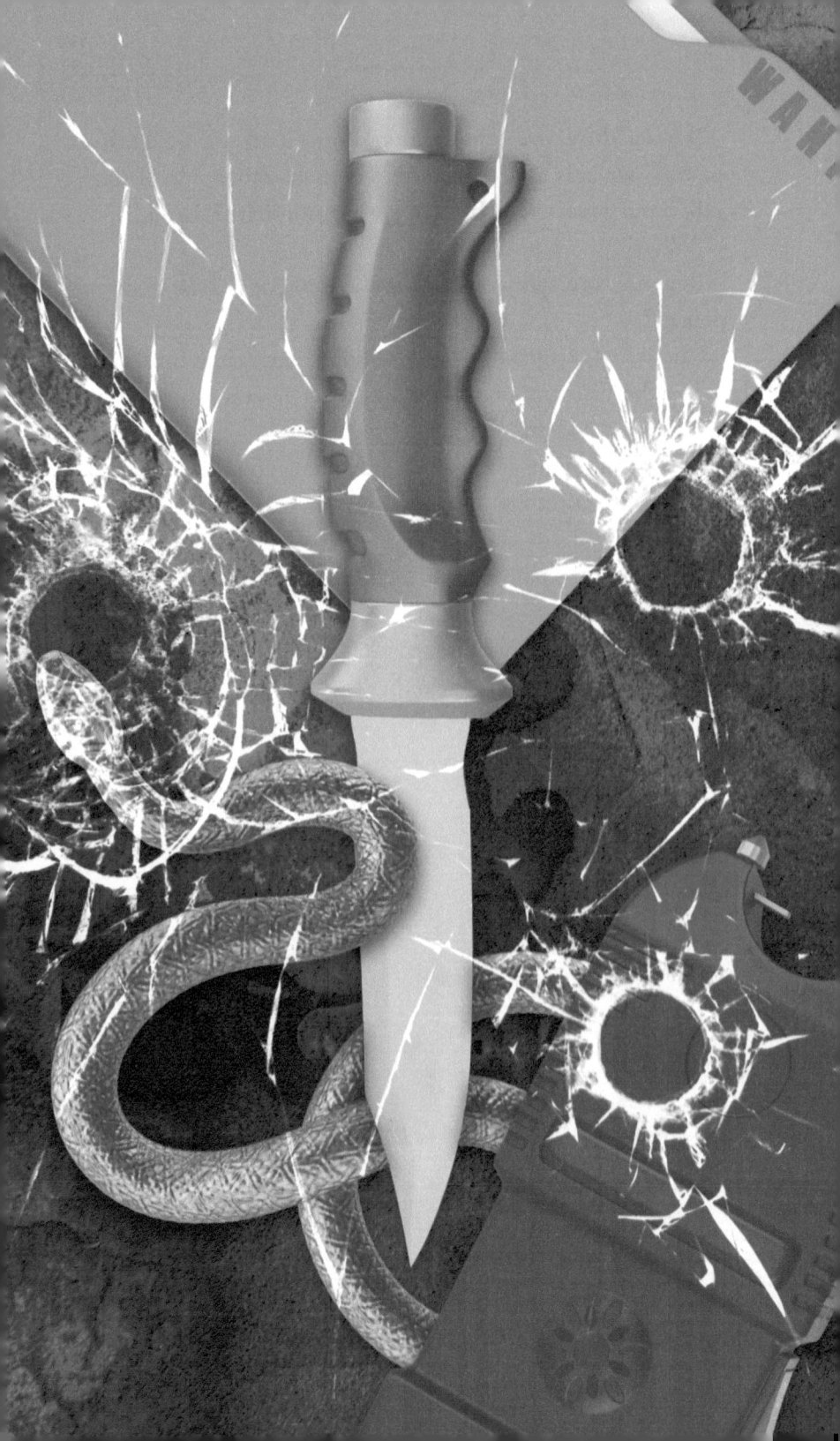

CHAPTER FIFTEEN

SHILOH

The morning had gone by in a slow blur. My feet hurt from stomping around in high heels last night, and the house was oddly quiet since Mom picked up a shift at the hospital and Dad was spending the day at the station. I had migrated to the living room couch and turned on the TV an hour ago, but the movie wasn't holding my attention.

Something pointless played—car chases, forced one-liners, explosions that barely registered. I curled up on the couch an hour ago, hoping to shut my brain off with a movie, but I'd been zoned out for half of it. My muscles refused to relax, my leg bouncing beneath the thick blanket.

The sound of the doorbell startled me before I left the couch to answer it.

"Shy-girl!" I heard as I swung it open.

Uncle Miles was already reaching for me. His arms wrapped around me before I could take a step back and I stiffened. My brain froze, but I didn't fight it. I gave him two light pats on his back before he pulled back.

He rested his hands on my shoulders. "You look good. Still pretty as ever."

I nodded once. "Thanks."

He squeezed my shoulders before stepping around me and

into the house, walking into the living room and plopping down in my spot like he owned the place.

I suppressed a full body shiver at the feeling of his hands on me and moved to sit on the edge of the couch, opposite him.

"You've been eating?" he asked. "Sleeping alright?"

"Sure."

He didn't let the silence grow. "You're working for Aaron, right? Your mom said you started working for him at the gym."

"Yeah. I like it there."

He hummed like he wasn't convinced. His gaze settled back on me, sharp and a little too focused for my comfort.

"You seeing anyone?"

I blinked at him. "Seriously?"

He laughed, too loud for the silence of the room and waved dismissively.

"Oh, come on, you gotta live a little eventually."

"I guess so."

"Well, I wanted to as—"

He was interrupted by a knock on the wall, and Creed appears from the hallway.

"Hey, Shiloh?"

"Yeah?"

"Can I steal you for a second?" He ignored Miles completely. "I need your opinion on the camera placement in your room."

I didn't question it. "Sure."

Miles turned his head slowly to look at Creed, eyes sharp and assessing. Creed met his gaze and didn't so much as blink. Just lifted his head in a lazy nod.

I stood and walked toward him, looking over my shoulder at Miles. "Be right back."

As I passed Miles, he murmured, "Friend of yours?"

"Security," I said simply, and kept walking.

Creed waited until we were up the stairs and in my bedroom before he spoke.

"There's no camera," he said casually, leaning against my dresser. "We would never put a camera in your bedroom, just to be clear."

"What did you call me up here for then?"

"You looked like you needed an out," he said with a shrug.

I exhaled, letting my shoulders drop. "Yeah."

"You looked like you were about ready to bite him."

"I was considering it."

A slow grin spread across his face. "I'll come back down with you and watch."

I snorted at him, sitting on the edge of my bed and flopping backwards.

"He's the uncle, right?"

I propped myself up on my elbows to look at him. "Yeah, he doesn't come around a whole lot, but when he does, he can be a bit much."

Creed nodded, busying himself by fiddling with the latch on my jewelry box.

"Open it."

He raised an eyebrow, but lifted the lid, showing me the inside like he was waiting for further direction.

"See the obnoxious string of pearls?"

He hooked his index finger around the necklace and pulled it out of the box, dangling them in front of his face.

"A gift from dear Uncle Miles."

"Is this... the kind of thing you would typically wear?"

"Not even if you paid me. They've been sitting in that box for months now."

Creed smirked, setting the box aside and unclasping the necklace before bringing it to his throat.

"Oh god, don't."

But he'd already looped it around his neck, letting the small pearls settle against his black hoodie. I stared. Why was that... hot?

"How do I look?"

"Like you strangled an elderly woman and looted her corpse."

He tilted his head side to side like he was considering it, turning to the mirror and adjusting the necklace with mock seriousness. It actually looked good on him. The contrast shouldn't work, but it did.

"I'm keeping these," he said.

I rolled my eyes. "Fine, they look better on you anyway."

The words slipped out before I could stop them. Too honest, too fast. He stilled, turning back to me slowly and smiled. Not a smirk, not the little crooked smile he displayed when he was getting under my skin. This one was brighter. Softer. Dangerous in the most obvious way.

"You think I look *good* in pearls, Red?" he asked, his voice warm and low.

"No," I lied.

He stepped forward. "You sure?"

I scoffed, but I didn't move from my reclined spot on my bed as he advanced slowly.

His boots were quiet on the carpet, his steps slow and sure. By the time he stopped moving, his knees brushed against the edge of the bed, our legs touching. Just barely, just enough.

His hand lifted slowly. He didn't ask, just curled his fingers under my chin and tilted my face up to look at him.

"Why did you keep them?" he asked softly, brushing his thumb along my jaw.

"I don't know."

"Try again."

"I felt like I had to."

"You do not ever have to do *anything* because a man wants you to."

"Does that include you?"

"Yes."

My breath hitched at his proximity and the finality in his voice.

"So, you will stalk me, but I don't have to obey you?"

A flicker of something dark and satisfied passed through his expression. "No," he agreed, voice lower. "Unless, of course, you would like to."

The air between us was thin, charged. I could have pushed him away, given myself space to breathe, but I didn't.

"Do you know that you stiffen under his touch, but lean into mine?" he asked, his hand still gently cupping my face..

I realized he was right. I had shifted on the bed so that I was leaning into his palm. Heat flared in my cheeks, but I still couldn't bring myself to move.

He smiled wide, and something electric shot down my spine. I hated how much I liked it. He didn't lean in. He didn't kiss me. He just held the moment—like he was content to let the tension build until I snapped first.

"I-I don't know how to do this." The words fell from my mouth, barely louder than a whisper.

Creed's expression shifted. The grin softened. That sharp, cocky edge dulled into something quieter. Steadier.

"You don't have to," he said, his voice low. "I don't have expectations for you, Shiloh."

I couldn't look away from him. "I want to... I just don't—"

His thumb ghosted over my jaw, barely there, not even a real touch, and his eyes tracked the movement like he was watching for a flinch.

"I'm not asking for anything," he said. "Not tonight. Not tomorrow. Not ever—unless *you* want it."

The heat was still there, simmering beneath his voice.

But the pressure? Gone. He was giving me space in a moment where men had always taken advantage.

"You've had too many choices made for you," he added. "I'm not going to be another one."

My chest ached. "I'm not scared of you," I said quietly.

He leaned in, placing a soft kiss to my forehead before pulling back, easing out of my space.

"No, but you are scared. I intend to ease that, Red. Never to add to it." He smiled at me as he moved to the door, opening it just wide enough to slip out, and close it behind him.

CHAPTER SIXTEEN

CREED

The door to her room clicked shut softly behind me. I gave myself a second to catch my breath and shake the scent of her from my head.

She always smelled like fucking strawberries from her shampoo; it drove me insane. I headed downstairs, threading through the dark hallways like I'd been here for years. By the time I reached the security room, Aaron was already at the console, watching the monitors.

"You look like shit," I said, pushing the door shut behind me.

"You look like a man wearing pearls," he replied dryly.

I glanced down. Forgot about that. "Charming, aren't they?" I said, pulling the neck of my hoodie out so they fell to my chest. "Shiloh gave them to me."

Aaron raised an eyebrow at me. "You're really into her?"

I met his gaze. "You asking me as her pseudo big brother, or as my boss?"

He smirked faintly. "Both."

"Yes."

He considered me for a moment before nodding. "Fuck it up and I'll hurt you, Creed. I mean it."

"I know."

He gestured toward the table where a file laid open.

Three photos were spread out—mugshots, surveillance stills, and grainy shots pulled from traffic cams. New suspects.

"Waynes gave us something before he died," Aaron said. "A list of names. Code names, most of them. We've identified three possibilities connected to this new ring."

I leaned over the table to study the names. Milo Grant. Caught twice with ties to trafficking rings overseas. Slippery. Wealthy. Untouchable, no charges ever stuck. Released from police custody this morning. Selene Vale. Worked front-facing operations at a youth rehab center—the kind that rich people shipped their kids off to and didn't ask any questions until they returned.

Dominic Price. Tech guy. Hid behind a screen, but he was the reason these bastards didn't leave a digital footprint.

"I've seen Milo before," I muttered, tapping his photo. "He hangs around the crowd downtown."

"Yeah, he's bold. He has connections though; the senator might be one of them for all we know."

I flipped through all the photos again, looking for anything else that stood out.

"Did she tell you where she got the pearls?" he asked, not looking up from the monitors.

"Yeah, she did."

"She never wore them," he said softly. "Didn't even touch half the stuff in her room after she got back either. She's trying, Creed, but... it's different. Just because she *is* safe doesn't mean she knows how to *feel* safe."

I nodded once. He wanted to make sure I knew where she was at, mentally. I did; I made sure I did.

"Did that dickhead leave?" I asked.

Aaron sighed. "Yeah, David walked him out a few minutes ago."

The door creaked open and David stepped in, looking exhausted.

"Aaron," he said. "We've got something across town. Attempted grab, similar profile. We need to go."

Aaron stood without hesitation, grabbing his gear.

"Creed, you got the feeds?"

"On it." I slid into the chair as they left, the soft hum of the equipment settling around me.

It was going to be a long night.

THE HOURS BLED BY SLOWLY. The feeds rolled in from multiple monitors along the desk in front of me—each one displaying quiet hallways, locked doors, and still views of the street. Until midnight.

Until Shiloh's scream echoed down to my ears. It punched through the silence like a gunshot—raw and jagged, muffled through her closed bedroom door, but still too loud to mistake.

I jolted upright, eyes already on the feed from the camera outside her door. Nothing out of place.

Just her, screaming through another one of the nightmares she's been having lately.

I shot a text to Nate.

C:

I need you in ops. Shiloh's having a bad one.

His reply was instant.

N:

On my way. Go.

I was already out of the chair by the time his response came in.

HER DOOR CREAKED as I opened it, the sound swallowed by another scream. She was caught in it—some memory she couldn't wake from. Her hands were clenched tight in the sheets, knuckles white, legs tangled and trembling.

I sat down on the floor by her bed, close enough to reach her, but I kept my hands on top of my bent knees. Her breathing grew harsher. Panicked. Desperate. A whimper escaped her, so full of fear and sorrow that it tore something inside me.

"Shiloh," I whispered. "You're safe. You're home."

She didn't hear me.

I shifted forward, laying my arm on the edge of the bed and resting my chin on it.

There was a sheen of sweat forming at her temple, her eyelids fluttering, jaw clenched tight.

Carefully—so fucking carefully—I reached up and brushed the hair from her face. My fingers trembled, and I didn't know why.

"Breath, baby," I murmured. "It's just a dream. It's not real anymore."

Her lashes twitched, her body stilling just slightly.

"I'm here, Red. I'm not going anywhere," I whispered. "Not tonight."

Her hand curled against the sheets but loosened; the ragged edge of her breath softened.

I kept my fingers in her hair, gently rubbing her locks between my thumb and forefinger. The tension bled out of her in slow waves; the release was evident in her body as the nightmare faded. Long after the screams stopped, long after her breathing evened out, I still found myself sitting on her floor. Watching the steady rise and fall of her chest, the way she unfurled from the fetal position I found her in. And I swore, when I found the people who took something as precious and simple as sleep from her, they would beg for mercy I didn't have.

CHAPTER SEVENTEEN

SHILOH

I woke slowly for once. Warm. Still. The blankets weren't tangled around my legs, and my chest didn't ache from running in my sleep. No screaming. No cold sweat. Just... quiet.

I blinked up at the ceiling for a second, rested but disoriented. Something was different. Off.

Then I hear the sound of paper shifting across the room.

I turned my head, finding Creed sitting in the armchair by the window, coffee mug balanced in one hand, a file folder in the other. Just sitting there, casually, like he was in his personal office and not my bedroom. He stretched his legs out in front of him, completely at ease like he hadn't been watching me sleep.

"What the hell are you doing?" I croaked. Maybe there was some screaming, based on the scratchiness of my throat.

He didn't even look up. "Working. You snore, by the way."

"I do not."

"Sounded like a symphony of chainsaws in here," he said, turning the page with one finger.

I reached behind my head and flung a pillow in his direction, sighing when it hit the ground a full three feet to the left of him.

"And she's athletic? Be still my heart."

"Hilarious," I said, sitting up to run a hand through my

hair. The sunlight streaming through the curtains brightened the room, making Creed's presence here seem more out of place, and causing me to feel even more off-balance.

Creed finally glanced over. "You okay?"

I squinted at him. "Yeah. Why wouldn't I be?"

"You had a nightmare last night." His voice was even, like he was talking about the weather. "Bad one. Kicked half your blankets off. Screamed loud enough to wake the dead."

My stomach twisted. "I don't remember."

"You slept through it." He set the folder down on the windowsill and took a sip of his coffee. "I sat with you. You calmed down after a bit."

"You sat with me?"

He shrugged. "Didn't want you to wake up alone."

I stared at him. He didn't meet my eyes this time, just reached into the file and pulled out a thin manilla folder.

"Anyway. Thought you might want to see this." He stood, walked over, and held it out to me.

I took it cautiously. "What is this?"

"Information I'm sure you were going to find out on your own anyway," he said, watching me closely. "Milo Grant was released this morning. Early deal, sealed record. Back out on the street."

The name punched straight through my chest. I flipped the folder open, and his face stared back at me. Cold eyes. Arrogant smile. The lazy smirk of a man who knew he wouldn't be held accountable for his crimes.

"What's the catch?" I asked, glancing up.

"No catch..." Creed said. "I thought you would want to know. That's all."

I narrowed my eyes. "Why?"

He didn't blink. "Because I know what it feels like when

the system fails. And because I trust you know what to do with that."

His words settled somewhere beneath my ribs. He trusted me. He didn't pity me. Didn't treat me like glass. Didn't even ask what I planned to do. Just gave me the information and left me the choice. And somehow, that made it harder to breathe.

I looked at the folder again. "Where is he?"

"Downtown. Registered at a high-rise under a fake name, but he's not hiding." Creed stepped back. "I marked the address."

I flipped through the last page—sure enough, there it is. Address, car model, building security details.

All laid out like an invitation. I glanced up again. He was halfway to the door, mug in hand, back straight, like this was nothing.

"You're not going to stop me?" I said.

"Would it work if I tried?

I frowned. Creed paused in the doorway, one hand on the frame. "You're smart, Red. I'm not worried about what you'll do, just worried all of this might get in your head."

My throat tightened. "It already did. A long time ago."

Creed nodded once. Like he understood. Like he wasn't going to ask me to explain.

Then, with a sharp exhale, he said, "Then you do what you need to do to root it out. I'm here if you need help."

He disappeared down the hall, leaving the faint smell of coffee and my thundering pulse in his wake. I flipped the file back open. Creed's handwriting was tight, efficient, red ink circling the address. He left notes in the margins—entry points, potential blind spots, security guard rotations. He must have pulled intel hours ago. He'd been planning. Preparing. For me. I stared at the page longer than I needed to. Then I grabbed my phone and scrolled to Lottie's name.

. . .

> **S:**
> You awake?

L:
Unfortunately.

What's up?

> **S:**
> Need a ride downtown. And a distraction.

L:
Trouble distraction or fun distraction?

> **S:**
> Both.

L:
💀

I TOSSED the phone on the bed, changed out of my pajamas, and grabbed my worn black hoodie from the chair, pulling my hair into a low braid. The mirror caught my reflection as I moved, and for a second I paused. I didn't look like the girl I was a few weeks ago. I barely looked like the one who escaped The Manor. This version of me had something... *alive* behind her eyes. A brightness that wasn't there before. A purpose. By the time I headed downstairs, the house was quiet. No sign of my parents, no sign of Creed. I gripped the file tight in my hands, the plan already writing itself in my head.

Lottie pulled up twenty minutes later, her red convertible obnoxious and perfectly fitting for her personality, despite the price tag. She draped her arm over the passenger seat as I got in, turning her body toward me expectantly.

"What are we getting into?"

"What do you know about the Marlowe Towers?"

Her brows lifted. "High-end, fake-name, money-laundering type place?"

"That's the one."

"And we're... sightseeing?"

I handed her the file. "More like gathering intel."

She whistled low as she skimmed it. "This guy sounds like a real winner."

"He's a waste of flesh."

She tossed the file into the backseat before meeting my eyes, her tone softening slightly. "Was he part of it?"

"Yes."

Her fingers drummed against the steering wheel. I didn't need to look to know she was grinding her jaw.

"Say less," she muttered. "Let's go fuck up a scumbag."

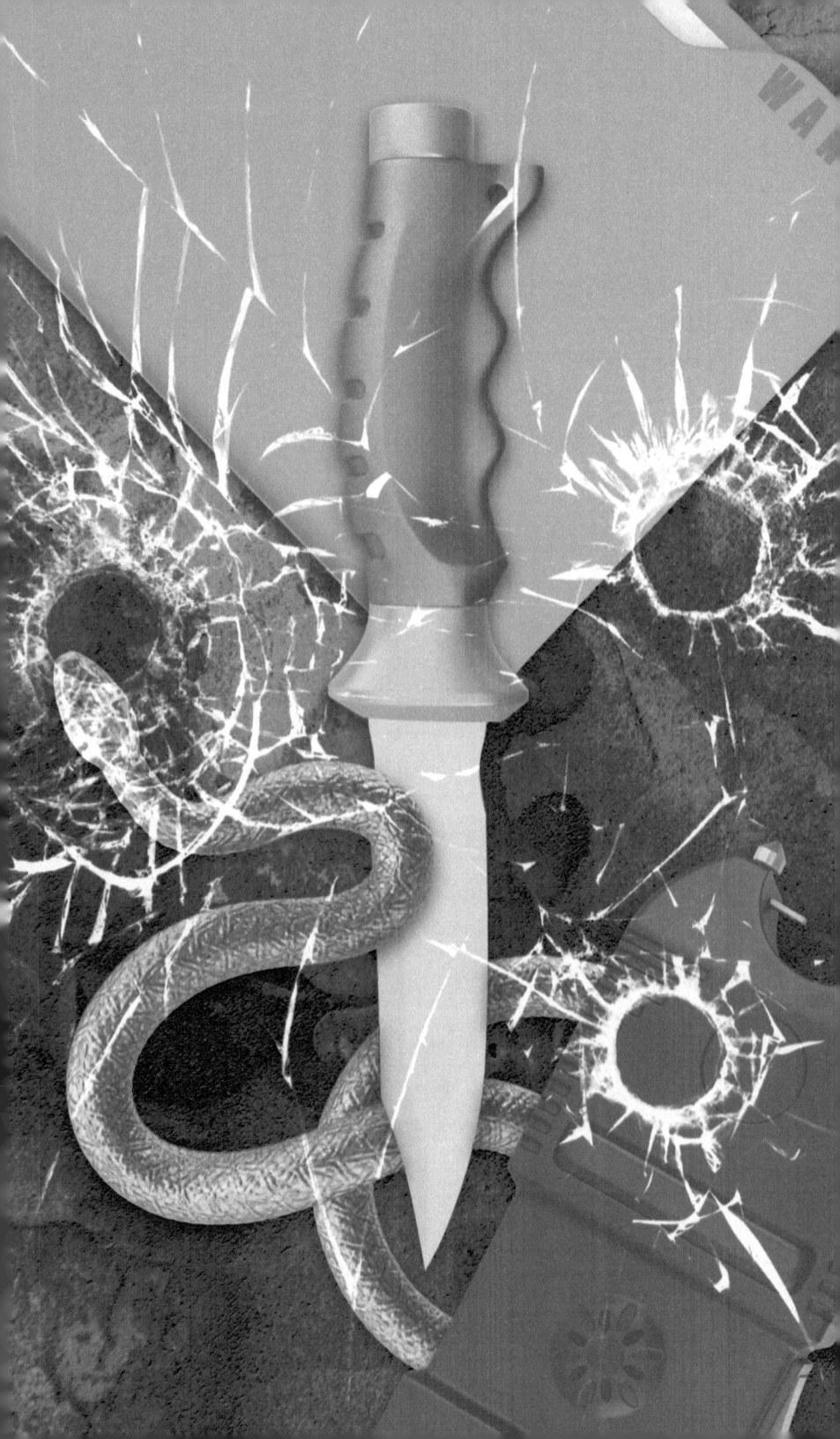

CHAPTER EIGHTEEN

SHILOH

The Marlowe Towers rose like a middle finger to the rest of the downtown area. Made of glass and steel, it was an obnoxious display of wealth in a predominantly low-income community.

Lottie parked across the street, killed the engine, and leaned forward over the steering wheel to get a better look.

"Bougie as hell," she muttered. "What's the plan?"

I was quiet for a beat, watching the entrance. A doorman stood just inside the glass doors, stiff-backed and looking bored as fuck. A single front desk clerk scrolled through his phone. Security cameras—three outside, two inside that I could see.

Tight, but not impossible.

"I'm working on it."

Lottie shifted to look at me. "You know what apartment he's in?"

I shook my head once. "Not yet."

"Hmm." She tugged down the neckline of her shirt and tossed me a wink. "Then I guess I'll go find out."

"Lottie—"

Too late.

She was already out of the car, flipping her hair over her shoulder and strutting across the street in her worn-in converse. I sunk lower in my seat and muttered a curse under my breath.

Through the tower's massive windows, I watched her approach the front desk. The clerk perked up immediately as Lottie leaned in, effortless charm and manufactured innocence rolling off her in waves. She tapped her nails along the marble countertop as she talked. He ate it up. I could almost see the hearts in his eyes from here.

She tilted her head, laughed at something he said, and trailed her fingers along the edge of the desk like she was tracing letters into fogged glass. Ten seconds later, he turned the screen toward her and pointed. Got him. She sauntered back out like nothing happened, slipping into the car with a triumphant grin.

"Suite 1607," she said, buckling her seatbelt. "He's apparently a gym bro who hits the weight room on the bottom level every night around nine before heading to his suite."

I blinked at her. "You got all that?"

She shrugged. "Just the basics."

I snorted. "You're unhinged."

"Please. We wouldn't have anything in common if I wasn't."

She wasn't wrong. I stared back at the building, running through what I'd just learned. Time window, access points, potential entry. I could feel the plan forming in the back of my mind piece by piece.

"You gonna tell me what you're thinking?" Lottie asked, eyes narrowed.

"Soon."

Her mouth twitched. "I'll be here when you're ready."

She always was.

The high-rise faded behind us as we pulled back into traffic, the air in the car settling into a comfortable hush. Lottie drummed her fingers on the steering wheel and stole a few sideways glances, like she wanted to ask what I was planning but knew better than to press.

When we got to my house, she rolled to a stop at the end of the long driveway.

"You'll call me if you need anything?" she asked, eyes serious now.

I nodded. "Thanks for today, Lottie-Lou."

She winked. "Always down for a little espionage with my favorite trauma-riddled bestie."

I flipped her off with a half-smile and stepped out.

Inside, the house was quiet. No chatter from the kitchen, no heavy footsteps upstairs. I made my way down the hall, the hum of electronics drawing me to the security room. The door was cracked so I pushed it open. Empty. The screens glowed softly in the dark, cycling through camera feeds. I spotted Creed on the patio, a coffee cup in one hand, the other tucked into the pocket of his tactical pants as he surveyed the backyard. Still as a statue, watching the trees like they might make a move.

A demented kind of thrill filled me as I watched him, knowing he was unaware that I was getting a live feed of his every movement. That I could see every errant strand of jet-black hair get tousled in the light breeze. I slid into the chair, allowing myself just a moment to appreciate him without his smirk to tell me I'd been caught.

I traced the way his tight black shirt clung to his body, the sleeves snug around his biceps with all the black ink on his arms on full display. He rolled his neck, giving me a perfect view of his sculpted jaw, the way his Adam's apple bobbed as he took a swig from his cup. His tongue flicked out to catch a drop left behind on his lip, and I leaned in.

God he was so fucking—

"You looking for something in particular?"

I flinched away from the screen, spinning around in the chair to see Kane leaning against the doorframe, arms crossed, face unreadable.

"No. Nope, just—"

"Relax, Shiloh. You're allowed to be in here. It's your house."

"Right."

He stared at me for a second, then pushed off the doorframe and took a seat at the small table covered with thick files.

"Is Aaron around?"

"He's in a meeting with your dad." His eyes flicked toward the screen behind me. "Creed is outside. Your call."

And with that, he grabbed a file and flipped it open, relaxing into his seat and dismissing me.

I hesitated for a moment, staring at the two options laid out like forks in the road. Aaron would tell me to slow down. To think things through. To let them handle it.

But Creed... Creed let me move at my own pace. I left the room and headed for the patio door.

THE GLASS DOOR slid open without a sound, and the scent of late-summer rain hit me. The clouds overhead were dark and fat with an incoming storm—bringing my favorite smell of rain before it hits the ground. Creed didn't turn right away—just lifted his cup to his lips and kept his eyes on the treeline at the edge of the yard.

I stepped out and shut the door behind me.

"You look like a statue. Have you even blinked today?"

A smirk pulled at his mouth. "I wouldn't be very intimidating if I paced nervously in circles."

I walked over and leaned on the railing a few feet away, letting the quiet settle between us before I spoke. "We went to the high-rise. The one from the file."

His gaze cut to me, sharp but patient. "Learn anything useful?"

I paused. Lottie got us a door number, a timeframe to work with. But I don't say that.

"Still working on it," I said instead.

Creed didn't press. Just nodded once like that was enough. "If you want backup, or eyes on the building... I'm not far."

I glanced sideways at him, unsure if that was meant as an offer or a warning.

"Do you—umm... do you know..." I couldn't get the words to form properly. Did he know what I was doing? He knew enough to hand me the file, but if he knew what I was actually doing with the information, would he turn me in?

"I know enough. I might be observant, but I'm not a cop, Shiloh. Whatever you do with the information you have, that's up to you."

The silence returned, heavier this time. I stared out past the lawn, fists tightening on the railing. There was something venomous curled in my chest. Something new. Or maybe not new—just no longer chained. It started when I killed Joseph. The moment my knife slid into his flesh, something in me stopped pretending to be gentle. Taking his life didn't feel like vengeance; it felt like clarity. And now?

Now it felt like a fire burning low and slow, waiting to be fed more kindling.

I wanted to find Abigail. I wanted to dismantle every remaining limb of The Manor and anyone who ever had a hand in the creation or resurrection of such a vile thing. Maybe that made me dangerous, or maybe it just made me human.

"Is there something you'd like to tell me?"

I looked up. He watched me now, coffee forgotten in his hand.

"I don't know what you're talking about. I'm just curious."

He stepped closer, just enough that I could feel the weight of him in the space between us.

"Little liar," he chuckled. "Just be careful. I have no doubt you can take care of yourself, but these people are not solitary creatures. They work in packs."

I swallowed hard and looked back out to the yard, anything to avoid the thinly masked concern in his eyes.

"I will." It was the most honest thing I'd said all day.

CHAPTER NINETEEN

CREED

She was good at slipping away. Silent in a way that only people who have spent time hiding in plain sight could be. She made it out the side door, managing to avoid every single camera, with a black hoodie pulled over her head and her mind working overtime.

I let her think she'd gotten away with it, like none of us were watching. But I never let her out of my sight for long. Not when I knew what was out there.

I followed at a distance, letting the dark swallow the quiet hum of my car's engine. It was easier this way, watching her from the shadows. Safer. For her, for everyone.

She parked a few streets down from the high-rise, slipping out of her car with a bag slung over her shoulder before disappearing through the alley behind the building.

I left my car and followed on foot. She didn't see me, never does. She was focused, razor-sharp, like she was made for this. Which she wasn't. Not really. She wasn't born this way; she was created. Each day that ticked by in that place changed something vital inside her. Little by little. Piece by piece. Until she was something completely new. Until she was the girl running through dark alleys to rip life away from men who didn't deserve it.

I slipped inside the service entrance behind her. There were no cameras at this entrance yet. I made sure to double check that and then left that little bit of information in the file I gave to her. The elevator dinged down the hall. I heard her steps, soft but sure, moving toward her next ghost. I found the stairwell and climbed. Her target lived on the sixteenth floor, a useful piece of intel I got from her conversation with Lottie. That tap on her phone really was proving to be worth it.

The man she was after was arrested during the raid at The Manor. He was a 'recruiter'. In other words, his M.O. was to lure in runaways with the promise of food and somewhere to stay. Most of them were sold within the week. They weren't nearly as lucrative as the elite targets, but they brought in enough extra cash to float Milo's coke habit.

I'd have taken this one out myself if I hadn't already seen the look in her eye when she studied his photo. No, she deserved this one. By the time I made it to the hallway outside his suite, her work had already begun. I heard the muffled thud of a body hitting the ground, the sound of furniture shifting, a sharp cry cut off almost as fast as it started. I hovered outside of the apartment for a few seconds, listening. Silence. She was brutal. Efficient. The kind of quiet rage that simmered beneath the surface until it burned through everything.

I waited a few more seconds, enjoying the sound of Shiloh dragging the man across the floor.

His pleas were weak as she took him to what I assumed was the bedroom, barking questions at him as she went. I slipped inside, easing the door closed and sticking to the shadows in the dark hallway.

"Where is she?" Her voice was so calm, so steady.

"I don't know! I don't even know who that is! I haven't been in touch with anyone since I got out, I promise!"

She was quiet for a moment.

"You know, I think I actually believe you. Unfortunately, someone has that little girl, and tonight, that's going to be your problem."

I peered around the doorframe just in time to see her suppress a gag as she rammed her knife through his left eye, putting so much force behind it that she rocked forward on her toes before pulling back.

The knife was firmly planted in his skull, blood pouring into his open mouth. Dead. For fucking sure.

She braced one foot on his shoulder for leverage and yanked the knife free, exhaling heavily before wiping the blade against his clothes and shoving it back in her bag.

I ducked back into the hallway, listening in amusement as she opened the window and shuffled down to the fire escape. Clever girl, considering she was drenched in blood. I moved into the room, taking in the scene before me.

The man laid face down across the floor, blood pooling beneath him, dark and sticky on the hardwood. She showed neither mercy nor hesitation. I moved quickly, gloves on, wiping down any surface she might have touched. Door handles. Counter. Bathroom sink. The window. I gathered anything that might link back to her and tossed it into the trash bag I brought. Then I kneeled by the body, pulling the king of hearts card from my pocket.

The Red King claimed another. A diversion, really. A failsafe in case she slipped up. A message to the others. Shiloh's kills just happened to be in the same target pool as mine, so claiming them as my own, upping the body count of the boogeyman to the rich and disturbed, seemed like a good move. This way, these kills traced back to The Red King, not Red.

When I was done, I moved just as quietly as she did, retracing her steps through the fire escape and out into the alley. She was already long gone. By the time I got back to the house, it was close to two in the morning. Most of the lights were off. Aaron's car was gone, probably still out working on one of the multiple leads we received in the last two days. I cut the engine and walked toward the side entrance, stopping when I heard rustling a few feet away.

I took a few steps toward the sound, pulling my flashlight from my belt and shining it in front of me. Nate was crouched near the bushes by Shiloh's window, a taser in one hand and the wildest fucking grin on his face. He didn't flinch when the light hit his eyes, just lifted the taser in a wave like he was proud of it.

"Evening." he said casually, nodding at the body twitching on the ground beside him.

I sighed, pinching the bridge of my nose.

"What the hell, Nate?"

"Guy had a gift box. Was looking through her window." Nate nudged the box with his boot.

"Highly suspect. Also, the feeds went black for five minutes. That's why I came out."

I crouched down, checking the guy's pulse. He was alive, but he wouldn't be getting up for a while. Nate had a thing for tasers, and his didn't exactly emit a legal voltage.

"What's in the box?" I asked.

"Didn't open it," Nate said, "just tased him in the jaw and then I thought I'd wait for you. Y'know, in case it's a bomb or a head or something unsavory."

I rolled my eyes and peeled back the lid. It wasn't a bomb. Or a head. It was a small nightlight shaped like a unicorn. Plastic, cheap... There was a note tucked inside with the words: *Too late.*

My stomach turned. Shiloh didn't have an admirer. Other than me, anyway, so who was leaving gifts outside her window?

"Recognize him?" I asked, nodding at the man on the ground.

"Not really. Might have seen him at a bar once? Who knows. He's very ugly and not at all memorable." Nate scratched the back of his neck, then gave me a sideways look. "You wanna question him when he wakes up, or should I play bad cop again?"

"I'll call Kane, we'll figure out where to hold him. Better we interrogate him than the cops. I think our methods will be more efficient."

Nate shrugged and started humming to himself, flipping the taser in his hand like a fidget toy.

"Did she hear anything?" I asked, nodding to Shiloh's window.

"No, she came in and went straight to the shower. Should I tell her?"

"No. She doesn't need anything else on her plate tonight," I said quietly.

Nate laughed. "Fickle pickle we're in, hmm?"

He disappeared inside to find Kane, leaving me alone in the dark, the nightlight in one hand and questions clawing at the back of my mind. This was getting messier. And Shiloh was already in too deep.

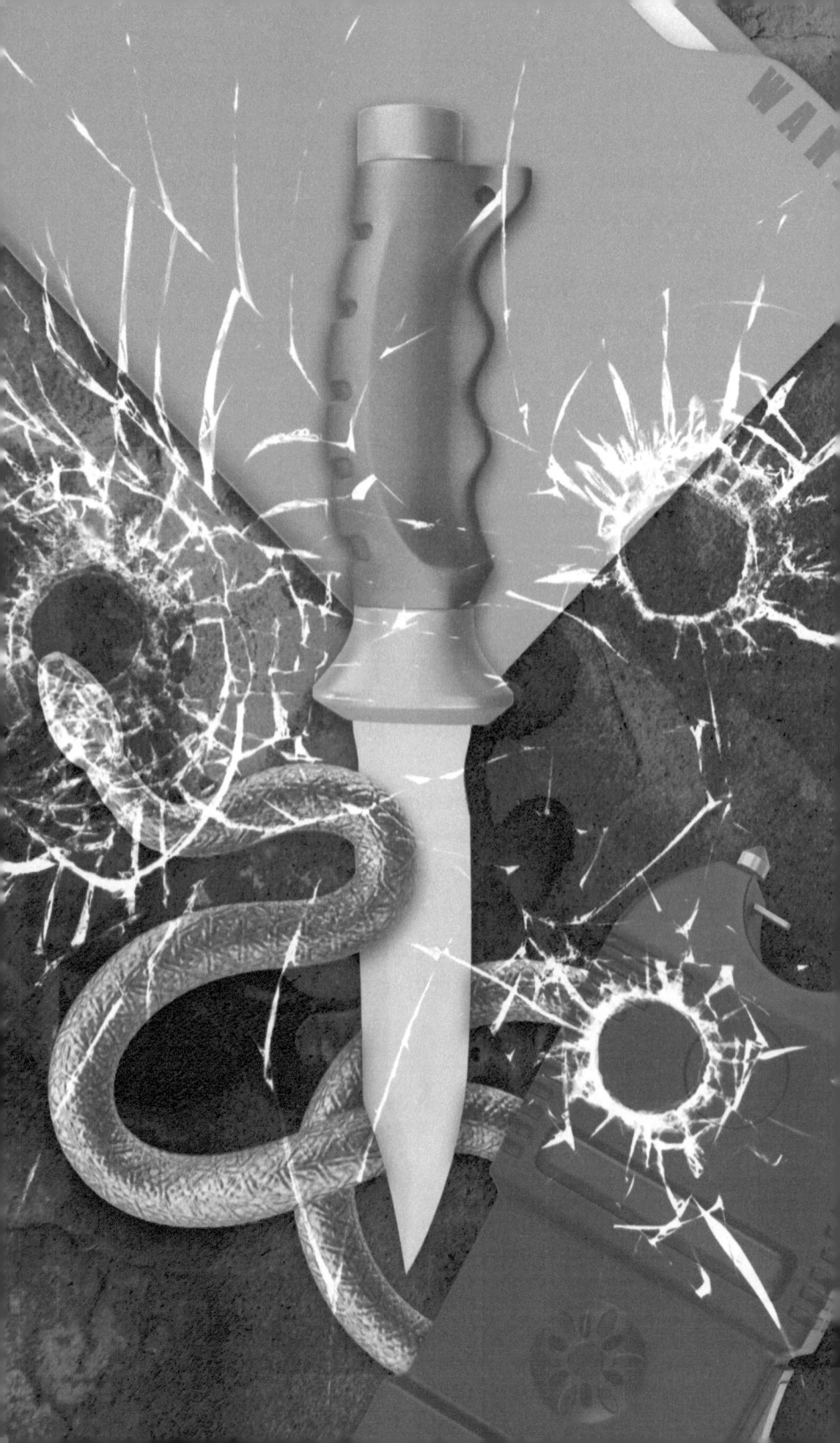

CHAPTER TWENTY

SHILOH

The sun warmed my face as I lounged in one of the Adirondack chairs in the backyard. With my legs kicked up on the edge of the firepit, I scrolled on my phone with a mindless flick of my thumb. Lunch sat half-eaten on the plate beside me, and for once, I wasn't obsessively planning my next move. I was just... existing.

Until I saw the headline.

"The Red King Strikes Again: Another Man Found Dead, Signature Card Left at Scene."

My stomach dropped. I sat up too fast, phone clutched in my hand, and blinked at the photo beneath the headline. Grainy image. Crime scene tape. The streetlight from the alley near the high-rise.

I killed that man. The report went on to detail how the victim was found in his apartment, no witnesses, no security footage. Only the card left on his chest—the king.

A familiar rage boiled in my chest, crawling up my throat, bitter and hot, leaving the taste of acid on my tongue. He fucking did it again. The Red King—whoever the hell he was— has taken credit for my kill, again.

I was so stunned I didn't hear the footsteps approaching until Creed stood behind me, casting a shadow over my chair.

"You okay?"

I glanced up. His voice was calm, lazy. He held two glasses of lemonade, offering me one with a raised brow.

I took it automatically, eyes narrowing. "Do I look okay?"

He sat in the chair beside me, one ankle resting on his knee. "You look pissed off, but that's sort of your default."

I tossed him a glare and gestured to the phone. "This asshole did it again."

Creed leaned closer, squinting at the screen. "The Red King?"

"Yeah."

"You have beef with a serial killer?"

"He's a thief." The words slipped out sharper than I meant them to. I covered it with a sip of my drink.

Creed didn't respond right way. Just watched me. The corner of his mouth twitched like he knew something that I didn't and it made my skin prickle.

"You seem awfully angry," he said finally. "Something you want to talk about?"

"No," I shot back. "I just don't like the idea of some psycho getting praised in the news for doing the right thing."

His laugh was low and smooth. "Killing bad people is the *right thing*?"

My heart stuttered. Shit. "I mean..." I shrugged, casual, but I felt anything but. "If someone's got it coming."

He tipped his head to the side, amusement clear on his face. "You're a little crazy, aren't you?"

"Better than boring, I guess," I muttered and his smile widened.

He let the silence stretch for a moment before leaning back again. "You know, if you ever needed help..."

I narrowed my eyes. "Why would I need help?"

He shrugged. "Just saying. My services are available."

The words dug in deep. I should have brushed him off. Should've reminded myself that trusting anyone was a bad idea with an even worse outcome. But there was something in the way he talked to me, watched me. It didn't feel wrong and it didn't feel fake. It felt like he cared. Before I could say anything else, the back door slid open. Aaron stepped out, his face serious.

"Shiloh, we need to talk."

I glanced at Creed, who already stood, the easy grin wiped from his face.

Inside, the mood shifted. The security room was heavy. The guys were all gathered around the small table, my dad included.

"What's up?" I asked.

My dad frowned at me, whatever he had to tell me, it wasn't good.

"Shiloh, early this morning the feeds went down. Nate noticed and went outside to patrol while Kane got them back up and running."

"Okay?"

"While he was out there, he saw someone. Outside your window."

My heart sank. "What time was this?"

"Around two in the morning"

I was home. I had just gotten home, actually. Had someone followed me? Was it the Red King?

"It was a single suspect; he was carrying a small gift-wrapped box. This was inside, along with a note." Kane opened the box on the table in front of me, pulling out the familiar nightlight.

I choked back the nausea and reached, taking it from him

and cradling it in my hands. Why would they send me this? They had to know I was looking for her, which was a stretch already because I hadn't left anyone alive after I questioned them, but it was also a bold assumption that I would even remember the nightlight to make the connection in the first place.

I glanced at Aaron who visibly shook with anger. His jaw locked tight as he stared at the small light in my hands. It was a message, but it was so detailed, thought out and personal that I felt afraid for the first time in weeks.

"We are working on getting information about the sender, and anything else he may have out of him," Kane replied.

"Where is he?" Surely, they took him into the station.

"He was arrested, but he was able to bail out within a few hours," my dad said, agitation clear on his face.

"However," Kane interjected, "Nate picked him up and we are currently... holding him in the cellar. For questioning."

"Which I will deny if anyone asks." My dad looked around the room with a raised eyebrow, making eye contact with each of the guys. Considering he was the chief of police, the trouble he would be in for kidnapping and holding a man hostage would be astronomical.

"You said there was a note?" I asked, already feeling the edge sharpen in my voice.

Kane nodded and reached into the small box on the table, pulling out a clear evidence bag and passing it to me. Inside was a small scrap of paper with loopy handwriting in blue ink.

"Too late."

I read the words twice, my skin crawling with disgust and fear. Two simple words to say, 'We have her, you fucked up, and we know where you are.'

"I don't recognize the handwriting," I muttered.

Creed stood silently across from me, arms crossed, expression closed off. I felt his eyes on me as the guys talked, waiting for cracks to appear, or for me to finally just fucking lose it and snag a gun before jaunting off on a rampage. My father was watching me in a similar manner.

In fact, all their faces, save for Nate who just looked manic as usual, held varying degrees of concern. Like I was made of glass and each word they spoke was a pebble tossed against me. How long until I shattered? Maybe they expected me to breakdown.

But I didn't.

I couldn't. All I could feel was the dull burn in my chest that had replaced most of the other human emotions a long time ago.

"We ID'd him," Kane said. "Local guy. Name's Reid Martin. No prior arrests, no connection to the ring that we can find."

"So, he was hired."

"Most likely."

That did it. The burn flared.

"So, someone wants me bad enough to hire someone to drop presents at my window in the middle of the night?"

No one spoke. It wasn't really a question anyway. A violent kind of anger flared to life inside me. Who the fuck was after me? Why? Sending someone else just felt like a game. Someone with the means to get a whole other person past our security measures surely had the ability to just come to me themselves. A game. That's exactly what this was. This was psychological. They wanted me scared, cornered, broken. Tough fucking shit.

"So, you have him?" I asked Kane.

He nodded once. "He's downstairs."

"Good. I want to see him."

Aaron shifted. "Shiloh—"

"No." My voice came out hard. "He left something at my window. He knew where I sleep. He gets a visit."

There was a beat of silence thick enough to choke on.

Creed spoke for the first time, steady and with an air of finality. "Then she sees him."

Something about the way he said it grounded me. Made the breath settle in my lungs. Not protective, more like confirmation. I was still in control. I didn't know who was doing this; I didn't understand what they wanted from me. But I didn't need to understand it to burn it all to the ground.

CHAPTER TWENTY-ONE

CREED

We had moved Reid into the small room off the gym downstairs, a fairly roomy space, though it was nothing but pipes and concrete. He was tied to a chair in the middle of the room, his jeans and black shirt dirty from his tussle with Nate. He was a thin guy, no bulk to him whatsoever.

His sharp eyes landed on Shiloh as soon as she entered the room, a gleam to them that rattled something in my chest. Nate and Kane went to the back wall, Aaron and David standing near the doorway. I followed Shiloh, staying just a few steps behind as she moved just out of reach from Reid.

"Who sent you?" she asked.

He didn't answer, just leaned back against the chair like he had all the time in the world.

"Nice setup you've got here."

She didn't blink. "Who gave you the box?"

That made him smile. Slow. Creeping. "Word on the street is someone wants their girl back."

"I'm not anyone's *girl*." Her words were pure venom.

"Sure. I didn't catch his name. Just took the job, sweetness. He told me where you'd be. Said you'd be surrounded by men.

Called you a whore, actually. Figured I'd take the job and see what all the fuss was about."

Her hands curled into fists at her side. Reid leaned forward like he was sharing a secret.

"I heard about you, you know. From Ruben. We used to hang out in the same clubs. Said you used to cry the first few times, then you started begging for it like a bitch in heat. That's how it goes, right? Girls like you—"

"*Get out.*"

Shiloh's voice was level, but lethal. Kane turned to look at David, who was red faced and fighting the tears building in the corners of his eyes.

No one moved.

"I said GET THE FUCK OUT." The sound pierced through the air like a bullet, and feet started shuffling toward the door.

I took a few steps backwards, but Shiloh turned, locking her eyes on me. She swallowed hard, a flicker of emotion passing over her face before she choked it down.

"Not you." It was a plea. Barely a whisper.

I nodded, moving to the door and closing it after Nate exited, then walking up behind Shiloh who hard-turned back to face Reid. I stepped closer, until I could feel the heat of her body brushing against my chest.

"Nothing he says means a goddamn thing," I whispered, leaning my chin against her shoulder to whisper into her ear. "You do whatever you need to do."

She leaned back, just a fraction, just enough that I could feel the rapid pace of her heartbeat against me. Her head bobbed up and down gently with a nod, and then she took two steps forward, her arm swinging out on the last step. She punched Reid right in the fucking face.

A smug grin tugged at my face as she stepped back,

brushing the hair out of her face.

"Let's try this again. Where did you get the box?"

He spit a wad of blood-tinted spit at her feet, meeting her eyes with a stupid level of vitriol.

I didn't move from my spot behind her. Didn't speak, didn't intervene. Just watched the way her shoulders rose and fell with a heavy sigh, the way her neck rolled to the left before straightening as she locked her eyes on him.

She was silent. Still. And somehow, that made the room feel colder than it already was.

Shiloh crouched beside him, slowly, deliberately. Her fingers brushed the arm of the chair, tracing the wood right next to where his wrists were tied to it. He flinched. She smiled.

"Let's make this simple," she said, voice flat. "You give me a name, and I will let the police handle the rest of it."

Reid didn't respond. He stared at the wall past her head, like if he didn't meet her eyes, he could pretend he was in control. He wasn't. I knew it. She knew it.

"I don't know his name," he muttered finally. "I never met him. Just a call. A wire transfer for the money. I did what I was paid to do."

Her expression didn't change. "You're lying," she said softly.

"I'm not," he insisted. That smug tone crept back into his voice like he forgot what kind of girl he was dealing with. "But I get it. You're used to needing control. That's what they always said about you. Ruben especially. Said you wanted it, so he made sure you never had any—"

She linked her fingers with his, her palm resting against his. I blinked.

"I've always wanted to try this, I read about it once," she said quietly.

Her hand curled around his—fingers threading together

like lovers might do—and she looked at him for a moment. His brows pinched. Confused. Maybe even hopeful, like he thought she was about to break. Like this was some secret soft spot he had found in her.

Then—*crack.*

His scream split the silence as she pushed her hand forward, hard and fast, the angle of it folding his wrist the wrong way. Bone snapped. The chair jerked under him, the wooden legs rocking on the concrete as he howled. I didn't think I breathed. She stood slowly, shaking out her hand like touching his had left something unpleasant on her skin.

My heart beat out of rhythm, or at least it felt like it did. Watching her take control, watching her take her pound of flesh after the shit he spewed at her, it altered something in my brain. She was a fucking force. A hurricane of resentment and retribution, destroying everything in her path. She was goddamn gorgeous. I watched her turn, her eyes meeting mine and searching them.

What are you looking for, baby?

Fear? Disgust?

You won't find it here.

I winked at her, savoring the slow smile that crept across her face. And that was it. This would be the moment I would think of when people asked us, years from now, 'when did you know?'

A mean, jagged kind of affection for her simmered in me. Not the kind people wrote love songs about, but the kind that makes you willing to carve the world up and drop the pieces at her feet if she asked.

She didn't flinch, didn't shake. Just stood there, watching him squirm and cry into his shoulder while his broken wrist dangled from the side of the chair.

And I wanted her more than I had ever wanted anything.

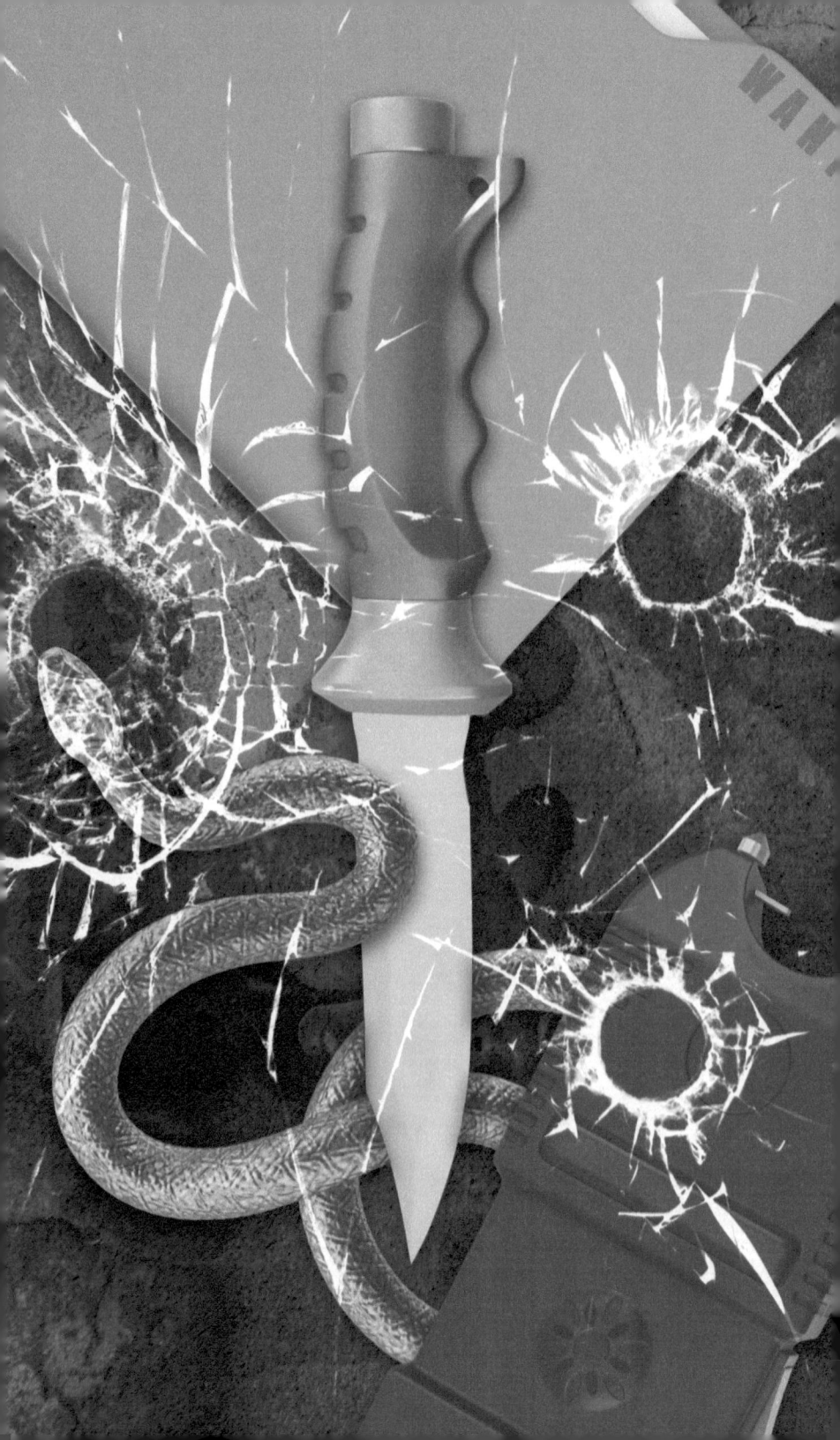

CHAPTER TWENTY-TWO

SHILOH

I stood still in front of Reid, letting the sounds of his pain echo off the basement walls, my hand flexing like I was resetting the bones in my own fingers.

His were bent backward further than they probably should be, the skin around his wrist now pulsing and red where it had started to swell.

He sobbed into his shoulder, mumbled something about me being a 'crazy bitch' but I didn't listen. He wasn't going to give me a name. Not because he didn't have one, but because he didn't see me as worth the trouble.

"I gave you a choice," I said calmly. "That's more than you gave anyone else."

He spit near my boots. Missed.

"You think you're better than me because I got paid for it? You're not. You were just as—"

I flinched at that one, instincts flinging my fist toward his face and snapping his head to the side. Anything to keep him from finishing that sentence. His breath caught, but he didn't speak again. The worst part was that he was right. I didn't make any money off it, but I was given the same jobs he was. I sabotaged the few that I was handed, but if I hadn't been able to screw the plans up, would I have gone through with them? To save myself, would I sell out another kid?

That old familiar feeling of self-hatred returned with a fury. No. I would not.

No matter how many times I reminded myself of that, the disgust I felt didn't ease.

His words had hit their mark. Behind me, Creed moved forward, placing himself in between me and Reid, just a few steps to my left. Anger poured off him; I could see it in the harsh set of his jaw. The way his hands clenched. The way he wouldn't look at me. I knew he wanted to go after Reid for himself, and honestly, he might get more out of him than I have. But he didn't. He was using every ounce of self-control he possessed to stay by my side, to let me handle this how I needed to. That mattered more than I expected.

I turned away from Reid without another word, walking toward the door with my face carefully blank like I'd just wrapped up a business meeting. My blood buzzed, my hands still shaking slightly.

"Creed," I said, pausing in the doorway, my voice flat, "leave him as he is. Don't feed him. Don't set the bones."

He looked at me, meeting my eyes and nodded once.

"If he talks, let me know. If he doesn't... I don't care."

I don't remember walking up the stairs. Don't remember shutting the door behind me or walking into my bathroom. But the faucet was running, and I was standing in front of the sink, wrists deep in steaming hot water. The soap was nearly gone, lathered into a thick pink foam under my nails, around my knuckles, bleeding into the cracked skin. I kept scrubbing.

My hands burned. Red. Raw. The sting didn't feel like enough. I wanted to take layers off my flesh until I found something clean and pure underneath. I heard the door open but didn't bother looking up. My body had tuned itself to his at some point, relaxing instead of tensing when it felt his presence. He moved slow and silent like smoke, his body creeping closer to mine.

My focus stayed on my hands, on the way they wouldn't get clean, no matter how hard I tried.

His hands came around me and settled on top of mine.

"Shiloh," he pleaded. "That's enough, sweetheart."

I didn't answer.

His thumbs rubbed over my hands, firm, slow strokes as he eased them out of the water.

My breath caught but I didn't pull away. I couldn't look at him either. Just stared at the sink, at the swirling water and smeared soap and raw skin.

"I can't scrub it off." My voice cracked over the words. "It's still on me."

"Shhh. It's alright." He turned off the faucet, and I let him.

I let him guide my hands out of the sink, his touch firm but patient. Like he knew what I was trying to erase. I waited for the instinct to kick in. The one that told me to cower away from him or run. To kick him out and lock the door. To protect what was left of me. It didn't come. When I turned in his arms, it was slow, but deliberate.

My head barely reached his shoulder, but the warmth of him soaked into my skin like sunlight through glass. I stood there, still as stone, while his arms came around me. He guided my head against his chest and held me there. Solid as a rock.

And for the first time in as long as I could remember, I felt it. Safe.

I left out a shaky breath and leaned in closer as the first tear slipped down my cheek. Creed didn't ask questions; he just held me like he had been waiting for me to let him.

"You are not dirty, Red." The venom in his words was

drowned out by the soul-shattering sorrow I could hear on my behalf. The emotion coming from him pulled a sob free from my chest. It tumbled out before I could lock it down and swallow it whole like I always did. It wasn't quiet. Wasn't graceful. It was the sound of all my broken pieces being tossed on the floor for him to see.

Creed's arms tightened around me. His breaths coming heavier as I cried, like he knew what it cost me to fall apart in front of someone else. At some point my legs gave out, and he caught me without a word.

"Got you," he whispered into my hair, his voice rough. "I've got you, Red."

He lifted me like I weighed nothing and carried me out of the bathroom. I didn't fight him. Instead, my arms and legs wrapped tightly around him on their own, clutching him to me like he would disappear if I let go.

My hands were curled into the fabric of his shirt, my knuckles white, and I couldn't make myself let go even when he eased us both onto my bed. He gently pried my fingers off him, setting me on my feet just long enough to pull the covers back and ease me into the bed. Then he slipped under the blanket beside me, rolling onto his side and pulling me close until my back met his chest. His arm slid around my waist like a shield.

"I'm sorry." The words came out in between hiccups, but he just squeezed me tighter against him.

"There is nothing for you to be sorry for, Shiloh," he said, pressing his lips to my shoulder. "There is no right way to do this. Someday, you're going to find a way to let go of the parts of the past that hurt you. You just did, even if it feels small now."

I nodded through a sniffle, but the words stuck.

Was that what I was doing? Was I letting it all go?

Maybe. Maybe I didn't want to. Anger had been the only

thing keeping me going lately. The devastating *need* to get rid of people like Ruben and Reid.

Who would I be if that was gone?

"Rest. I'll be here when you wake up."

My swollen eyes fell closed a few minutes later, and for the first time in a long time, I felt safe while I fell asleep.

CHAPTER TWENTY-THREE

CREED

The knock came just after sunrise. Quiet, hesitant. I didn't move. Shiloh was still tucked into my side, her breathing soft and even. The last thing I wanted to do was wake her. The door creaked open anyway. I glanced over to see Aaron frozen in the doorway. Tension filled the room as he ran his eyes over her, noting the way her body was plastered to mine. I had kicked off my shoes and tossed my shirt to the floor sometime around two in the morning, and she had immediately curled into me, resting her head on my chest. She had been sleeping in that same position for hours now.

Aaron wasn't the type to lose his temper, but I knew that protective look in his eyes. He loved Shiloh like a little sister, and he wasn't happy to see her tangled up in a man like me. I raised a brow at him. His arms were crossed, jaw tight.

"You sleep in all your clients' beds, Creed?" he asked, keeping his voice low.

"Nope. Just her," I replied evenly.

He shifted like he wanted to say something else, but then his eyes flicked to Shiloh. She was peaceful for once. Her face half-buried against my chest, her hand flat against my stomach instead of curled into a fist.

He exhaled through his nose and nodded once. "She okay?"

"Getting there."

I watched him hesitate, then step back out of the room. He didn't close the door all the way. Just left it cracked, like he was giving me the benefit of the doubt but keeping one foot in line just in case. Smart man. I looked down at Shiloh again. There were faint shadows under her eyes, but she looked softer this morning. Her guard hadn't slid back into place yet.

Gently, I shifted from beneath her. One hand brushed her hair back from her face, fingertips trailing along her temple.

"Red," I murmured. "Time to wake up."

She stirred with a small groan, her brow pulling slightly as she blinked up at me. And then—right on cue—the realization hit. Her eyes widened, her body tensed, and the color in her cheeks turned a shade darker.

I smiled.

"Don't panic," I said. "You just used me as a very warm, very charming pillow."

She blinked. "I—"

"I'm honored, really."

A soft huff escaped her, somewhere between a laugh and a groan. She turned her face, pressing it into my shoulder and mumbling something I couldn't quite make out.

I let my hand glide down her arm before I shifted away, slowly untangling myself. Her hands lingered on my abdomen a second longer than necessary, like her body wasn't quite ready to let go just yet. I stepped into my shoes, forcing the smirk off my face as I caught her eyes gliding over my exposed skin while I fished my shirt off the ground and pulled it over my head. When I looked back up, she had shoved a pillow over her face.

"For what it's worth," I said, smiling, "you drool a little in your sleep."

A pillow smacked into the door right as I pulled it shut behind me.

I PASSED Aaron on the stairs. He didn't say anything, just nodded and moved toward Shiloh's room as I headed down to the security room.

Nate was already there, slouched in one of the chairs with a protein bar hanging out of his mouth like a cigarette and his boots kicked up on the table. He looked up when I walked in and let out a low whistle.

"Well, well, if it isn't our own little lover boy," he said, grinning around his food. "Now where could you have disappeared to, hmm?"

"Grow up, Nathaniel," I said, but I didn't bother hiding the small curve of my mouth.

Kane looked up from one of the monitors. "She alright?"

I nodded. "Cried herself out last night. But yeah, she'll be alright."

There was a beat of silence before Kane spoke again. "David called."

I leaned against the wall, arms crossed. "Yeah?"

"He wants us to release Reid. Says he'll have his patrol keep an eye on him, and if he so much as litters, they'll pick him back up."

I stared at the monitor a long moment, jaw tightening. "No."

Both of them turned to look at me.

"You didn't hear the things he said to her. Even after she

snapped his wrist, he was still trying to get under her skin. If we let him go, he'll come back."

Nate crumpled a wrapper in his first and sat up straight. "So, we get to kill him?"

Kane gave a slow nod. "We have to make David think we did what he asked. We'll take him somewhere outside of the city."

Nate's grin turned manic. "I'm going to collect his kneecaps."

Kane looked at me with an expression that clearly read, "*What the fuck?*"

But I didn't have any more explanation for Nate than he did. If he wanted kneecaps, it was best to just let him have at it.

"We don't leave him breathing. He talks to someone else, this shit escalates. He decides to come back with reinforcements, this shit escalates. We don't tell David, or Aaron."

"What about her?" Kane asked.

"She deserves to know, but we tell her after. If she's pissed, she can take it out on me."

Kane shook his head, but turned back to the monitors.

I pushed off the wall and walked over to the table, reaching for the file we had on Reid. "Pick somewhere out of the way, no cameras within a three mile radius, low traffic."

Nate leaned back in his chair, smirking. "I love this fucking job."

We would get it done, but we wouldn't make it easy on him. I wanted to kill him last night. Quick. Efficient. Cold. But this wasn't about me. This one was making it personal. For her.

And he was going to know exactly how I felt about that.

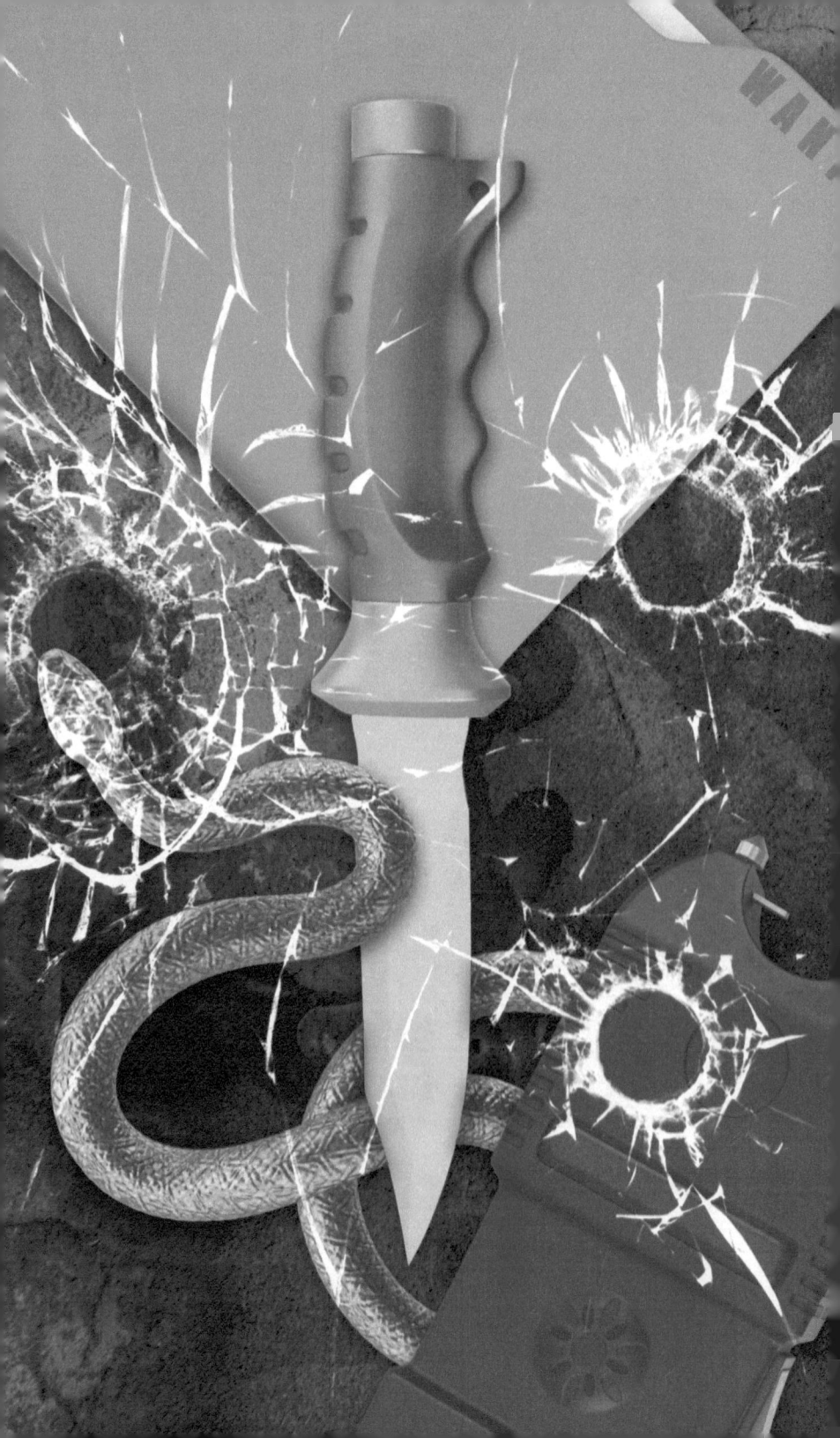

CHAPTER TWENTY-FOUR

SHILOH

The knock on my door was enough to make me flinch.

"Yeah?" I called, already knowing Aaron would be on the other side.

He poked his head in, brow furrowed with that concerned older brother look he wore so well. His eyes flicked over the bed, to the tossed sheets, and then to me still sitting upright on top of them, fully clothed. I hadn't moved much since Creed left.

He cleared his throat. "Didn't mean to interrupt. Just checking in."

"I'm fine."

His mouth pressed into a line. "Creed was in here all night?"

I blinked at him slowly. "Yeah."

"You let him stay?"

I shrugged, my arms crossing loosely over my stomach. "I kind of snapped, and then he just...stayed."

Aaron looked like he didn't know what to do with that. His hand rubbed at the back of his neck while he lingered in the doorway like he was deciding whether to say something else.

He settled on a heavy sigh. "They're good guys, it's just scary letting anyone that close to you."

"I'm sorry, did I miss the part where you became my father?" I laughed. I thought I had noticed his protective streak getting worse lately, apparently, I was right.

He walked over to sit on the edge of my bed. "You know, I've known them most of my life. Kane and I, we grew up in the same foster home. We went through the same hell, made it out together. Creed and Nate came along the year Kane and I graduated high school, and that was it. We were a package deal. They're all like brothers to me, but if it came down to it, Shiloh, I would choose you over them in a heartbeat." His eyes darted between mine, searching for something that told him I understood. "Whatever happens with you and Creed, I just want you to be happy. Okay?"

"Yes, Dad," I replied.

He sighed. "You haven't been to the gym in a few days," he said. "Thought maybe you'd want to come in today. Get out of the house for a little bit."

I nodded, already scrambling out of bed to get ready. "Yes. I'll meet you downstairs in five."

He chuckled at the way I rushed around as he shut the door. I grabbed a random shirt and a pair of athletic shorts from my closet, slipping into a pair of sneakers. I brushed through my hair before tossing it in a loose ponytail, giving myself just a few seconds in the mirror to make sure no leftover makeup had smeared across my face during my sobfest last night. I didn't need to dwell on how swollen my eyes were.

Downstairs was already getting chaotic when my shoes hit the bottom step. Kane and Nate were in the living room, messing with something that had a metric shit ton of wires coming off it. Aaron was in the kitchen with my father fixing thermoses of coffee, and then there was Creed.

He was waiting for me beside the staircase, his eyes finding mine as I entered the room. He stepped forward like he was just passing by, but his hand caught mine and he gently tugged me around the corner.

"Walk with me," he murmured.

I followed without thinking as he led me out the front door and to the passenger side of Aaron's truck. He opened the door and waited while I climbed in, then reached into his back pocket and pulled out a slim black pocketknife, folded neatly in his palm.

"Keep this on you," he said. "Always. Don't care where you're going or who you're with."

I stared at it. "Is something wrong?"

"Nothing immediate." He hesitated, then placed the knife into my hand. "Just want to make sure you're prepared at all times."

My fingers curled around the knife as I pulled it toward me to inspect it closer. "K.C.?"

"My initials. It's my favorite one, so don't lose it. If you stab someone, make sure you pull it back out of them before you leave." He winked at me, shutting the door and walking back into the house before I could reply.

Or ask him what his first name was.

THE GYM FELT the same as always. The fluorescent lighting and faint smell of sweat and metal, the soft thump of Aaron's expertly curated playlist in the background. We worked side by side for a few hours—cleaning weights and wiping down benches, handling front desk check-ins. It was good. Mundane. It was the routine I was used to, and I fell back into it easier than I expected.

I was folding a stack of clean towels when I saw the door open.

Uncle Miles stepped through, his face blank until he spotted me, and a wide grin split his face.

Jesus Christ.

He was dressed sharp, like usual. Expensive jeans, loafers that cost at least a couple grand, and a tailored shirt. Definitely not dressed for the gym, which meant he was here to see me.

"Shiloh!" he said, just a touch too loud. "There you are."

I stared back at him. "Here I am. What are you doing here?"

He chuckled, stepping closer. "Well, it's hard to catch you at the house these days. Your security makes it feel like Fort Knox around there."

Aaron walked over to us from the other side of the gym, standing so close to me our shoulders nearly brushed.

"Miles. Everything alright?"

Miles smiled at him too, but it didn't quite reach his eyes. "Everything's fine. Just wanted to steal my niece for lunch. We haven't caught up in a while."

My stomach twisted. I didn't want to go. But the words stuck in my throat, too hard to shape them into a 'no.' Miles had never done anything wrong, he was always overly polite, actually. He was just too much. Most people were, but he didn't seem to notice the way I recoiled when he got too close.

Aaron stepped in before I could say anything. "Yeah, give us a few and we'll all head out together. I'm starving."

There was a flicker of annoyance in Miles's face, but it passed quickly. "Of course."

Aaron gave me an encouraging smile and yelled for Sam, one of the other employees to take over for an hour. We decided on the sandwich shop across the street, which meant this thankfully shouldn't take long.

I slid into a booth, Aaron taking the spot at my side, leaving Miles to sit across from us. They made small talk after we ordered, Aaron forcing the conversation to continue right up until our food came to avoid any awkward silences or openings for Miles to grill me. I'd have to remember to thank him for that later.

He managed to sneak in a few as I chewed on my sandwich.

"How have you been? Really."

"I'm fine," I replied around a mouthful of B.L.T.

"You sure? I know it must be strange... living with all those men. Big house like that, full of strangers. Do they ever make you feel uncomfortable?"

Aaron stiffened beside me.

"It's not my first time living in a big house full of strangers. The difference is that these ones care about my well-being. So no, I don't find it strange or uncomfortable."

Miles held up his hands. "I'm just asking. I worry about you. All that testosterone... You're a pretty girl, Shiloh. It's not hard to imagine that someone could get the wrong idea."

My skin crawled. I stared down at my sandwich, the remnants of the last bite I took turning to ash in my mouth. I felt Creed's knife against my leg as I shifted in my seat, and to my surprise, it steeled my nerves a fraction.

"They have never made me feel anything other than safe," I said flatly. "That's better than I can say for most people I have encountered in my lifetime."

Miles smiled again, but this one was tighter. "And Creed? He seems extra protective of you."

Aaron pushed his plate away. "We should head back. We've got a shipment coming in."

I didn't say anything. I stood, and followed Aaron out, the weight of Miles's stare pressing into my back like a brand.

CHAPTER TWENTY-FIVE

CREED

He was already bleeding when we dragged him out of the car. Nothing life-threatening, but Nate had landed some punches during the drive that had definitely cracked something in his face.

The place we brought him to used to be a cabin—maybe even a nice one at some point. Now it was just rotting wood and rusted metal, the thick scent of damp earth and decay clinging to everything around us like smoke. Remote enough that no one was close enough to hear us. A good spot to take our time.

Kane opened the door without a word. Nate hummed along to what I was positive was a Beach Boys song as he yanked Reid inside by the back of his shirt. Reid was shaking, his face pale and slick with a mixture of sweat and blood, hair plastered to his forehead like it was glued there. His mouth had been taped shut for the drive, but it hadn't stopped him from rambling incoherently the entire time like we could actually make out what the fuck he was saying. Not that we cared.

We tied him to a metal chair in the center of the room—arms out, wrists cinched tight to the armrests, ankles bound to the legs. I circled him slowly, letting the silence stretch long enough to get under his skin. Kane leaned in the far corner, arms crossed, jaw tight. Animated for him meant both eyebrows were raised. Maybe a twitch in the jaw. But he was excited for this.

Nate had a knife out already, spinning it between his fingers like a coin. "Think he's gonna piss himself before or after the first bone breaks?" he asked casually.

"After," I mused. "He's too proud." I crouched in front of Reid, meeting his gaze.

I reached out and grabbed the edge of the tape that covered his mouth, ripping it free in one smooth motion. He swore under his breath, working his jaw back and forth to ease the ache I'm sure was building there.

"You're making a mistake," Reid spat, his voice hoarse. "She's not worth this."

Poor bastard. I backhanded him hard enough to crack his lip open. Blood splattered the floor at my feet.

Nate let out a low whistle from behind me. "He's a slow learner, huh?"

Reid sneered at me as he spoke, "You think hurting me is going to change anything? I'm not the one who wants her. I'm just the messenger."

"And yet," I said coolly, "you were outside of her window. You had help getting past our security. Messenger or not, you didn't act alone."

He shrugged...or tried to. "I did what I was paid to do. That girl's a whore, and you're all just another—"

I grabbed his face with both hands and slammed the back of his head into the chair so hard the metal screeched against the floor. The fury burning in my chest was molten. I had been on fire since last night when I saw her flinch at his words. Rage had been beating like a war drum in my head ever since.

I stood up and leaned in close, whispering near his ear. "I'm going to give you some free advice," my voice was dripping in warnings I knew he would ignore, "do not talk about her."

His mouth opened to say something else, but I drove my fist into his ribs before he could, hearing something crack under my knuckles. Then another hit—sharp, clean, just under his eye. Blood poured freely now, and I felt nothing but pure satisfaction.

"She deserves peace," I whispered. "And I'm going to make sure she gets it. Even if we have to kill every single one of you to do it." I turned Reid's head toward me, forcing him to look at me through his swollen eye. "Who paid you?"

Reid laughed, a wet, broken sound falling out of his mouth. "You're wasting your time." He shook his head, sending little droplets of blood across the floor.

I took his hand. The same hand Shiloh had held before she snapped his wrist. I held it up, turned it palm out, the rope holding it to the chair grinding against his skin with the movement.

I bent one finger back until it snapped.

He screamed.

"That's one," I said.

"I don't know a name!" he shouted.

"Two," I said, snapping another. "You better try harder, or you're going to have to hire someone to scratch your ass in the morning because you won't have a single working finger on either hand."

"I swear—I swear! I don't know who he is. I just took the goddamn job!"

"Three."

His cries turned ragged as he looked down to see three of his fingers bent at unnatural angles. The fourth finger broke louder than the rest.

"Okay! Okay." He was borderline hysterical. "If I tell you what I know, will you let me go?"

"Yes." Kane's voice came from the corner.

Reid looked between me and him, his eyes carefully avoiding the blonde maniac behind me.

"It's a website, okay? All the information is on my phone. People post...jobs on there. You accept one, they wire the money and message the details. It's all encrypted so I don't see how it would even help."

Kane nodded, then looked at me. "We'll get into it."

Reid slumped, shaking now as blood and spit painted his chin. "So, I-I can go?" he asked. God, he sounded pathetic.

Nate grinned, stepping closer and flicking his knife open. "Not quite." He laughed.

Reid's eyes widened as he gaped at us. "But you—you said—"

Poor fucker couldn't even get a sentence out.

"I lied." I shrugged.

I took a few steps back until I reached the kitchen counter, pushing myself up to sit on top of it. I leaned forward; my hands clasped between my knees as I watched Nate get to work.

As it turns out, he was incredibly serious about the kneecaps.

CHAPTER TWENTY-SIX

CREED

I went to Shiloh's bathroom as soon as we got back to the house. She was still out with Aaron, so instead of fighting the guys for the guest bathroom, I snuck upstairs and hopped in her shower to wash the blood off. My knuckles were cracked and bleeding, leaving a copper tint in the water that trailed down my body and circled the drain.

Once all traces of Reid's DNA were washed away, I stepped out of the shower and wiped the fog off the mirror with the side of my arm. I tied a clean towel around my hips and stepped out into her bedroom. Her scent lingered everywhere—warm and soft like strawberries and vanilla—and I gave myself a moment, just to stand there and breathe her in.

Whatever this was for Kane and Nate, Shiloh was the furthest thing from a job to me. I knew the night I saw her climb out of that van that she was going to be trouble for me. Her blue eyes lit up like beacons when I opened the back door, just the tiniest hint of fear in them, and then she grabbed the girl and went right back to the stone faced soldier she needed to be in that moment. She knew what sabotaging that mission would cost her, and she still did it. I saw the slight tremble in her hands as she turned and started walking back to that hell-hole with Aaron, and I snapped. I was outside Ruben's window as quickly as I could get there, slipping inside and putting a bullet through the skull of the man stupid enough to lay a finger on her.

That was it. That was the night I realized I believed in soulmates. The door creaked, snapping me out of my rambling thoughts, and I turned just as Shiloh pushed the door open.

She froze in the doorway like she had walked in on something illegal. Her eyes traveled slowly from my chest, down the line of my abdomen, to where the towel sat low and barely clung to me. Her throat bobbed as she swallowed.

"Well," I said, grinning, "if I'd have known you were coming back so soon, I might've put on pants."

She blinked, finally dragging her gaze back to my face. "I didn't know you were in here."

I hummed in response. "You sure you weren't just trying to see me naked? All you have to do is ask, Red."

Her mouth popped open, shut, then opened again. "That's—God, you're so full of yourself."

I stepped closer, clutching the towel to my hip. "Only when you look at me like that."

"I wasn't—"

"You were."

She looked flushed, and fuck if that wasn't the cutest thing I'd seen all day.

I moved to the dresser, grabbing the pair of sweats and loose shirt I had laid there.

She whirled around to face the door as I reached for my towel, pulling a deep chuckle from my chest. I stepped into the sweats and pulled the shirt over my head, clearing my throat to signal to her that I was, once again, proper.

Her gaze dropped to my hands as she turned around, and her expression changed. "You're bleeding."

I glanced down at the torn skin across my knuckles. "It's fine."

"What did you do?"

"Occupational hazard."

She took a step toward me, brows drawn. "From what, cage fighting?"

I didn't answer. She didn't really need me to.

Her voice softened. "Did it help?"

I met her eyes, watching the way her pupils dilated the closer I got to her. "No. But it was necessary."

The way she looked at me, fuck. I would swear she could see right through me. That those eyes were examining every black spot inside me, cataloging them, organizing them by degree of depravity, and then choosing to move closer anyway.

"You're so goddamn beautiful, Shiloh." I didn't mean to say it out loud, but I didn't regret it either. How many times had she heard that in her life? How many times was she told about all the good things that made her *her*?

Her eyes moved to the wall behind me, avoiding the compliment as she chewed at her bottom lip.

"And you're brave. Strong. Smart as hell."

Her chest rose and fell faster with each word from my mouth, her hands twisting in the fabric of her shirt.

"Look at me." I waited until she did what I said, the vulnerability in her eyes enough to knock the wind out of me. "Do you want me to stop?"

"No. I don't want to stop." Her words were shaky, but she leaned in closer. Close enough for her hands to grip the fabric of my sweatpants at my hips as her feet shuffled forward a step.

I cupped her jaw with one hand, resting the other on her lower back and bringing her in closer.

"Creed?"

"Hmm?"

"I want you to kiss me." It was a whisper. A barely audible request. But beneath the hesitation, there was a fire burning in those blue eyes of hers.

"Yes ma'am." My mouth met hers, softly. Just the slightest bit of pressure.

Then her hands slid up my body, finding my shoulders and grasping onto them. She moved her lips against mine, her hands gripping onto me like she wanted to crawl into my skin. And I let her.

There was the sweetest taste of desperation on her tongue, like she'd been holding back and suddenly forgot why. I kissed her back just as fervently as her hands moved to my hair, tugging just enough to make me groan into her mouth. I backed her into the wall without breaking the kiss, bracing one hand beside her head, the other still aching and raw as it skimmed her waist. She gasped as I pressed my hips against her, and I drank in the sound like it belonged to me.

Because it *did*. This wasn't a game. Not some conquest. I wasn't doing it out of boredom. It was something else entirely. I broke the kiss, forcing myself back before we went further than she was ready for, and rested my forehead against hers.

"Okay?"

She nodded, her lips parted, eyes blown wide.

"We move at your pace, Red. Always."

A shaky laugh escaped her. "I got a little... caught up in—" She gestured toward me with one hand.

I smiled, pressing a kiss to her cheek, then the corner of her mouth. "You and I both." I pushed off the wall, backing out of her personal space to clear my head, and trying to subtly rearrange myself before she caught sight of the wood in my sweats.

Her eyes dropped to my hand, then flicked back to my face, a flaming red heating her cheeks as she giggled.

Busted.

"Sorry about that," I said, rubbing at the back of my neck.

"No, don't be. It's not scary like I thought it would be, you know?" She seemed surprised.

And while I was over the fucking moon that I didn't terrify her after pinning her up against the wall, her shock over that fact felt like a punch to the gut. A good reminder to let her have control in this area, at least until she was completely comfortable.

"Can you hang out for a little bit? We could watch a movie." She seemed nervous to ask, which was precious.

Kane and Nate were already downstairs, and if she was home, then Aaron was around here somewhere too. I'd talked to the guys already about taking on a more bodyguard kind of role with Shiloh, while they handled the majority of the surveillance. It worked out.

"I'd love to." I smiled at her, watching her face split into a grin in return.

Twenty minutes later, we were sitting in a nest of blankets on her floor, an oversized bowl full of popcorn in her lap, and an array of candy spread out before us. She laughed at some cheesy joke in the movie that played in front of us, but I couldn't keep up with what was happening on screen. I was too busy listening to the sweet tinkling sound of her laughter and wondering what that feeling was in my chest that had suddenly made my entire body feel warm and light.

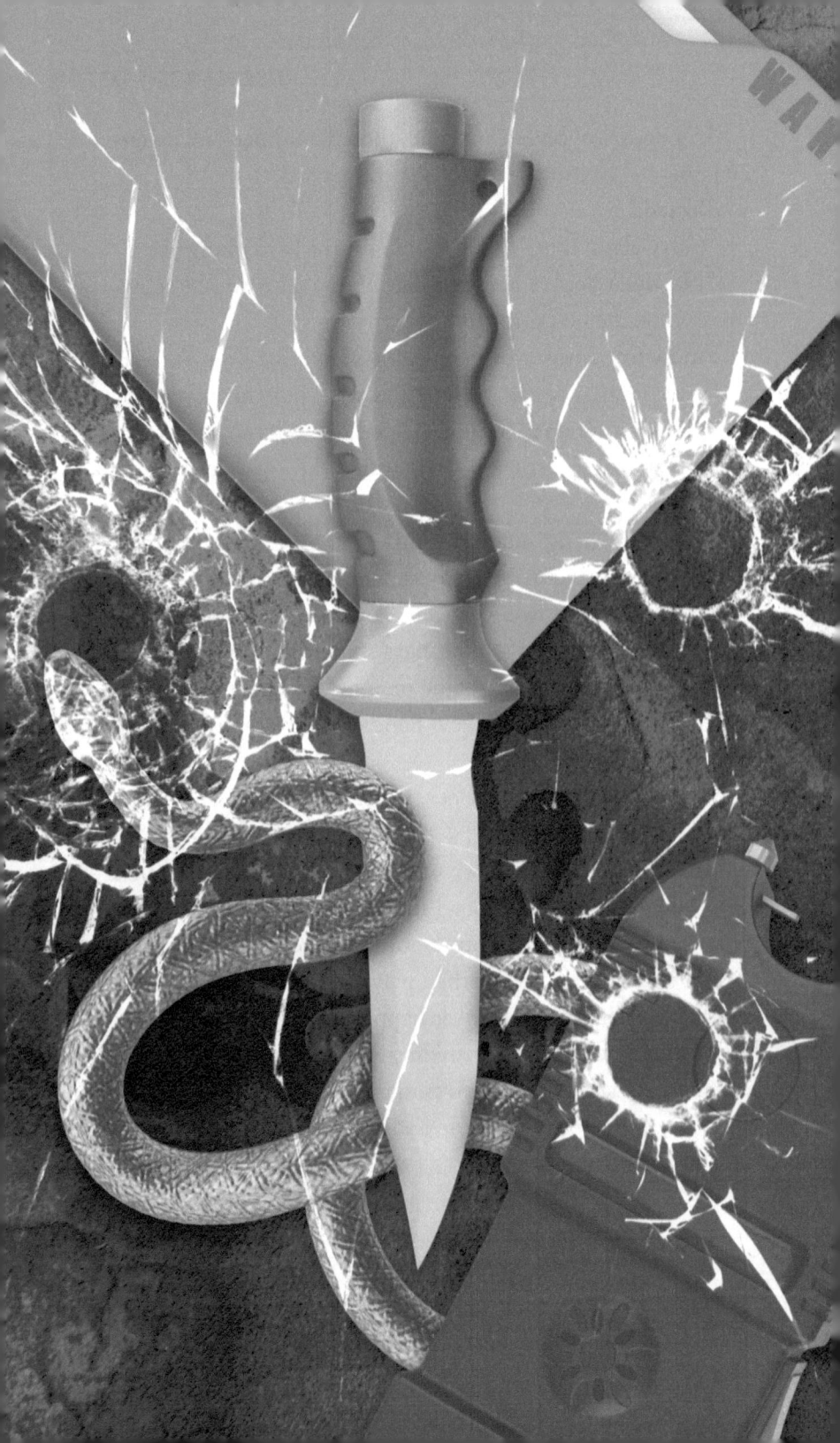

CHAPTER TWENTY-SEVEN

SHILOH

I woke up to the faint scent of Creed's cologne lingering on the pillow next to me, though the bed was empty on that side. My fingers curled into the spot where he had slept last night, his body curled against mine. Solid. Safe. A sigh slipped through my lips. *Safe*. I hated that word. Hated how easily it slipped into my vocabulary lately. Nothing about the world we lived in was safe. It wasn't a feeling I was comfortable experiencing.

I shoved the blankets off and sat up, scrubbing my hands down my face. My skin still tingled where he'd touched me when I came in last night. His hands had cradled my jaw as his lips met mine, his hands holding my hips like he couldn't get me close enough to him.

The tension between us had snapped, the feelings I'd been attempting to choke down burst to the surface, and next thing I knew, we were against my bedroom wall. Last night, it hadn't seemed scary. In the light of day, I was feeling a little less confident.

I tugged on a hoodie and a pair of leggings, slinging my hair into a low ponytail. I could hear the faint voices downstairs— Aaron, maybe. Or my dad. Probably both. I padded down the stairs and found them in the kitchen, mugs of coffee in hands and their uniforms already on. My dad looked up when I entered, his smile easy and warm.

"There she is," he said. "Was just about to come check on you."

Aaron raised a brow but didn't say anything. He gave me a small nod and excused himself, mumbling something about checking in with the guys. I didn't miss the glance he tossed my way before he left.

He knew Creed had been spending time in my bedroom, but I think he was starting to worry it was going further than just security. And he was right. A little behind on the whole situation, honestly.

My dad pointed to the coffee pot. "Want some?"

I nodded, grabbing a mug from the cabinet and filling it halfway with hot coffee and the rest of the way with some sweet creamer my mom had bought. I wasn't a big coffee drinker, but it was nice to have something to occupy my hands.

"Thought maybe we'd grab breakfast," he said, tossing me a set of keys. "There's a diner near the station I haven't been to in a while. If you're up for it."

I was. I hadn't gotten to spend much time with him lately, plus I was hungry. "Sounds good."

He smiled. "Good. You okay to follow me? I've got to get to work when we're done."

"Sure." I shrugged, following him through the garage and climbing behind the wheel of my car. I waited for him to pull out and then followed him down the driveway and across town, passing the police station and pulling in behind him at a small diner.

It was a tiny place tucked between a dry cleaner and a pawn shop. Not my father's usual scene, but the smell that hit me when I walked in explained his choice.

The vinyl booths were cracked with age, the table tops set

with menus so old the laminate was yellowed and peeling, but it smelled like fresh pancakes and hot bacon. My stomach growled loudly, pulling a deep laugh from my dad as we took our seats.

We both ordered the morning special, a large plate with a pile of scrambled eggs, toast, bacon, and a stack of pancakes that I promptly drowned in syrup.

Dad made small talk around his food while I nodded and mumbled responses as I shoveled my food into my mouth.

He was talking about a recent arrest—some drug charge, nothing major—but I wasn't really listening until he said something that made me freeze mid-bite.

"...guy we booked the other night, part of the string of missing kids cases. Supposed to be just another delivery driver, but he had some weird receipts in his glove compartment."

I blinked at him carefully, keeping my face blank. "What kind of receipts?"

He shrugged, cutting into his pancakes. "Unmarked deliveries to random warehouses. No real business names. Most of them were abandoned. Could be nothing, but we're thinking it's connected, Shy."

The food turned to lead in my stomach. "Did you run his name?" I asked casually, hoping he couldn't hear the anger seeping into my tone.

"Already in the system," he said. "Jason Lyle. Minor priors, nothing that stuck out until now."

Jason Lyle.

I filed it away, pretending to sip at my juice. "And he's in custody?"

"Released on bail. We didn't have enough to keep him, but we're looking into it and if we find anything, we'll pick him right back up. Don't worry about that."

I pushed my plate away and leaned back. "Do you think he's still in town?"

Dad nodded. "We're keeping an eye on him. Can't arrest him on gut feelings, Shiloh. But we'll get these monsters."

Not if I got them first. I let him finish his breakfast, playing along with the small talk, nodding and smiling when appropriate. But my mind was already miles ahead, planning exactly what I was going to do when I found Jason Lyles. I was itching to get more info.

I slipped my phone from my pocket while Dad finished his coffee, typing 'Jason Lyles' in the search bar and scrolling quickly through the photos that popped up. A little digging around gave me a few pictures he was tagged in on someone's social media account, unsurprisingly, he was standing outside of Sinner's.

That place really was a cesspool.

Note to self: Make sure Dad and Aaron know that place needs to be bulldozed and declared a biohazard scene when all of this was over.

I waved to my dad as we pulled out of the parking lot and went our separate ways. I made it back to the house just as Aaron was leaving, Kane and Creed following behind him.

"Where are you guys headed?" I asked.

"Not far. We're doing a full perimeter sweep. Need to check some of the cameras we've got set up on the back lot. Nate's still inside, so you aren't alone," Aaron assured me.

Not sure that made me feel any better. I didn't feel 'unsafe' around Nate, but my god was that a strange dude.

"Got it. I'll be fine." I smiled at Creed who looked torn between doing his actual job and following me back into the house.

Before he could decide, I turned and walked through the front door, closing it softly behind me.

I slipped down the hallway toward my dad's office. He never locked it—not even when the guys got here. The doorknob turned without any resistance, and I hurried in, shutting the door behind me.

Guilt bubbled in my chest. He had never once told me I wasn't allowed in this room, because he trusted me. I was about to break every ounce of that trust. The computer booted up with a soft hum as I pulled out the plush leather desk chair and sat down. I opened the precinct's database, entering my birthday when it prompted me for a password. And then I was in.

I clicked on the search log like I'd watched him do a hundred times over the last year—hovering around him when he thought I wasn't paying attention, clocking his passwords as he typed one-handed while sipping on coffee.

It was a habit to observe everything around me and catalog the important details. I never really thought I would need the information until now. I typed in *Jason Lyle*, and pages of info popped up—arrests, interviews, evidence logs from a drug arrest. But it was the most recent note that caught my eye.

Current address: Guest of record at Horizon Motel, Rm 209

Known associate: Brandon Keene

Unconfirmed link to ongoing trafficking investigation. Surveillance recommended.

Unconfirmed? What more did they need? A video? A body? My jaw tightened.

They were watching him, planning to build a case that, despite their best efforts, would likely end in a plea deal and minimum jail time. And then he would be back out here, doing the same vile shit he was doing now.

A sour taste spread through my mouth as anger turned into a headache, pulsing behind my eyes. A soft knock at the door startled me. I hit escape on the keyboard and pushed the power button on the monitor just as the door creaked open an inch.

Nate leaned in. "Not spying," he said calmly, holding his hands up like I might throw something at him for intruding. "Promise."

I narrowed my eyes but said nothing. He stepped inside anyway, one slow step at a time like he was approaching a wild animal—which, honestly, was fair.

"I was just passing by, and..." He reached into the pocket of his hoodie and held something out. A small black taser rested in his outstretched palm.

"In case you, y'know," he said with a half-grin. "Find yourself needing to give someone a little jolt."

My fingers hovered over his hand before I took it. It was warm from sitting so close to his body, the metal prongs at the top gleaming in the light.

"I didn't say I needed it."

"I know," he said with a shrug. "Didn't ask." His grin tilted sideways, but something about his gaze sobered—a deeper part of him surfacing for just a moment. "It's powerful, okay? And it's there if you need it. That way you don't feel alone, even when you are." He winked, turned, and strolled out, whistling something off-key as he went.

The door clicked shut softly behind him. I stared at the taser for a long moment, my grip tightening. Not alone.

But this part? The decision, the action, the weight? That was all mine.

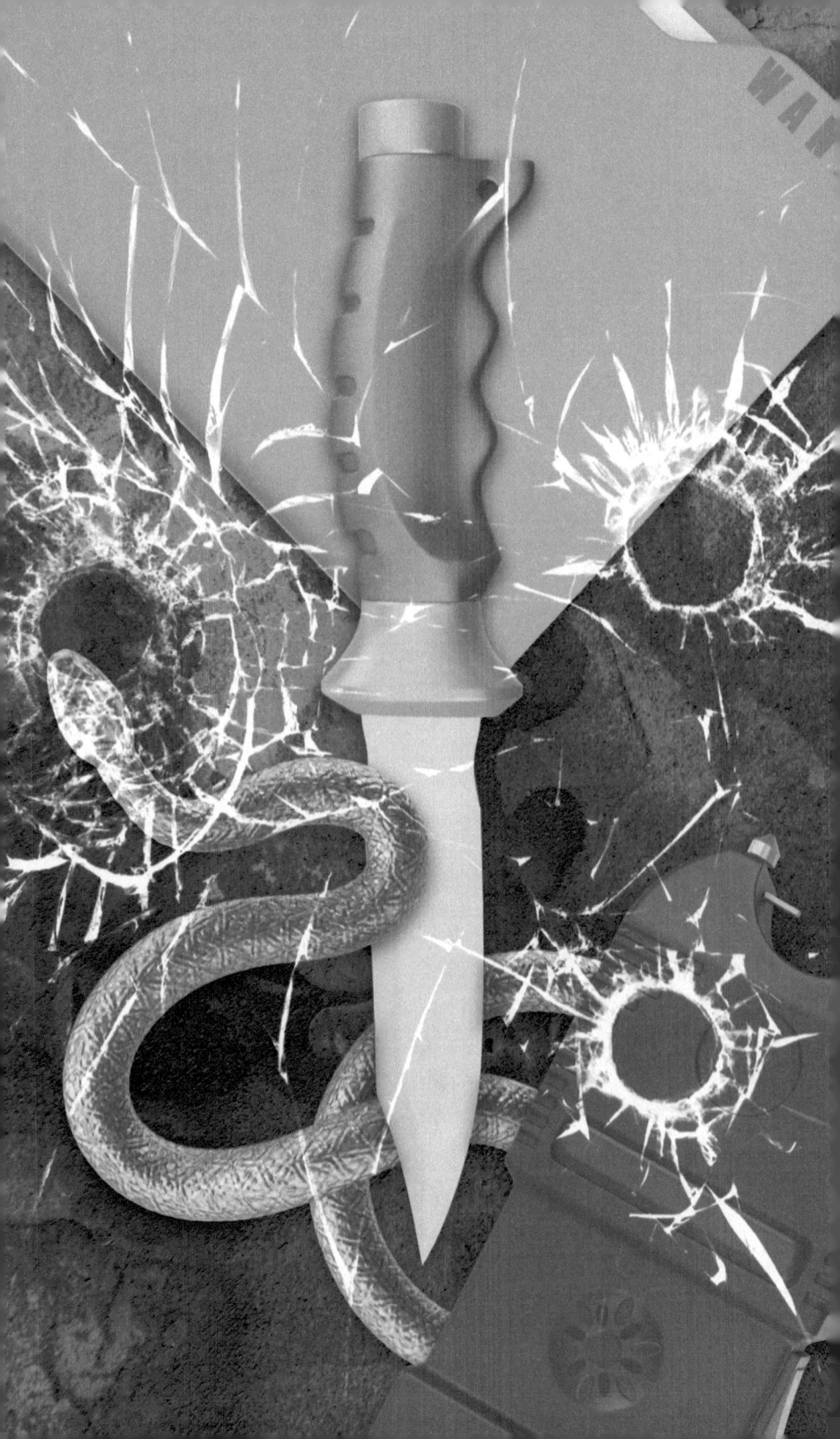

CHAPTER TWENTY-EIGHT

SHILOH

I tucked the taser into the waistband of my jeans, hoodie falling over it as I pushed away from the desk. Every second I stayed in this room, the air seemed to grow thicker, suffocating me with the things wasn't supposed to know. I heard the front door open and close, voices carrying down the hall as I scrambled to exit the office, rushing into the small bathroom and closing the door quietly behind me.

I could hear the distinct voices of Kane and Creed, Nate and Aaron I'm sure weren't far behind. There was no slipping out unnoticed with half the team parked in my living room like the security detail from hell. Not unless I waited them out. So, I did. Hours crawled by. I showered. Changed into leggings and got my bag ready before stashing it behind my door. I ate half a sandwich I barely tasted and tried my best to appear engaged in conversation when Creed and Aaron found me in the kitchen, but my mind was already miles away.

"Shiloh?" My mom's voice came from the bar stool next to me, startling me as I turned my head to face her.

When had Creed and Aaron left? When had my mom come in? I was going to have to start scheduling dissociation time, so I didn't look like a weirdo sitting here, a stale sandwich clenched between my fingers, while I stared right through the kitchen cabinets.

"Yeah?"

"Honey, are you doing okay?"

"I'm fine, why?"

Why? Are we serious? Because you have been sitting there like a murderous mannequin for the last who knows how long, Shiloh. Get a fucking grip.

"Just checking in. There's been so much going on lately, and I feel like we haven't had much time to sit and talk."

Fair. It had taken some time to build our relationship back when I got home, but weekends of shopping trips and Friday nights on the couch while we watched cheesy rom-coms and made fun of the dialogue had mended our bond stitch by stitch. Now that I was thinking about it, I couldn't remember the last time we had spent time together, just the two of us. Work kept her busy, and I kept myself busy. It had to have been at least a few weeks before hell broke loose for the second time around here.

"I know, I'm sorry. What if we went shopping next weekend? I think some time out of the house might be good for me."

Her eyes crinkled in the corners when she smiled at me, her soft hand patting the top of mine as she nodded. "I would love that."

Guilt tugged at my stomach. She had no idea what I was doing tonight, or what I had been doing the other nights I wasn't home. While the men I killed deserved every bit of it, I knew it would kill her if she ever found out.

"If you ever just need to talk to someone," she said, waving her free hand around the air between us, "about all of this, I'm here."

"I know, Mom. Thank you."

She nodded, content enough with my responses to drop it for now and leaned in to kiss the top of my head.

"Goodnight, Shiloh."

"Goodnight."

I stayed cemented to the barstool I sat on, forcing the guilt out of my system and focusing instead on my plan for tonight. I knew Jason was staying with someone, but I was confident I could handle it. The taser Nate had given me was apparently illegal to own in most countries due to the voltage. Thank you very much for that bit of information, Google. I had slipped Creed's knife into my waistband, the taser would stay firmly in my palm, and the rest of the items I might need were piled into my bag. I was ready.

When the guys all went their separate ways to man their posts, and the house finally fell silent, I moved. I cracked my door open and waited. No footsteps. No rustle of movement. I made it to the staircase without a sound, my bag slung over my back and my shoes quiet on the carpet. The kitchen light was off, the living room too.

The only sound on the bottom floor was my rapid heart-beat, pounding in my ears like it was trying to give me away. I veered down the long hallway to my right, going to the window in the laundry room and wedging it open. I landed in the back-yard, taking a single second to listen for the sound of approaching footsteps, before sprinting toward the gate. Lottie had left her car down the street with the keys in it, zero questions asked. One of these days, she was going to interrogate me. But so far, she had been there every time I called, helped me regardless of how shady my favors sounded, and didn't say a word to anyone about any of it.

I hurled myself over the gate, landing less than gracefully on the other side, and then ran as fast as my legs would carry me until I reached her sleek red car. I stabbed the key in the ignition, thanking whatever gods might be listening that her car was so much quieter than mine, and pulled out onto the street, driving away from my house and toward my destination.

The drive was quiet—only a soft hum from the tires rolling over the road, the static of my thoughts, and the sound of my nails tapping against the steering wheel filled the small cab. I knew where I was going; the images I'd found online of the motel were burned into my mind.

It was exactly what I expected when I pulled into the nearly empty lot—cracked pavement, a flickering vacancy sign, and a row of vending machines glowing like beacons in the dark. Room 209 sat near the corner, a busted porch light casting shadows across the door.

My hands were steady as I got out of the car, hefting my bag over my shoulder and walking toward the room in front of me. Voices drifted through the thin walls. Muffled, but there were obviously two people in there. I slipped the taser out, thumb hovering over the trigger, and knocked on the door with my free hand.

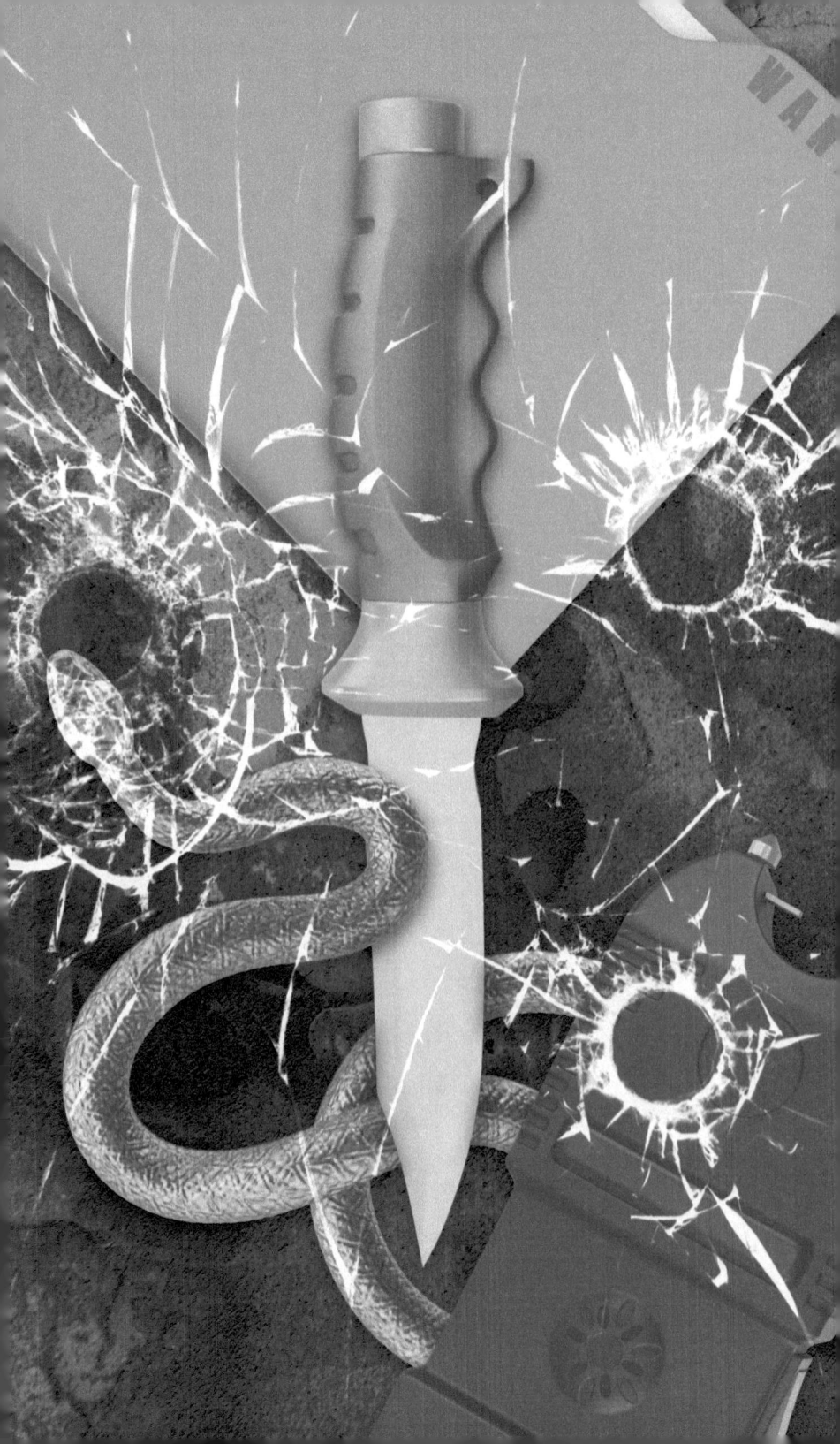

CHAPTER TWENTY-NINE

SHILOH

The door swung wide open with no hesitation from the man on the other side. His brow furrowed as he looked at me. "Can I help you?"

"You can, actually." I pushed my arm out, the prongs of the taser landing against his neck as I hit the button and watched his body crumple as it convulsed. I pushed him forward with both hands, giving me enough room to scoot inside and shut the door. I slung my bag off my shoulder and yanked it open, reaching for the metal cuffs just as the bathroom door opened and another man stepped out. His eyes widened as he took in the situation his friend was in, but I was ready. I snatched Creed's knife from my waistband and flicked it open, jumping over the body at my feet and lunging at the other man.

"Who the fuck are you?!" he shouted, catching my arm a second before I made contact with my blade.

"I'm here for your friend," I gritted out, wrenching my arm free of his grasp and darting to his left. He was slower than I was, sluggish like he had been drinking. I could use that to my advantage. I spared a second to look at Jason on the floor, he was beginning to stir, but Nate hadn't lied. That taser was strong as hell. I had maybe another minute before he got his bearings, and then I would be really outnumbered here. I lunged at his friend again, my knife finally meeting his skin and carving a nice long line across his abdomen. Blood trickled out of the cut in a steady stream, which he attempted to staunch with his dirty hand pressed against the wound.

"You little bitch!" He swung out with his free hand, nearly catching me by the hair, and swearing incoherently when I ducked just in time.

"I didn't come here for you; you can leave if you'd like."

He lunged. I ducked and pivoted on my heel in a tight circle as I felt the sting of his fist clip my jaw. I swung back out with the knife, desperation beginning to build somewhere deep in my chest as he blocked it.

We crashed into the nightstand, a lamp tipping over and shattering across the floor. I straightened up and drove my knee into his gut, right over the only mark I had managed to leave on him so far. He howled, doubling over just enough for me to get on top of him. I jumped on his back, wrapping my arm tight around his neck and pulling back as hard as I could, the knife still clutched in my hand.

"Stay down," I snapped, breathless.

Blood pounded in my ears, but I still heard shuffling behind me and a sharp breath that matched mine as I realized what was happening.

Too late. Arms wrapped around me, yanking me back. I thrashed, twisting, kicking, swinging the knife in every direction, but one of them grabbed my arms while the other slammed my head against the floor. Stars exploded behind my eyes, my fingers loosening around the knife.

"No—" I gasped. Panic turned to dread, dread into silence. I couldn't move. I couldn't fight. My body screamed, but everything else just... shut off.

The absurdity of me thinking I could take on two grown men by myself finally hit me.

I wasn't a serial killer. I wasn't trained in any kind of fighting. The only thing I had was my anger and I wore it like a cloak, deciding it would be enough to take out whoever I needed to.

It wasn't. I let my eyes fall closed, rather than stare into their sweaty, red faces.

I tuned out the conversation between the two of them, refusing to let myself acknowledge the mixture of rage and excitement that pulsed through their hands on my body.

A loud bang from across the room made me jolt. The second bang came seconds later, louder, followed by a spray of something warm across my face.

I opened my eyes just in time to watch the man at my side slump to the floor, a third bang echoing off the walls had the hands on my wrists falling away. And then it was still.

I tipped my head back, finding Creed in the doorway, gun in his hand, and his face harder than I'd ever seen it. He wasn't angry. He was rage personified. The harsh set of his jaw, the cut of his eyes, seemed to amplify the hatred that rolled off him in waves.

"Shiloh." He walked over to where I lay on the floor, kneeling next to me as he ran his eyes over my entire body, checking for injuries if I had to guess. His chest was rising and falling fast, each exhale coming out short and harsh through his nose.

"How did you find me?"

"It's not hard to find something you never lost, Shiloh."

I blinked up at him. Feeling the tacky blood on my face as it began to dry. I'm sure I looked insane right now. I pushed myself up, forcing my legs underneath me, looking around the room at the mess we had made. What if he hadn't gotten here in time? What if he hadn't come at all? I would be dead. Abigail wouldn't be any closer to safety, and my parents would be destroyed for a second time. The weight of my naivety settled in.

"I'm sorr—" I started, cut off by Creed's thumb as it brushed a drop of blood from my bottom lip.

"Don't apologize to me for this. I don't know what it feels like to have years of your life stolen from you, but I would imagine I would want retribution for it too, if I were in your shoes."

I nodded.

"Let's get you home and cleaned up, hmm?"

I forced myself to nod. Creed scooped me up and planted me in his car before pulling out a duffle bag from the trunk and going back in to clean up the mess we had made. Every ounce of DNA from either of us was gone by the time he came back to the car.

"Nate is going to get the car back to Lottie." He said gently.

I wasn't thinking about the car. I was thinking about the nightmares I would have about tonight once I fell asleep again.

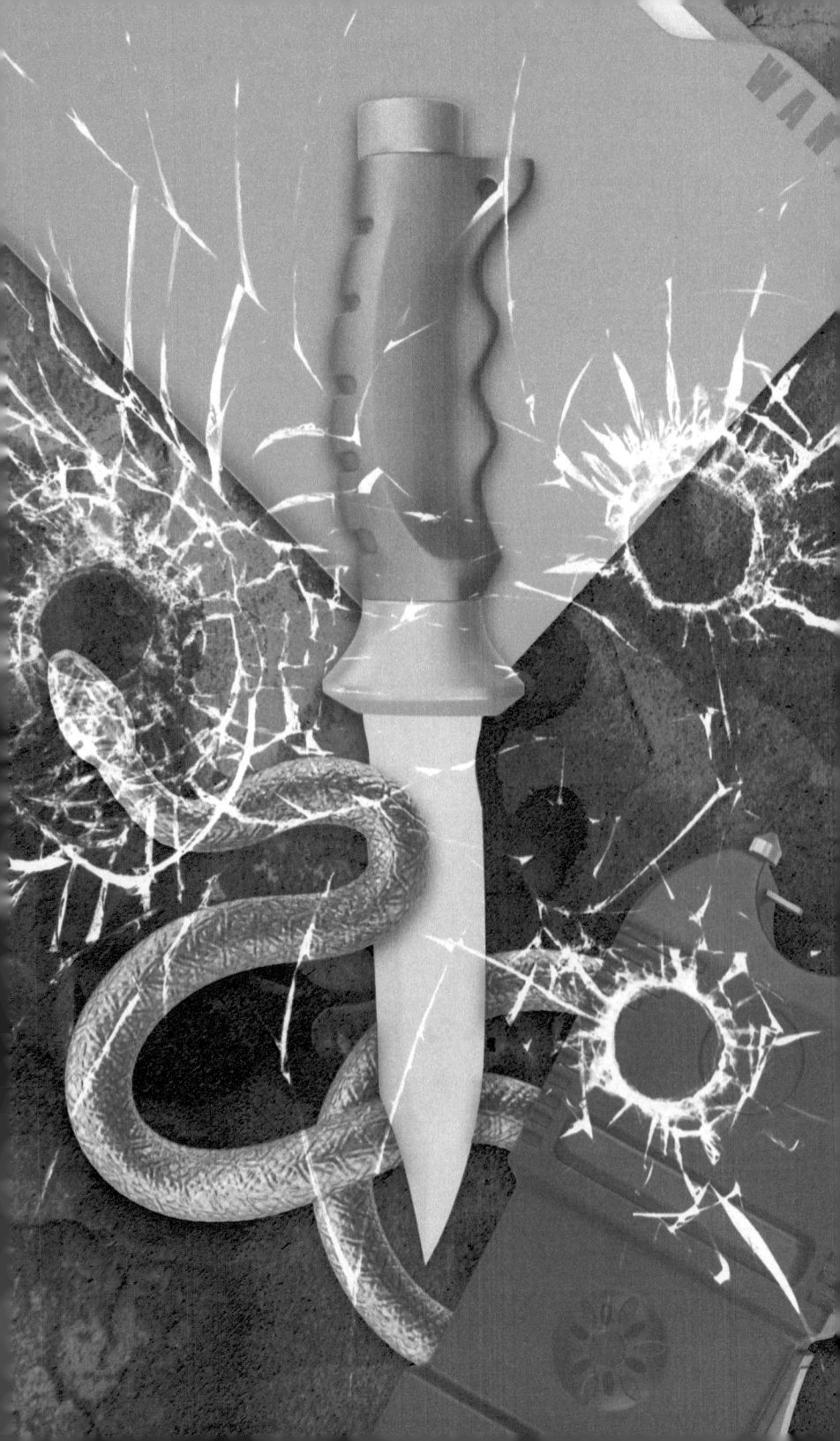

CHAPTER THIRTY

SHILOH

I focused on the way the stitching felt on the seat beneath me as Creed drove us back to my house. My fingers rubbed against every seam, the thread against my skin keeping me present in this car with him.

"What can I do?" he asked, both hands gripping the wheel so hard his knuckles were white.

"You already did it," I mumbled. "While I just... laid there."

I saw his head whip toward me from the corner of my eye, but I kept my gaze focused on the seat.

"Shiloh," he started.

"It's the truth. I froze."

"You had two grown men on you, Shiloh, your mind did what it needed to do to protect you. That isn't a fault."

"It felt like one!" The sudden change in volume startled even me. Creed just raised a brow in my direction.

"I knew there would be two of them. I planned for it, and they still got the upper hand. And then, when it mattered most that I fight back, I just shut down."

"You left your mark on both of them, that matters."

"No. Because inside I'm still a teenage girl in Ruben's office with no control over my own body."

"Then we will work on it. Have you had any training?"

"No. Which makes it even crazier that I thought I could take them both out. I've never even been in a fight."

Creed was quiet for a moment, his jaw working back and forth as I caught glimpses of his profile under the streetlights.

"Do you trust me?"

My instinct was to scoff at him, to tell him 'absolutley fucking not.' But that wasn't really true.

He was occasionally overbearing, tended to stalk me, but he was there when I needed him. He protected me without an ounce of hesitation. He didn't chastise me for my little revenge spree. How could I not trust him?

"Yes."

He nodded. "When we get home, I want you to go change into loose clothes. Long sleeve shirt and sweats."

"What? Why?"

He pulled into my driveway and turned off the engine. "Trust, Red. Change and meet me in the gym."

Apprehension rattled through me, but what choice did I have? I couldn't have a repeat of tonight. If either of those men had been sober, I wouldn't have lasted long enough for Creed to get to me. Their sluggish movements and delayed reflexes were the only things that allowed me to feel control for the short time I did. Whatever Creed had in store, I would just have to endure it.

I ran up the stairs, digging through my drawers until I found a pair of black sweats and a matching hoodie that fit two sizes too big. I shucked off my clothes and pulled them on, tying my hair into a ponytail and slipping downstairs.

The gym took up the left side of the basement. It hadn't been nearly as nice when I was little, but my father had apparently spent a good bit of time down here in my absence.

The wall separating it from the rest of the lower level was made entirely of glass. I pushed through the door and looked around the massive space. Weight benches and a treadmill took up the left side, a few punching bags dangling in the corner. The entire floor was covered in thick black mats, just like the ones at Aaron's gym. The back wall was all mirror, floor to ceiling. I locked eyes with Creed in the mirror as he stepped through the door, Kane right behind him. I swiveled around to face them.

"So, what are we doing?"

Kane took a seat on one of the weight benches, his eyes darting from me to Creed and back again.

"Kane is a former MMA fighter. He's been professionally trained, and he's trained multiple others. We aren't going to force you, but I think it would be a good idea to let him work with you. Teach you at the very least some self-defense tactics."

My pulse pounded in my ears. I wasn't afraid of Kane, but he was huge. Built like a tattooed tank, he stood at least a solid foot and a half above me, and if I had to guess, he outweighed me by about a hundred pounds. The thought of having him tower over me was paralyzing.

"Shiloh."

I snapped my head to meet Kane's eyes.

"I will not hurt you."

I nodded out of instinct. Of course he wouldn't, but still.

"But I will make you think I'm going to."

Creed looked like he wanted to interject, but he knew it was necessary. We all did.

"You need to be scared, in an environment that is safe, so that you can work through your response. It's normal to freeze up, but it won't do you any favors."

"I know." I chewed at my thumb nail, my foot tapping nervously on the mat beneath my feet.

Kane stood and walked toward me until he stood close enough to reach out and touch me. "We're going to walk through what happened tonight, and then we're going to recreate it."

I pulled at the hem of my hoodie, making sure it was tugged as low as possible.

"That's what the clothes are for. I will not touch your skin, Shiloh. I promise. That fabric is the barrier. Eventually we will work through that too, but for tonight, if I see skin, I stop. Okay?"

I forced a steady breath in and out. I knew what he was saying was true. I knew Creed would intervene if needed. For all intents and purposes, I knew I was safe in this room. My body, however, was not on board. Adrenaline had already caused beads of sweat to form at the base of my neck, my fingers curling painfully into the fabric of my hoodie.

The pounding in my ears morphed into a steady *whooshing* sound, drowning out the sound of Kane and Creed's hushed conversation. I uncurled my fingers, feeling the numbness that was spreading through them, climbing up my hands like a trellis.

Just breathe.

I closed my eyes tight, focusing on the monumental task of breathing while I rocked back and forth on my feet. Two warm hands cupped my face on either side as someone stepped into my space.

"Red. Open your eyes."

I opened them slowly, finding Creed's icy blue eyes looking back at me.

"A panic attack is the only danger to you in this room. Breathe. In and out, slow and steady."

I matched his pace, forcing my chest to rise and fall with his. My eyes flicked to my left where Kane had been standing, only to find him back on the weight bench, his hands clasped in front of him as he purposely looked anywhere but in my direction.

"Look at me."

I snapped my gaze back to his. He grabbed my left wrist, bringing it to his chest.

"Just like this. In, out."

My hand rested over his heart, the steady thump of his heart beating against my palm. And then the shadows at the edges of my vision began to fade. With each deep breath, the ocean waves in my ears ebbed away, the feeling returning to my body as the panic eased.

"There you are." His hand came to the back of my head, pulling me against his chest and squeezing me to him tightly. The smell, the feel, the warmth of his body was like a salve. The comfort of having a body against mine that didn't want anything from me was a revelation.

"Thank you," I whispered into his shoulder. The deep breath he released in response told me he had heard me. I pulled back, shaking out my limbs and turning to Kane.

"Okay."

"Okay?" he repeated.

"Let's do it." I nodded.

CHAPTER THIRTY-ONE

CREED

I watched Kane roll up the sleeves of the hoodie he wore, walking slowly toward the mats at the far side of the gym while Shiloh followed behind him. She was terrified; that much was clear. But I trusted Kane. He would push her, but not further than she could handle.

"Walk me through it."

She stretched her arms above her head as she spoke. "Jason came up behind me while I was on the other guy's back. He wrapped his arms around my shoulders and pulled me off of him."

Kane walked around so that he was behind her, but he didn't touch her. "And then?"

"Then he pivoted, so that he was facing me, and slammed me on my back. My head hit the floor so hard it rattled. Then they both kneeled down, pinning my arms and legs. One of them had his hands on my stomach, but I had closed my eyes by the time I felt them."

"Is that everything?"

She nodded sharply. "Creed came in after that."

"Alright."

He stepped forward, wrapping his arms around her shoulders, though I noticed the space he left between their bodies. While his arms were making contact, there was still a good six inches between his chest and her back.

"Pick a word. Any word you want, but when you say it, we stop. No questions asked."

She scoffed, a pale pink color tinting her cheeks. "I don't need a *safe word*."

"I do. I'm not in the habit of hurting women, Shiloh. When you need a break, I need you to be able to tell me before it goes too far."

"Okay, okay. Black?"

"That works. Are you ready to start? I'm going to go slower the first time. After that, I'll move at the same pace an attacker would."

"Am I supposed to fight you off?"

"No. You are supposed to focus on the moment the fear locks you into place and then figure out how to break through it."

"Okay." Her wide eyes found mine, apprehension coloring her face.

I nodded in reassurance. "*We've got you*," I mouthed to her, noticing the way her shoulders lowered slowly as she let her guard down just a fraction.

Kane moved with a practiced precision, his arms tightening around her as he hooked his boot behind her ankle, releasing his grip just in time for her to spin around, and then he took both of them to the floor. They landed with a loud thump, the thick mats absorbing most of the impact. Kane's hand slipped out from behind Shiloh's head where he had cushioned her fall as he pushed his body between her thighs and pinned each of her wrists in one of his hands next to her head. Kane jerked his head at me, signaling it was time for me to come closer. I crouched down beside them, noting the flushed color in her face and the way each exhale came out harshly from her nose.

"Can you move?" Kane asked.

"No," Shiloh grunted the word out, panic swimming in her eyes.

"I have your wrists and hips locked, but an attacker isn't going to hold this position. Whatever they want, they aren't getting it by keeping you pinned like this. Either their hands or their legs will move, that is your opening. You following?"

"Yes."

Kane let go of her wrists, moving his hands to rest around the base of her throat.

"Try to hit my face."

She swung out instantly, missing each shot as Kane used his size against her and leaned back out of her reach.

"It's... useless!" Her breaths were coming in short pants now, her feet kicking aimlessly at the mat beneath her.

"Correct. Unless I lean down into your space, you won't be able to reach, and punching up is a hell of a lot less effective than punching down. We are going to go step by step. Lift your hips as high as you can."

She followed his instructions, planting her feet and bridging her hips beneath him.

"Now drive your arms down, hard. You will need to combine both of those things next time."

She blew out a harsh breath as she drove her arms down, sliding them between Kane's arms and down to her waist. He nodded, letting it happen as he nodded in approval.

"Good, now sit up, and wrap your arms around my back."

Kane was still as he went over the next steps with her, making sure she nodded in understanding before he continued. Shiloh shot up, gripping onto his back and holding him in a bear hug. Her knuckles were white from where she held him, her breaths coming in heavy pants.

"That's it. Now, I am on top of you, but we're on equal footing because I'm off balance. Trap my foot and roll us over."

Kane had barely gotten the last word out of his mouth before Shiloh threw all her weight into rolling their bodies across the mat. She grunted in frustration, shoving against his shoulder, and flipping him on his back. I hadn't noticed the shake in her hands until she braced herself against his chest. Each exhale came out ragged, the flush in her face spreading to her neck. Kane threw his arms out straight at his sides, avoiding any extra contact with her.

"Take a minute. Whatever's going on in your head right now, you have to find a way to lock it down," Kane instructed.

Her head bobbed, but her panic was so palpable I could taste it. "What now?" The tremble in her voice felt like sandpaper against my skin.

"Now you hit. Wherever you can, as hard as you can. If you have a weapon, you will aim for my neck, my chest, or my abdomen. If all you have is your fists, go for my throat. One solid punch right here," he tapped his Adam's apple, "And you will have time to run, or at least get off the ground."

Shiloh dug the heels of her hands into her eyes, releasing a breath laced with frustration. "Black." It was a whisper. A single world laced with so much disappointment.

"Go get some water. When you're ready, we'll run through it again, faster this time," he said softly.

She was up in an instant, bolting from the room without a word to either of us. Kane got to his feet, standing in place with his hands on her hips.

"She's fine, Creed," he drawled.

"I know."

"Then stop looking at me like you're going to murder me, it's distracting."

"She's fucking terrified, Kane."

He shrugged. "She's going to have to do it scared. She's small. Unless we teach her how to use that to her advantage, she doesn't stand a chance against a guy the size of me."

"How do we help without fucking her up any more than we have to?" I added, my jaw aching from the way it had clenched during their tussle.

"I'm not going to use kid gloves with her, Creed. Trust me to help, but if you keep staring at me like that, I'm gonna have to kick your ass out." His eyes said he was serious, but there wasn't a chance in hell I was leaving this room unless she told me to herself.

I opened my mouth to respond right as the door to the gym flew open again. Shiloh stormed back into the room, her hair smoothed back into a tight ponytail, and the hoodie exchanged for a tight, long-sleeved shirt.

"Okay, let's get this shit over with."

Guess they were going again.

CHAPTER THIRTY-TWO

CREED

Shiloh finally loosened up around the fifth run through. Kane stopped holding back, using his full body weight against her and moving at the speed an attacker would, but she held her ground. Each time he got her on the floor, she would freeze, her body naturally wanting to fall into the familiar response it had created for her at The Manor. By the third time he pinned her, she managed to shut that response down. Would she be able to do the same when it was a stranger? Probably not. Not yet anyway. She had a long way to go until men didn't immediately cause her fight or flight system to kick in, but she was working on it.

I followed her upstairs and made myself comfortable on her bed while she showered. Kane had helped her regain a feeling of control, but the adrenaline from sparring was taking its time leaving her, and the events from earlier were still fresh in her mind.

The bathroom door opened, revealing Shiloh through a cloud of steam. Her long red hair hung in wet strands that trailed over her shoulders. The tank top and shorts she wore did little to hide her skin, including the bruises that lingered along her thighs and wrists.

"They're from the guys at the hotel," she said as she caught me staring at them, plopping down on the bed beside me.

The silence stretched for a moment as she picked at a loose thread in the hem of her shorts.

"Thank you. It actually helped a lot."

"Anytime. Kane is a scary looking motherfucker, but he would never hurt you. Anytime you want to train, we'll work it out."

She turned to face me, crossing her legs in front of her and meeting my eyes with a determined look.

"How did you know?"

I raised an eyebrow.

"About me. About why I was at the hotel."

"I pay attention."

She huffed out a breath. "That's not an answer."

"It's the only one I've got. You haven't left my sight for long since the night of the Raid, Shiloh."

Her brow furrowed as she mulled that over. "You've been stalking me?"

"That's a harsh term."

"Then explain," she demanded.

I dragged my fingers through my hair, searching for the words to describe how her very presence had hit my brain like an atom bomb the first time I laid eyes on her. "Something clicked inside me when you jumped out of that van. I followed you back to that hell hole and saw what was happening and that was it. Whatever had clicked into place was not a gentle thing, Shiloh. It was a pin being pulled from a grenade."

I cut myself off. There wasn't a way to explain what I felt for her without sounding like I was completely insane.

"After you killed Ruben, I didn't see you again. Not until you came here."

"Just because you didn't see me, doesn't mean I wasn't there. I've been within reach for the last eleven months."

My heart thudded hard, too loud in the quiet of her bedroom. This would be where she told me to get the fuck out. That I had scared her. That I was crazy. That she—

"You could have at least said hello," she said, a sly smile creeping across her gorgeous face.

I grinned back at her. "Hello, Red."

"Hello, Creed," she said with a laugh, the sound so light and full of life I wanted to bottle it and snort it in lines. "So, I have a stalker in my bed," she said, flopping onto her back next to me, the sweet smell of her shampoo hitting me as her head found its place beside mine.

I chuckled. "Says the murderer."

Her head snapped to the side, eyes wide. "How much do you know?"

"I know that we had cameras in Joseph Waynes's apartment before you got there."

"Oh." She tucked her bottom lip between her teeth, her eyes searching mine.

"I know that we watched from the moment you entered, to the moment you left out the fire escape. I know you are a devious little thing with a taser."

I matched her position as she rolled to her side, both of us propped up on one arm, our bodies close enough to share heat between us. Her fingers reached out, catching the pearls around my neck between her forefinger and thumb.

"You're still wearing it," she mused, absentmindedly.

"I was told they look good on me."

She tossed her head back and laughed, the motion causing

her to pull on the necklace, resulting in a surprising hitch in my breath. It didn't go unnoticed.

She narrowed her eyes slightly, tugging at the strand intentionally, her fingers grazing the hollow of my throat. My hand moved to her waist, squeezing at the soft skin between the band of her shorts and where her tank top had ridden up.

"Shiloh." It came out like a warning. Like a plea.

Her teeth latched on to her lip again as she slowly twisted the pearls in her fingers, pulling the necklace taut against my throat before tugging downward.

The pressure hit me just right. Not enough to cut off the blood flow, but just enough to send heat crawling up my spine. Her eyes flicked up to mine, holding them for just a moment before she moved. Her fingers stayed wrapped in my necklace as she slid a leg over my hips, using her weight to roll me on to my back and straddle me.

"What do we have here?" I asked, screaming at my dick to lay back down. The feeling of her smooth skin sliding across mine had sent the blood in my body south in record time.

"An offering."

Fuck.

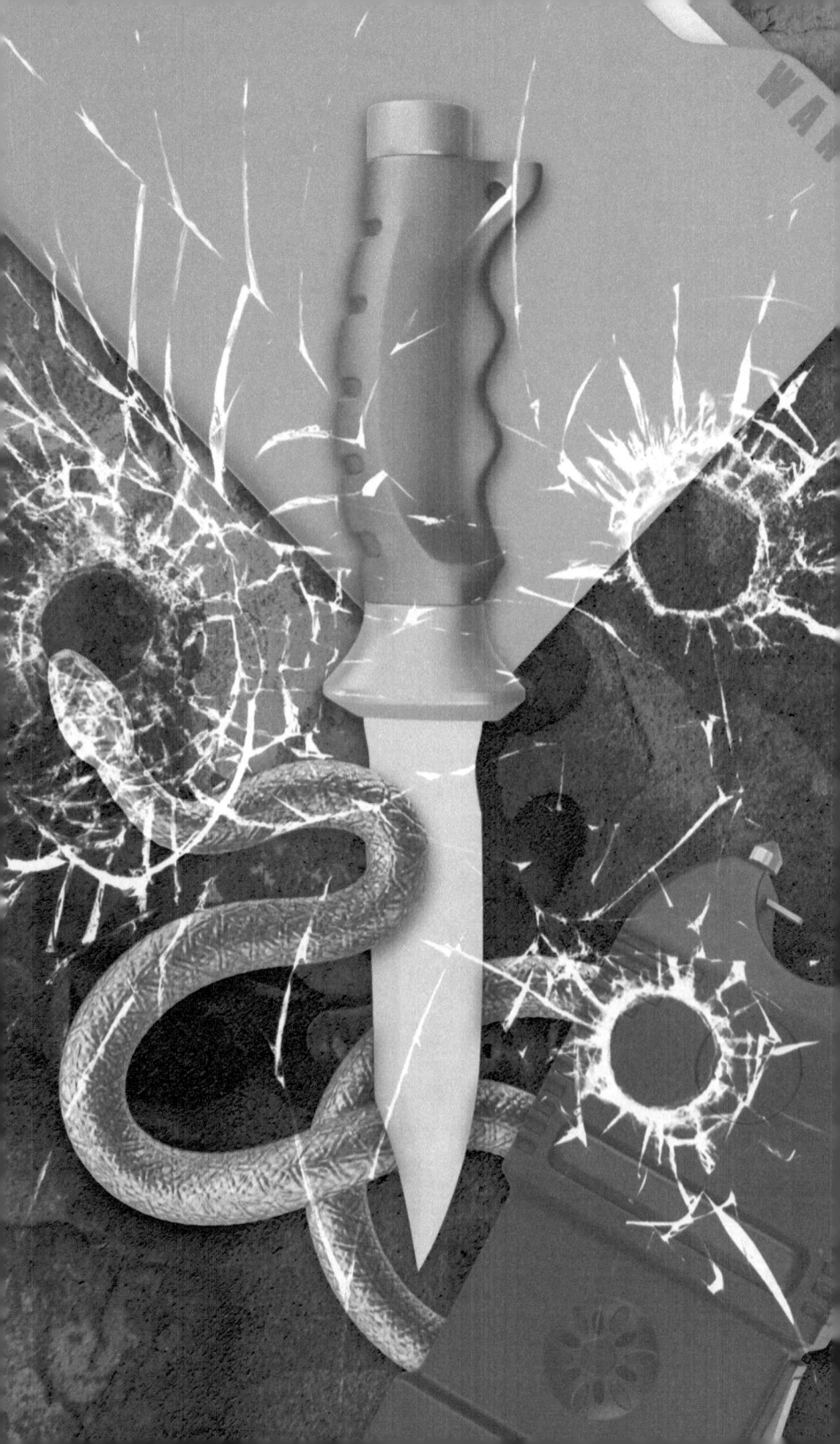

CHAPTER THIRTY-THREE

SHILOH

"Yeah?" he asked, his hands coming to rest at the tops of my thighs. His thumbs ran smooth circles over the sensitive skin.

"Yeah."

His grip tightened, and then he rolled. Quick, seamless, practiced, and I was beneath him.

One hand caught the side of my face, his thumb brushing beneath my eyes like I might disappear if he looked away. The other slid down, slow and confident, over the curve of my waist to grip my thigh and hook it around his lap.

"This is what you want?" he asked, voice tight. "Say it."

I could barely breathe, let alone speak. The weight of him settling between my thighs had my brain short circuiting. I nodded; my eyes locked on his as my heart tried its hardest to punch its way out of my ribs. I did. I was scared to death, but I wanted to be as close to him as possible. I craved the feeling of him against me.

"I need to hear it, Red."

"I want you. Please," I whispered, fingers curling into the soft hair at the back of his neck.

His mouth was on mine before I finished the sentence. Soft at first, but with so much heat I felt like I was being consumed. I arched into him as his hand slid up my shirt, dragging the fabric with it until I had to lift my arms to let him tear it off. His eyes tracked every inch of bare skin like he was memorizing the map to a lost city. Reverent, possessive, dark. He dipped his head, his mouth finding the skin beneath my collarbone, then lower, lips grazing the tops of my breasts before his tongue flicked against a sensitive nipple. I gasped, a sharp, involuntary sound that earned a groan from him in response.

My hands slid down his back, fingers digging into the hard muscle there. I could feel every inch of him, heavy and hard against my thigh, still hidden by the thick tactical pants he wore.

I shifted beneath him, grinding up just enough to feel the friction right where I needed it.

"Shit," he muttered, rolling his hips against me in a move that made my eyes roll back in my head.

"Creed, please take off your fucking pants," I begged. I knew I sounded desperate, but I was. Every nerve ending in my body screamed for him.

He sat back, his eyes blazing as he ripped his shirt over his head, then flicked the button open on his pants and lowered the zipper. I swallowed hard as I took him in. His body was gorgeous. Tattoos covered the expanse of his abdomen, shoulders, and arms. But the definition of his muscle was visible even through the ink.

"Got your fill?" he asked with a smirk.

"For now."

"Good." His hands gripped my shorts at the waist and slid them down my legs, the cool air of my bedroom hitting my skin before he leaned back over me. His teeth met my neck, biting hard enough to leave a mark before his tongue soothed the sting. "How long has it been, Shiloh?"

"Over a year." I hadn't been with anyone since I had been home. I had a few toys in my nightstand, but I hadn't felt desire like this in... ever. Sex had never been something I had any say in, and by the time I got home, my view of it was so skewed, I just never sought it out on my own.

He hummed approvingly in my ear, his hand skimming down my stomach until they met my center.

"Jesus, you're soaked," he groaned, sliding his fingers slowly across my slit before pushing gently against my entrance.

I gasped at the feeling that had nearly become foreign to me, but he moved back upwards, swirling his fingers in tight circles over my clit.

"Oh god." My hips arched against his hand on their own, chasing the pleasure he was building.

He planted soft kisses across my chest, his hand working between my legs while I laid beneath him, panting.

"Deep breath for me, baby."

I inhaled just as he sucked my nipple into his mouth, pulling hard at the same time he pressed a finger inside me. My breath caught somewhere between a gasp and a moan, the sensation bordering just close enough to pain that stars burst behind my eyes.

"Okay?"

"Yes. More," I breathed.

He chuckled as he slid his finger out, coating himself in me before pushing two fingers back in. He pumped them in and out, his pace increasing along with my pulse. My heartbeat ratcheted higher with every passing second, my nails digging into the muscle of his forearm. It had never felt like this. Nothing in my life had ever felt this good. It took less than ten minutes, and I was riding the edge of something I had never experienced with a man before.

"Fuck. Creed!" I felt myself spasm around his digits as he slowed, each pulse sending a new wave of chills skittering across my body.

He sat up as I came down, retrieving his wallet from his pants before pushing them off his hips.

"You carry condoms around?" I asked.

He smirked, pulling out a foil packet and tossing the wallet to the floor.

"Just one." He lifted it to his mouth, tearing the corner. There was an "R" scribbled across the front in black marker.

"Did you... label it?"

"I put it in there the day after I had you pinned against the wall. And yes, I labeled it," he said matter-of-factly.

"This is for you and me. In case it ever came up, I didn't want there to be any doubt. I don't sleep around, Shiloh. I don't bed hop through my clients, and this isn't just sex. If you ever have doubts about that, you tell me, and I'll straighten them out. This is me and you, Red. Just me and you."

I nodded through the wave of emotion that had hit me like a hurricane. This was safe. The nerves eased a fraction, and my eyes tracked his hands as they lowered to roll the condom over his length. The size of him nearly making me choke. My sexual experience was limited partner-wise, and Ruben wasn't packing anything impressive under the starched suit he always wore. Creed was easily twice as long, the girth alone making my thighs clench together on instinct. He noticed, of course, smoothing his hands over my legs reassuringly as he smiled down at me.

"Slow and steady."

"Slow and steady," I repeated.

He lowered himself over me, my legs parting to fit his hips between them. The fear I anticipated hadn't come. There was nothing but a desperate need inside me to have him as close as possible.

He guided himself to my entrance, the first brush of him against me making us gasp in unison. He moved slowly, my body stretching to accommodate him with a delicious burn until his hips met the backs of my thighs. He groaned, his hips rolling against me while his hand gripped the flesh of my hip in a viselike grip.

"Okay?"

"Yes. Faster."

"So much for slow and steady," he chuckled, pumping his hips harder, the muscles in my lower stomach tightening with each thrust. "Fuck you were made for me, Red. Look at how good you take me."

His hand grasped the back of my neck, pulling me forward as he leaned back so I could see his length as it moved in and out of me.

"Every inch, like a goddamn glove." His hips moved faster, his thumb pressing into the skin on the front of my thigh.

"I watched every bit of your first kill, do you know that? I saw you sink your knife into him, right here." He pushed harder, before sliding his hand up to rest on my throat.

I gasped, either from the feeling of his finger digging into my skin, or from the fact that he watched me take a life, and didn't run the other way.

"Then you stabbed him here." He bit into the skin of my shoulder, right where I had stuck Joseph Waynes.

A loud moan tumbled from my lips. This was not right. It wasn't normal. Why was it so fucking hot?

"And then, I watched you slide your knife across his throat. No hesitation, no fear." His thumb slid back and forth across my throat.

"Just." *Thrust.* "Pure." *Thrust.* "Fucking." *Thrust.* "Rage. My beautiful, bloodthirsty girl." *thrustthrustthrust.*

My heart rate peaked, my core clenching around him like it wanted to keep him there forever, and I hurtled toward the edge. He leaned down, claiming my lips in a searing kiss, hips moving in time with his tongue as it slid against mine.

My body was on fire in a way I'd never experienced before. Each brush of his tongue, his hands, his skin against mine was like gasoline on a flame. He wrapped one of my legs around his waist, holding it there in an iron grip while the other hand kept its hold on the back of my neck.

"You liked what you saw?" My words came out breathless between the sounds he was pulling from me.

"I fucking loved it." His voice was rough in my ear as his pace increased, his hips slapping against me nearly matching the pace of my frantic heartbeat. "Goddamn, Shiloh."

I could feel myself peaking, the ripples of pleasure turning into full-on waves that had a shiver racing down my spine. "Creed..."

"Oh, I know, baby. I can feel you." His hand slipped between us, rubbing circles across my swollen clit, and I lost it.

I cried out into his mouth as my body shattered beneath him, electricity racing from my head to my toes. He groaned into my mouth, slamming against me twice more before stilling with my name falling from his lips.

He held his weight off me while we came back down to earth, my fingers trailing along the ridges of his back until he lifted his head to meet my eyes. One hand came up to brush a rogue strand of hair that had fallen in my face, the move so tender and at odds with the way he controlled my body that it made my chest ache.

"You truly are the most incredible woman I've ever met."

I smiled up at him, delirious and satiated. "No. I'm just the same kind of twisted that you are."

"Same thing." He smiled, rolling off me to dispose of the condom in the trashcan beneath my nightstand.

He held his arm out, nodding his head for me to snuggle up against him, so I did. And God, did it feel good.

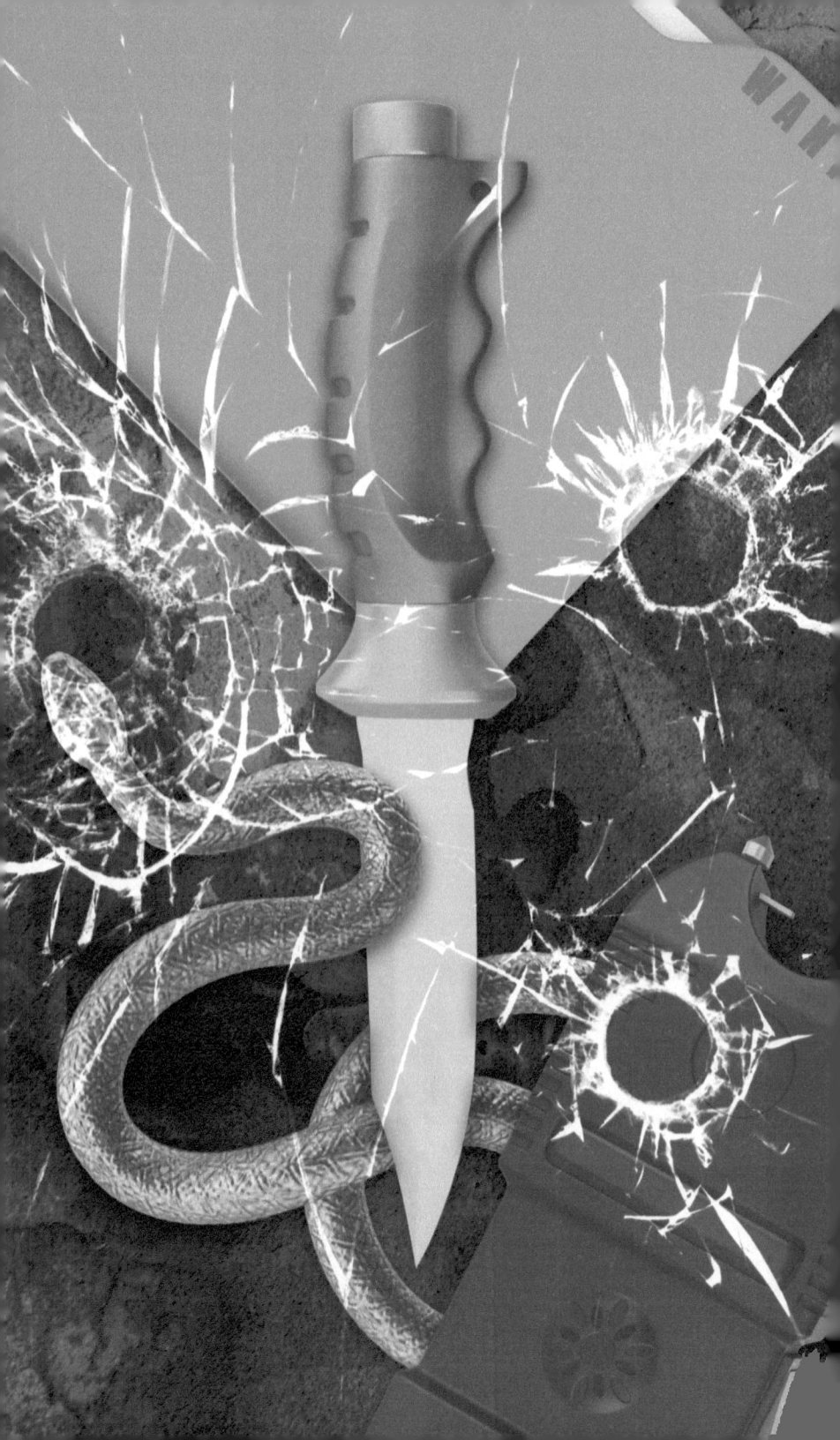

CHAPTER THIRTY-FOUR

SHILOH

Sunlight trickled in through the blinds on the window across from my bed. The warmth against my back had a smile spreading across my lips. He stayed. I knew the guys had a job to do here, but I wasn't sure how they split the responsibilities, considering Creed was with me or apparently following me most of the time. Every time I walked past the security room, Kane or Aaron were usually sitting behind the monitors.

Since Aaron was an undercover officer, he didn't go in everyday like my dad did. He worked certain cases, but a lot of his time had been spent around the house lately with everything going on. It was oddly comforting, knowing that in some corner of the house, there would be at least one of them keeping an eye on things.

Creed pressed a soft kiss to the back of my neck, his arms circling tighter around me.

"Goodmorning, Red," he said, nudging my ear with the tip of his nose.

I shifted in his arms to face him. His hair was a mess, his jaw dusted in stubble that highlighted the smirk on his face.

"Goodmorning. You look smug."

His face broke into a slow wicked grin. "You look wrecked."

I shoved at his chest, laughing as he caught my wrist and

kissed the inside of it. For a man capable of doing the things I'd seen him do, Creed looked awfully soft laying in my bed.

Someone knocked on the door, then cracked it open before either of us could answer. Nate leaned in, fully dressed in all black, sipping from a mug that said *Miss Orlando Bikini Pageant*. That was not our mug.

"Well, don't we look cozy?"

Creed groaned and flopped back on the pillow like he'd been shot. "Don't you have better things to be doing, Nathaniel? Committing arson? Stealing candy from children?"

"I had planned on robbing a nunnery, but Kane made me go to the briefing instead." Nate took a long sip of his coffee. "Speaking of which—lover boy, you're needed downstairs."

Creed ran a hand through his hair and sat up. "I'll be down in ten."

Nate's grin widened. "Make it five. Boss man's pacing."

He winked at me, then disappeared down the hall, whistling the Hannah Montana theme song. The door clicked shut behind him. Creed stood and stretched, displaying every glorious inch of his bare skin in the process. He grabbed his shirt from the chair and pulled it on in one fluid motion. He looked every bit like he belonged here—my room, my bed, my life. He kissed my forehead before heading toward the door.

"I'll be back," he said, voice low.

"I'll be waiting," I teased, propping myself up on my elbows. I watched him walk out, letting out a long breath. My body ached in the best way. But more than that, I felt *settled*. Which was terrifying in its own right.

After a few minutes of rotting, I got up and padded across the room, pulling on a hoodie and shorts. I crouched to grab my phone that had been knocked off the nightstand at some point and noticed Creed's wallet half-tucked beneath the edge of a discarded blanket, lying next to the foil wrapped from last night. Maybe he would want to keep it. I grabbed his wallet and the wrapper to stuff it inside when something fluttered out and landed on top of my bare foot.

A playing card. White background. Red border. A king. My breath caught in my throat as I stared at the card like it might be a hallucination. I bent and picked it up with shaky hands.

I was holding the same calling card that had been left at all those crime scenes. Even *my* crime scenes. Creed's calling card. My Creed. The man who had followed me, watched me, tampered with the scenes I'd left and claimed them as their own was the same man whose body heat still warmed the right side of my bed. And he never told me.

He *knew* what I was doing. That wasn't some shot in the dark hunch he had; he knew. He didn't stumble into the motel or give me that file by chance. He'd been watching this whole time, leaving his signature behind like we were playing some twisted game of tag.

Was this card for Jason? Had he stuck it in his wallet before he followed me last night so he would be prepared to leave his little clue? Rage bloomed under my skin like wildfire.

I squeezed the card between my fingers, heart pounding hard enough to hurt. He lied. He let me think I was the only one dancing on this line. And he had known the whole time.

CHAPTER THIRTY-FIVE

CREED

The security room was beginning to smell like stale coffee and testosterone. Aaron paced from one wall to the other, Kane sat half-hunched over his laptop, and Nate had taken it upon himself to doodle smiley faces on the whiteboard.

I leaned back in the chair across from Kane, arms crossed, still riding the high that came from waking up in Shiloh's bed with her body curled against mine.

"So," Nate said, spinning a pen between his fingers, "you look mighty refreshed. Good night?"

I didn't take the bait, just grinned and stretched my legs out in front of me. "Wouldn't you like to know?"

"Oh, I *do* know. Thin walls, brother."

Aaron made a disgusted noise. "Jesus, Nate."

"What? I'm not the one playing hobby horse with the client while we've got multiple security breaches happening."

I arched a brow. "Hobby horse?"

Nate bobbed his head. "You know, the mattress mambo? Conducting a headboard symphony? Giving the ol' ham candle a home—"

Kane, without looking up from his screen, muttered, "Can we focus, please?"

Aaron stopped pacing. "Thank you."

Kane adjusted his screen so I could see it and clicked on a file.

"I decrypted more from the black site forum tied to Reid's burner. Two confirmed admin accounts, both accessed from IPs, bouncing off relay servers. But last night, I got a hit."

I leaned forward. "Where?"

He pulled up a map. "Vacant property outside of city limits. Been on the market for five years. Last month, a trust company leased it under a shell corp."

I let out a low whistle. "Classic."

Nate leaned over Kane's shoulder. "You think this is the new manor?"

"Could be," Kane said. "We won't know unless we check it out."

Aaron rubbed his jaw. "And the other thing."

Kane nodded, his eyes dark. "Yeah. The house security system picked up two attempted breaches overnight. Someone tried to loop the surveillance feed and trigger a remote override."

My jaw tightened. "They get in?"

"No," Kane said. "But whoever it is knows what they're doing. I've added more redundancies, but we're gonna be glued to the monitors for a bit."

"Which means," Aaron said, "we can't let our guard down."

I nodded. "Where do you need me?"

Kane glanced at me. "You're coming with me."

"To the site?"

"You've got the best field read. And you're weirdly charming when people have guns in your face."

"Aw," I said, mock-touched by his words. "You noticed."

"Just keep your head straight. This isn't over, Creed. Not even close."

I stood, stretching. "Always do, boss."

Nate rolled his eyes. "Except when your head's buried in—"

"*Nate,*" Aaron and Kane said in unison.

I waved them off, already heading toward the door. "I'll tell Shiloh I'm heading out. Meet you in fifteen."

The house was quiet as I bounded up the stairs and down the hall to Shiloh's door. I didn't bother knocking, just turned the knob and stepped inside.

"Hey, I've gotta run with Kane for a bit—" My words died in my throat.

She was sitting on the edge of the bed, her back to me. Her posture was stiff, rigid almost. The kind of stillness you see right before a storm breaks. My heart slowed.

"Shiloh?"

She turned slowly, and when our eyes met, my stomach dropped. Something was wrong.

Her expression was unreadable—calm on the surface, but the sharpness in her eyes set me on edge.

I took a cautious step forward. "What is it?"

She didn't answer, just lifted her hand, and held up a playing card. More specifically, the card from my wallet that I had planned on leaving on Jason's corpse last night. I worked my jaw back and forth to ease the tension building there.

"Shiloh—"

"You could have told me." Her voice was quiet, controlled, and laced with betrayal so sharp it could split muscle from bone. "I would have understood," she added, still not moving. "But you didn't give me the chance."

I took another step. "I was going to."

"When?" Her voice cracked. "Before or after I found out

for myself?" She looked down at the card, then back up, and this time, her hands were shaking.

"I trusted you, Creed."

Fuck.

"I would have told you anything you wanted to know about what I've done. You knew it all anyway. Why would you keep this from me? You were there. You were there and you let me think some random psycho was following behind me."

I didn't realize how badly I'd miscalculated until that moment. Until I saw the look on her face and the weight of my secrets punched straight through my chest. I wanted to fix it. To explain. But the way her eyes wouldn't meet mine told me she wasn't ready to hear it. Not yet.

She lifted the pocketknife I had given her, holding it in the air while her thumb traced my initials etched into it.

"What's your real name?" she asked dryly.

I sighed. "Kingston Creed."

"The Red King." It was a whisper, to herself more than in response to anything I had said. The pieces were clicking together in her mind by now—the name, the cards. But there were missing parts that she didn't know about.

"I'm sorry. That I didn't tell you, that I hurt you by not telling you, and that I made you feel unsafe. There are reasons behind the cards, Red."

"I don't really care what your reasons are right now," she answered absently.

"I know. I'm going to go with Kane, and when I come back, we are going to finish this conversation, because this? This is not how we end. Do you hear me?"

She shook her head, moving to the chair by the window and sitting with her back facing me. "Just go."

"I am. But I'm coming back, Shiloh. You are sadly mistaken if you think it's that easy to get rid of me."

She scoffed. "I've been sadly mistaken about a few things, as it turns out."

I closed the distance between us, bracing my hands on either side of the chair and leaning in to speak into her ear.

"While I'm gone, consider the fact that you aren't mad that I'm a serial killer; you're mad that I didn't tell you I was. I'll be home soon." I placed a kiss to the top of her head and left her room, closing the door behind me. This day had gone to shit incredibly fast.

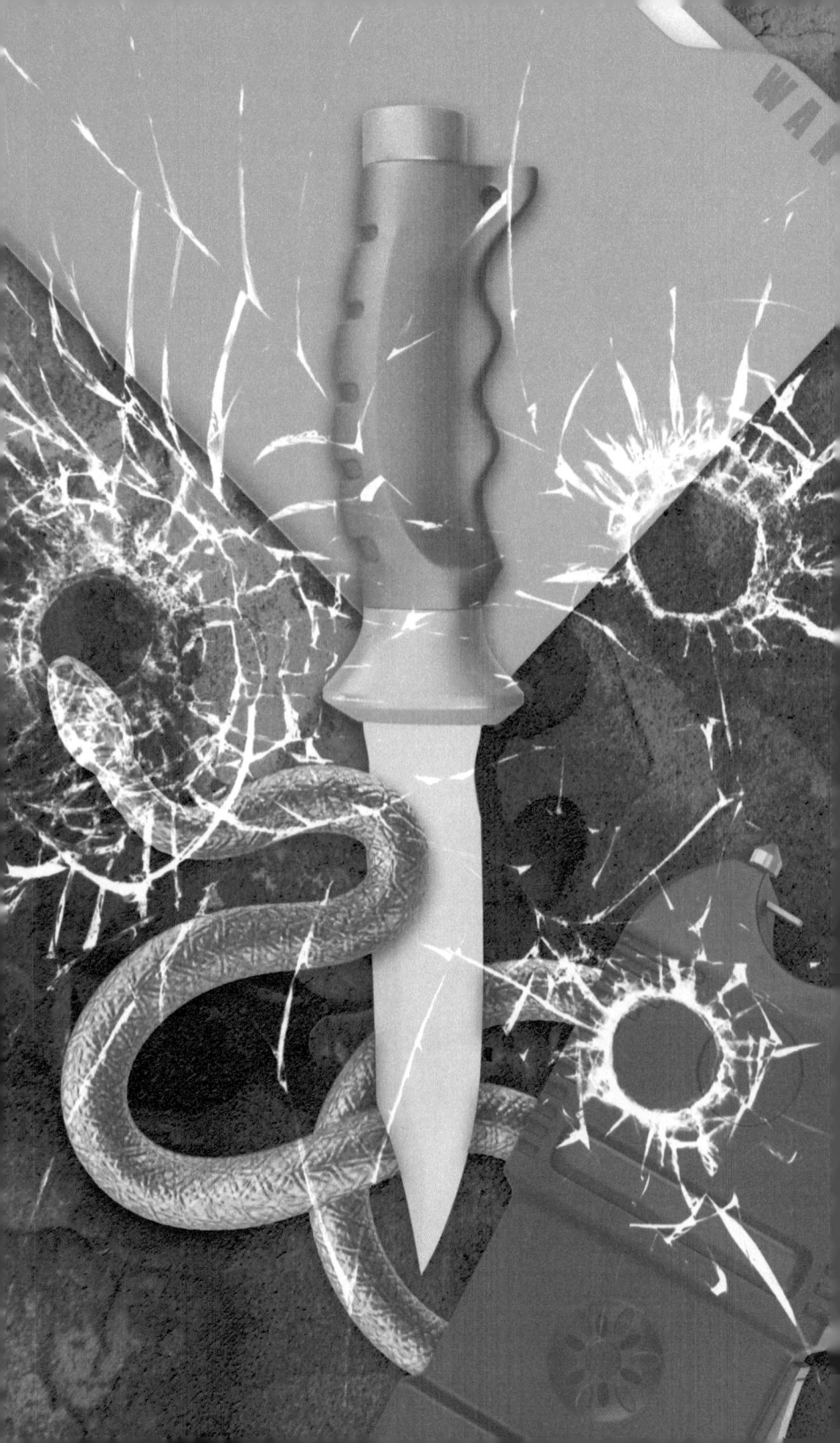

CHAPTER THIRTY-SIX

SHILOH

I sat in front of the window, flipping the card between my fingers while I watched Nate do his patrol lap around the back yard. Of all the emotions running through me, rage burned the brightest. The Red King.

Of course it was him. He might as well have worn a neon sign on his forehead last night when he told me he saw me kill Joseph. The hormones that had swarmed my head had muddied my brain enough that I didn't connect the dots. He saw the entire thing; he had cameras placed around the apartment. If someone else had come in, he would have told me. The realization that it was so obviously the man in front of me made me sick to my stomach.

I prided myself on being observant, on my ability to notice everything around me, and I somehow overlooked every clue he left behind. He knew when he saw me washing the blood from my clothes on his first day here. He knew when he handed me that file. He'd always known, and I was the fool in the dark.

The worst part was the nagging voice in the back of my mind that said *I did know*. Somewhere inside, I knew it the same way I knew my own pulse. Maybe I just hated the way it felt to be right this time. I grabbed my phone off the nightstand and hit Lottie's name. She answered on the second ring.

"Helllooooo," she drawled.

"Can you come over?" I asked, swallowing the lump in my throat. "Like...now?"

Lottie paused, just for a second. "On my way, babe. Give me twenty."

She showed up in fourteen. I heard the knock, followed by the door opening without permission—which was on brand—and her voice carried through the house like a thunderclap.

"HELLO? I brought snacks. Where is my bitch?"

Aaron's voice answered her, sharp and unamused. "You can't just walk in here."

"Relax, Sheriff Biceps, I was invited."

I peeked over the stairwell to watch the scene unfold. Aaron stood at the base of the steps, arms crossed, in full cop stance. His face was tight, like he'd bitten into something sour.

Lottie tilted her head at him and smiled. "You're hot when you're agitated. I'll make a note of that."

Aaron didn't move. "Don't flirt with me."

"If I were flirting with you, I would have much less clothing on."

"You're nineteen."

"Legal, hot, and emotionally available," she said, stepping past him with a wink. "Triple threat."

Aaron shook his head. "This house doesn't need any more chaos right now."

"Too late." She turned, walking backward. "Chaos has arrived, and she's wearing glitter eyeliner."

I snorted and waved her up.

Lottie took the stairs two at a time, arms open and a bag of snacks dangling from her hand. "Tell me everything. No filters."

We went to my room, shutting the door and locking it behind us. I curled up on the bed with a pillow in my lap while

Lottie kicked her shoes off with a dramatic flair before flopping down on the bed next to me, crossing her legs and dumping the bag in her hand upside down.

Chips, sour straws, a dozen different kinds of candy bars, and a pack of cigarettes fell on the bed between us. I raised a brow at her.

"I didn't know what we would need, so I grabbed everything."

I chuckled, her familiar antics easing the burn in my chest by a fraction.

"I need you to promise me," I said quietly, "that whatever I tell you, you'll still look at me the same way."

She blinked once, then reached over and bopped me on the forehead with the heel of her hand. "No one's ever accused me of being a good person, Shy. I'm not gonna get all judgey."

"It's not just bad," I murmured. "It's... it's really bad."

She took my hands in hers. "I'm listening."

So, I told her. Everything. By the time I was done, the room was still. A heavy silence hung around us while she processed, and I recovered. Her thumb had run soothing circles over my hand the entire time I spoke, pausing to squeeze it reassuringly during some of the heavier parts of the story.

"So, that's everything."

She stared at me for a moment, then smiled softly. "I would have done the same," she said finally. "And probably worse."

And that was why everyone needed a Lottie. She could see every disgusting part of me, every terrible thing I'd done, and would still stand next to me with a smile on her face.

"And Creed?" she added. "You love him?"

I didn't answer. I hadn't told her I did. I hadn't even thought about it. I never had a normal relationship, so I had no clue what it felt like to be in love. I wanted him next to me. His presence calmed the worst of the voices in my head. He made me feel like I was alive, instead of just surviving. Was that love?

She smirked, her eyes glinting. "I'll take that as a yes."

I sighed. Leaning my head on her shoulder. "I feel like I shouldn't," I admitted. "It makes everything worse."

"Does it make it worse, or does it make it feel messy? You haven't let anyone get that close to you before, Shy. How much of it actually feels wrong and how much of it just scares you?"

"I hate that you're so good at this."

"I'm your ride-or-die bitch. Whatever you decide, I'm here. But I think once the dust settles, you'll realize you and him aren't all that different."

"I know."

She wrapped her arms around my shoulders. "I can key his car though, if that makes you feel better."

A genuine laugh slipped out of me, and I felt a little better than I had before she got here. This morning had shattered my carefully constructed illusion of control, but I didn't feel like the floor was falling out from under me anymore. Because I wasn't alone.

CHAPTER THIRTY-SEVEN

CREED

The property was an old warehouse tucked between two defunct factories on the edge of the industrial district. Far away from town. It was quiet and rundown, the perfect place to set up shop for people who didn't want to be found. I clicked my flashlight on, scanning the loading bay. Rusted out scaffolding, a side entrance covered in graffiti, and a busted security camera dangling from exposed wiring were the only things I'd found so far. Charming place. Kane walked a few steps ahead, his boots silent on the cracked concrete. He had his tablet out, infrared scanner connected and running a sweep for hidden surveillance signals. I was keeping an eye out for physical trip-wires or motion sensors. Anything that told us someone had been here.

"Right side's clean," I muttered. "They haven't reinforced the access points, either. Looks abandoned."

"For now," Kane replied, his tone clipped. "But that changes fast when they're cycling kids through. We set cameras now, we'll catch movement when they get cocky."

He crouched by a utility box and started wiring the first cam into a crack near a gutter pipe.

"You hear from her?" he asked, not looking up.

My jaw flexed. "No."

"She's not gonna stay quiet forever. I anticipate you getting your ass handed to you when we get back."

"She's pissed," I said flatly. "She has every right to be."

Kane let out a grunt. "Yup."

I kneeled beside one of the interior doors and drilled into the corner to mount a sensor. My hands were steady, but the burn in my chest hadn't let up since I left the house. Since I left her.

"I didn't want to lie to her."

"Didn't stop you though," Kane said, pulling out the tablet to sync the feed. "Not judging, just stating facts."

I exhaled through my nose. "I didn't know how to tell her. I figured when she found out, it would be *after* all this shit was over, and I could explain."

"Yeah? That how it worked out?"

I shot him a look, but he didn't return it. Just kept working.

"I know why you leave the cards, Creed," he said, standing with a sigh. "I don't agree with it, but I get it. She would have too, if you'd given her the opportunity."

I knew he was right. That pissed me off. "I knew she was putting the pieces together; I just didn't know how to explain it. So much shit had happened, and she just needed me. Not the fucking King."

"All that girl wants from you is the truth. Give it to her and let her decide what she does with it. From what I've seen, I don't think she'll run screaming."

I leaned back against the brick wall, closing my eyes against the torrent of *what ifs* that ran through my mind.

"Give her time, alright? In the meantime, help me with these last couple cams so we can get out of here."

We finished the setup in silence. Cameras mounted, lenses

angled, feeds streaming directly to the team's encrypted server. Kane ran a final diagnostic while I walked the perimeter, checking for exposed tracks, tire marks, anything that suggested movement. Nothing.

I made my way back inside, checking the loft of the warehouse before we headed out. My feet froze in place as I reached the top step.

"Kane."

"Yeah?"

I blew out a heavy breath. "You need to come up here."

His boots pounded up the stairs until he came to stand behind me, muttered curses slipping out of his mouth as he looked at what was in front of us.

At least a dozen sets of bunk beds, still in the boxes. Thin mattress pads laid in a stack on the floor, next to a pile of boxes with sloppy duct tape holding them closed.

I walked over to them, swiping my fingers across the top of the closest box, and then turning my hand up. Not a speck of dust.

"They're new. Someone put these here recently."

"They're coming. We'll be here when they do. Let's go tell the team."

We trudged back down the stairs. The feeling of excitement for having found their new stash house was muffled by the pit of dread that had formed like a rock in my stomach. They would come, but where were they now? How many kids did they have? We hadn't been able to track down whatever safe houses they had to be stashing them in, and that ate at every tender part of my soul that I still had.

We knew there were six girls from Sunbridge, but they could have been taking them from all over. There were certainly more accommodations in the loft than needed for the girls they took from here. Kane was already on the phone, calling Nate and Aaron and telling them to be ready to brief when we pulled in. Would we be able to take this on on our own?

We could pull in the local PD, no doubt Shiloh's dad could pull strings, but they wouldn't handle it the same way we would. Everyone they pulled from this building would be booked and processed, and then we would wait for years for a trial. What could they prove? How many traumatized children were we willing to force onto the stand? How could we sit in courtroom after courtroom and listen to seven-year-olds describe their abduction?

No. There was a better way, and it only worked if everyone involved agreed that we didn't abide by the law. Certain kinds of people weren't fit for prison; they weren't capable of rehabilitation. They just needed to be put down. So that's what we would do. The drive back was silent, both of us working to swallow the weight of the responsibility laid on our shoulders.

"We'll handle it, Creed," Kane said, his voice low. He always had to be the voice of reason, the one we looked to when shit got serious. Part of me wondered if that was why he was so closed off most of the time.

"I know."

And I did. We were a solid team, and we weren't fighting for the same things these guys would be. They were in it for money. We were in it for blood.

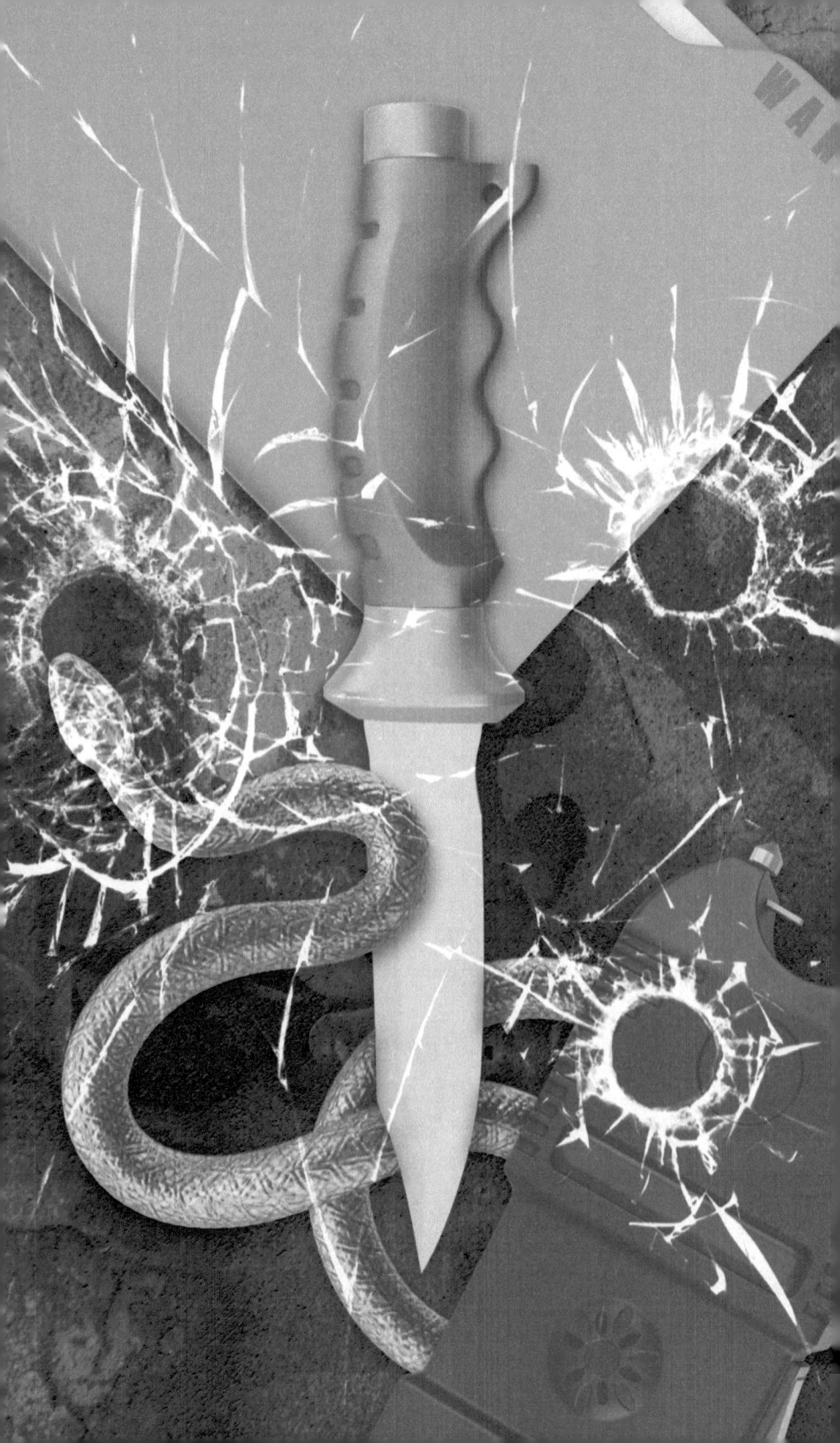

CHAPTER THIRTY-EIGHT

SHILOH

The mood in the house changed as soon as Kane and Creed stepped through the front door. Lottie and I had moved downstairs where we were curled up on the couch watching a movie when the door slammed shut. Whatever they had found had their jaws tight and their eyes sharper than usual. Creed didn't look at me, not right away. Kane gave me a nod; one of those 'brace yourself' kind of looks as I got up and followed them to the security room, leaving Lottie on the couch.

Nate was already in the room, spinning around in one of the desk chairs with a toothpick hanging out of his mouth. Aaron came in behind Kane and Creed, the air around them taut with tension.

Kane pulled a small remote from his jacket pocket, clicked it, and the screen on the far wall lit up with grainy images from what looked like drone camera footage. Warehouse exterior, rusted metal siding, a busted fence. Then a slow pan around the inside.

"There's a loft here," he said, pointing to the top corner of the video. "We found supplies up there. Beds, mattresses, boxes of what I'm assuming are supplies."

Someone was preparing.

"They've been there," Kane said, his voice low. "Not for

long. No dust, no cobwebs. They moved in fast and quiet, probably testing the space."

Creed finally looked at me. "They're rebuilding The Manor; that's our best guess based on the information we've pulled together so far. New location, same basic operations."

My chest tightened painfully.

"We've already rigged the place with motion sensors and cameras," Kane continued, flipping to another slide of a grainy photo showing the stairwell leading to the loading dock. "We're watching twenty-four-seven now. The minute they bring girls in, we go."

Creed nodded. "Everyone needs to be ready to move at a moment's notice."

Aaron rubbed at his jaw, his brows drawn together as he studied the photos. The room fell quiet, and that sickening feeling of inevitability crawled down my spine. They were coming. It wasn't a maybe. It was a countdown.

Kane cleared his throat. "Shiloh, hang back a second?"

Nate whistled at me like I was being called to the principal's office as everyone filed out of the room, Creed turning to look at me over his shoulder as he left.

Once the door clicked shut, I turned to look at him. "What's up?"

He didn't answer right away. He walked to the desk and picked up a tablet and turned it so I could see the screen. A blurry photo of a man with greasy blonde hair and a round face stared back at me.

"Recognize him?" I squinted at the photo.

"No, I don't think so."

Kane set the tablet down. "Samuel York. His name came up in the files we cracked from the website on Reid's phone. I cross referenced with a list I got from the bartender at Sinner's."

"Sinner's?"

"Did you know they run a gambling night out of the back room?"

"No, I didn't know that." That wasn't surprising though. You could throw a dart at a board full of criminal activities and odds were, whatever it landed on was taking place in that bar.

"Most of the guys we'll be looking for will turn up at a place like that. Anyway, there's a game going on tonight. Guess whose name was on the invite list?"

That sick twist of my gut came back with a vengeance. "So, what—you want me to take him out?"

Did Kane know? I should have paid more attention to the wording Creed used when we were talking. Did they know he was the Red King? Of course they did. They were almost constantly with him. They'd have to be dumber than I was to miss that. Kane and Nate were a lot of things, but oblivious was not one of them.

"I want you to go check it out. See who's there. What they're saying. If he's involved in the ring, odds are he's working with whoever is rebuilding The Manor and this is the kind of setting where lips loosen and we get intel."

I nodded slowly, already calculating. "I can go alone—"

"No," Kane's voice cut in fast. "You'll take Creed."

I blinked. "What? No. Kane, I don't need—"

"Yeah, you do." His tone wasn't sharp, but firm. He wasn't going to give in. "I know you two are dealing with your own shit right now, but I'm not sending you in there alone. And like it or not, Creed would have that entire place stripped down to the foundation in a heartbeat if someone laid a hand on you. He's the best option for back up."

I looked away, my jaw so tight it hurt.

"Shiloh," he said, his voice a little softer. "I'm not going to get into your business, but you and Creed? You have a lot in common. Neither one of you does what you do for fun. He's got his issues but give him a chance before you cut him off." He handed me a folded piece of paper.

"Both of your names are on the list. Go in, be discreet. Creed will handle security; you scan for anyone that looks familiar. Change what you can about your appearance—a wig, makeup, whatever. You're the only person that will recognize these people if they're in there, but we don't want them to recognize you if we can avoid it."

I took the paper and nodded. "Got it."

Kane stepped back. "Good. Because if they're hosting events like this, they're already lining up buyers."

The words made my skin crawl. I left the room and turned toward the stairs, the mission burning hot beneath my skin.

CHAPTER THIRTY-NINE

SHILOH

"Honestly, this is some of my best work," Lottie announced, tugging the wig forward on my head and adjusting the strands around my face.

I caught my reflection in the vanity mirror and barely recognized the girl staring back at me. The black wig she had picked out was straight and sleek, hitting just below my shoulders with bangs that covered my forehead. The makeup was heavier than I'd ever worn—charcoal-lined lids, thick lashes, and red lipstick that made my blue eyes look like they were almost glowing.

The dress... well, if you could call it that. It was black, skintight, and barely held together with strategic cutouts and a zipper that ran all the way down my spine.

"Are you sure this isn't overkill?" I asked, standing slowly so I could see the full thing in the mirror.

Lottie tilted her head and handed me a pair of red bottomed heels like she was handing me a knife.

"You're going into a den of degenerates. Blend in. Seduce the room. Stab someone if needed. That's your holy trinity."

I huffed a laugh. "Should I bring a rosary?"

"Only if it doubles as a garrote." She waggled her brows.

I slipped the heels on and gave a quick twirl. The dress hugged every curve. I probably wouldn't ever dress like this again, but the wig and makeup felt like a mask. I wasn't Shiloh. I was someone else entirely, and that's exactly what I needed. Lottie stood back, arms crossed, appraising.

"You look amazing. Someone's gonna choke on his drink."

As if summoned by her words, a knock sounded at the door. Lottie sauntered over and opened it wide, revealing Creed. He froze as he took me in. His eyes dragged over every inch of me, slow and stunned. I watched his chest rise as he took in the final look. His jaw clenched; his hands flexed at his sides.

"Jesus Christ," he muttered.

"Close," Lottie said breezily, "but I think she's more of a goddess. Don't you?"

Creed didn't even blink. "She always is."

My stomach flipped. He was wearing a pair of fitted black slacks, a button up shirt in the same shade tucked into the waist. He had slicked his hair back, all but one stubborn piece that fell close to his eyes. He looked lethal. Beautiful. He stepped into the room and all the air inside it was sucked out. God, he always looked so good

"You're going to get us both killed looking like that," he said.

"Is that a complaint?" I raised a brow.

He stepped close enough that I could feel the heat rolling off him. "Not even close."

Lottie clapped once. "And that's my cue to leave. If you're not back by dawn I will assume you kissed and made up and are ravaging each other's bodies in some weird serial killer lust fest. Bye!" She swept out dramatically, closing the door behind her and leaving me alone with Creed. He still looked at me like I wasn't wearing anything at all.

"You ready?" he asked, his voice rougher now than when he came in.

I nodded. "Let's go break into hell."

THE NEON SIGN for Sinner's buzzed overhead, casting red light across the rain-slick pavement like fresh blood. Creed pulled the truck into an alley two blocks down and killed the engine. For a second, neither of us moved. I adjusted the hem of my dress, checked my reflection in the visor mirror. A stranger stared back—confident, cold, unrecognizable. That was the point, so why did it freak me out so much?

"You sure about this?"

I met Creed's eyes in the dark cab of the truck. "Do I look unsure?"

His lips twitched. Not quite a smile, but close. "You look like trouble," he said, leaning closer. "Which means I'm absolutely fucked."

I rolled my eyes and opened the door, high heels hitting the pavement with a click. "Come on, Red King. Let's go play."

We slipped into the club through the front, our names already on the list thanks to Kane's mystery bartender. The bouncer waved us through without so much as a second glance. Creed kept a casual hand on my lower back, guiding me through the crowd with quiet authority.

Inside, bodies moved in groups on the dance floor. Bass thumped through the entire space so loud I could feel it through the soles of my feet. We moved to the bar, looking for the person Kane had told us to find. The gambling ring was private. Password protected and invite-only. The bartender was our connection.

I leaned over the sticky surface in front of us enough to catch the attention of the brunette at the end. All Kane had told us was it was a 'dark-haired woman.' He had been incredibly cagey about the entire thing, which was something I was most definitely going to pry into later.

Her brown eyes found me, and she walked over. "What can I get you, babe?"

"I'm looking for Fallon?"

"Well, you found her," she said with a smirk. She reached into her apron and pulled out two poker chips, sliding them across the bar and into my hand. She pulled my hand, leaning across the bar until she was close enough to whisper.

"The password is Bishop. Down the hall past the bathrooms, black door on the right. Be careful."

I slid one chip into Creed's pocket, earning a look from him and smiled at the woman in front of me.

"Thanks."

"Enjoy the rest of your night."

As we turned to leave a man slammed his glass down on the bar next to me.

"What the fuck is this shit? I asked for whiskey, and you gave me watered-down piss!"

"I can assure you, I did not," she said wryly.

"Fix it, bitch."

She just shrugged. "Okay." She reached beneath the bar, grabbing the water sprayer, and aimed it right at his face. I ducked behind Creed just as the water smacked into the man's face.

"All better!" she said cheerily. "Now get the fuck out of my bar." She whistled, the sound ear piercing even in the loud room, and the bouncer from the front door appeared beside us, snatching the man by his collar and dragging him out as he yelled a string of insults toward the woman. Fallon blew him a kiss as he went.

I turned to Creed. "I like her."

He rolled his eyes, ushering me toward the back room. "You would."

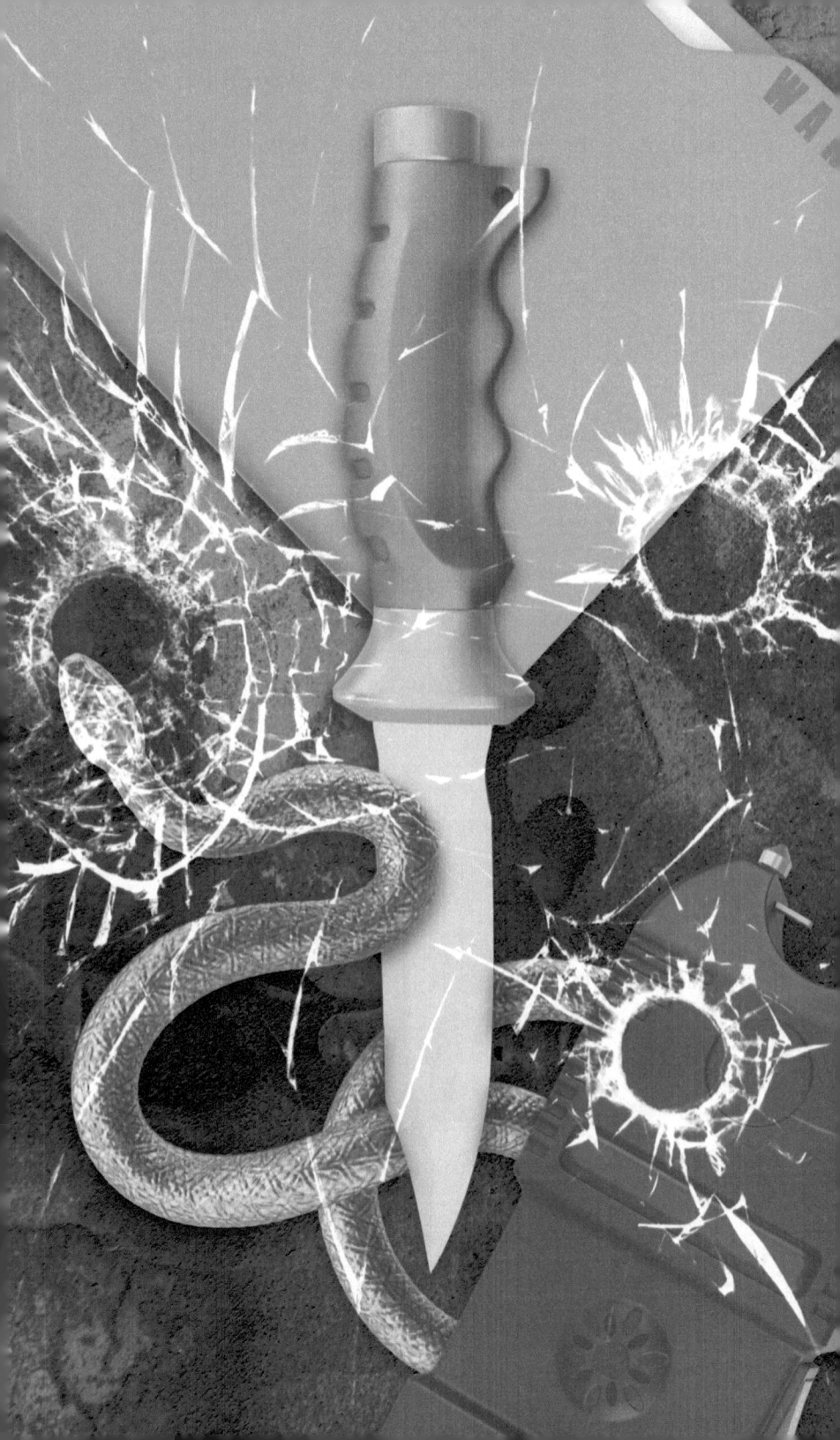

CHAPTER FORTY

SHILOH

There was a man waiting outside the door when we arrived. He held his hand out without saying a word. Creed and I placed our chips in his hands.

"Bishop." I forced my voice to stay calm despite the nerves that were building. He scanned the chips, then pushed open the door.

We stepped inside, taking in the smoke-filled room. It was quieter back here. Poker tables dotted the floor, the room lit with overhead lights that cast long shadows across the walls. Men in suits and watches worth more than my car shuffled chips and laughed like they owned the world. They probably did.

I scanned the area, my gaze zeroing in on the table to the far left. I recognized the man from the photo Kane had shown me and nudged Creed, nodding carefully. The man was laughing, but there was the slightest shake in his hands. The suit he wore looked cheaper than the ones of the men around him, and a thin sheen of sweat had formed on his forehead. That was our target.

Creed leaned in, his breath brushing my ear. "You good?"

I nodded, but my pulse was climbing, "Let me sit in. Get him comfortable."

"I'll be ten feet away."

"Try not to kill anyone."

He didn't smile back. "No promises."

I approached the table like I belonged there, hips swaying, and my chin held high.

"Room for one more?" I asked sweetly.

Samuel York looked up at me, his eyes taking their sweet time traveling from my chest to my face. I wanted to peel his skin off.

"You got cash to burn, sweetheart?" he asked, taking a puff from the cigarette between his lips.

The chair creaked as I lowered myself into it, placing a hand on York's shoulder like we were old friends.

I smiled. "Only if you're worth taking it from."

The table laughed and York's grin turned predatory.

I bought in with the wad of cash Creed had handed me before we walked in, and the game started. Chips clacked; cards slid around the table. I let the man to my left talk my ear off about boats and bourbon, nodding along and keeping my voice light.

But my ears were tuned into the conversation taking place across the table. Two men were whispering low, their chips barely moving.

"...four new shipments last week—"

"Clean. No IDs, no noise. Said they'll rotate them by Friday."

York chuckled, clearly in on it. "Make sure they're worth the price tag this time."

My stomach turned but I kept my face blank, my nails tapping lightly on the cards in front of me. I flicked my gaze toward Creed. He leaned against the wall by the bar, dark eyes locked on mine like a sniper lining up a shot. I tilted my head just slightly, giving him a small nod.

Target acquired. I stayed long enough to win a few rounds —just enough to boost York's interest. When I stood and slid my chips toward the dealer, York stood too.

"Heading out already?" he asked.

I smiled at him. "I've already gotten what I came for."

I turned and walked, my pace slow and deliberate. I heard his chair scrape back, and the echo of footsteps behind me. God, men were predictable. Creed was already moving. Walking parallel to us and reaching the door just moments after my shadow and I did. I continued out the back door, into the alley. The second I was through the exit, I stepped to the side and let York push past me.

"Where are you headed in such a hurry?" he asked, grabbing for my arm. That was a mistake.

Creed's hand slammed into his shoulder, spinning him around, and then York was pinned to the brick with Creed's forearm across his throat. I stepped close, letting him see my face clearly now that the pleasantries had been stripped away.

"What do you know about the new Manor they're building?" I asked softly.

His eyes widened. Bingo. "I-I haven't done anything! I haven't even seen the girls!" he stuttered.

I looked at Creed. "Do we need this one?"

He shook his head. "We'll get any info he has off his phone. We've also got the tapes from the poker room being transferred to us so we can ID the other guys at the table."

"Wanna leave a message then?" I asked, a buzz building in my veins that matched the fire in Creed's eyes.

He swung out, hitting York in the temple hard enough to make him crumple to the ground.

"You know what? I do." He pulled a knife from his pocket, offering it to me.

I took it, feeling the weight of the handle in my hand before crouching so I was level with York's body. The blade slid across his throat. Sharp as a scalpel, it cut through flesh and tendon like I was slicing butter. I wiped the blade on his shirt before handing it to Creed and digging one final touch out of my purse.

A red queen playing card.

Creed barked a laugh as he flipped open his wallet and pulled out the matching mate card. We flicked them out of our hands, watching as they landed in the pool of blood collecting in his lap. We didn't speak as we moved toward the truck a few blocks down. Creed tensed as we turned the corner in front of the bar, his breath catching.

"What is it?" I asked, looking around the empty street in front of us.

I followed his line of vision to the entrance to the bar and the man talking to the bouncer. Miles was laughing at something the other man had said, his hair slicked back, suit pressed, smiling like a snake as they talked. He stepped through the front door of Sinner's like he'd been there a million times before. My blood turned to ice. What if he had? What was he doing in a place like that?

"We need to go," Creed said. "Now."

I swallowed my panic and moved, letting Creed guide me away. But alarm bells were blaring in my head.

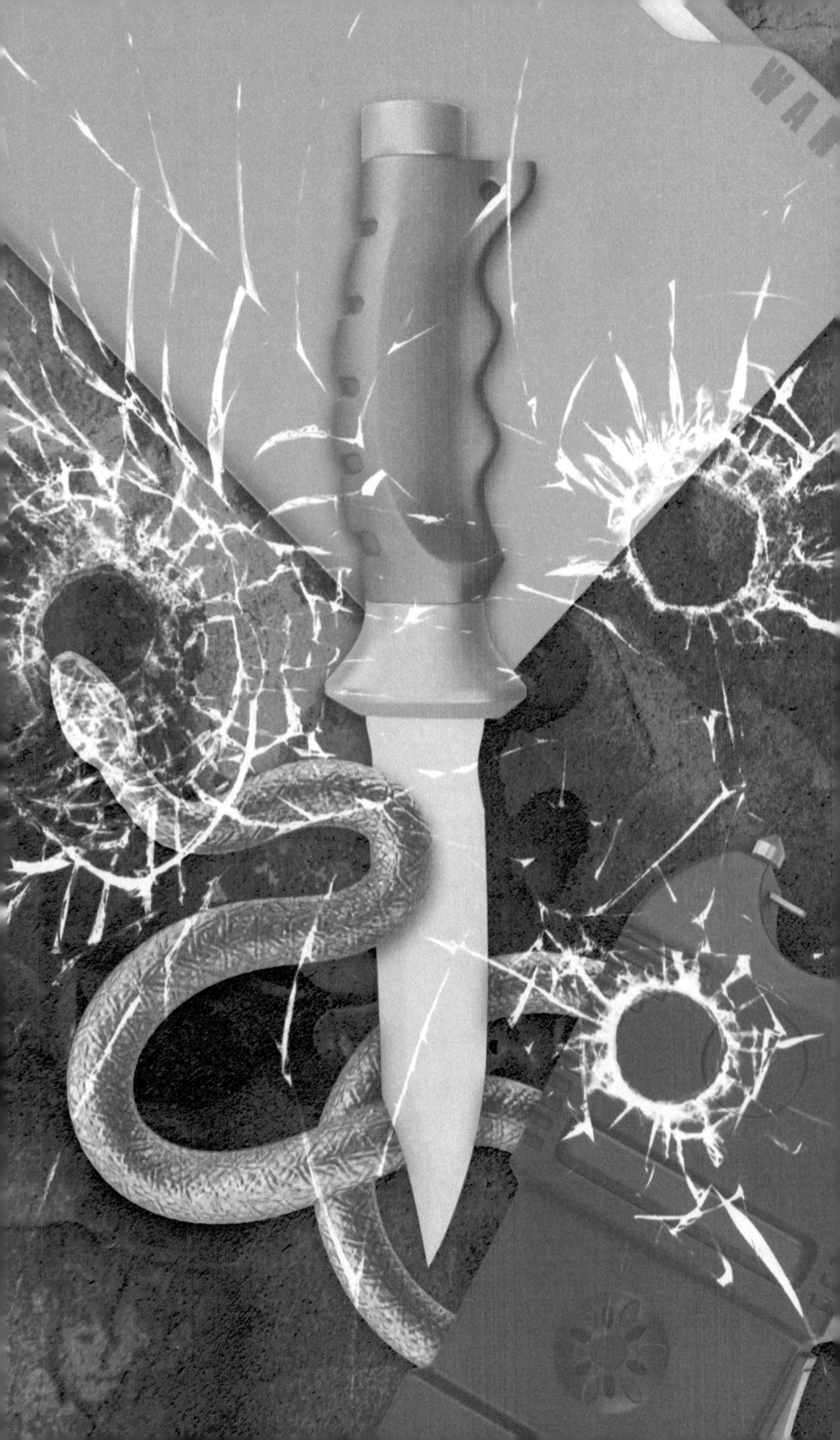

CHAPTER FORTY-ONE

SHILOH

Kane didn't believe in gentle warm-ups. The second I stepped onto the mat, he swept my feet out and I hit the floor hard enough to see stars. I rolled, popping back up to my feet, and went at him again.

"Lead with your elbow," he said, blocking the jab and spinning me by the wrist. "Your height's an advantage, use it."

"I'm five-five, Kane."

"Exactly." He shoved me in the shoulder. "Nobody expects the short one to take their throat out."

We went another round. Hip toss, shoulder lock, me cursing, Kane not even winded. Sweat burned my eyes, and my bruises throbbed, but every time I hit the mat, I pictured a different face from The Manor and got up faster. When Kane finally tossed me a towel, Creed was leaning in the doorway like he'd been there the whole time. His usual all black outfit was distracting enough that I was glad I hadn't noticed him there while we were still sparring. Men in tactical pants and tight black t-shirts were becoming a weakness of mine. Or maybe that was just Creed.

"You gonna keep tossing my girl around, Kane?" he drawled.

Kane flipped him off. "She's improving."

"Obviously." Creed's eyes tracked the new bruises blooming on my thighs, heat sliding into protectiveness. I'd decided on shorts and a long-sleeved shirt for today, and surprisingly, it hadn't been an issue. "But she needs more than grappling. She needs to learn how to take someone down."

Nate strolled in, twirling a combat knife in his hand. "Speaking of taking people down, Shiloh, you ever shoot a gun?"

I wiped my face with the towel as Creed and Kane groaned in unison.

"No."

Nate's grin was feral. "Field trip."

KANE DROVE and Nate rode shotgun so he could play DJ with the radio, and Creed sat beside me in the backseat of Kane's Jeep, knees brushing mine every time we hit a pothole.

"You comfortable with this?" he asked quietly.

"I need to learn."

He didn't argue, just slipped his hand over mine on the bench seat so the guys couldn't see.

The private range was tucked in an abandoned quarry. Steel targets, plywood silhouettes, and a bunker of borrowed weapons.

"Jesus, is this all yours?" I asked, looking between the guys.

"Yup!" Nate smiled. "Nice, huh?" He grabbed a bag from the back of the Jeep and set it on a rickety looking table, unzipping it and unloading its contents onto the surface. He explained the guns to me as he set them out. A Glock, a Sig, even a sawed-off that he insisted was 'for the vibe.' Kane handed me ear protection and a matte-black 9mm. "Stance first. Thumb over thumb, squeeze, don't tug."

Creed moved behind me, his chest brushing against my back, arms bracketing mine. "Lean forward," he murmured in my ear. His hands corrected my grip, gentle, patient. Inexcusably intimate.

I looked to Kane who stood to my left, waiting for him to nod, signaling me to shoot, then I sighted the outline of the man on the plywood, exhaled, and squeezed. The kick surprised me, my shot landing at the very edge of the wooden man's shoulder. Creed stepped up beside me and nodded.

"Again," he said.

Ten rounds later and there was nothing but splinters where the silhouette's chest had been.

Nate whooped. "Look at the little assassin go. Proud of you, tiny terror," he said as he rubbed his fist against the top of my head.

Kane came over to get the gun from me. "You aren't going to be a sniper anytime soon, but I think you could take someone out with one of these if you needed to."

"Easy, big fella. You're gonna make my head big with the compliments," I replied as I tugged off the ear protection and handed it to him.

Creed's hand found the small of my back as we walked back to the car, his gaze finding mine just long enough to ask a silent question. Had the wall I'd slammed between us budged at all? Maybe a little. But I wasn't ready to let him back in all the way just yet.

Back at the house, the mood had shifted. Aaron's Charger wasn't in the drive. No note, no text, just an empty spot where his car was usually parked.

"Patrol," Kane said, but it sounded like he was guessing.

Creed's jaw ticked. Nate tried to joke about Aaron finally

downloading a dating app, but we all worried anytime one of us was out alone. There were too many variables, too many ways things could go wrong if we didn't stick together. I headed upstairs to shower off the smell of gunpowder, Creed catching my wrist halfway up.

"You did good today," he said, eyes searching mine.

"Thanks, it was kinda fun."

He nodded, but the worry on his face was evident. "Stay close tonight. Without Aaron here, I'll need to help run cams with the guys."

"Fine."

He released my wrist, standing at the base of the stairs as I disappeared into the hallway.

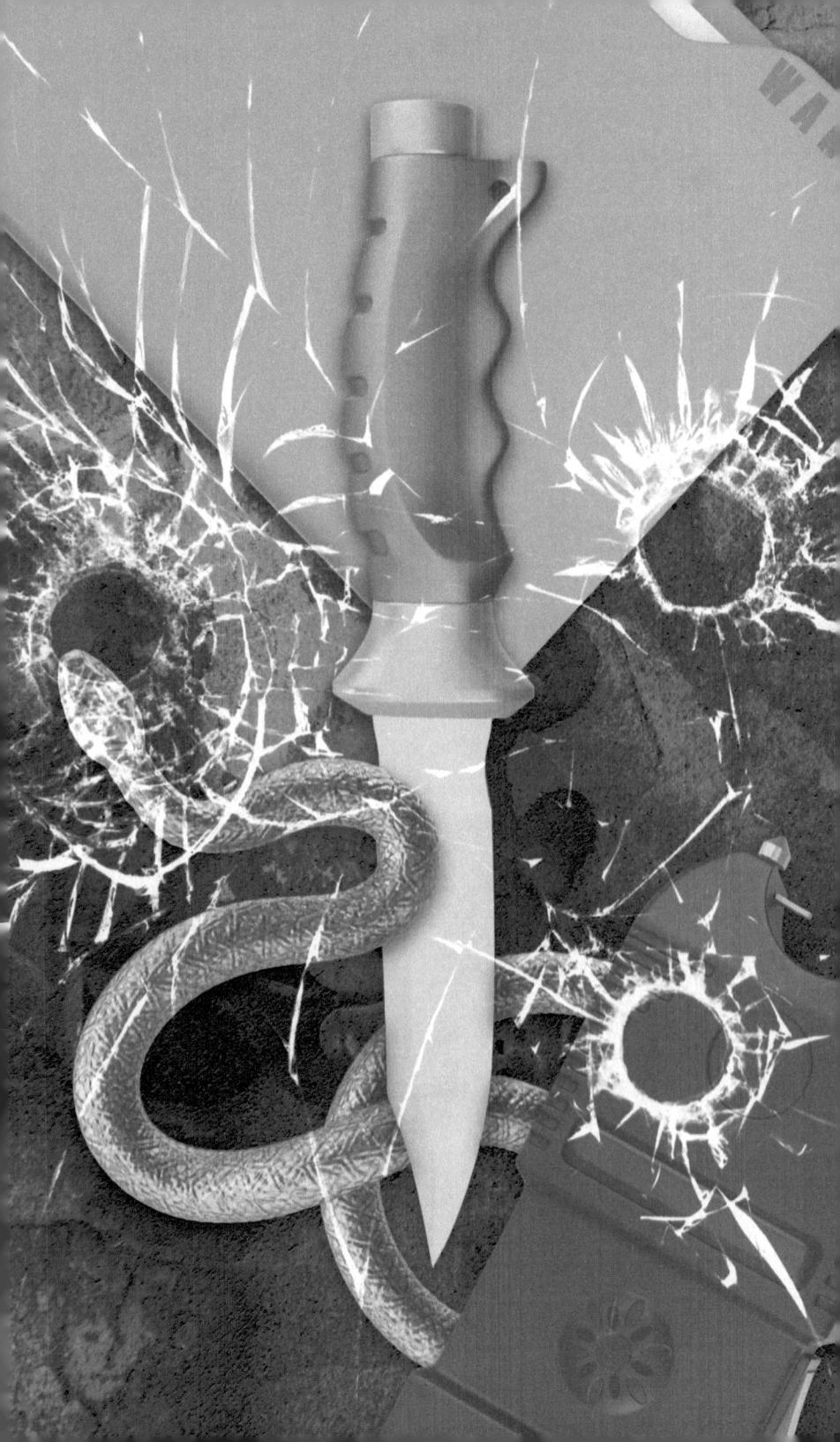

CHAPTER FORTY-TWO

SHILOH

I tossed and turned all night, finally giving up on sleep around six in the morning. By the time Mom came knocking on my door, I was dressed and ready to go. She loved shopping, though she only wanted to do it when I went with her. So, it had become our thing. We tried on ugly dresses, bought things we didn't need, ate pretzels, and then collapsed on the couch with our bags spread out all over the living room until Dad came home.

The mall was packed. People milled around in groups as we bobbed and weaved, ducking into one of our favorite stores.

"How's work going? I know you haven't been able to get to the gym much, but Aaron said he'll make sure you get some hours in this week."

"It's good, same old same old really."

"Are you sleeping better?"

I lied, "A lot better."

She held up a crimson dress that looked suspiciously like blood under the lights.

"How about this one? You'd knock them dead in this." She grimaced at her phrasing. "Sorry, bad choice of words."

I laughed—actually laughed—and the tightness in her shoulders eased. Small victories.

While she tried on cardigans, I scrolled through my phone.

KANE:

Motion on loft cam #2. Possible furniture
delivery. 4 a.m. time stamp.

So, they were moving into the warehouse already. That was
a good thing; the sooner they got in, the sooner we could get the
girls out. The reality of the work ahead of us still made me
nervous, though I'd never admit it out loud. The truth was, I
wasn't trained for this. Not really.

Sure, I had been working with Kane, but him, Nate, and
Creed had been sparring and shooting for years. They were
trained, efficient, and calculated. Would I be an asset to them?
Or would I be in the way? If I couldn't hold my own, then that
meant one of the guys would be distracted trying to cover my
ass and his. I couldn't let that happen. I would just have to work
harder, train with Kane more often, bribe Nate to sneak me off
to the range until I could hit the target with my eyes closed.
When the time came, I was going to be a weapon, not a
weakness.

Mom emerged in a soft gray sweater and pirouetted.
"Honest opinion?"

"Perfect." I smiled. We got her sweater, a pair of jeans I
didn't need, and an espresso to keep the nightmares at bay. We
walked in circles, sipping, chatting about nothing. The kind of
day normal daughters have with their normal mothers.

Outside, dusk bled into violet. Creed texted:

CREED:

Everything going okay?

ME:

Yeah, heading home now.

We drove home to the soundtrack of one of Mom's favorite musicals, something I had missed during the time I was gone, and she was determined to get me into it. To be honest, I was zoned out for most of the ride. My eyelids were already drooping, and I knew what waited for me when I closed my eyes. Unless—unless Creed was there next to me. He was like the antidote for night terrors. Somehow, when he was there, I slept through the night without so much as stirring. I craved that kind of peace so badly that it hurt.

Back at the house, Nate was on the porch, phone pressed to his ear, his face uncharacteristically grim. He saw me, forced a grin and pocketed his phone.

"Have fun shopping, ladies?"

My mom smiled and nodded, as we walked past him into the house. Aaron still wasn't back, but Creed stood by the living room window, his silhouette black against the sunset, watching the driveway.

I went to him, letting our distance shrink. He didn't move to touch me, but our shoulders brushed, contact that felt better than it should have.

"Ready to storm the gates?" he asked softly.

"Can I sleep first?" I joked.

But his eyes drilled into mine, reading the need in them, and he nodded, slipping his hand into mine and leading me upstairs to my bedroom. We slid into bed, his arm opening for me in an invitation. And I took it. I needed to sleep more than I needed to hold onto my pride for tonight.

CHAPTER FORTY-THREE

CREED

Kane's voice crackled through Nate's walkie talkie as we walked the perimeter of the house, sharp and demanding.

"Briefing. Now."

Nate and I exchanged a look. He raised an eyebrow that said, 'this better be good' and then followed me inside and down the hall. Shiloh appeared at the top of the stairs, pulling her braid tight, eyes already narrowed like she could smell trouble.

In the security room, Kane had the TV screen split four ways: a local news broadcast, crime scene photos edged in the Sunbridge police watermark, a blurry still of a card tucked into a corpse's jacket, and grainy security footage outside of Sinner's. Shiloh's breath caught. Nate swore low under his breath, and Aaron was already on the laptop screen, his face tight as he looked between all of us.

Kane didn't waste any time jumping in. "SPD just leaked this to every precinct within a hundred miles. They've linked eight murders by M.O and calling cards. Task force is live as of an hour ago, and they've flagged the warehouse district as 'an area of interest.'"

I straightened. "How close are they?"

"Close enough." Kane tapped the still of the security footage. "That's a partial plate on the truck. They haven't run it yet, but it's only a matter of time."

The room felt like someone had sucked all the air right out of it. All of us were silent as we considered what this meant for us. "So, on top of The Manor 2.0, we now have cops hunting us?" Shiloh asked.

Kane's gaze flicked to me. "They pull surveillance from Sinner's, see you two together, it goes sideways fast. I've already reached out to my contact to see what we can do about erasing it; we just have to hope we got the footage from inside before the cops did."

Nate plopped onto the couch, hands linked behind his head. "Love a new sub-plot right before the climax."

"Focus," Kane snapped. "We move on the warehouse tonight, but we do it quietly. No stray brass, no cards, no faces on tape."

The last line hit harder than he meant it to. I could feel Shiloh's stare burning a hole through the side of my skull.

Kane killed the screen. "Get prepped. We roll out at dark."

"I'll meet you guys there, let me finish up here and I'll head that way." Aaron said before the laptop screen went dark. All of us had been split a million ways trying to track down leads. It felt like tracing wires to a live bomb and trying to grab the right one before it exploded in our faces. Our best shot was that he could pull together a few of the guys he knew to help storm the gates tonight. If not, we were on our own. Nate sauntered off muttering about suppressors. Kane followed, phone already in his ear. The minute they were gone, Shiloh rounded on me.

"You said the cards were a message," she hissed. "You didn't say they came with a police task force."

"It's under control," I began.

She laughed, a sharp, incredulous sound. "Control? They have evidence stacking against you as we speak."

I ran a hand through my hair, swallowing the sigh building in my throat. "That was always the plan."

"Excuse me?"

I closed the door to the security room so we could speak privately. She stood there, arms folded tight, her chin held high as she faced me head on.

Fuck. Here goes nothing.

"I leave the cards," I said, "so if the murders ever connect, they land on one person—me. Not Kane, not Nate, not you." I held her gaze. "It's a shield. I built the myth so the cops would chase a ghost while the people I care about stay off their radar."

Her eyes flicked to the hallway where Kane's footsteps faded. "You're protecting them."

"And you." I pulled a card from my pocket, flipped it between my fingers. "That night you snapped Jason's wrist? If someone finds that body, the card says I did it. Not Shiloh Hale. That keeps you clean."

She stared at the card, lips pressed thin. "You branded my kills."

"I claimed them," I corrected. "So, you wouldn't have to carry the rap sheet along with the scars."

Silence swelled, heavy with the things I wanted to say, and the things I already had.

I closed the distance, slipping the card back into my pocket.

"I will never let the world take you down for finishing what it started."

Her throat bobbed as she looked away. "And if they catch you?"

"Then they catch me." I brushed a knuckle under her chin, coaxing her eyes back to mine. "It's my weight on my shoulder, Red. My job, my choice."

She leaned in just a fraction, the wall between us cracking —a spiderweb fracture as the trust slowly began reforming. I felt it like the first breath after nearly drowning.

"We still hit the warehouse?" she asked.

"Tonight."

"And if the cops show?"

"Then we deal with it. One thing at a time." I wasn't worried. This had always been the plan. If they come for me, and only me, then I did something right.

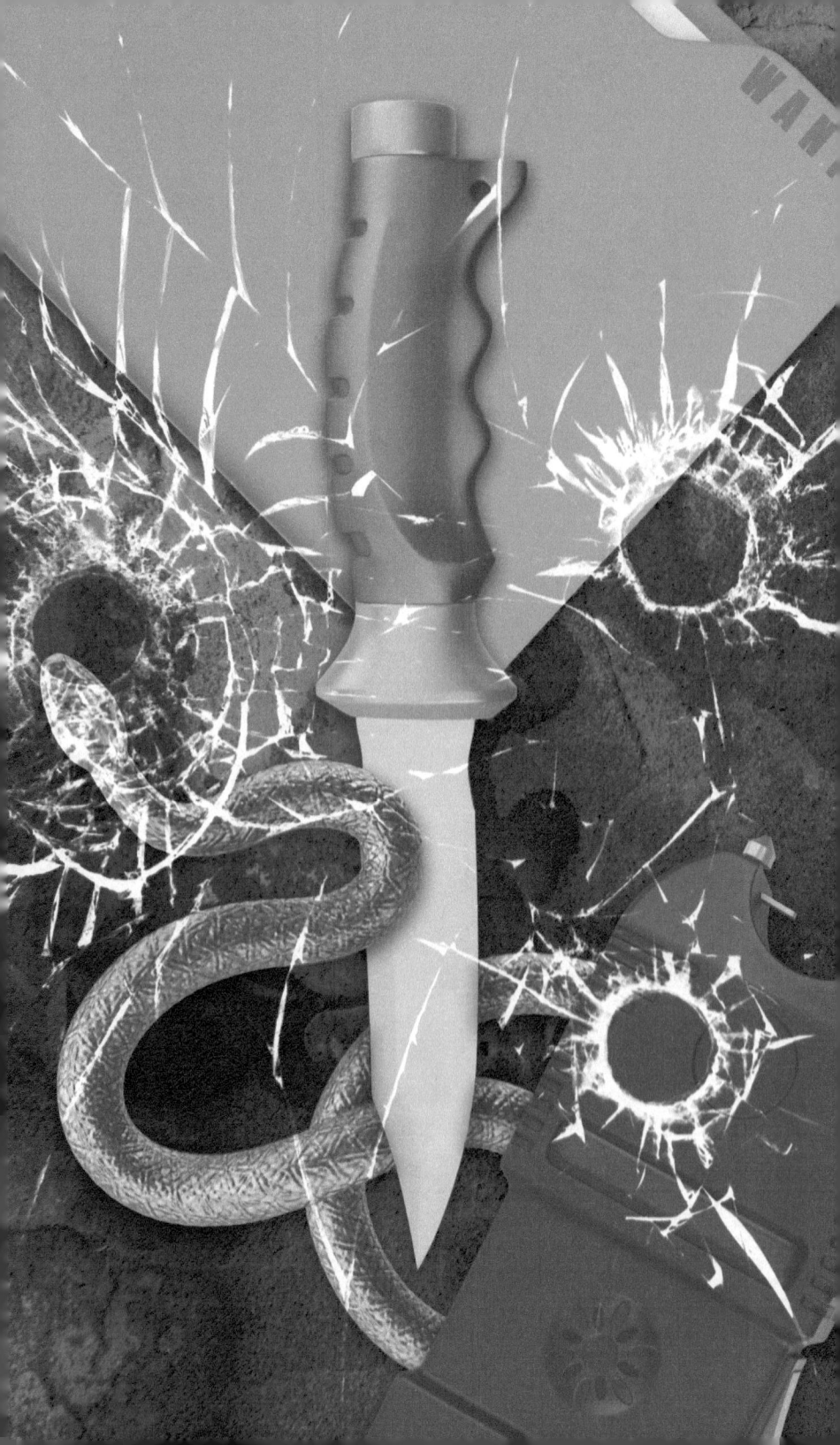

CHAPTER FORTY-FOUR

SHILOH

By nightfall, the house was buzzing. We had convinced my parents to take a night for themselves and sent them off on a date I planned out. They would still be working their way through courses at a five-star restaurant when we pulled out of the driveway. Nate was pacing circles in the living room, periodically walking over to the open duffle bag on the coffee table to toss things inside. Spare mags, extra earpieces. The large TV on the wall showed a silent feed of the warehouse. Figures moved like shadows through the darkened rooms, at least a dozen of them. They had moved in fast.

Kane stood in the middle of the room, his hands on his hips as he looked at all of us.

"I'm not going to get soft, and I'm not good with motivational speeches. Keep your head on a swivel, watch each other's backs, follow the plan. We are better than these fucks in every single way, let's go prove that."

"Hear hear!" Nate yelled before running to wrap his arms around Kane's abdomen in a bear hug. Kane batted him off, and they quickly went back to work.

I double-checked the Glock Creed had handed me earlier. Safety on, bullet chambered, and slipped it into the holster at my hip. I had a knife in my waistband and extra ammo tucked into the thick Kevlar vest I wore. The body armor was heavy, and I could already feel bruises forming under the pressure of the straps, but it was a small price to pay for safety. I was still adjusting the second holster on my thigh, attempting to get it to sit comfortably, when I heard the familiar footfall behind me. Quiet, deliberate, and always just a little too smooth. Creed. He stepped into my space like he had always belonged there, heat from his body brushing against my shoulder.

"Strap's loose," he murmured, his deft fingers ghosting over the edge of the vest where it met my side. I didn't even flinch. As much as I had wanted to hold onto my anger, I couldn't deny the peace I felt at his touch.

He crouched slightly, tightening the buckles on my thigh holster without looking up. When he stood, he was closer, his face inches from mine, and stoic as a statue.

"I know why you were angry with me," he said, adjusting the second strap, his voice low enough for only me to hear. "I should have told you. About the cards, about all of it."

My eyes met his. "Yes. But I also understand now that you were trying to protect me."

"I still am." His hand settled on my waist, flexing as he spoke. "No more secrets, Red."

The heat that swelled in my chest didn't feel like anger anymore. It was steadier. Gravity finally pulling me toward something I wasn't afraid of crashing into.

I stepped into him, my fingers curling into the belt loops of his tac pants. "No more secrets. We do this together."

He let out a slow breath, a sound of pure relief falling from his beautiful mouth. "Together," he agreed.

His lips met mine, his hands curling around my face to anchor me to him. If things went south tonight, then this would be the last time I got to be this close to him, to feel his skin on mine, to taste him. I yanked him back to me by his waist when he started to move back, swallowing the chuckle that tumbled into my mouth as he pressed his lips back to mine more fervently.

A throat cleared across the room, and we finally separated. Kane and Nate were already loading bags onto their shoulders and heading for the door. Creed met my eyes and nodded. Enough to say 'we can do this.' I picked up my duffle and followed them out the garage door, climbing into the back seat. Creed settled next to me, and Nate sprawled out in the passenger seat, singing quietly to himself while he cleaned a knife. No one said a word. There wasn't anything else to say.

We were going in, we were getting the girls out, and we were hoping to any god that would listen that we all came out with them.

CHAPTER FORTY-FIVE

CREED

The warehouse sat like a carcass at the edge of the industrial strip, the metal exterior rusted and rotting from the inside out. It was the perfect place to hide a nightmare like this.

Kane slowed the SUV to a crawl a few blocks out. We killed the headlights and coasted the last hundred yards behind a wall of fog. It was still out here, the only movement coming from the tall rows of weeds that swayed in the field to our left.

Nate cracked his knuckles in the front seat, his leg bouncing in anticipation. He had enough trauma to make a therapist cry, but this was his outlet. Hurting those that hurt others, it was almost soothing for him. Shiloh sat beside me with her fingers drumming along her thigh, the tension growing thicker in the cab of the SUV the longer we sat here in silence.

"Comms check," Kane said softly, pressing a hand to his earpiece.

"Copy," I answered.

"Copy," Shiloh followed, her voice steady and controlled.

"Copy Captain." Nate was already smiling, just waiting to be unleashed on the men inside.

There was still no new camera footage. The last sweep of

the warehouse had shown movement, shapes flitting past the bunk beds and crates, but the feed cut out shortly after. No exterior security meant nothing to intercept, and that only made it worse. No cameras meant they weren't expecting to be there long, and they didn't want to leave a trail. The odds that they already had a second location ready to move to after this one were high.

I grabbed my mask, slipping it over my head and sliding the gas mask over it, letting it rest on top of my head until we needed it. My gun was already chambered, my knife laced down in my boot with the blade sharp enough to cut through bone. We didn't know how many people were inside, thanks to the camera footage being grainy. We also weren't sure how many girls were in there. But it was time to find out.

We moved in silence as we exited the car. I took point with Kane while Shiloh and Nate trailed behind us. Two sets of steel double doors with heavy chains hung in front of us.

Unlocked. That was a nice surprise. That was either very dumb or very deliberate. I glanced at Kane, and he gave me a nod. Time to get this show on the road.

"Gas masks," I murmured into comms. "On three."

I pulled mine into place and the world muted, filtered through lenses and breath.

"One."

"Two."

"Three."

Kane's boot hit the door like a battering ram. I slammed my foot into the second panel, and it caved with a screech of rusted hinges.

Smoke filled the space in seconds, acrid and thick. Nate's first grenade rolled through the opening like a silver marble, hissing as it went. Shiloh's followed, perfect and precise, exploding into a cloud of dense cover.

Shouts and movement surrounded us on all sides. Fuck there were a lot of people in here.

"MOVE," Kane barked into the comms, and we did.

I followed Kane as he split left, guns raised. Two men rushed us from the back of the building, I dropped one with a shot through his forehead, Kane had the second one down right after.

"Left bay," Shiloh's voice said in my ear. "We've got eyes on the girls."

"Get them out," I answered.

"I'll stick with her," Nate added.

I caught a glimpse of her running through the smoke, her gun raised in front of her as she ordered terrified girls to run. Kane and I cut deeper into the warehouse. The farther we went, the more makeshift it looked. Like someone had thrown together a replica of the old Manor using scrapes and night-mares. Men came at us, stumbling half-blind through the smoke. We didn't slow down.

A few ducked out the back, but Kane was a solid shot and took them out one by one as they reached the door. We hit the back hallway, a busted office door hanging on one hinge, papers scattered everywhere, a laptop open on a rickety desk. The man inside was mid-escape, arm reaching for a gun under the desk while he moved toward the window.

"Try it," Kane said coldly.

The man paused. I stepped in, kicking the desk away from him, and had his hands bound in seconds.

"Where's the rest?" I asked.

He coughed, spit hitting the floor. "Fuck if I know, you've probably killed them all by now."

I tightened the zip tie until he winced.

"Where's the real operation? There's no way this is where you decided to set up headquarters."

He smiled through blood. "Oh! You think I'm in charge? I'm just logistics, buddy."

"Then give us a name."

His brows drew together.

"Surprised he isn't with you."

Kane and I exchanged a look. We didn't have time to do this here.

"Bring him," I told Kane.

Kane grabbed the back of his collar and dragged him out like the garbage he was.

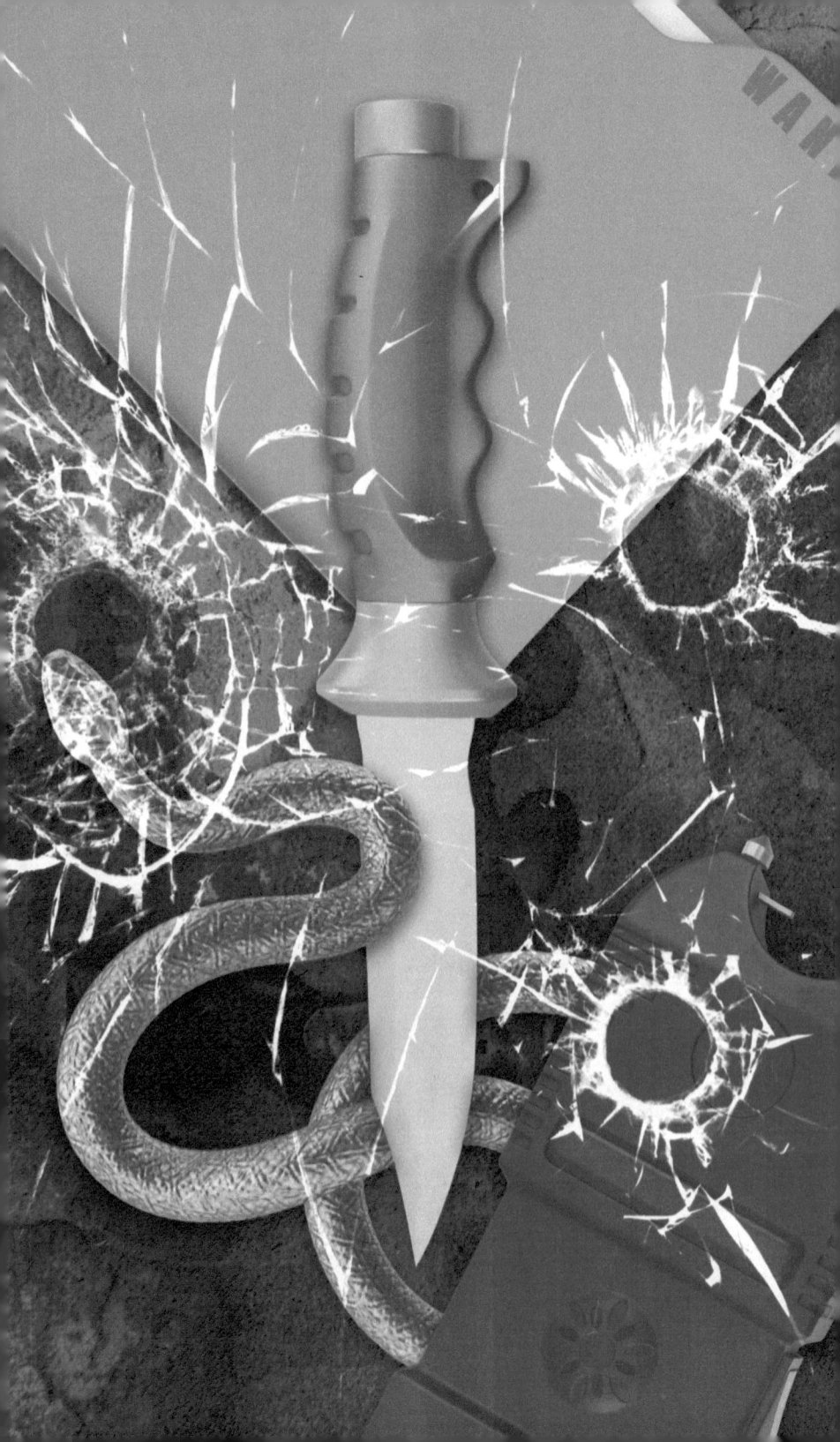

CHAPTER FORTY-SIX

SHILOH

The smoke stung, even through the gas mask. I moved like a shadow behind Nate, gun up, heart pounding out a rhythm that didn't match my feet. Not fear. Not panic. Just adrenaline.

Get in. Get the girls. Get out alive. The warehouse was a maze of crates, busted mattresses, and rot. Dim lights flickered overhead like the power itself couldn't stand what was happening inside. Nate peeled left, I went right, following the sound of muffled cries. Two girls were huddling behind an upturned mattress, trembling so hard I could hear their teeth click. I pulled my mask up and crouched low.

"Hey, I'm here to help," I whispered. "I need you to run, straight ahead, through the door with the light over it. There's a van outside. A girl named Lottie is waiting. She's safe, you'll be safe."

One nodded, the other started crying. I grabbed her hand, pulling her to stand with me and nudged them toward the door. "Go. Now."

I turned and ventured further into the building as they ran for the exit. I found more in the next bay. Six of them, some barely older than when I was taken. Some fought me, some clung to me. Some didn't even speak. But one by one, I got them out. One after another, ushering them toward the loading dock. Lottie's voice echoed from outside, calm and firm. The van was filling fast.

Nate met me halfway through the last row of beds. "Kane found three more. He's sending them out."

I nodded. "I'm heading upstairs to check the loft."

He hesitated. "You sure?"

"I haven't found Abigail. I need to know she's not here."

That was all it took. He nodded. "I'll finish this last row and then I'll be right behind you."

The stairs groaned under my boots as I climbed to the second floor. The air was clearer, less smoke than the first level, but it was still thick with the smell of sweat and the sharp tang of gasoline. I covered my mouth with my sleeve, pushing through the maze of boxes. The rooms up here were smaller. Offices, maybe, before they were turned into cages. I checked three. Nothing. Then the fourth. A flash of pink caught my eye —pastel hair, bright against the grimy walls. A girl sat with her back to the wall, legs curled protectively around a smaller figure. She didn't look much younger than me.

"Abigail," I breathed.

She looked up at the sound of my voice, tears streaming from her big blue eyes.

"I remember you." Her bottom lip trembled as she spoke, the sight of her cracking my heart wide open.

I dropped to my knees, pulling my mask fully off my face. "Hi, sweetheart. We're gonna get you out of here, okay?"

The pink-haired girl stood, instantly on guard. I realized she must have been around the same age as me. How long had she been here?

"She knows you?" she asked me.

"She's my friend," Abigail whispered. "She saved me before."

The older girl nodded once, tight and defensive, still eyeing me like I might sweep them both away to something worse. I grabbed Abigail's hand. "Let's get out of here."

She nodded and jumped into my arms; her small hands clutched together around my neck. The pink-haired girl stuck close behind us as we stepped into the hallway. The smoke had mostly cleared, but the dim lighting of the loft was difficult to navigate. I kept putting one foot in front of the other, my arms wrapped tight around Abigail. That's when I heard it. Boots pounding across the floor toward us, the sound was so loud it felt like it shook the floor beneath my feet. That wasn't Nate. He wouldn't barrel in, not at the risk of frightening the girls more.

"DOWN!" I yelled, shoving Abigail into the girl behind her and turning just in time to see the muzzle of a gun flash in front of me. Pain exploded across my shoulder. Once, twice. Both bullets penetrating the skin just above my vest and leaving a searing path through my skin.

The shock registered after the pain did. The hallway tilted sideways as I hit the ground with a thud. I heard the girls scream as I tried to sit back up, trying to focus through the burn long enough to reach for my gun. The man stepped forward, raising the gun again, but before he could fire, a shot rang out behind him and his body dropped in front of me, a lifeless heap in a fast-forming puddle of blood just inches from where I had landed.

Nate tore through the smoke, gun still raised.

"No no no—Shiloh—" He shoved the gun back into his waistband, his hands frantically running across the top of my vest, trying to find the wound in the dark.

"Fuck. Fuck. I'm sorry, Shy. I'm sorry. I'll fix it."

His hands shook as he tried to stop the bleeding, dragging me up against his chest, he began to rock back and forth.

"CREED! KANE!" he screamed, his voice breaking. "SOMEONE HELP! Please..."

CHAPTER FORTY-SEVEN

CREED

"CREED! KANE!"
"SOMEONE HELP!"

Nate's voice tore through the warehouse like a bullet. Time stopped and sped up all at once, the air around us thickening in an instant. Something was very, very wrong. Kane's head snapped toward the loft where Nate's voice had come from, and we both took off in a dead sprint for the stairs, Kane dragging the man from the office behind us. I hit the stairs at full speed, stomping up them as fast as my feet would carry me. I could feel the way the panic was making my chest tighten beneath my vest, desperation sinking its claws in as we got closer to the sound of Nate's cries.

The smoke had thinned just enough to see Nate on the ground, cradling Shiloh in his arms, her arm slick with blood. Two girls stood behind them—one I didn't recognize and Abigail, pale and shaking as she stared at Shiloh on the ground. I dropped beside her, fingers already searching the wounds while Kane rolled the man on the ground over with his boot, checking his pulse and nodding at me. There were two bullet holes. Through—and through. Upper shoulder, nothing fatal. We got lucky. Her eyes fluttered.

"Okay baby, you're okay. We're gonna get you out of here." I smoothed the hair back from her face, her blood slick on my hands and coating the hair I had touched. The sight of it made me wince.

"I'm okay," she said.

"No, you're not," Nate snapped. I noticed the shake of his hands, the tears that streamed steadily down his face. This was too much for him.

"Get her out, Nate." I told him, panic hot in my throat. He hesitated.

"Nate, look at me." His eyes met mine, wide and panicked. "I need you to get Shiloh out of here, so she's safe." He finally nodded; jaw clenched tight like steel. He lifted her off the ground, cradling her like she was glass, and took off toward the exit, Kane motioned for the girls to follow after him.

I pressed the heels of my hands into my eyes. It was taking every ounce of control I had not to chase after her, to hold her in my arms and make sure she was okay. But we had to finish the job. No one was safe, not until this was all truly over. Kane dragged the man back down the stairs, zip tying him to a pipe while we moved back toward the office to gather anything we could use. Laptop, papers, all of it was stuffed into a duffle bag and slung over my shoulder.

We took out the horde, but there was still someone missing. Whoever had started this, whoever was in charge, they were nowhere to be found. The bodies littering the floor of the warehouse were all replaceable. Vile men were a dime a dozen, and if we didn't find the head of the snake soon, he would just rebuild again. A clock was ticking down in the back of my mind. We were running out of time. I shoved the rest of the papers from the desk drawer into the duffle bag and zipped it shut.

"Clear," I yelled to Kane. "Let's go, Shiloh needs a doctor right fucking now."

The smell hit me as I exited the room. Volatile and acrid, with an almost sickly-sweet tinge to it. A heady, rich oily scent clung to my nose, hitting the back of my throat with a bite so strong it made my head spin. I looked up, noticing for the first time the wires that snaked through the rafters. Motion triggers. A tripwire. Homemade explosives stitched into the beams. The building was rigged. Sometime between us scanning the place, and the smoke bombs we tossed that obstructed our view, they had planted enough gas tanks in the rafters to blow the warehouse out of existence.

I barreled toward Kane where he stood in the center of the room.

"MOVE!" I shouted, wrapping my arms around his waist and shoving him as hard as I could toward the exit. He looked down at me, confusion written on his face, and as he took his mask off, he must have smelled it too.

"Kane GO. It's going to—"

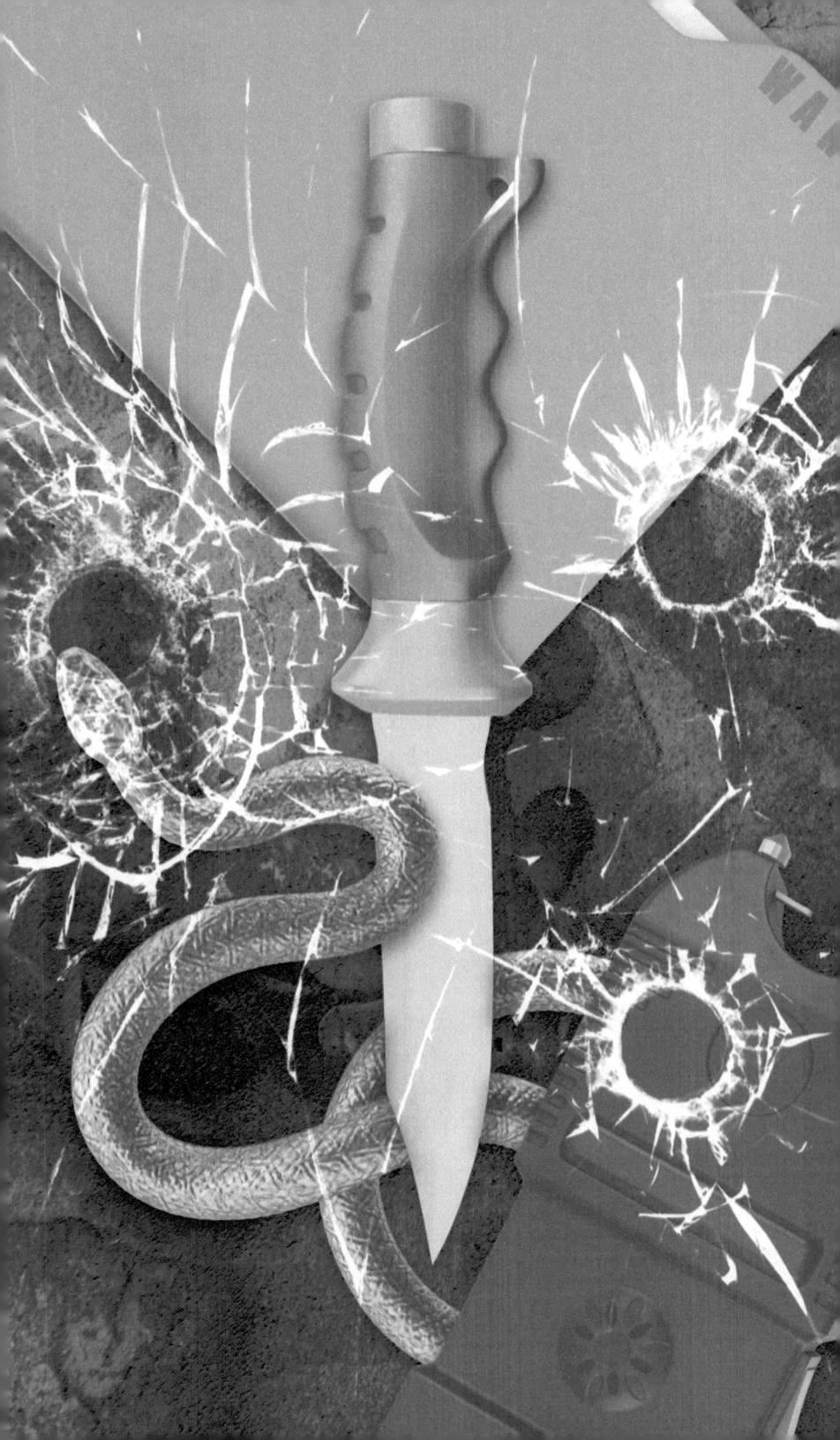

CHAPTER FORTY-EIGHT

SHILOH

The clear night air hit me in the face as Nate bounded through the exit, my body jostling in his arms. I could hear Lottie talking to the girls by the van, coaxing them all into their seats as gently as she could. We had actually done it. I looked up at Nate, searching for the right words to bring him back from whatever place he was currently in, but anything I could have said died on my tongue in the next instant. The world around us flashed white—then orange.

FWOOM.

A concussive blast lifted us off the ground. Nate shielded my head as we rolled, and debris rained down around us. Heat rolled over my body like a tidal wave, scorching the exposed skin as my mind fought to process what was happening. All I could see were the flashes of light that flickered across the sky from where I laid on my back. Someone cried, but I couldn't tell if the sobs were coming from me or Nate. His chest pressed against mine, pressing me into the rough gravel of the parking lot. I struggled in Nate's grasp, managing to lift my head just in time to see the thing that will haunt my dreams for the rest of my life. The warehouse roof ballooned before collapsing in on itself altogether. The lights around us blurred into streaks of red and orange, pulsing against the fog in my vision.

Every heartbeat came slower. Louder. My shoulder felt like it was on fire, and then it was just... numb. I think sometimes you experience something so awful, so life altering, that your brain won't let you acknowledge it in that moment. I stared at the cloud of smoke pouring out of the front entrance, but there was a solid wall in my mind when I tried to make sense of it. There was fire, there were tears streaming down my face, but I couldn't manage to accept the worst part of it all.

Nate's arms were tight around me, and I could tell he was yelling by the way his chest vibrated against me. But I couldn't hear him. The blood pounding in my ears drowned everything else out.

I twisted in his arms, desperate to see Creed running toward me. "Where's—"

"Don't," Nate rasped. "Don't move, Shiloh."

They hadn't come out. There were no footfalls, no silhouettes racing toward us, away from the flames.

Somewhere in my chest, I felt something crack. A jagged feeling that tore through my body, ripping at the bone and muscle as it made its way to my heart. Creed and Kane were still inside. The fire roared as if it were taunting me.

Nate tipped his head back and screamed like a wolf howling at the moon. "I can't do this alone!"

The fog in my brain was increasing, everything around me blurring at the edges like I was sinking into murky water. I was slipping.

"Stay awake, Shiloh," Nate cried over me, his green eyes locked on my face as he sobbed. "Please. Please don't leave me too."

I tried. I really did. And then the world went black.

CHAPTER FORTY-NINE

SHILOH

I woke up choking on my own breath. Bright, sterile lights blinded me from above my bed while somewhere in the room, a steady beeping noise grew increasingly louder.

I tried to sit up, feeling the rustle of a thin hospital gown against my thighs. Hospital. I'm in the hospital. Images of the warehouse rapid fired through my mind.

I lurched forward, desperate to find Creed, but a hand on my arm stopped me.

"Hey—whoa."

Lottie.

She sat in the chair beside my bed, her legs curled up, a hoodie swamping her frame. "You scared the hell out of me, you bitch," she said, her voice thick. "Seriously, you flatlined for, like, three seconds."

I tried to sit up, slower this time, but each vertebra in my spine felt like a rusted hinge.

"How long?" I managed. My throat was raw, and the words were little more than a croak.

"Almost sixteen hours since surgery," she said. "You were shot twice, and you had some shrapnel in your leg from the explosion. They cut out the metal, sewed you shut, and left you with a couple gnarly souvenir scars. You'll terrify TSA." I tried to smile, but I could feel on my face that it came out crooked.

"Everyone... the girls?"

"All safe." A flicker of relief softened her mouth. "Kane has a legit bunker ready—security, beds, trauma counselors. I got them dropped off and settled in. Abigail's already asking when she can see you."

The weight on my chest eased—until another name slammed into the forefront of my mind. "Creed? Kane?"

Lottie's gaze slid to the floor. "That's...complicated."

Panic crackled across my chest. "Lottie—"

"Listen," she sat up straight, hands lifting in surrender, "Your dad and half of Sunbridge PD are outside playing PR whack-a-mole. The cops pulled footage from Sinner's. Creed's face is on their corkboard under 'armed and extremely danger-ous.' Your dad's moving heaven and probably a few felonies to make sure they don't storm this room looking for The Red King."

I tried to push up, but pain flared in my shoulder. "So, he's—"

"I don't know." Her voice dipped. "Kane either. The EMT's only brought you and Nate. The warehouse was still burning when the firefighters called off the search."

Nate. I pictured him screaming for Creed, blood on his hands and his eyes so full of terror. "Where is he?"

"Interrogation—involuntary ," she added quickly, "trying to convince your dad that you two aren't the problem, but until someone sees those two breathing..." She let the sentence die.

The world seemed to tilt on its axis, and for a moment, I wasn't in the hospital bed anymore. I was under the collapsing roof of the warehouse. Smelling the gasoline, hearing the metal screech. I'd promised Creed we would make it out together. And then the world exploded around him.

It seemed like every time we took a step forward, something shoved us five steps back. We saved the girls. That was the goal. But in doing so, I had lost something I never thought I would get the chance to have to begin with.

Creed rolled into my life like a hurricane, flooding everything in his path, and when the storm faded, a new version of me stood in its wake. A stronger version of the girl I was in The Manor. I owed a part of that to him, and I couldn't stomach the thought that I would never get to look into those crystal blue eyes and tell him that he helped heal parts of me that I'd thought were irreparable.

"He can't be gone, Lottie. He just can't. Tell me he's okay," I begged, I choked down logic and reason and I begged her to lie to me.

"Oh, babe," she whispered back.

My vision began to tunnel, the edges of the room around me fading to black as the machine next to me picked up the pace with its beeping.

A nurse entered the room, scanning the machine before laying a soft hand over mine. "Vitals are normal honey, it's probably a pain spike which is to be expected. Deep breaths."

I obeyed until my pulse slowed, realizing too late that the tube she was fiddling with was connected to my arm, and she had just stuck a syringe into it.

"Just a little morphine," she added. The drug pulled me backward feet first until everything in front of me was one big blur. Lottie squeezed my hand reassuringly.

"Rest," she whispered. "If anyone can crawl out of hell, it's those two."

I wanted to fight the morphine. To rip off all the tubes and wires connected to me and storm through the hospital demanding answers. But the darkness felt like water, and I was so tired of swimming.

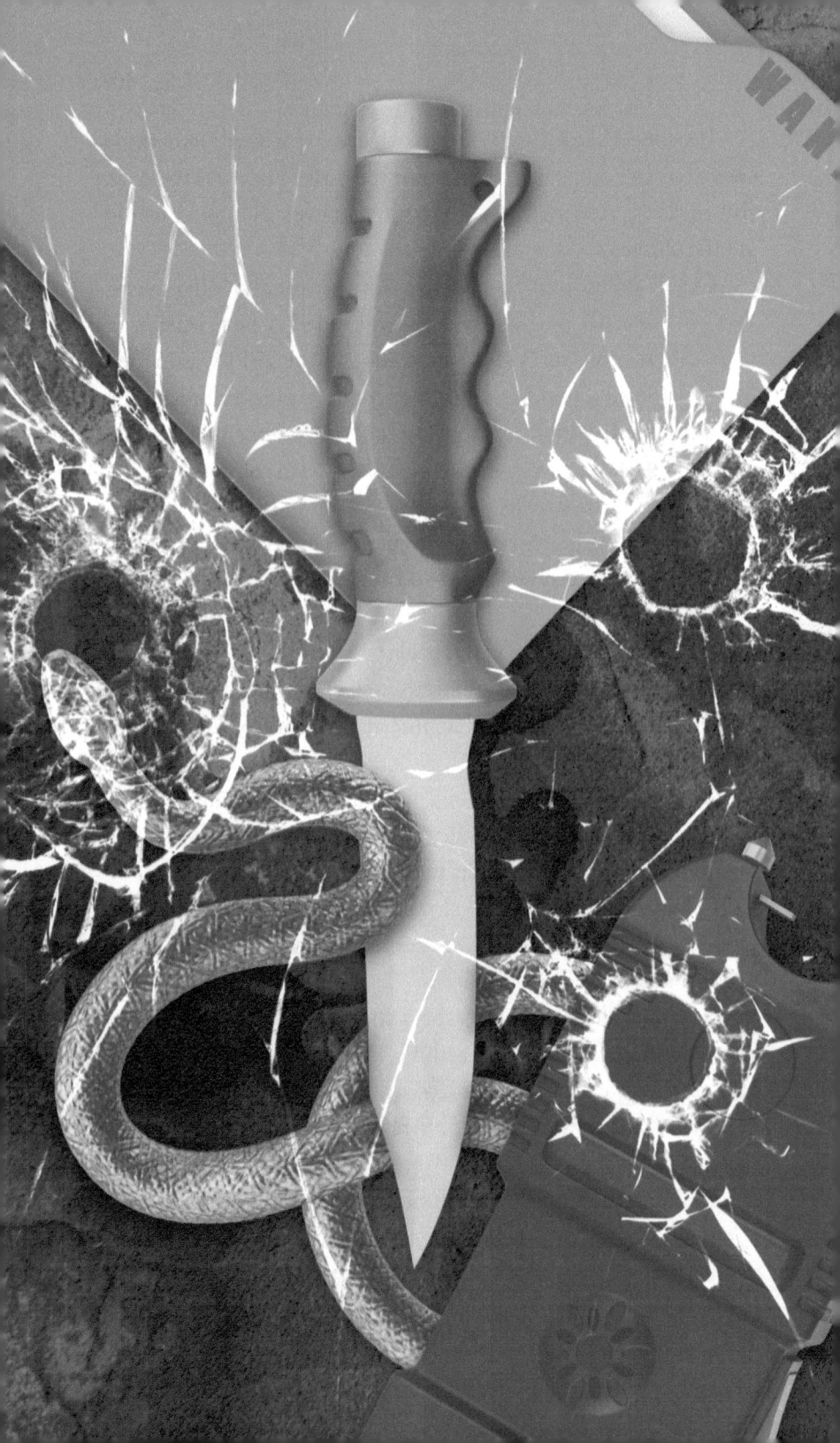

CHAPTER FIFTY

SHILOH

By the time the morphine-haze had thinned, my room had turned into a battle bunker. Kane occupied the chair by the window, boot propped on the sill like he owned the place. Nate had sprawled across the visitor's couch with three IV hooks he'd cannibalized into something vaguely knife looking because according to him, 'boredom is deadly.'

Creed refused to sit anywhere but next to me or the foot of my bed. Every few minutes, his gaze would stray to the door like he was expecting a SWAT raid to take place any time. He had every right to worry about that. Voices rose outside, my dad's filtering through the door—firm and clipped, before he stepped inside, my mother right behind him. He entered in rumpled khakis with bags under his eyes. He looked as exhausted as I felt. Mom ran over to my side, her scrubs crinkling as she bent down to hug me, kissing the top of my head. "How are you feeling, honey?"

"I'm okay. The food here sucks though," I joked, trying to lighten the mood and ease the lines around her eyes.

"I'll see if I can't get something better sent up for you. I know you guys have a lot going on in here, but I got transferred to your floor, so I'll be in and out, okay?"

"Okay." I smiled as she cupped my cheek, tears shining in her eyes as she stepped back to let my dad scoot in closer.

"Kiddo," he said, bending over me to wrap me in a gentle hug. "Wish I had better news."

His gaze slid to Creed and lingered. "I can keep the task-force off your back tonight, maybe 'til morning. After that, the DA's filing subpoenas. They'll call every witness. Even you, Shy."

Cold fear trickled down my spine. Creed nodded but stayed silent.

"You shouldn't even be in here," Dad added, his voice low. "But I owed you a few minutes." He squeezed my good shoulder gently, then straightened. "Whatever is going on here, Shy, I trust you. I trust your judgement..." His eyes slid to Creed again then back to me. "I've got your back. We have maybe a few hours at most before people start coming in that I can't keep out, so make it count." The door shut, plunging the room into a heavy silence.

Nate whistled. "Well, that sucks. Hard."

Creed was focused on me. His eyes locked onto mine, like they might be telling him something my mouth wasn't, and he didn't want to miss it.

"I'll lie on the stand," I said. "Say I don't remember what happened."

"They'll tear you apart in court," Kane said. "You're on every security camera between your house and Sinner's. If they call you in, there's no hiding the truth."

Nate shrugged. "Unless, of course, you had the legal right to just shut right up." He wiggled his eyebrows at me. "You know, like a wife would."

The room fell dead silent. My heart raced as I considered that. That was how it worked right? They couldn't force spouses to testify against each other. Heat bloomed in the center of my chest at the thought of marrying Creed. Not in a bad way, not coated in fear or apprehension, just a solid warmth that trickled through my bloodstream. I actually wanted it.

I looked at Creed, the corner of my mouth kicking up in a smile. He straightened, turning his body to face me with a serious look on his face.

"Shiloh." His voice was low. "We don't have to do that."

"What if I want to?" I countered.

"That's not just a loophole, it's not just about testifying. It's...us. Tied together. Permanently."

I met his eyes. "And?"

His jaw flexed tight. He was fighting it. The urge to want it too much.

"You want that?" His voice was so quiet, softer and more uncertain than I had ever heard him. "To be mine like that?"

"I already am," I whispered. And it was the truth.

Through all the shit I had been dragged through in my life, Creed had been like a beacon of light. A solid presence beside me while I faced whatever came next.

He breathed hard through his nose, his hand coming up to brush the hair back off my face. "I'm not great at this, you know that," he said. "I'm not a very good man. I can promise you I will always try to be the best for you, but you don't have to do this for me to keep that promise."

I pushed myself up, ignoring the ache. "You once told me that I wasn't dirty. That you saw me, all of me. So don't back down now."

He hesitated, and then like gravity had snapped its hold, Creed leaned in, one hand gripping the rail beside me, the other brushing along my jaw.

"I love you." His voice broke on the last word, like he could finally breathe again now that he'd said it. "Jesus, Shiloh, I love you so much its fucking dangerous."

The air crackled around us. Kane and Nate had vanished from my line of vision. There was just Creed and I, and he loved me. That was all.

I hadn't realized I was crying until his thumb brushed a tear from under my eye.

"I love you, too." It was raw and honest, and heartbreaking in the most beautiful way. A confession and a vow, all at once. Creed released a heavy breath, leaning in to kiss me with a smile on his face.

"Oh, thank fuck," he mumbled just before his lips met mine. There was a reverence in the kiss, a promise between the two of us. We were doing this. Nothing had ever felt more right.

"So, this," Kane gestured between us as we separated, "is this happening? You're getting married. As in legally?"

I nodded. He blinked at us a few times before tilting his head back toward the ceiling and sighing.

"Fuck it. Okay. Let's go. I guess I'm going to go kidnap a pastor."

Nate grinned from his spot on the couch, sticking his hand in the air like a kid in class. "Actually, as luck would have it— I'm ordained." Three pairs of eyes whipped to him.

"Come again?" Creed asked.

Nate just shrugged. "So, I had these two guinea pigs in high school, Susan and Lasagna Jones. I wanted them to be married, but you know, legitimately. So, I didn't half-ass it."

Kane stared at him. "You're telling me your ability to perform legally binding ceremonies stems from a guinea pig wedding?"

"That's exactly what I'm telling you," Nate said casually.

All I could do was laugh. Even with the sting in my shoulder, it felt good. Lighter than anything had felt in weeks. Kane whipped out his phone, facetiming Aaron and handing it to me.

"You're doing *what?*"

I laughed at the shocked look on his face. "It's a good plan, but it's also something we want. Can you get here soon?" I asked.

Aaron sighed. "I wish, Shy. I'm three hours away meeting with some undercover guys from Bramwell, I'm hoping one of them might give us a lead."

"Okay. Well, I'll have Lottie record it for you."

"Enjoy it, Shiloh. You deserve all the good things."

I smiled at him and hung up, handing the phone back to Kane who immediately started barking orders at Creed and Nate. "The hospital chapel is on the second floor. Nate, get paperwork. I'll find rings or steal them off a nurse. Creed—clean yourself up."

Nate winked at me as he hustled past. The room quickly turned into a bustling mess as they all skated around, securing the things we needed to get this done. I searched my mind for doubts but found none. I was sure. The world was about to try to tear us apart, and we were going to fight like hell. Starting with a wedding, in a hospital, officiated by a psychopath with a guinea pig complex. And somehow, it still felt like the most *us* thing in the world.

CHAPTER FIFTY-ONE

SHILOH

They wheeled me into the hospital chapel like it was a combat op. Kane pushed me into the room, parking my chair in front of the altar before taking his place next to Creed. Nate was already there, sunglasses on, holding a tiny bible he'd stolen from the drawer in my room. A bouquet of stolen cafeteria flowers sat in a coffee mug on the altar. The whole place smelled of antiseptic and holy water. Incredibly romantic.

My mother stood near the back, looking like someone had hit her with a frying pan. My dad next to her was rigid, jaw tight, arms crossed, clearly deciding whether he wanted to walk me down the aisle or arrest someone. Lottie flounced in five minutes late wearing hospital scrubs tied into a crop top, hair wild, and holding a half-empty red bull. "Did I miss the vows? Wait—is this actually happening?"

"It's happening," I told her with a small smile as Creed helped me out of the wheelchair and steadied me on my feet. "We're doing this."

"Oh my god. You got shot and decided to elope. What a bad bitch. I love that for us," she squealed.

Creed shook his head at her. He had cleaned up, but the marks from last night were still all over him. There were bruises blooming on his neck, and his knuckles were raw. He'd found a black long-sleeve shirt somewhere and brushed most of the dirt from his pants. He stood beside me now, one hand resting gently on my hip, the other finding mine. When I looked up, his eyes were already locked on mine. We hadn't even started yet, but the gravity of the feelings between us were enough to tilt the whole chapel sideways.

"Alright, degenerates," Nate called, flipping through the bible like it had footnotes for quickie weddings. "We're gathered here today to bind this unholy union in front of God, multiple security cameras, and two slightly confused but ultimately supportive parents."

My mom blinked. My dad muttered *"Jesus Christ"* under his breath.

"I'm licensed in all fifty states and one international waters loophole," Nate went on. "So, unless someone has a good damn reason to object—"

"I swear to God, Nathaniel—" Kane hissed from the corner.

"I'll keep it legal." Nate winked.

Creed's thumb brushed against mine. I turned slightly toward him, heartbeat thudding under the weight of what we were doing here. Nate nodded.

"Kingston Creed, do you take this woman—this semi-feral, mildly unhinged, terrifyingly hot assassin-in-the-making to be your lawfully-wedded wife?"

Creed's voice was steady. "I do."

"And do you promise to protect her, fight beside her, teach her how to stab people cleaner—"

Creed's mouth twitched. "I do."

Nate turned to me, his eyes mischievous but soft. "Shiloh Hale. Do you take this man—this brooding, morally bankrupt, violently handsome man—to be your lawfully-wedded husband?"

"I do." The words came out stronger than I expected. Certain. Like I'd known them all along.

"Do you promise to keep him from appearing on any other FBI most wanted lists, to cut him when he misbehaves, and to call him a dumbass to his face when necessary?"

"I do."

Creed squeezed my hand tight, a grin ghosting across his lips. Kane stepped up with the 'rings' which were actually two pieces of copper wire he'd fashioned into circles. "Best I could do," he muttered. "Now take them before I cry."

I slipped the makeshift ring on Creed's finger. His hands trembled slightly as he did the same to mine. Nate took a step back, clearing his throat. "Then by the power vested in me by getordainedfast.org, and the guinea pig gods of yore... I now pronounce you husband and wife—"

Creed didn't wait for Nate to tell him to "kiss the bride." He pulled me close, one hand on my waist, the other sliding up to cradle my jaw, and kissed me like he had the rest of our lives to make up for lost time. The room faded. The pain in my shoulder disappeared. All I could feel was him. Solid, certain, and mine.

Applause broke out somewhere and Lottie whooped loud enough to be heard on the next floor. My dad cleared his throat very loudly. Creed finally pulled back, resting his forehead against mine. "You okay?"

"I'm married," I whispered, dazed and breathless, but so incredibly fucking happy.

"Yes, you are," he said, his smile so soft and raw that I craved his lips against mine again just so I could taste it.

Kane handed us our paperwork, or the forged equivalent of it and signed the bottom as our witness. Nate took a selfie with the entire group before getting choked up and muttering something about how he's "always been an emotional officiant."

"So, I call dibs on maid of honor when you two have a real ceremony that isn't surrounded by IVs and criminal charges, okay?"

"Deal." I laughed. My parents walked over to hug me, confusion still blanketing both of their faces.

My father leaned in close to whisper in my ear. "I'm not entirely sure what in the hell is going on here, and we will be discussing it later, but you look happy, Shiloh. So, I'm happy for you."

"Thank you, Daddy."

He turned to Creed, extending his hand to shake. "If you ever hurt her, I will hurt you. Is that clear?"

"That's if you get to him before we do," Kane added.

"Understood, sir." Creed nodded, shaking my dad's hand firmly. We all made our way out of the chapel, Creed walking me back to the room while the rest of the group scattered to find food that didn't come on a brown plastic tray.

"Is this how you pictured your wedding day?" I asked him, leaning into his shoulder as he laid next to me in the hospital bed.

"Before you, I never pictured it at all. Someday, I will give you the most obnoxious wedding money can buy. But for today? This was better than anything I could have dreamed up, Red."

I felt the same. It was messy, rushed, hilariously thrown together. But somehow, in the wreckage of our lives, we'd found each other and stolen this moment. This vow. This righteous act of defiance.

They would come for us, but we would be ready.

Together.

CHAPTER FIFTY-TWO

SHILOH

The hospital released me begrudgingly, with a sling, a bottle of pills, and a warning about 'avoiding strenuous activity.' Creed signed my discharge papers proudly, while Kane cleared the hallway and Nate pushed my wheelchair. We caravaned straight to my house—Creed, Lottie and I in my mom's SUV, the guys following in Kane's jeep. Creed's hand found mine over the center console, his thumb running soothing circles over my hand, while his eyes tracked every street camera like a hawk. Dad had gone to the precinct when Mom was called in for questioning.

Apparently, having a serial killer living under your roof was frowned upon, even if they had no clue who he was until now. We had a small window to get to my house, get enough clothes to tide me over, and get to the guys' apartment outside of town to hunker down and make a plan. We slipped through the front door, the locks already busted from multiple raids during my stay. Kane posted at the living room window, a rifle slung low over his shoulder, and Nate prowled around the foyer talking to himself about 'bad vibes and worse wallpaper.' Creed didn't speak, he just took the corner by the patio doors, eyes on the backyard, his whole body coiled tight like a wire.

Lottie nudged me toward the stairs. "Come on, Mrs. Red King. Let's pack your apocalypse wardrobe."

The climb hurt, every step tugging at stitches in my leg, but Lottie filled the silence with off-key singing until we reached my room. It looked smaller than I remembered, as if the life I'd lived here no longer fit. Maybe it didn't.

She rummaged through my closet, grabbing an empty duffle and tossing it on the bed.

"Essentials, right? Guns, panties, sweatpants."

I shook my head at her as she got to work, riffling through drawers and tossing stacks of hoodies, sweatpants, sports bras, and hair care products into the bag. I moved to my jewelry box, pulling out the king card I had found on my bedroom floor the day I found out who Creed was, and slipped it into the inner pocket of the bag. A keepsake. Morbid, maybe, but mine.

"So," Lottie started, "married a wanted man, survived a couple bullets, staged a wedding in a hospital gown. How's the honeymoon glow?"

"It's more of a blood spray," I said, slipping a pair of slippers into the side pocket. "But I'm happy."

The word felt strange on my tongue, like speaking it out loud might jinx everything. Lottie's grin softened.

"Good. You deserve reckless, chaotic happiness." She paused, picked up a framed photo of me and my parents on my sixth birthday. Before The Manor came and tore everything apart.

"Think they're going to freak when you finally tell them everything?"

"My dad is probably drafting a prenup as we speak, but they were surprisingly...supportive of the whole thing. I think they trust me enough to get the facts later."

She nodded. Lottie had known my parents since we were in preschool, they weren't the kind to steam roll me into doing what they thought was best. Even when they probably thought I had lost my mind. We stuffed toiletries into the bag, zipping it closed before Lottie snagged a glitter pen from her purse and scribbled MRS. RK in huge letters on the tag. She smiled at her handy work, hefting the bag over her shoulder and looking at me. Thunder boomed outside the window as rain began falling against the glass panes.

"Ready to bail on suburbia?" she asked.

"More than ready."

We headed downstairs, the guys all looking up in tandem, three pairs of eyes assessing everything from the bruises on my arms to the size of the duffle bag on Lottie's shoulder. Creed's lips twitched at the sight of the tag as he grabbed the duffle from Lottie and helped me down the last step.

"Truck's clear," Kane said. "It's about fifteen minutes from here to the apartment. Got everything you need?"

"Yeah, I think I'm good to go." I had plenty of clothes for however long our hideout would be. Creed's hand brushed along my arm. "You good?"

"Yeah." I breathed in the smell of the house. It had been so foreign when I finally came back from The Manor, but over the last year it had started to smell like home. I was going to miss it more than I thought I would.

"Let's roll out," Kane said. We all moved toward the foyer, but we never made it to the door.

CHAPTER FIFTY-THREE

CREED

I'd been staring out of Shiloh's living room window for fourteen minutes when the world tilted. Rain started, heavy and fast. The perfect cover for sirens if the cops were closing in. Kane had drifted into the kitchen, checking the back door locks for the third time while Nate stood in the foyer flicking a butterfly knife around in his hands like a nervous metronome. Shiloh and Lottie reached the bottom stair, and I turned, just in time to catch the tired set of her shoulders before she straightened up and plastered on a smile. I moved over to her and took the bag from Lottie, easing Shiloh off the last step.

We were heading for the front door as a group when a click echoed from the rear of the house. Kane's head snapped toward the hallway where the utility room sat.

"Back latch," he hissed. Shiloh tensed as Nate gently guided her behind him, bracing his feet wide against whatever was coming down that hall. Kane and I moved in tandem, gliding toward the living room on silent feet, the barrel of Kane's gun leading the way. A tall figure emerged from the hall, rain dripping off a long coat. Every muscle in my body coiled as he moved into the light, stopping when he noticed he wasn't alone. And there he was. Uncle Miles standing in a puddle of water.

"If you've got a good reason for being here, you better say it now," Kane barked, clicking the safety off on his gun.

The thing we hadn't mentioned to Shiloh yet was that we'd been digging into Miles. The man was in debt up to his eyeballs, and according to Kane's contact at the bar, he spent the majority of his time at Sinner's in the back room with the same kind of men we spent our time looking for. There were too many overlaps, too many coincidences. Something was off with Uncle Miles.

Miles raised his hands. "Relax, I was just coming to say goodbye to Shiloh." He peered around me, looking for her where she stood behind Nate.

"Not happening today. Go back out the way you came," I told him evenly.

His face was already doing that weird, red mottling thing it did when he was angry. "I want to see my niece, and you won't stop me."

"Your niece?" I laughed as I circled around behind him, drawing his focus away from my girl. "You mean my wife?" Miles's expression curdled. Before he could answer, the living room TV behind me flicked from muted weather reports to breaking news. My own face filled the screen, a grainy still from Sinner's. The banner below my headshot read:

"WANTED SERIAL KILLER—'THE RED KING' IDENTIFIED."

Miles saw it over my shoulder, the color draining from his face at a comical rate as he sputtered, "You."

"The devil himself." Nate sing-songed from the foyer.

I took two steps into his personal space and leaned in close. "Boo."

He stumbled back, his legs hitting the back of the couch and causing him to fall onto the cushions. Kane stepped up behind him, pressing down firmly on his shoulders with both hands when Miles tried to stand back up.

"While you're here, let's have a chat," he said, sliding his hands into the inner pockets of Miles's coat and retrieving a small pistol. Thunder rolled over head like a warning.

"What do you know about who's running the new manor?" I asked him casually. There was no way he didn't know something. Even if his hands weren't directly in it, he spent too much time around the clientele to not have some idea of who was behind all of it.

Miles pressed his lips into a thin line. "I have no idea what you're talking about."

I crouched, pulling my knife from my boot and placing it on the armrest next to him. "Wrong."

He swallowed hard. "You don't scare me, Creed," he sneered my name like it was a curse. Maybe it was.

"Good. Fear is inefficient." I leaned closer. "Truth, though? Truth can save a lot of time and pain for you."

Nate perched on the back of the couch, knife still twirling around in his hands. "Let him explain the gambling debts first."

Miles flinched. Shiloh stepped beside me, her eyes trained on Miles as he squirmed under the scrutiny.

"Gambling?" she asked.

Miles's gaze skittered. "I-I had some rough years."

"Try again," I gritted out. I had a hunch, but if I was right, he was going to be the one to look her in the eyes and say it.

He sucked in a shaky breath. "I owe some—" Kane smacked the back of his head. "Okay! A lot. I owe a lot. Sinner's... they have back-room games. High stakes. I thought—I thought I could win big."

Shiloh crossed her arms. "So, you bet against the house and lost. How much?"

"Half a million," he mumbled.

Silence cannonballed through the room. I don't think Shiloh even took a full breath.

"Who fronts that kind of credit?" Nate asked.

Miles hesitated. "People—people who traffic in more than chips." He swore into his hand, dragging it over his jaw.

Shiloh's voice was sharp as a blade. "And when the debt came due, and you couldn't pay up?"

He wouldn't meet her eyes. His leg was bouncing wildly as he sat. "They offered... an alternative."

Realization crawled over her features. Horror lighting her eyes like a slow sick fog. "Alternative like... me?"

Miles crumbled, a desperate sound breaking free from his chest. "They promised you'd be cared for! They promised—"

A sound ripped from Shiloh's throat, somewhere between a sob and a snarl. "YOU! You took me to the park that day. You sold me because you couldn't pay your poker debt?" Lightning flashed, thunder cracking so loud the windows rattled. It still didn't drown out the sound of her heart breaking.

We had considered it, theorized. But now it was out there, and there was no taking it back. Her own family, flesh and blood, had sold her soul. Shiloh swayed, and Lottie rushed over to her, wrapping her arm around her shoulder and ushering Shiloh to the other side of the room.

I straightened. "Names, Miles. Who's in charge over there?"

His shoulders sagged. "Man calls himself Bishop. Runs the high-limit games on Fridays. Same symbol on all the chips."

Kane's eyes flicked to me, a confirmation. He had been digging through everything he could find, and that name had rung a bell. We had a lead. I pulled a pair of cuffs from my belt, securing one to Miles's wrist, and the other to an insanely heavy coffee table in front of him.

"Wait, you can't—" he sputtered.

I leaned in close. "You're safer here than where you're headed if the Bishop finds you, and the only reason I'm not skinning you alive myself is because I'm short on time." I got close enough to his ear that only he could hear me. "But I will be back for you. Pray the cops find you before I do."

I turned, gathering Shiloh's bag from the door and opening my arm as she stepped into my side. Silent tears streaked down her cheeks, fury shaking her frame. I wanted to tear him apart, bit by bit until he laid in pieces at her feet, but we needed to move right now, or I wouldn't have the chance. Kane's phone buzzed and he answered, eyes flicking to us as he hung up.

"Patrol in-bound. Five minutes." He grabbed her duffle from me and nodded at her. "Time to disappear."

I turned my wife in my arms, wiping the tear streaks from her beautiful face. "You ready to finish this, Red?"

She wiped her face, rage settling into something sharper. "I am now."

CHAPTER FIFTY-FOUR

SHILOH

We slipped into the rain, leaving Miles behind to deal with the interrogation. The cops could have him, for now. I made it about halfway to the SUV idling in the driveway before I felt my knees start to shake. The familiar panic clawing its way through my body.

This whole time, it was Miles? The years I spent in The Manor ticked through my mind like a slideshow. The things I endured in that place while he smiled at my parents like he wasn't the reason I was there. The rain pelted my shoulders as they shook involuntarily. I closed my eyes, squeezing them shut while I forced air in and out of my mouth. This was not the time to fall apart. Creed's hand met the small of my back just as another hand grabbed my wrist. I opened my eyes to find Nate, his brows drawn together in concentration as he slid a rubber band off his wrist, and onto mine, nodding to himself once he had it in place. He straightened, holding out his own arm in front of me and displaying the dozen rubber bands that covered his wrist.

"Snap snap," he said, pulling one upwards before letting it snap back into place against his skin. "When you feel it coming, snap. It helps."

I gave the band a small tug, letting it thwack against my arm as I released it. It didn't hurt, not really, but it stung enough to pull my attention toward the sensation, rather than the panic I was feeling.

"Thank you, Nate," I whispered.

"Always got you," he said, giving me a salute before running for the shelter of the SUV.

Creed smiled down at me softly. "He might be better with the panic attacks than I am, if you ever want to talk to him about it," he said, ushering me into the back seat.

I nodded, reaching for the band on my wrist. Snap. Snap. Snap.

CHAPTER FIFTY-FIVE

CREED

We ditched Kane's SUV four miles from the high-rise, swapping to a nondescript sedan waiting under a streetlamp. Nate called it 'clean' which meant the plates likely belonged to a dead man. Kane drove under the speed limit, his eyes darting back and forth across the road as we slowly made our way home.

Lottie and Nate were turned toward each other in the back seat, bickering softly about whether Red Bull could be sufficiently used as intravenous therapy, while Shiloh laid across the middle bench with her head in my lap. The drugs were taking their time leaving her system, and the events of the last few days were settling in. She was living one nightmare after another. She perked up as we pulled into the underground garage of a pale brick building. It wasn't flashy on the outside.

Wrought iron balconies wrapped around the higher levels, a few bushes dotting the landscape. It looked plain, boring, safe. The rent, however, would make a hedge fund manager blink. We all trudged toward the elevator, nothing but the sound of our breathing filling the small space as we rose to the seventeenth floor.

The thing about this building was that we owned most of it. The seventeenth floor was ours, the fifteenth and sixteenth were both covered in security cameras and guarded by a few of Kane's old MMA buddies who did routine checks through all three floors. This was the safest place any of us could be.

The elevator doors opened, revealing walnut floors and three large metal doors. I nodded to the one at the end of the hall. "That's Nate," I said, sticking my key into the door in front of us. "Kane is at the other end; you and I are here."

Her brow lifted. "All three units?"

"We don't like neighbors."

Inside, soft track lights revealed the living room and kitchen. Matte-black cabinets, quartz counters, leather sectional and a wall of glass overlooking the river. Lottie dumped Shiloh's bag near the coffee table, wandering into the kitchen with Kane and Nate and pretending not to watch Shiloh's reaction.

"This is..." She walked in a slow circle through the living room, pausing at the massive window. "You never mentioned you were loaded."

"Ahh. We prefer to think of it as being 'funded.'"

She turned, one eyebrow arching. "Explain."

"We drain the accounts of the guys we take out. Kane gets into their phones, transfers the money, we launder it, invest it, and he makes sure it doesn't track back to us." I gestured toward the view. "Buildings like this keep the cash clean. The rest goes to tech, safe-houses, resources we need to get the jobs done."

"And the leftovers?"

"Donations. Three orgs, every year. Trafficking Recovery Network, Clean Horizon Rehab, and The Home Center. They work with homeless teens." I thumbed toward the study where the ledgers sat on my desk. "Paper trail is bulletproof. The IRS thinks we're saints."

Her lips pressed together, eyes softer now. "You steal from monsters to help kids like me."

"Yes," I replied, my throat tight.

Nate padded over, setting a black Amex on the side table next to her. "This one is yours. In case you need it for anything or just feel like having an online shopping spree," he said.

"A credit card? No, I don't—"

"Nonreturnable, I'm afraid. The only stipulation is that if you book a flight to Bora Bora, you have to take me with you. I only fly first class, by the way." He nodded once, like he was glad he had cleared that up, then moved back to the kitchen where Kane had started pulling things out of the fridge to cook.

I jerked my head toward the hallway. "Want to see our room, wife?" God, I loved being able to call her that. Was the wedding rushed? Sure. Was it a strategic move? Yes. But she was mine, I was hers, and the circumstances couldn't take that away.

My bedroom was less polished than the living space with a concrete ceiling and exposed brick accent wall. A king bed with black linens sat in front of two floor to ceiling windows.

"This place is more... you than I expected."

"You thought I slept in a coffin?"

"I figured maybe a pile of knives."

"That's next door. Kane hoards blades like a crow with shiny things."

My single nightstand held nothing but a lamp and a picture of Kane, Aaron, Nate and I at nineteen, grinning like idiots in front of a broken van.

Shiloh stepped in, moving straight to the photo and picking it up. "You look like babies." She laughed.

"That was right after our first target. We were kids. We had no idea what we were doing, just young and full of rage. No one else was stepping in, so we did."

She looked over her shoulder at me. "And that's when it started?"

I leaned against the wall, crossing my arms. "Sort of. I was seventeen when my parents died. A drunk driver clipped their car while they were headed out to dinner. I was supposed to be with them that night, but I decided last minute to stay with Kane instead."

Her expression shifted, a quiet understanding in her eyes.

"I spent a lot of time being angry. Aaron and Kane, their dad was the kind of man that taught them to be violent before they could spell it. We looked out for each other all through high school. Then came Nate. His story isn't mine to tell, but his dad... it's hard to stomach some of the things Nate's dad did."

Shiloh's face hardened. Her and I had been building something between us, but she had gotten close to Kane and Nate over the weeks too, and I recognized the way her jaw set as I talked. She felt as protective of them as I did.

"We realized if no one was coming to save us, maybe we could be the ones to save someone else. Not the way the world wanted, not clean and shiny. But we did it anyway."

She sat on the edge of my bed, still dressed in the sweats and hoodie Lottie had brought her in the hospital. "Did it ever get any easier?"

I walked over, crouched in front of her, hands braced on her knees. "No. But it started to matter more than the pain did. Maybe we haven't made a dent, but we've kept kids from living the kind of life you guys had to live. That's something. That's worth it."

Shiloh looked down, her voice soft and low. "And now you've got me"

"And now I've got you." I reached for her hand, gently curling my fingers through hers. "And you've got all of us."

There was a moment of silence between us. The quiet stillness that comes when someone truly sees you, all the ugly, dark parts, and doesn't flinch.

"Do you regret it?" she asked finally.

"Which part?"

"Any of it. The kills, the cards, this life."

I held her gaze, refusing to even blink before I could get the words out and make sure they sunk in. "No. Not for one damn second. Every choice I've made in this life led me here, to you."

And that was worth it. While most people would have us crucified for the way we handled things, we were making a difference. Maybe not a big one, but for each kid that we saved, each predator we took down, we were tipping the scales. Bit by bit, we were correcting the wrongs that we saw. That was worth it. This family that we had built, was worth it.

She exhaled, a little shaky, a little relieved.

I brushed a lock of her hair behind her ear, letting my thumb linger along her jaw. "You want to shower? Change? I'll go see what Kane is cooking in there."

"Yeah," she said, pressing her face into my hand. "And Creed?"

"Yeah, baby?"

Her voice dropped. "Thank you for saving me. Not just from The Manor. From everything."

I stood, kissing her temple. "You saved me, too, Red."

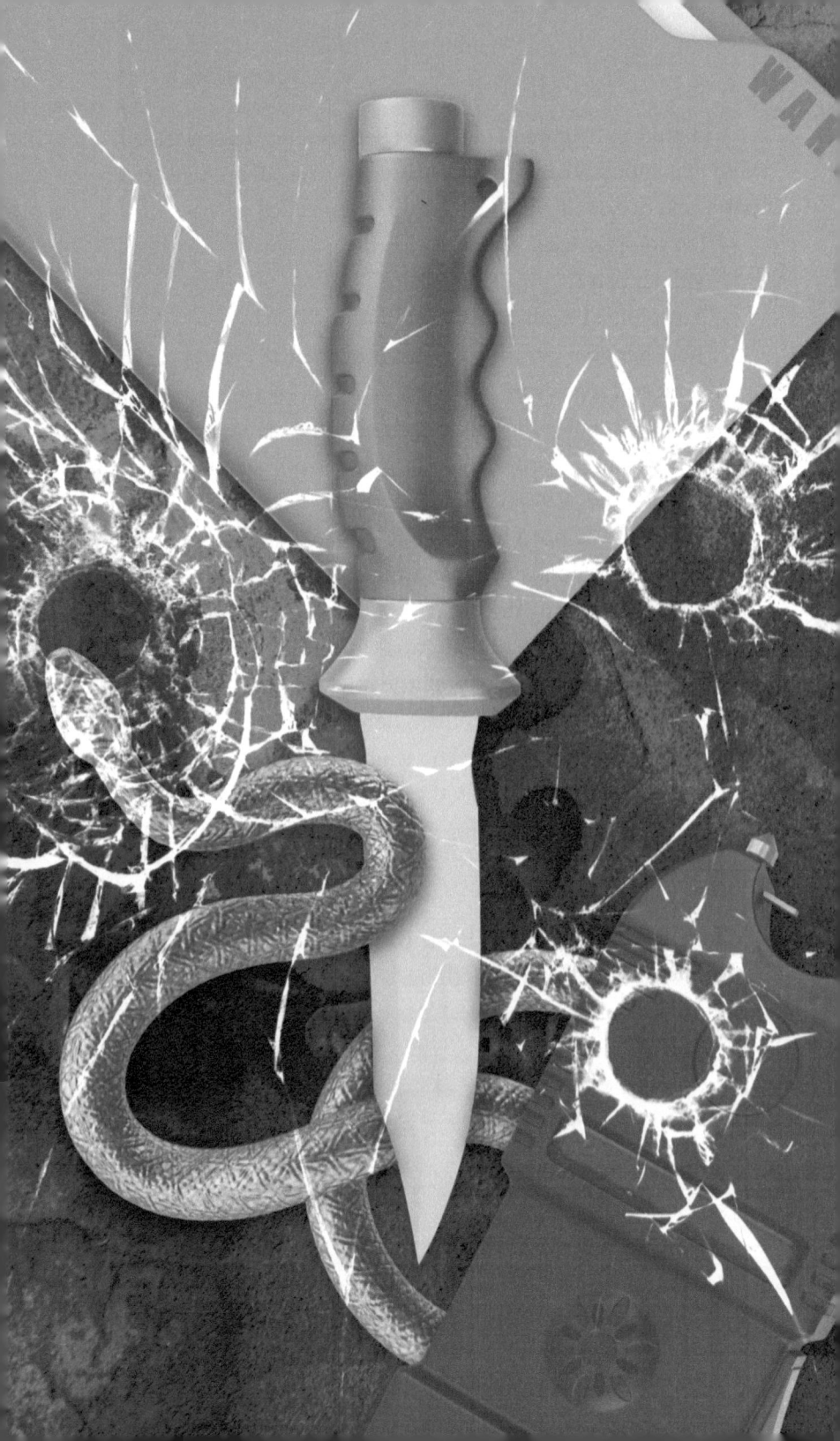

CHAPTER FIFTY-SIX

SHILOH

I don't know what I had in mind when Kane said they had moved the girls into a "safe house." Maybe a steel box, or an underground bunker. Turns out, it was just a weather-bleached Victorian house wedged between a library and an accounting office uptown. Inside though, every square inch had been gutted and rebuilt. Reinforced doors, bullet-resistant windows, and enough surveillance to rival a government building.

Abigail pressed herself against my good side the moment we crossed the threshold, her thin arms circling my waist like she had been waiting for years to see me again. I gave her a gentle squeeze.

"You're safe. I promise," I whispered to her. The pink haired girl, who I had been told was named Sabrina, hovered behind us in a hoodie that was two sizes too big, scanning the corners like she was already mapping out exit strategies.

Kane was already stationed at the dining room table, three laptops open, fingers flying over the keys. We had decided to spend the day in here with the girls, getting to know them and figuring out which ones would get sent home, and which ones we needed to find permanent placement for.

Lottie commandeered the living room couch, unpacking blankets, colorful bottles of nail polish, and bags of toys she'd grabbed on the way over. "Abby, come help me set up Barbie HQ!"

Abby grinned at her before bolting over and sitting cross legged at her feet, shucking dolls from their packaging.

I gave her a wave, then turned to find Sabrina leaning against the kitchen island, watching Nate rummage through cabinets for snacks. She tilted her head. "You always armed when you cook?"

Nate, knife still tucked under his belt, straightened. "I'm always armed, always, Pinkie Pie."

She snorted. "It's more of an insult to you that you know My Little Pony than it is to me for having pink hair, big guy." Creed passed between them with a box of bottled water, one brow raised. "Play nice, children."

"I'm nineteen," Sabrina said, her eyes cut into slits. She snagged a protein bar from Nate's hand, ripped it open with her teeth, and sauntered into the living room. Nate visibly rebooted, staring after her like he had just seen God, and God was a five foot two pink-haired woman.

I nudged him. "Careful, she seems like she bites."

"Swear to God I'll schedule my rabies shot tomorrow."

I suppressed a laugh and drifted back to Kane. Whatever was going on there, I wasn't getting in the middle of it. Sabrina seemed like she had enough fire in her to let Nate know if he was bothering her, and maybe not everyone left that place as immune to men as I did.

"Any updates?" I asked Kane.

"Nothing solid. I've been sorting through everything we've compiled so far and—" his voice trailed off as he clicked on a new window and froze.

"What?"

He zoomed in on the file signature stamped into the precinct upload log. A. Cross—Level-6 Access Granted.

Kane's jaw worked back and forth. "Weird."

"What's weird?"

"That access level is internal affairs—Maybe he's scrubbing evidence, but I haven't gotten him on the phone today so I have no idea what he's doing in there." He shook his head, minimizing the window. "Probably nothing."

"Kane?" I whispered.

He plastered on a calm that didn't reach his eyes. "We'll figure it out, don't worry about it, Shy."

I wanted to probe for a better answer than that, to figure out what had spooked him, but Creed called me over to the stairs. "How are you feeling?"

"Fine, my shoulder is a little tender, but I can manage."

He handed me a bottle of aspirin and my prescription from the hospital. "I wasn't sure which one you'd want so I brought both. I'll grab you some water."

As he moved to leave, I caught his wrist. "Something's off with Kane," I murmured. "I think he found a breadcrumb that scared him."

Creed's face was still, not a single movement to tell me what he thought about that.

"I'll talk to him." He brushed his lips against mine, tossing me a water from the kitchen before pulling out a chair next to Kane and leaning in to speak in hushed tones. I wandered down the hall to the bathroom, bracing my arm on the sink and breathing through the sharp sting I was beginning to feel in my thigh. Stitches were a pain in the ass. Once this was all over, I was going to take the longest, most expensive bubble bath in the history of the world.

My phone buzzed with a text from Aaron:

Update me after. Be careful.

He was helping at the station as much as he could, which meant he wasn't around as much as I'd like, but we all had a role to fill. I splashed water on my face, then hobbled out to the living room. Lottie had built a blanket fort, and Abigail sat cross-legged inside, carefully brushing glitter polish onto Nate's left hand while his right held a Barbie wearing combat boots and a duct tape uniform.

"—and that's why Barbie needs a flamethrower," Nate explained. He wore a rhinestone tiara crooked on his head, his expression dead serious.

Abigail nodded sagely. "Flamethrower. Good."

Sabrina lounged on the nearby couch, eating popcorn out of the bag, smirking at the scene. "He's a menace."

"I heard that," Nate said, wiggling freshly painted fingers. "I'm actually a delight."

I laughed. The sound catching me by surprise. For one heartbeat, the world wasn't burning. It was glitter, tiaras, and a little girl painting the nails of a self-proclaimed psychopath.

We were enjoying the few minutes of peace we'd managed to steal for ourselves. The world could come crumbling down tomorrow, but we had this. At some point, I still needed to sit down with my parents and come as clean as possible without risking one of them having a stroke.

We were all aware that our moral compasses didn't exactly point north, but to survive in this world, that seemed like a necessity. There were certain ways to deal with certain problems. Our way worked. It was brutal, lawless, efficient. And while we were criminals in the eyes of the law, right now, in this room? All I saw was my family.

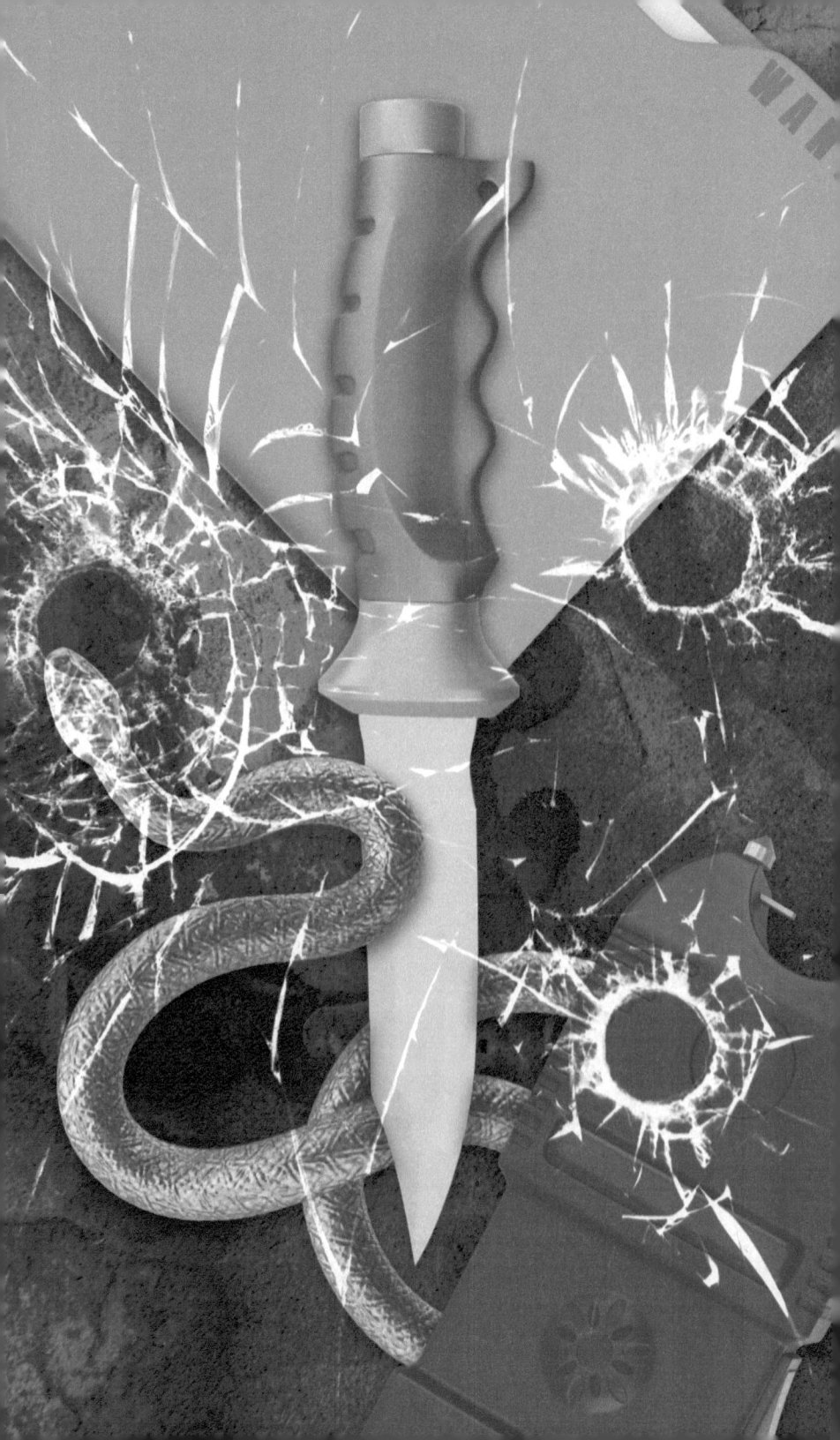

CHAPTER FIFTY-SEVEN

SHILOH

Creed's apartment was starting to feel more like a home. There was laughter in the next room that didn't feel forced, Abigail's toys littered the living room floor, and I woke up this morning with Creed curled around my back like a human heating pad. Sabrina was barefoot on the kitchen counter when I walked into the kitchen, shoving chips into her mouth and discussing which flavor of Pop-Tarts should be considered "superior" with Lottie. Abigail, meanwhile, had claimed Nate as her best friend. He sat on the floor of the living room with her as she drew stars across his knuckles in blue marker and lectured him about the Barbie cinematic universe.

"Wait, hold on," Nate said, raising a hand. "There's a Barbie movie with fairies and mermaids?"

Abigail nodded seriously. "Yes. And princesses. And a Pegasus. Her name is Brietta."

"I'm gonna need a chart," Nate whispered to himself. I leaned back against the couch, letting the scene sink in.

My body ached, the stitches still tight and bruises fading, but something very close to peace was settling over our little band of weirdos. Kane and Creed were in the office, going over the files again. The plan was to lay low, figure out who was really behind the warehouse. We had all agreed that Sabrina and Abigail would stay with us for now.

Abigail hadn't wanted to be away from us, and we hadn't been able to get her parents on the phone yet. Sabrina just didn't have anyone. She was nineteen and way too feral to let her loose on the streets, so she was staying in Creed's spare room for the time being. The moment she and Nate locked eyes, I knew we'd never be rid of her anyway. I wasn't mad about it. She was batshit insane, but she fit in here.

The exhaustion crept in slowly. Not just from the stitches and bruises, but from the whiplash of the last few days. So much had happened with so little time to process that I could physically feel the weight of it in my body. Footsteps padded softly across the floor, and I looked up to see Kane walking toward me, holding a water bottle in one hand and a prescription bottle in the other.

"You're overdue," he said gently.

I sat up just enough for him to hand me the water and shake two pills into my palm. I had quit the stronger pain meds the day I left the hospital. I remembered from my days in The Manor how easy it was to depend on them to take the edge off the world around me, and I didn't want to depend on them like that again. A couple super charged Tylenols seemed to take the worst of the ache away, anyways. "Thanks."

He dropped onto the couch beside me with a sigh. "Been a fucking week, huh?"

"It hasn't been boring," I replied with a smirk.

I chased the pills with a long drink of water while he watched Nate attempt to braid Abigail's long hair.

"She picked the craziest one in the group and stuck to him like glue." He laughed in disbelief at the bond that had bloomed between Nate and Abby in virtually no time. She was enamored with him, and he seemed softer, saner, with her.

"I think it's good for him. And her, to see that not all men are scary."

Kane nodded, his lips pressing into a thin line.

We sat in comfortable silence for a minute, nothing but the sound of whispered giggles coming from Abigail and Nate before Kane nudged me with his elbow. "Creed's in the office. If you want to escape the glitter princess slumber party for a bit. We'll watch her."

I glanced down at her, noting the bright smile stretched across her face before gently shifting off the couch. "Thanks, I think I'll take you up on that. Better run if she comes near you with the nail polish."

"I'm secure enough, I think I could make it look good."

"Abigail! Did you hear that, Kane said you could paint his nails!" Nate grinned.

I quickly scooted down the hallway as Kane tossed a pillow at Nate's head. The office door was cracked slightly, the light spilling into the hallway. I pushed it open and stepped inside, finding Creed at the desk, going over what looked like surveillance feeds and a stack of notes written in Kane's aggressive chicken scratch handwriting. He didn't look up, but he spoke immediately. "Kane get you your meds?"

"Yes, thank you," I said, easing the door shut behind me.

Creed turned toward me, his eyes scanning my face like he was checking for damage. "You look tired," he said quietly.

"So do you."

"Touche." He leaned back in the chair, scooting backwards and patting his thigh. "Come here."

I padded over to him, sliding onto his lap where he pulled me tight against him, one hand still taking notes while the other wrapped around me to rest on my thigh.

"Busy little serial killer, aren't you?" I joked.

He hummed under his breath, setting the pen down and

adjusting me on his lap so that I faced him more fully. "Well, when I'm not dipping into the same victim pool as you, I do also have a company to run."

"How much therapy do I need for finding that a little hot?"

He chuckled as his hands found my waist, gently lifting me and setting me on top of the desk in front of him.

"Only a little?" he asked with a smile. "You find the idea of me killing bad men, and stalking around the outside of your house with a gun to keep you safe, only mildly arousing?"

My heart stuttered in my chest as he brushed his lips across my jaw, trailing them lower until his tongue met the sensitive skin behind my ear.

"Slightly more than mild, I suppose."

He chuckled, a wicked grin flashing on his face as he slowly sank to his knees in front of me. Due to his height, it put him eye level with my waist.

"Here you are, with the big bad Red King of Sunbridge on his knees for you. What will you do with me?" he asked, lifting my feet one at a time and unlacing my shoes before setting them beside him.

"Oh gosh, I don't know. I'm just so scared I'm shaking!" I gasped, clutching at my chest and putting as much fake fear into my voice as I could manage.

He smiled as his hands curled into the waist band of my sweatpants. "When I make you shake, it won't be from fear. Lift your hips, baby."

I arched my hips off the desk, watching with rapt attention as he pulled the sweatpants down my legs and tossed them on the floor.

"Prove it," I whispered.

His hands spread my legs wide, careful not to touch the stitches along my thigh as he lowered his head between them. The wet heat of his tongue through my thin panties was enough to send my heart rate skyrocketing. My hands instinctively curled into his thick black hair, guiding his mouth as he moved against me. He hummed in approval.

"More," I panted. I wanted him. All of him.

"I've got you, Red." He stood, grabbing my hand to help me slip off the desk, then turning to grab a long throw pillow from the reading chair in the corner. He laid it across the top of the desk, gently guiding me to lean on it. With my arms resting in front of me, and the pillow so close to the edge, there was no pull on either the gunshot wounds or the mess on my leg from the shrapnel.

"Good?"

"Yeah, this is good."

The sound of his belt buckle clinking as he worked his pants open sent goosebumps up and down my limbs and spine. He traced the ones along my back with one finger, stepping up behind me. I turned my head so I could see him.

"I'm not fragile. Don't fuck me like I'm made of glass," I said firmly.

Creed had lit a fire inside me; I didn't want to be babied. I wanted to feel the primal parts of him that only came out when he was naked with me, or hunting someone down.

"So bossy. One of these days, Shiloh—" he muttered, tsking his tongue as he lined up with my entrance. "I'm going to fix that. For now, I just want you to remember that I love you."

"Why—" I started, but the question died on my lips as he slammed forward, my pussy stretching to accommodate him. His hands gripped my hips, pulling me back against him so that my thighs never touched the desk.

He groaned as he slowly pulled out, and slammed back in. Over and over. The desk shook with his movements; the sound of our skin meeting was probably loud enough to be heard in the next room, but I didn't care. I couldn't focus on anything except how good it felt to be filled by him. His hands slid down my arms, grasping each of my wrists and pinning them together in front of me while his hips worked against mine in a steady rhythm.

He bent low so that his lips grazed my ear as he spoke, "Do you have any idea how many nights I watched you, wishing you would just open the goddamn door and let me ruin you like this?"

My heart pounded against the wooden desk.

"How many times I caught your eyes on me and imagined what it would feel like to have you under me? This sweet little pussy wrapped around my dick, my name falling from your lips?" He adjusted the angle of his hips, hitting that magic spot inside me that nearly had me coming out of my skin as I panted his name.

"My twisted girl. My little killer. My wife."

"Yes!" I screamed, attempting at the last second to muffle the sound against my arm. He made a satisfied noise as I came down, his lips trailing over my shoulder.

I lost count of how many times he made my vision tunnel, pleasure so hot I thought it would burn me alive coursing through me. By the time we had defiled his desk, the chair, the floor in front of the window, and the windowsill, I was a boneless, sated heap on the ground in his arms.

A sheen of sweat clung to both of us, Creed's heart thumping excitedly beneath my ear.

Some of the adrenaline from the last few days felt like it had been expelled, but even now, with Creed's hand rubbing soothing circles across my naked back, I still felt unsettled.

I rubbed at the scars across his knuckle. "Creed?"

"Red." He smiled. The words weren't forming right to tell him what I wanted to say, but if I didn't get it out, I was going to combust.

"I'm... I'm angry," I said finally.

He shifted, turning his face toward me with his brows drawn.

"At me?" he asked.

"No, not at you. At everything else. I'm trying to focus on the good, on the fact that we're all safe. But—I don't know how to breathe with this in my chest."

He looked at me like he was trying to figure out what part of me hurt the most.

"I trusted Miles. Not like I trust you, but like you would trust anyone you're related to. I trusted that there was a certain level of decency that would be upheld there, and I can't stomach the truth." His jaw clenched hard as I swallowed. "I want to hurt him, Creed. I want to tie him to a chair and set it on fire. I want to scream about all the things that happened to me in that place and make him hear it."

Creed leaned forward, placing a soft kiss to my shoulder. "You were owed that. You deserved to feel safe in your own home, with your own family, without having your life turned upside down."

"I don't know what to do with this." My voice cracked over the words. "It's like this balloon in my chest that just inflates and inflates, and it's going to pop and I'm going to end up in pieces all over the floor."

His thumb rubbed circles over my thigh as his eyes bounced between mine. "What can I do, baby? How can I help?"

I blinked fast, trying to hold back the rush of emotion building in my chest. "I don't know. I'm so tired of being angry. It feels like a live flame in my chest, and it's scorching every-thing inside me. I just want to push it all out and let it burn something else for a little bit."

He nodded like he understood, even though I'm sure I

sounded insane. It was becoming unbearable. I felt heavy. Like each new thing had added a hundred pounds to my body and my mind.

"I have an idea. Get dressed and meet me in the living room in five."

I arched a brow at him. "Where are we going?"

He smiled softly. "We're going to go make your world a little less heavy. Do you trust me?"

"Yes." No hesitation this time. I trusted him with my life.

He pressed his lips to mine before standing and pulling me to my feet. "Go. I'll be ready when you are."

CHAPTER FIFTY-EIGHT

SHILOH

The tires hummed in a low, constant growl along the textured road. My head rested against the window, the cool glass against my temple doing nothing to quiet the fire under my skin. Something ugly had taken root in my chest, and it was spreading, slow and poisonous, through my veins. Creed hadn't said much since we got in the car, but neither had I. I was lost in my head, and he was lost in thought beside me.

"What am I walking into?" I finally asked. We had crossed the city limit over two hours ago. He glanced at me, one hand loose on the wheel.

"Whatever you need it to be. If we get there and you want to leave, I will turn around and drive us back home. No questions asked."

That was vague. I nodded, laying my head back against the window and letting my eyes drift shut. Not because I was tired, but because I didn't trust myself not to crack right open.

When we finally turned off the highway, I recognized the road instantly. My body was rigid, and Creed must have felt it because he reached over, resting his hand gently on my thigh.

"You don't have to, Red. This is an offer, a choice. If it feels like it will help, then we go in."

I sucked in deep breaths as he parked in front of the old

Manor. The massive brick exterior extended three stories into the sky. It was an old historical building that Ruben had bought and turned into his house of horrors. Now most of the windows on the bottom floor were shattered, the weeds were waist high, and there was faded crime scene tape clinging to the fence that waved to me in the wind. Someone had dismantled most of the tech, I'd guess soon after the raid happened. The massive gate and fencing around the building were long gone, along with the obnoxious number of cameras that used to line the driveway. It didn't look like the Manor I grew up in anymore, it just looked like...bricks. In the light of day, it looked like any other abandoned building. Thick vines stretched along the windows, the grass and bushes overgrown and messy.

"It's different than it was," I whispered.

Creed nodded. He had seen it up close the night of the raid, the first time he ever came to my rescue, gun in hand.

"I want to go in, but what—what do I—" What was I supposed to do in there? What if the inside was preserved? What if seeing those hallways again was what broke the final thread of my sanity? What if I lost myself so bad this time, I couldn't get me back?

"Shiloh," Creed said, waiting for me to turn and face him before he continued. A tattooed hand cupped my cheek as he spoke. "You do whatever feels right. We can go in and have a moment of silence to take it all in. We can smash the windows; we can tear it apart brick by brick or burn it to the ground. I am here; whatever you choose, I will still be right here."

I swallowed hard.

"Okay. Let's go." I unbuckled my seatbelt before I let the fear talk me out of it and exited the car.

Creed came around to my side, lacing his fingers through mine, and kept step beside me as we ducked under the police tape and entered through the broken front door.

Leaves skittered across the ground in the foyer, every single visible window had been shattered, letting in dirt and debris from outside that danced across the marble floor in the wind. It was jarring. This place was always pristine when I lived here. There was never any dust, dishes, or laundry piled up. Ruben had staff that made sure of that. I tugged on Creed's hand, leading him down a familiar hallway, and into the last room on the right.

My room. Or at least, it used to be. The light was dim in here; there were no windows in the dorms. It looked... roughly the same. The mattress had been stripped, just a box spring and wires left like a ribcage in the corner. The walls were bare, but then again, they always had been.

"This was yours?" he asked.

I nodded. "It looked just like this when I was here, except there was a mattress and a blanket on the bed."

Creed studied the room. "It's very... bare."

"No personal touches allowed. 'It makes people soft,'" I quoted.

He didn't answer but I could feel the heat rolling off him. Rage disguised as stillness. We walked silently through the halls, my fingers trailing along the wall and coming away with enough dust that it soothed some of the anxiety. No one had been here. In all the worst nightmares I had for the first few months, it was always Ruben who came back for me.

Sometimes he was alive, sometimes it was his gray corpse that chased me through these halls, the bullet wound in his head seeping a viscous black fluid as he screamed. I shook off the memory.

"There's only one more room I want to see." I turned and left the room, Creed's footsteps following behind me. I took the longer route, weaving through the now empty sitting room. This is where the clients would sit and drink until Ruben was ready for them. The amount of bourbon that had been consumed in this room could flood a small city.

Dust choked the light filtering in from outside. I could still see outlines on the floor where the furniture used to be, but it felt just the same as the rest of the house. Empty. Barren. A shell of what it once was. I could relate to that. I kept walking down the hall to the far door.

"This was Ruben's office." The door creaked as I pushed it open. Everything was overturned, like the cops had stormed in and gutted it in a hurry. Drawers hung open; the old rug was curled up at the corners. I stepped inside, but the room fought me. Every breath was too heavy. The walls were too close. A very telling blood stain in the middle of the room nearly sucked the breath from my lungs. If the rest of the house was a ghost of its former self, this room was possessed. The urge to shut down and brace for impact was so tangible I could taste it. The rage inside me was so hot it burned right through that instinct.

"This is where he... where I never got to say no," I said. "Everything that made me me, was peeled away in strips right on this carpet."

Creed's hand curled around mine. I didn't even remember reaching for him.

"Do you want to leave?" he asked.

"No." I shook my head. I did want to leave, but I wanted to leave my mark first. I walked over to the massive oak desk in the center of the room, opening the top drawer and pulling out the same lighter I'd seen Ruben use to light his cigars so many times before. I flicked it, watching as the flame sparked and danced in front of me.

"Burn it all down it is then." He smiled at me, reaching for a stack of papers on the ground and holding them out between us. I held out the lighter, touching the flame to the corner of the paper, and watching as Creed moved toward the windows, laying the stack of burning paper against the fabric curtains that pooled on the floor. The fire bloomed fast, greedy and orange and flickering up the wall like they were as hungry as I was to watch this place be stripped down to the foundation. I stepped back as smoke filled the room, thick and black and curling like fingers around the ceiling.

"Ruben, I hope you are having the worst time in hell," I whispered to the room. The flames seemed to roar in response, climbing faster along the ceiling as Creed and I walked out of the room, and exited the building without looking back: Creed leaned against the front of the Jeep, pulling my back flush against his chest and wrapping his arms around me as we watched.

The structure groaned, a piece of the roof caving in with a cloud of smoke and embers. The fire crackled hot in front of us. I didn't scream; I didn't cry. I just breathed. And it seemed a little easier than it had before. My phone buzzed in my pocket, and I slipped it out, checking the text before putting it back and relaxing into Creed's hold.

"Aaron says he'll be at the apartment for dinner."

"How do you feel?" Creed asked, resting his chin on my shoulder.

"I feel like all of my pieces were stolen," I said, "and I just took one back."

I felt his smile against my skin as he leaned in, placing a tender kiss to my shoulder before ushering me into the passenger seat and fastening the seat belt across me. I watched in the rearview as the distance grew and the fire turned the sky orange.

I hope hell itself opened up and swallowed the charred carcass of Ruben's empire.

CHAPTER FIFTY-NINE

CREED

We hadn't made it two steps into the apartment before I felt it. Something was off. The air was charged, a tension lingering around the edges. Shiloh stopped short in front of me, either she felt it too or she noticed the way Kane stood at the end of the hall. His face was tight, jaw locked, and his arms crossed in front of him. "You both need to come into the office," he said.

Shiloh glanced at me warily, and I nodded. We followed him into the office, Nate already leaning against the far wall, his hands tapping frantically against his legs. A rare look of genuine unease had settled in his eyes, and that alone nearly stopped my heart. Nate rarely looked unsettled. Unhinged? Sure. But seeing him shaken was a sure sign something was wrong.

"What's wrong? I asked, shutting the door behind us.

Kane sat at the desk, his laptop still glowing. "I've been digging. Cross-referencing the phones we recovered. York, Lyle, Martin."

Shiloh stepped closer, her eyes scanning the screen.

"There are two numbers that appear on all three phones,"

Kane said, his voice flat. "Twice on York's, once on the burner we pulled off Lyle, and five times on Martin's."

Kane spun the laptop around to show the log. "This number called each of those men within twenty-four hours of major movements. Raids. Transports. It's not just a burner—they masked it behind an encrypted routing system. Took hours to trace."

"And the other?" I asked, though I already knew. Something icy crawled up the back of my neck as I fought the realization of what was happening here.

Kane stared at me. "The second number? Same encryption. We broke part of it and pinged a location."

"Where?" Shiloh asked.

He hesitated, his eyes flicking to mine before moving back to Shiloh.

"The station. The gym. Our house. And the warehouse."

I didn't move. I could see the wheels turning in her head, her mind desperately trying to connect the dots in a way that didn't cause her world to fall to pieces beneath her.

Nate spoke up, unusually quiet. "One of them we think is the Bishop. The other one... the other one is Aaron, Shy."

Silence punched through the room. Shiloh's head shook side to side like she could physically dispel the information from her brain. Nate slid down the wall, sitting on the ground while he stared straight ahead at nothing.

"No," she whispered. "Aaron wasn't at the raid. He wasn't there, so it's not him."

"He's been to the warehouse," Nate muttered. "Before we ever found it."

Shiloh looks to me, then back to Kane, her voice trembling as she spoke, "Are you sure?"

Kane just nodded once. "I'd bet my life."

The sound of the front door opening and closing made all of us freeze. Abigail's voice carried down the hallway. "Hi, Aaron!"

Shiloh was the first to bolt. We all followed, the office door slamming into the wall as we barreled out. He stood in the living room, casual, smiling like he didn't just walk into a war zone. Shiloh grabbed Abigail's hand, pulling her away from Aaron.

"You know him? From that night?" she asked her urgently.

Abigail tilted her head. "Which one? The place with the bunk beds?"

That did it. Sabrina, standing off to the side, tensed like a spring ready to snap. She watched Aaron like she wasn't sure if she should jump him or wait for us to. Shiloh was already moving, turning to Nate.

"Give me your keys." Nate handed them over without question. She tossed them to Lottie who watched the situation unfold from the kitchen.

"Take Abigail and Sabrina to Nate's place. Stay there until I call."

Lottie nodded, looking between all of us as she moved to usher the girls out the door. Sabrina threw one last sharp glance at Aaron before stepping out. The door clicked shut audibly behind them before Aaron finally spoke.

"What the hell is going on, Shy?"

Four sets of eyes burned into him, each second stretching like wire as we all tried to figure out the best way to approach this. The tension in the room was so thick, I could hear it hum around us.

"You tell us," Kane said coldly.

Aaron's eyes shifted, just slightly, but I caught it.

"Say it," Nate snarled, his hands shaking violently at his sides. "Tell us you didn't fucking do this."

Aaron didn't speak. That's all we needed to know. His eyes darted between us, his mouth opening and closing without sound before he finally pressed his lips into a thin line.

What was there to say at this point? Everything around us was burning to ash.

CHAPTER SIXTY

SHILOH

I couldn't breathe. The world seemed to move in slow motion, the shock registering across everyone's faces as the last good thing crumbled in front of us. Betrayal was not a new concept to me. Evil men were not a new concept to me. But Aaron? *My Aaron?*

He just stood there, not meeting anyone's eyes. He was supposed to be my best friend. He was the only person I could count on in that place, and here he was, resurrecting it. For what? It didn't matter. There was no excuse or reasoning that would absolve him from this.

He finally met my eyes, and all I could see was a stranger. My feet carried me across the floor before I even remembered telling them to move. One second, I was near the kitchen, the next I was in front of him, looking into eyes I didn't recognize anymore.

"You did this?" I asked. My voice didn't even sound like mine. Where I had expected to sound heartbroken, it was flat. Dull.

He didn't answer. Kane took a step forward, coming to stand beside me as he stared holes through his brother. "Say something, Aaron," he said, his hands clenched into fists.

Still nothing. The silence was deafening. Had this been

anyone else, Creed would have put a bullet through him by now. Nate would have ripped him apart with his hands, someone would have done *something*. The reality that this was our friend, our brother, and also the ghost we'd been chasing for weeks was heavy. And we didn't have any time to come to terms with it. It was unraveling right in front of us.

"How deep are you in, Aaron? Are you the Bishop?"

He shook his head, his voice quiet. "No, I'm not the Bishop."

My pulse thudded in my ears.

"I'm quickly losing my patience, Cross. Tell us what you know. Now," Creed said. He was dangerously calm. The only one of us that wasn't constantly clenching their hands or tapping their feet. He was deadly still like a snake preparing to strike.

Aaron blinked slowly. "It's not—it's not what you think." He glanced at each of us, his throat working like it was hard to swallow his own actions. His mouth opened and closed like he might say something, like he might actually explain what the hell was happening, but he didn't.

I felt the first crack then, spiderwebbing down my spine. The feeling of white-hot rage that had become so familiar to me.

"I looked up to you," I said. "I trusted you."

"You don't understand."

"What is there to understand? Did you miss The Manor so badly that you had to help build a new one? What did you miss, Aaron?" My pulse was pounding so loudly in my ears I could barely hear my own voice. "Was it the kidnappings? The screams in the middle of the night? Was it the way I limped when I left Ruben's office?"

"I DID IT TO PROTECT YOU!" he roared. "If my hand was in it, then I had control! FUCK!" He slammed his hand against the wall, leaving a fist-shaped hole in the plaster. "I knew who was coming and going, I decided the ages, I decided where they went when they left!"

In the silence that followed, I think my heart stopped beating. There was a moment, just a split second, where I felt it give out. What had been a rapid drum beating in my chest, dulled until I felt nothing at all. An all too familiar numbness began leeching into my veins. I heard Kane yell something from beside me, and then his fist flew out above my head, connecting with Aaron's nose and sending him flying backwards against the door. The thud of his body against the floor snapped me out of it. He laid in a heap with his hands over his mouth, blood ripping between his fingers.

"You motherfucker—" Kane lunged again, but Creed grabbed his arm.

"Don't. Not yet," Creed said through gritted teeth.

I glanced at Nate, who looked like he was going to combust. There was a vibration in his body that prevented him from standing still, a mix of panic and anger in his eyes that made him appear younger than he was. Kane and Creed were visibly restraining themselves as we all stared at the man we had considered a brother. Were any of us going to survive this?

"When? When did you get involved?" Creed barked at him.

"After the raid. Someone was already rebuilding it, okay?" Aaron said, his voice muffled through his hands as he held his nose to staunch the bleeding. "It wasn't my idea. Someone was already well on their way to taking Ruben's place before the ink had even dried on his death certificate. I did what I could to make sure they didn't come back for Shiloh."

"The photograph, Abigail's nightlight. Was that you?"

He had the nerve to look offended. "Of course not. The

Bishop knew; he was toying with me. He was taunting both of us."

"Why? Why would you do this?" I asked, praying for a steady voice until this was over.

"I heard about it through some of the guys I met when I was undercover. I went to try and pinpoint a location or a leader, anything." He laid his hands on his lap, the blood on them providing so much irony in that moment that I thought I would vomit. "They found me first."

"Are you saying you were blackmailed?" There was the slightest flicker of hope in Nate's voice. Like that would be the cure. All of this could be forgiven, if he had no choice.

"No. I wasn't blackmailed. They told me they were coming for Shiloh."

"They did," Creed gritted out.

"I know that now. I thought—I thought if I could get in on it, I could keep them away. That was the deal."

"You made a deal?" Kane leveled a look on Aaron that hurt to see. All of us knew Aaron in our own way, we had all formed our own bond. But for Kane, this wasn't *like* family, Aaron *was* his family. I couldn't fathom how he was still standing.

"No one touches Shiloh, and I won't tell anyone what I know. It was a good deal, okay? You're all so pissed off at me that you can't see it right now, but it was. Shiloh was safe. My family was safe. That was all that mattered. That was all I was fighting for."

"You were fighting against ME! Everything that I was doing." My voice echoed off the wooden floors, "Everything *we* were doing, and you—you? How, Aaron? How could you do this?" My voice finally broke. "You saw first-hand what that place was like, and you let other kids go there..."

"No, no, Shy, no. I was—I was keeping you safe," he pleaded.

Kane turned away, disgust coloring his face. Aaron was shaking his head back and forth, his hands bracing against the floor as he braced to get up before Creed's boot on his shoulder pushed him back to the floor.

"At what cost? How many girls, how many children did you let take my place?"

"No! That was the rule. They weren't allowed to hurt them. It's different, Shiloh. They're okay." So much pleading. So much delusion in those eyes. I thought of Abigail, of every other girl we pulled from that place. They were taken; they were held in a rundown warehouse waiting to be sold like cattle *in my name.* A shudder rocked my body.

"There is no world in which children are taken and sold that anything is okay,'" I whispered.

He actually believed what he was saying. I could see it in the way his brow furrowed, as he frantically looked between all of us, waiting for a lightbulb to go off over our heads as we understood his reasoning. And the hardest part to swallow, the biggest pill of all was that we knew what he thought he was doing. He wasn't malicious; he was so incredibly fucked up that he thought this was the right choice. That hurt more than anything. All of us had our scars, and we all coped with them in our own ways. But this? This was unforgivable. It was horrid. It was heartbreaking.

I sat down. I couldn't stand anymore. At any moment, the world was going to fall right out from under me and swallow all of us whole.

"You knew we were looking for them," Creed said.

"I did. I thought the other guys would keep you busy. It seemed like it was helping you, so I just kept passing along names. I thought maybe that would be enough."

"You knew we were taking them out?"

"Yes."

"Do you know about me?" Creed asked, crouching down beside Aaron.

"Yes." He wouldn't look at Creed and a thick, sickening feeling churned in my gut.

"You knew we were at Sinner's that night." Creed dragged his hand through his hair, his eyes shut tight as he spoke. "You tipped off the police, didn't you?" Creed sighed. It was a statement more than a question and Aaron's silence was enough of an answer.

He had betrayed everyone in this room, turned on Creed, led the cops right to our doorstep, all while he erected an empire from the ashes of the place that broke me the most.

Everything we had fought for, every life we snuffed out in the name of the girls we were trying to save, and he was behind us undoing it all. The entire time.

Where did we go from here?

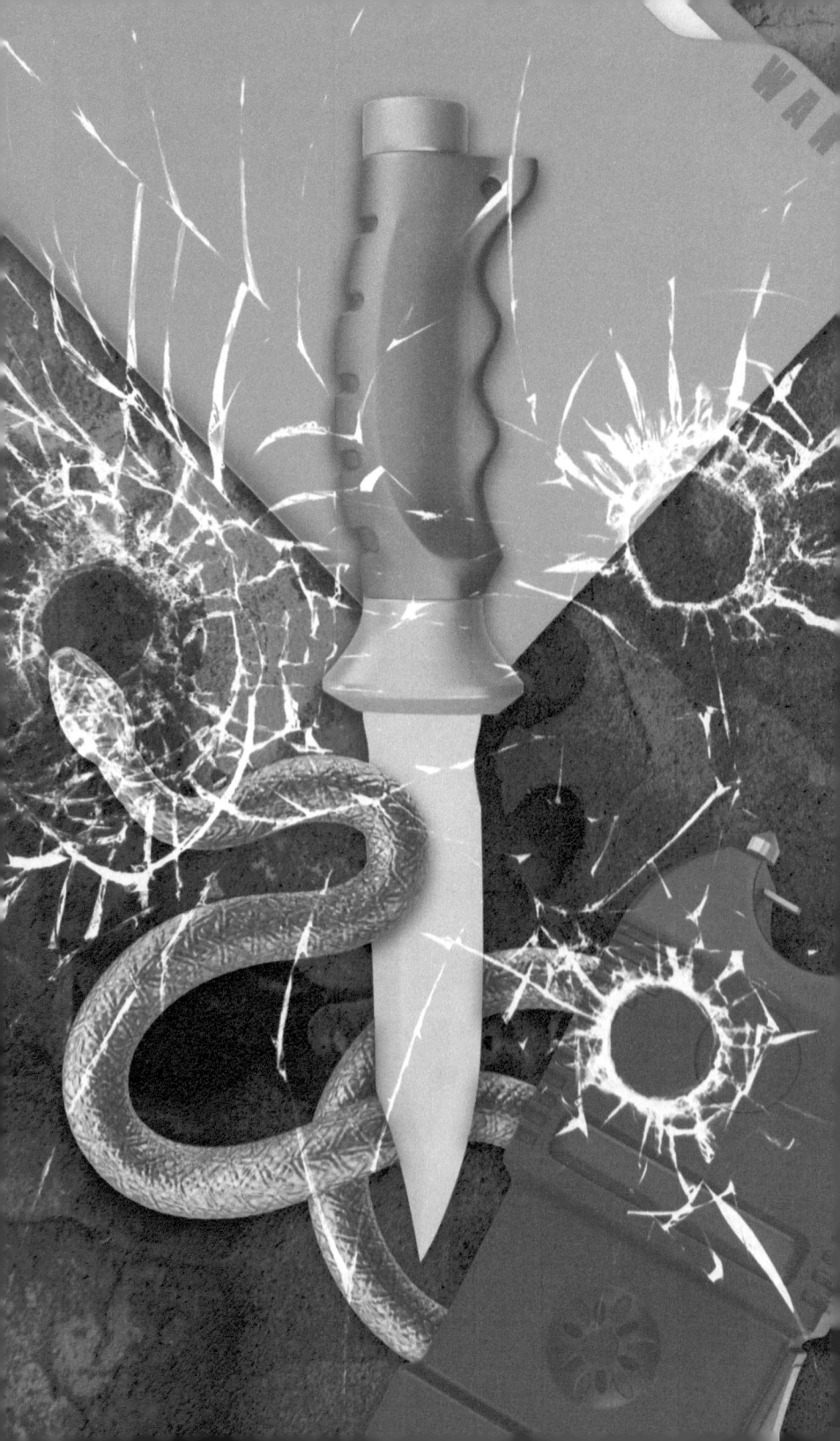

CHAPTER SIXTY-ONE

SHILOH

"Why?" Creed asked.

"I needed you to back off. I wouldn't have let them take you down, Creed. I would have figured something out, I just needed all of you to back off. You were getting too close, and I needed time to explain everything."

Kane had walked away; he sat at the kitchen island, his head in his hands. I didn't know how to explain the silent sound of three hearts breaking in unison, but it echoed around us like a gunshot.

"Get up," Creed muttered, locking eyes with Aaron.

"What?"

"Up. I can't fucking look at you right now and until we figure out what to do, you're going to get locked in the spare bedroom."

He sighed, getting to his feet and wiping the remaining blood from his face with the bottom of his shirt. He looked at Kane, but quickly averted his gaze when he realized his brother wasn't going to look back. I followed Creed down the hallway to the spare room, past where Nate leaned against the wall, the soft snapping of his rubber band matching our footsteps. Creed opened the door, moving aside to let Aaron enter.

He turned just before he stepped over the threshold. "Shiloh, I know it's bad. But you being hurt, that's worse."

"My life is not more valuable than anyone else's. You had no right. I never would have agreed to that."

There was so much turmoil in his eyes, regret and defeat drowning in the tears that were forming in the corners. I studied his face, looking for any sign that I had missed over the last few weeks. Had he always been this way?

"I'm—I'm so sorry. I thought I was helping. I thought—"

"It doesn't matter. You thought wrong. Creed is facing life in prison. I was shot, Aaron. There's a little girl across the hall who has been ripped from her bed by strangers *twice*, because of you."

His hand covered his mouth, his head shaking back and forth subtly as the weight of his decisions settled over him.

"I-I didn't think that far ahead, Shy. I just jumped; I just did what I thought was best to save—"

"You didn't save me. You helped create two dozen more girls just like me. And no one deserves to be this way."

I pulled the door shut, waiting for Creed to slip the keys from his pocket and lock it. There was a level of acceptance in Aaron's eyes. Understanding that told me he was beginning to see what he had done. It was just another knife in my back, and there wasn't room for any more.

THREE HOURS LATER, Lottie had curled up beside me on the couch. Her fingers wove into mine and stayed there, grounding me while my mind spiraled.

"You okay?" she asked, her voice soft.

"No," I answered.

She kissed my temple and got up. "I'm gonna use the bathroom and then I'll get you some tea, okay?"

I nodded. I didn't want tea. I wanted to erase the last two days of my life and make them better. I wanted to fix it. I wanted to throttle Aaron for being so fuck—

"Uh, guys?" Lottie's voice echoed down the hall. "Where the hell is he?"

Creed was on his feet first, Kane right behind him. The bedroom door stood open; the room empty. Nate growled, slamming his fist into the wall.

Kane walked over to the desk. "Wait—look." Aaron's phone sat open on the desk, a progress bar glowing on the screen.

Uploading... 97%

Nate reached for it, but Creed slapped his hand away. "Stop," he snapped. "We don't know what it is. Pulling it might make it worse." We all watched as the progress bar slowly ticked up. 98... 99...

Upload complete.

Time froze. Each of us froze too, scared to breathe too heavy like the phone was a bomb that would go off at any moment.

"What did he do?" I whispered. No one had an answer.

CHAPTER SIXTY-TWO

SHILOH

It took about two minutes for my brain to start working again. "Check the feeds at my house and the gym. If he's hiding out, he doesn't have a lot of places to go," I urged Kane, the air in the room was frantic.

What had he uploaded? Was he going to warn the Bishop that we were closing in? We still hadn't figured out what to do with him and now he had slipped through our fingers.

"Gym. The front counter camera caught him fifteen minutes ago," Kane said.

"Let's go." I was already racing for the door.

We all piled into Kane's Jeep, leaving Lottie to look after the girls after Kane handed her a small handgun and made her swear to shoot anyone that came in. There was no sound in the cab except for Nate's heavy breathing and the steady snapping sound of his rubber band popping against his wrist.

Kane kept glancing in the rearview mirror, looking between me and Creed like he wanted to say something, and usually, he would. He would know the right thing to say to keep us from unraveling. He would have a plan, a fix for whatever we had gotten ourselves into. Not this time.

There was the smallest hint of guilt in his eyes, like he was somehow at fault for not catching this sooner. I could feel the tension pouring off each of us. All of us shouldering the blame for not seeing the signs, not realizing something was so incredibly wrong. No one was to blame; no one except Aaron. We pulled up in front of the gym, Kane slamming the Jeep into park as we all filed out.

"Nate and I will take the back. You two go through the front and check the office," he barked before taking off at a full sprint for the rear entrance to the building. I followed Creed to the front door, scanning through the windows as we got closer. The bell above the door jingled when we pushed it open, Creed already scanning the area like he's expecting an ambush.

Nothing. No movement, just a silence and our heavy breathing until we heard the office door shut. Creed drew the gun from his waistband, pointing it straight ahead as Aaron emerged from the hallway, his clothes still covered in his own blood, his head hung low.

"I figured you'd come," he said, his hands raised in front of him in surrender.

"What was on the phone, Aaron?" Creed asked.

He glanced around the gym, then back to us. "Where are the others?"

"Circling the building. What's your plan?" I asked.

"It's already done."

"The file you uploaded, what was that? More evidence? Did you decide to take all of us down with you instead of just me?" Creed gritted the words out through his teeth.

Aaron exhaled heavily. "No. I fixed it. As much as it could be fixed, I fixed it."

I stepped forward. "What the hell does that mean?"

"It means that I get it. I fucked up, Shy. I know that now." I caught the tremble in his chin before the first tear fell. "I-I was trying, you know? But something—something in here—" his hands gripped the hair at the sides of his head, "isn't wired right."

His chest heaved as he hiccupped a sob. Creed stood to the side looking like he was trying to decide if he should shoot him where he stood or catch him when he fell.

"I thought I could keep everyone safe. But I didn't. I couldn't. So, I'm doing the only thing I can to help."

Kane and Nate came out of the back hallway, stopping short when they saw him.

"What was in the file?" Kane demanded.

"Evidence. Camera footage, fingerprints, a confession. All of it belongs to me, The Red King."

Creed's breath hitched, and Kane looked like he had turned to stone.

"You're taking the fall," I whispered. The front lot lit up with red and blue lights. At least a dozen police cruisers screeched into the parking lot as we all stood in a standoff not thirty feet away from them. We were running out of time. Kane moved, spinning Aaron around with a hand on his shoulder and jerking him into a hug.

"You really fucked this up," he said.

"I know."

"We-we'll figure it out, okay?" Kane's eyes were locked on the windows, watching as officers exited their cars and drew their weapons.

Aaron nodded, a sad smile on his lips. "I already have."

He pulled away from Kane, taking precious time to look all of us in the eyes, and walked toward the front door, turning to face us as he laid his hand against the glass.

"For what it's worth, I'm sorry." He pushed the door open, taking two steps forward before stopping. I realized what he was about to do a half-second too late.

"Aaron!" I screamed.

His hand slipped behind him, reaching for the gun tucked into his pants.

Kane barreled forward. "HOLD YOUR FIRE!" He ran past me, his hands up as he screamed so loud I thought my ear drums would burst. The pain in his voice was so raw it nearly knocked the breath out of me. "DON'T FUCKING SHOOT!"

It was too late.

Aaron pointed the gun toward the swarm of officers, and in seconds, I was on the ground with Creed's body covering mine as bullets rained throughout the gym.

Aaron's body hit the ground in front of me, but the only thing I could hear was the sound of Kane screaming.

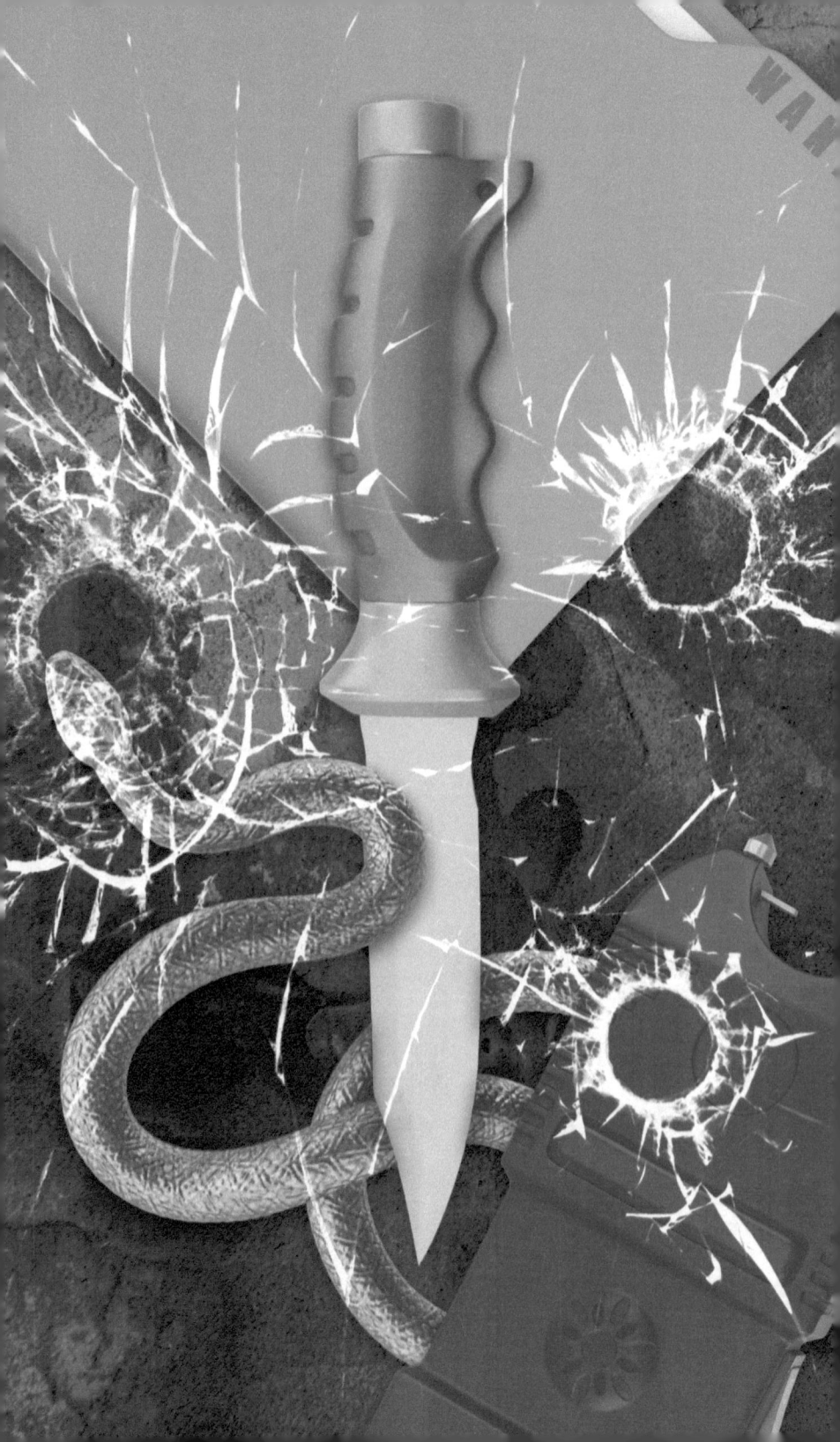

CHAPTER SIXTY-THREE

SHILOH

Two Weeks Later

The news hadn't stopped playing it.

"Red King Confirmed dead."

"Former officer Aaron Cross named as vigilante serial killer."

"Sources say he acted alone."

I turned off the TV. I hadn't gotten used to seeing his face plastered across the screen, and my hopes that they would report on it and quickly move on to the next big thing were slowly fading. Creed sat at our kitchen island, a cup of coffee in hand while he looked over a new file.

His holster was off, no tactical belt. He was just here. Barefoot, tattooed, tired. But safe.

The days leading up to Aaron taking the fall, we hadn't had time to figure out how we were going to keep Creed out of prison. Every time I looked at him, I was thankful for the things Aaron did right. It had been two weeks since he was killed. We realized too late that he never had any intention of going on trial or sitting in a cell, so we all watched as he took the only clean way out.

"Hey," Creed said softly. "You okay?"

I nodded, giving him a small smile. I thought we were all okay-ish. Probably twice as fucked up as we were a few months ago, but we were here. That had to count for something. Abigail's laughter echoed from across the hall, probably aggravating Sabrina which has become her favorite hobby aside from doing Nate's makeup. Turned out, Abigail's parents were the ones who sold her, *again*.

My parents signed her adoption papers last week. She was adamant she was going to live with me, but I was nowhere near emotionally stable enough to have a child around. So, we settled on her being my sister, who got to have sleepovers as often as she asked, complete with three big, tattooed criminals who catered to her every whim and Lottie who hadn't left our sides since the funeral.

One big mess of a family, but it was ours. Sabrina had also moved in; we offered her a safe house once things calmed down. She gave us the finger and asked which bedroom had the best lighting, so I assumed she was here to stay. Now she had a drawer full of glitter eyeliner in the bathroom and regularly threatened to shank Nate. He pretended to hate it, but he hadn't stopped smiling at her since she moved in.

I grabbed a mug and poured myself some coffee, sitting across from Creed. His eyes met mine. The storm I first saw in them, the one that used to scare me, it was quieter now. Still dangerous, still dark, but settled.

"You thinking about him?" he asked.

I nodded again. "Every day."

What Aaron did was unforgivable. But it was the things he did before that make it so hard to stomach. He was behind the warehouse operation, but he was also the guy who cleaned the burn mark on my hip when Ruben decided to brand me. He was the guy who helped me rescue Abby the first time. Complicated feelings swarmed my stomach anytime he was mentioned.

Creed reached across the counter, threading his fingers with mine.

"I still can't believe he did that," I murmured. "Framed himself, made sure we all walked away."

"He always thought he was protecting us; I genuinely believe that," Creed said. "Even when he was part of what we needed protecting from."

I blinked fast to keep the tears at bay. The ache was still there, dull but constant.

They buried him quietly. Only our group showed up. No honors. No flag. He didn't deserve a hero's ending, and as badly as that stung, we accepted it.

The others were still reeling. Kane was quieter, harder if that was even possible. I didn't think Nate slept outside of the cat naps he took on our couch when Sabrina curled up beside him and laid her head on his chest like she was trying to keep him anchored to the earth.

We were healing in pieces. There was only one thing we still hadn't figured out. The Bishop. We searched Aaron's files top to bottom. Looked through his texts, his calls, his private records. The number we suspected belonged to the Bishop was still bouncing off ghost servers. No face. No name. But he was still out there.

"You think he'll resurface?" I asked.

Creed didn't flinch. The topic stayed on his mind as much as it did mine. "He never left."

I sipped my coffee and glanced toward the window. The world outside looked normal today, safe. But I knew better. This wasn't the end.

It was the beginning of a new story.

AFTERWORD

To the readers,

Whew. That was rough, huh? Sorry about that. I feel like now is a good time to give everyone another warning—this is not going to be a lighthearted series. While I will NEVER have SA or abuse between my main characters, but there is a lot of back-story for each of them that might be hard to stomach in some cases that involve both of those things. The Sinners of Sunbridge were molded into who they are in these books, and I plan to show you every bit of it. Be cautious of your triggers, be careful with your mental health, and try not to hate me at the end of it.

As for Idle Hands, I'll let you in on a little secret: Aaron wasn't supposed to be the bad guy. I had planned for four books, one for each of the guys, but it just didn't happen that way. As I'm coming to realize, characters don't always behave the way I want them to. Sometimes when you're writing, the story takes a new path all on its own, and it feels right to follow it rather than try to change it. About midway through on the first draft, I called my sister over.

"The ending just doesn't feel right. I think I need to change something."

We talked and talked and talked some more.

"Aaron's character isn't fitting the way I wanted it to." And there was the issue. It was...off. The path I had laid out for him wasn't working.

"I think... I think Aaron is involved," my sister said.

I was shocked. A little defensive, if I'm being honest. But she was right. *That* fit. *That* made sense in the story. And so, I cried a little, and then I went back to the drawing board, and I realized I had already laid the groundwork for that outcome. The things Aaron had said, the choices he had made, they already lined up with his ending. I thought for a very long time about a redemption arc for him. Did he deserve one? Was it even possible? Would the other characters ever be able to fully trust him again? No.

While there are reasons behind his actions, there was no coming back from that. I think it's harder for me because I know his mind inside and out. I know the things that lead him to do what he did, and I know that the lack of malice on his end is probably the most heartbreaking part of it all. So, I have chosen to do something for him, and for you. I'm working on a novella from Aaron's POV. I know what was going through his head during each scene, but if you would like to know too, I'll give you that opportunity. Whether or not he was truly evil, that is for you to decide for yourself.

A huge thank you to everyone who helped bring this book to life. I had such an incredible team behind Idle Hands and I am forever grateful for them. Special thanks to Mallory, Anna, Samantha, and Shelby, for all of your help throughout this process! I'm so excited for this series and I can't wait for you all to follow the Sinner's on their next journey.

See you in the next one.

- Andi